TIME'S CAPTIVE

"*Time's Captive* is one of those rare books that will grab you and not let go until you finish the last page. Kate Lyon has created a sensual romance that is a time travel with fascinating historical details, paranormal elements and a suspenseful plot that will leave you craving for more."

—Romance Junkies

"Lyon weaves well-known history into a new legend."
—*RT Book Reviews*

"The author has done a fabulous job of research into this time in history. Her vivid descriptions pull the reader right into the scenes."

—A Romance Review

"Kate Lyon's debut novel is nothing short of a winner! Beautifully written with extraordinary lead characters and detailed research, *Time's Captive* captured my interest on page one and kept me riveted until the final, satisfying scene."

—Romance Reviews Today

"*Time's Captive* is sure to please all time-travel and Native American fans. . . . This is a dazzling start to Kate Lyon's career."

—Roundtable Reviews

"A well-written story that uses these tragedies to tell a wonderful tale of love and hope. Highly recommended."

—The Historical Novels Review

All Her Secrets Revealed

"You're clearly not as agile as you normally are, and you shouldn't be out of bed, let alone skulking about a strange house in the dark."

When he didn't back away, only sat staring at her with his glazed eyes glued to her chest, she glanced down. Her robe had come undone and the neck of her nightgown gaped away from her chest, revealing all her secrets. Every. Single. One.

"Oh!" She slapped her hand to her chest, luckily catching both robe and nightgown and restoring her modesty. She glanced up at him sitting there with his mouth open as if he'd been punched in the belly, and couldn't keep the asperity from her voice. "Do you think you could help me out?" She stuck out the hand not protecting her modesty. And wished she hadn't.

Like a snake striking, he caught her wrist with one mighty tug, pulled her up to his lips and simultaneously rolled, trapping her beneath him. "You're right, I'm not back to normal. Otherwise you'd already be naked."

When she opened her mouth to breathe—still debating whether to scream for help, lambast him or simply enjoy her sudden good fortune and ask questions later— he plundered her mouth. She gave up thinking. Instead, she focused on meeting his tongue stroke for stroke, on tracing the fluid muscles flexing in his back, arms and shoulders, on helping him untie her nightgown so he could . . .

Oh, dear! She dissolved in a shudder as his lips closed over one breast and his hand found the other. She wanted . . . No, she needed to be closer. How could she get closer?

Other *Leisure* books by Kate Lyon:

HOPE'S CAPTIVE
TIME'S CAPTIVE

Kate Lyon

Destiny's Captive

LEISURE BOOKS **NEW YORK CITY**

For Vern, for your unswerving faith, your patience when I falter, and your ambition on my behalf. This one's for you.

A LEISURE BOOK®

November 2009

Published by

Dorchester Publishing Co., Inc.
200 Madison Avenue
New York, NY 10016

ISBN 10: 0-8439-6283-6
ISBN 13: 978-0-8439-6283-3
E-ISBN: 978-1-4285-0759-3

Visit us online at www.dorchesterpub.com.

Destiny's Captive

Prologue

Alone in the dark of a moon-starved night, Chikoba banked his small fire and swung a blanket over his shoulders. Fingers of cold crept under his buckskin shirt, but he closed his mind to discomfort, thinking only of the task ahead. Already, he'd begun fasting. At dawn, he'd pray and begin dancing. Now he must rest, for the days ahead would be long and difficult, but his mind hummed with questions he must ask the Great Spirit.

Darkness shrouded him. Even the night creatures hid from it, leaving silence so deep that his thoughts shrilled like screams. He stared into the emptiness, searching for peace, but images of his beloved wife, Ekararo, her broken, lifeless body swollen with the child that had died within her, spilled across night's dark slate. He pulled the blanket tighter around his shoulders and pushed aside the wrenching grief that gnawed his gut, haunted his nights, and shadowed his days. Hatred burned inside him for the soldiers who had killed her, who had laughed as they turned and rode over her again, trampling the life from her and their child. Though eight moons had passed since her death, his hatred burned as bright as the day he'd found her body.

Part of him had died the day he'd buried her in a safe, secret place with her hands crossed over her belly to guard their child. That image got him through the brutal days that followed the attack, as he and the other warriors lured the soldiers away from the women, children, and old ones. But even in broken columns, the soldiers hunted like dogs on a blood trail.

Many of the old and sick had stepped off the trail, unable to run another step. What did they think as they watched their loved ones grow smaller in the distance? Did they beg the Great Spirit to take them quickly, before the bluecoats found them? Did they pray that their chief would give up the fight, good as it was, and surrender?

At the Palo Duro fight, soldiers had rounded up and shot the People's horses, then burned them. Soldier fire had taken their beautiful tipis and all inside them, stealing the People's spirits as well as their shelter, their precious belongings. Their chief heard his people's prayers and understood the message of the bluecoats. He surrendered. The Comanche—who had never before feared an enemy, who had ridden over their land free as the eagle soaring above it—surrendered and became captives. For the children, for the hope of their future, the warriors had given up their guns, but they hadn't given up the hatred in their hearts.

Weary of his circling thoughts, Chikoba stretched out on his stone bed, welcoming the discomfort. A warrior must suffer to prove his worth to the Great Spirit. Comanche in heart alone, Chikoba knew he must work harder, be stronger to help the Great Spirit see beyond the glare of his white skin to the truth in his heart.

He woke bathed in dew and mist, startled from sleep by the cry of the raven. Strands of dream crowded his mind with memories of Ekararo laughing in his arms. Her hair had rivaled the raven's wing in beauty. Like cool water tumbling through his fingers, it had gleamed even as she rose over him in the dark, and it flashed blue in the sun when she ran into his arms.

Chikoba swallowed the lump that choked him, rose from his bumpy bed, and shook his aching, empty arms. He took no food, no water, just lit his pipe and offered a thin, fragrant stream of smoke to the Great Spirit, then to each of the four winds, before pulling the smoke deep into his lungs. He climbed the highest rocky outcrop to greet the sun and when it crowned the eastern hills, he welcomed it with a glad cry, drew his knife, and cut new slashes in each forearm beside those he'd made in his grief for Ekararo and their child. One cut for Ekararo, one for his lost child, and these new cuts for his future—whatever it might hold.

Then he prayed, throwing everything that burned inside him into a heartfelt plea.

"Great Spirit who dwells on high, Father of all who walk upon this earth, heed your poor servant. I come seeking guidance and wisdom. Give me direction, for I am lost!

"The People cry, for the Great Spirit has turned his back on their suffering. The buffalo are gone, killed for the price of their hides and tongues. The stench of their rotting carcasses chokes Mother Earth. Can you smell it, or has smoke from burning lodges and dead horses seared your nostrils? Soon the People must surrender and live in humiliation on barren reservation land, prisoners for life.

"My own beautiful wife and unborn child have been taken in violence, their innocent lives snuffed out like fire blown before a cold wind, leaving me alone and broken, my heart bleeding.

"I can no longer live among the People, Father. Everywhere I look, I see her face, hear her voice. The People have no place for me, no need for a hunter, no fight for a warrior, and my white skin is dry grass on the fire of their hatred. Like the tumbleweed, I roll from rock to hill.

"Show me where to go, what to do. Give me wisdom to understand and accept the changes that must come in my life. Show me how to help the Comanche, if I can. And if I must live again among my enemies, give me strength!

"Hear me, Father! Please answer my prayers."

He tossed white sage on his fire and began dancing around it, chanting the medicine song he'd been given in a previous vision quest. The sun shone high and hot when he began singing of his long journey from Texas. There, a boy of only fourteen years, he'd seen his family killed, but he'd been sold first to Comancheros, then to the Kiowa, who took him to the high plains. There his Comanche brothers had freed him from slavery and made him a warrior to be feared.

His song carried him around his fire again and again, and the sun burned his bare skin as it followed its westward trail. His breechclout snapped against his thighs in the brisk wind—a sharp sting for every step. His shadow grew long, then disappeared. Still he danced and sang.

Sometime on the second day, Chikoba added new verses to his song, verses swollen with resentment for his father, the almighty Reverend Baldwin, who'd expected family and friends to live a pure life. More verses bled regret for the loss of his mother, sister, and two young brothers, all killed when their fort was attacked. His song ricocheted off nearby rocks long after dark claimed the night, rousing the wolf spirit that dozed inside him. His lament spoiled the silence, and all who heard it—animal and human—cowered in pain.

Nearly delirious by midday of the third, cloudless day, Chikoba at last sang of Ekararo, of his love for her and their joy as they awaited the birth of their child. The day was not long enough to tell his sorrow, and the sun hid its bright face behind rain-dark clouds as he relived the battle that stole his love. The sun set in the fire of his keening wail, a blaze of grief and anger thrown across the bruised sky. Even darkness could not cool the storm that raged inside him or stifle the growls of the beast within, now fighting to be free.

Still he danced, shuffling, barely able to lift his feet or turn his body, his parched lips unmoving and his dry eyes mere slits as he peered into the night. Fearing he might fall senseless on his rock bed before the Great Spirit answered his prayers, Chikoba clutched his medicine bag and prayed for strength. A long shudder wracked his body and he sighed as warmth flowed into every limb. His muscles stretched, lengthened, and his eyes narrowed as the night came alive with movement and sound.

A noise escaped him, whether grief or joy he could not say. More than a sigh of relief, less than a groan of pain, the beast inside snarled its pleasure and took hold. Chikoba welcomed it, opened himself and let it fill him, flowing deep, to his very fingertips. No longer content with his well-trod circle around the fire, he leaped onto the rocks and gazed out over the hills and valleys. There he threw back his head and gave a long, grateful howl, overjoyed by the rush of blood in his veins, the heady scent of prey scurrying for cover.

The familiar face of the black wolf, his spirit guide, filled the bright circle of the moon. "Your prayers have been heard, white son. Despair not. A full life lies before you, filled with the love you seek. Yes, even children to replace the son taken from you. Seek happiness where you first learned sorrow."

As the moon swallowed the wolf's face, Chikoba slid to his knees and hung his head, despairing. How could this be? How could he live among the whites and forget his hatred?

Staggering, he rose, only to fall onto his rock bed and into a deep, restless sleep. Vivid, intense images made him jerk and twist in his struggle to fight them off. Fast and bright, they continued until the sky blushed pink as Ekararo's cheeks. He stilled and smiled, then slept.

He woke, naked beneath the burning sun, to the cry of the raven and memories of Ekararo in his arms. For the first time, he welcomed them. Never again would he hold her in his arms, but as often as he wished, he could hold her in his mind. He had only to close his eyes to see her beloved face, watch her cheeks flush as he stroked her slim body, hear her sweet cry of release as he spilled his seed inside her. Many men died never knowing such joy. He had been blessed. And his hatred for all soldiers burned brighter.

Chikoba washed in a small creek nearby, gasping as the cold water hit his skin. Using the creek's glossy surface as a mirror, he cut his hair, leaving enough to tie at the back of his neck. He shaved, ran a hand over his smooth cheek, and frowned into the water.

He didn't look white. His skin was too dark from long hours in the sun. He shrugged. In time, he would turn pale again and look more like his enemies.

He opened the parfleche waiting beside his bed and scowled at the clothes inside—clothes he'd stolen from a sleeping cowboy. The man hadn't stirred, even when Chikoba had lifted his hand off his pistol. Smiling at the remembered pleasure of the coup, Chikoba pulled on the black shirt and scowled at its poor fit—snug in the arms and shoulders, loose about the waist. He couldn't fasten the top three buttons, not if he wanted to breathe. After a careful sniff, he sliced the legs off a pair of red flannel long johns, pulled them on, and hopped around adjusting his male parts.

"Damnation," he growled as he tugged the black trousers up his legs. They fit as close as a woman's caress. At the thought, his manhood reared its hungry head. With a grimace, he shoved it into his pants, cursing under his breath as he fought the buttons. Ekararo had been gone for many moons and, because of her difficult pregnancy, he'd been without a woman for over a year. When the last button was fastened, he braced his hands on his knees and breathed deep, silencing his squawking body.

He pulled on socks and low-heeled, tooled black leather boots, took a few steps, and sighed. At least the boots didn't pinch. He tossed the spurs into his dying fire, followed by a sky blue bandana. The bright color would draw too much attention.

Finally, he picked up the braided rawhide that had secured his breechclout. A sacred part of every warrior's clothing, it represented his very manhood. He held it lightly, considering where to wear it, then tied it around the brim of his hat.

"Ha!" he laughed, and pulled the braided cord free. Every Comanche—hell, every Indian—would laugh his head off. He could already hear their ribbing:

"Hey, hombre, why do you wear your nuts on your head?"

Not a question he wanted to answer. Still grinning, he unbuttoned his pants, shoved down his long johns, and tied the braid around his waist. Once everything was rebuttoned, adjusted, and patted down, he grimaced. Someday he might again feel at ease in white men's clothes. Today was not that day.

He poked up the fire enough to burn his buckskins, saving only a small white parfleche containing the tiny clothes Ekararo had made for their baby. It was time to become a white man. He must put the warrior, Chikoba, behind him and reclaim his life and his white name.

Jeremiah Baldwin. His mind shied away from his memories. He was no longer that boy; nor was he the man he had been. He must step off the Comanche path and put away the warrior.

That meant watching his back trail, leaving no shadow, drawing no attention. General Mackenzie and his bloodhound soldiers could still be tracking him for his part in last summer's Comanche raids.

At the creek, he stared at this new Jeremiah Baldwin in the pond's shining surface and frowned. He didn't look right. What was missing? With a slap to his hip, he remembered and pulled his prized possession—a holster containing a shining Peacemaker—out of his saddlebag and slung it around his waist, then tied it down on his thigh. He shifted it, settling it low, and smiled, pleased at the way it rode his hips. With the black leather gun belt snug around him, he felt like the best warrior in camp. Unbeatable. His hand rested easy on the butt, and the gun slid out of the holster as if it had been greased. He settled the black hat on his head and tugged it low.

The man staring back looked dark and angry. Too noticeable. He frowned. There, that was better. He'd pass as a white man, and the scowl would discourage the curious. He shifted his shoulders, trying to find some ease in the tight shirt, and cast a longing glance at his smoldering buckskins. He'd come too far to look back.

He tipped his hat brim at Jeremiah Baldwin, then yelped as he swung onto his horse. These damned clothes pinched in tender places. A few miles away, he pulled up and scowled over his shoulder at the column of smoke rising from his fire on top of the hill.

Should he have kept his buckskins? A warrior's clothing held great *pahoute*, Comanche medicine, and added to his strength. His horse danced under him as his knees tightened. He didn't hold with Comanche superstition, but the road ahead would be long and difficult. He'd need plenty of *pahoute* to find his place among the whites.

His fist tightened on the reins. He'd seen that place in the dreams that had kept him half awake all night.

A large white house had beckoned—candlelight shining from every window. A woman waited in the doorway, her features hidden by dusk and shadow. The woman, not the place, drew him. Did she wait for Jeremiah Baldwin, or was she a *haint*, a ghost from his past, sent to torment him?

Not long ago, he'd been told by a Comanche shaman

to head for Oregon. Maybe someday he would. For now, he'd follow his vision, and his gut. He reined his horse south and kneed it into a hard gallop, leaving his Comanche life behind. His future lay in Texas, in his past.

Tight-lipped and grim, Jeremiah faced it alone.

Chapter One

Jeremiah Baldwin rode into Cedar Creek with his knees clenched around his horse's belly and his gut tied in knots. He tugged his hat brim lower and headed for the livery.

The town buzzed and the people's pointed frowns stung like fresh stings on tender hide. A deep growl rumbled in his belly from the animosity pointed his way. The horses tied along the street tossed their heads as he passed, fighting their tethers. They sensed the wolf rising inside him. If he didn't calm down, there'd be a damn stampede. He'd considered circling town, but the warrior in him scorned the idea. What was it Quannah, his Comanche brother, always said?

Look your enemy in the eye, then spit.

Jeremiah returned the most piercing stare, turned his head, and spit.

The staring eyes narrowed. The man's lips tightened and the horse he sat pranced and tossed its proud head.

Jeremiah cast a jealous glance over the animal— flashy, but sound, the kind of horse a warrior lived to steal: sorrel with a striking blond mane and tail, a deep chest, strong withers, and a proud, arching neck. Too bad he'd given up stealing horses.

The man glared and the horse gathered itself to rear, but at a quick word from its rider it stilled, trembling but standing quiet.

Jeremiah took the man's measure as he rode by. Older, but fit, the man sat tall in the saddle, moving easily with the horse, his hands firm on the reins as he controlled the nervous animal. He wore the hat favored by wealthy

Mexicans, low-crowned and flat on top, narrow-brimmed, not at all like the wide-brimmed sombrero favored by the peasants. He dressed in the Mexican style, too: tight-fitting black pants; long-sleeved white shirt buttoned to the neck, fitted to his lean waist and tucked snugly into his pants; a waist-length, black leather vest decorated with metal studs; a bloodred scarf tied loosely at his neck; gleaming black, low-heeled boots. He carried a knife in a sheath at his waist, and a gun in his gun belt. His gaze was as sharp as a hungry hawk's.

Jeremiah continued down the street to the livery, ignoring the man's stare and the hostile townsfolk. He resisted the urge to flex his shoulders until he rode into the cool dark of the stable. Once out of sight, he sucked in a deep breath, only then realizing he'd been holding it. He dropped his reins and sat his horse, letting the aromas of hay and grain, liniment and fresh manure wrap him in welcome. Memories of his youth flooded him as his eyes adjusted to the dim interior.

"You're it, Jeremiah!"

"Hide, Christine," he shouted as she darted out of the stall behind him. She shoved him and ducked his grab for her shoulder. "Hey! No fair."

He smiled as her tinkling laugh rang off the rafters.

"What can I do for you?" A deep voice, thickened by a German accent, rumbled from the depths of the stable.

Jeremiah blinked and squinted to see past his shadowy memories, his heart squeezing as the elusive memory was swept away. A massive man approached from the tack room swinging a black leather saddle in one hand as if it were a blanket. Jeremiah started to dismount, but his horse ambled up to the stranger, sniffing his scarred leather apron.

"Ah, he's a smart one." The man settled the saddle on a nearby sawhorse, then reached into a pocket and came up with a small apple, which he offered to the horse on a palm the size of a small boat.

"*Gut Jung*," the man purred as he stroked the horse's neck. "Good boy. You could use some feedin' up." He raised a bushy brow at Jeremiah, who slid out of the saddle with a grimace. The damn contraption had worn his butt and legs raw. "Grain's extra. Max Biermann." Warily, Jeremiah eyed the big man's hand, before surrendering his own to be mauled.

"Jeremiah Baldwin." The name tumbled off his lips as easily as it ever had. He'd considered using a false name, keeping his identity to himself until he'd gotten a feel for this town that had sprung up so near Baldwin Fort, site of his father's dream. But he'd decided to hold his head high. He had nothing to hide, no reason to be ashamed of the name his father had given him. Other than his eyes and the color of his hair, it might be all he had left of his father. Let the people of this town know that he'd returned. Let the guilty among them tremble.

Jeremiah eyed Biermann's barrel chest and wide shoulders and returned the man's punishing grip without wincing. If the man was half as tough as his shoe-leather palm, Biermann would make a bad enemy, and a better friend.

"Baldwin, huh?" Biermann released his hand and stepped back to look him over, his expression wary. Jeremiah ignored the once-over while he untied his bedroll and saddlebags. He hadn't forgotten that a town's livery-man might as well be deputized; he was expected to watch for trouble and the vermin that brought it. But unless he recognized his name, Biermann would never guess why he was here.

"What brings you to Cedar Creek?"

"Passing through." Jeremiah glanced out the stable door, nodded at the busy street. "Looks like a nice town. Maybe I'll stay awhile."

"Looking for a place to settle?" Biermann asked. "Most land hereabouts has been bought up by European outfits for big cattle spreads. Not many small ranchers left."

"Just looking around." Jeremiah settled with the liveryman on the horse's keep, then turned to leave, but Biermann stopped him.

"Mrs. Maguire's boardinghouse takes male guests," he said, and gave him quick directions. "Less uppity than the hotel and quieter than the saloon."

"Thanks." Jeremiah strode for the door, feeling as if he were about to ride into a raid alone. He stopped short, sensing Biermann close behind him. "You move well, big man."

"Be careful looking over this town, Jeremiah Baldwin." Jeremiah didn't miss the emphasis of his last name. Biermann nodded down the street to the corner where the man with the flashy horse stood talking with another man. They started toward the livery. "Some folks aren't partial to strangers."

"I'll keep that in mind," Jeremiah said, and shook Biermann's hand. He thought about asking who the two men were but decided to make inquiries elsewhere. He didn't want Biermann alerting the men to his interest when they asked about him. And they'd be asking. Soon. Biermann couldn't tell what he didn't know.

Jeremiah tugged his hat brim lower as he walked into the bright afternoon light. He appreciated Biermann's warning but could have told him the last thing he'd expected was a warm welcome.

"Right on time," Angel said as she approached the livery, where her father was waiting for her with Mr. Biermann. She strapped her purchases on her horse and swung astride, then fixed a puzzled gaze on her parent. He and the liveryman had stopped speaking, but he still hadn't acknowledged her greeting.

"*Papá?*" she said, following his gaze down the street. "Is something wrong?"

A stranger stood there, his gaze fixed on her father, whose hand hovered near his knife.

"Do you know that man, Father?" She squinted, trying to make out the stranger's features despite the midday glare.

Her father started and turned, his smile stretched thin. He didn't look at her. "Good, you're finally here. *Vamanos.*" He stepped into his saddle, his voice and manner urgent.

"I'm ready," she said, and glanced again down the street. Her breath caught. The stranger stared at her, and he wasn't smiling. He wore black—black shirt, pants, boots, hat, even his gun belt was made of black leather, as if a long stretch of shadow had shifted into the shape of a man. She wished he was nearer, so she could identify him and verify her growing feeling that she knew . . . had known him before.

He had a strong, square jaw and deeply tanned skin made darker by the beginnings of a beard, a bold, pointed nose, and deep-set piercing blue eyes that met hers in an unblinking stare. Though she couldn't say why, she knew if she knocked off that hat and ran her fingers through his hair, it would be a deep, reddish brown.

Though at least fifty yards lay between them, she trembled, awareness pricking her skin, raising goose bumps. Even the hair on the back of her neck rose in appreciation.

"Who is he?" she asked her father in a whisper. She didn't want her voice to carry, didn't want the stranger to know he'd caused such a reaction. "I've never seen him before, but he seems familiar."

Her father tossed a too casual glance at the stranger, who turned away, his long, supple stride putting distance between them. His saddle and gear rode his shoulder, yet he didn't walk so much as prowl. Dressed in dusty black—the sunlight glinting off his pistol—he should have been of little interest, but his walk caught her attention and held her mesmerized. No man she'd ever met could match his height, his sheer masculine aura, even at this distance. His deep hat brim only added mystery, shadowing his face, veiling his intent, keeping his secrets.

"*Vamos, hija,*" her father said, not bothering to conceal his irritation with her as he fought his stallion. "We go. Now, daughter." He sank spurs and, with uncharacteristic disregard for the people forced to scramble out of his path, galloped out of town.

Puzzled by her father's behavior, Angel lingered, watching the compelling stranger. As he approached the intersecting street a block away, he tipped his hat to her and smiled—a brief flash of gleaming white—then turned the corner and continued his lonely walk. She smiled as she admired his rear view, knowing now where he was headed. She glanced up at Mr. Biermann, raised an eyebrow as she nodded in the direction the stranger was heading. Her smile widened when Max bobbed his head, confirming her suspicion that the stranger was headed to the boardinghouse at the end of the block.

A lone black wolf had come to town.

With her nervous horse firmly in check, she rode out of town with more than usual caution, apologizing to the people her father had left grumbling, then looped her reins around the saddle horn and let her horse set the pace for the long ride home. While she rode, she considered how to go about breaking through her father's bewildering silence to find out what he knew about the intriguing stranger. That might be more difficult than usual, given his intense reaction to the man.

Confident of eventual success, she turned her thoughts to the more difficult part: getting acquainted with the stranger. Fortunately, she had nothing pressing planned; she was free to spend some time in town.

As the daughter of the wealthiest rancher in the area, she was accorded a certain respect, but never demanded it. She preferred to live quietly at the hacienda, enjoyed a small circle of close friends—mostly women who lived and worked on their hacienda and people from the smaller, neighboring ranchos—and employed caution when faced with male attention. She didn't trust the men who came to call on her, suspecting that her father's money had spawned their interest in her.

She'd never before exercised what her friends called "feminine wiles," or pursued a man as she was considering doing with this stranger. Success was not certain. Even her father's wealth couldn't make up for her lack of beauty and sophistication. She preferred the outdoors and its many exhilarating activities—riding, hunting, simply enjoying the beautiful land—to traditional female pursuits. As a consequence, she had a lean, strong body and lacked the curvaceous appeal of most women. Worst of all, she was only pretty, not beautiful by anyone's measure, and because she was accustomed to giving orders to her father's vaqueros and the workers on the hacienda, she was far too direct, totally lacking in social graces.

Poise was as foreign to her as perfume to a rat. To compensate, she remained in the background at parties and public gatherings, avoiding unwanted attention. She prided herself on her useful skills: training and breeding horses, caring for many kinds of animals. She was an excellent shot with almost any weapon, and very good with the knife she always carried in a sheath in her boot.

However, men of her father's class, men with money and position, didn't appreciate her marksmanship or her grasp of ranching. They hired men who possessed those skills. They wanted a woman who looked good on her husband's arm, an ornament, not someone useful.

She suspected that, in the past, her father might have discouraged potential suitors whose social position and wealth didn't meet the high standard he set for his only daughter. He, too, was wary of fortune-hunters. Any man who attempted to sweep her off her feet found himself swept out of Caldwell County. Her father must be very convincing; none had ever returned.

She frowned. This stranger had done no more than nod at her, which her father hadn't seen. Why was Father upset? She'd gotten the impression—from the hum on the street and Max Biermann's interest—that the stranger had just arrived. Did Father already know the new wolf in town?

Still confused, but undeterred, Angel squared her shoulders and gave a tight nod as she reached a decision. She'd tell . . . no, she'd ask her father not to meddle as she pursued an acquaintance with this stranger. She was a woman now, not a child to be protected and guarded. She must be allowed to make her own decisions about her life. Father's concern was becoming stifling.

She chuckled at herself, wondering how the intriguing new man in town would react upon learning he was the point of her resolve. He'd done nothing to indicate an interest in her. Except for that fleeting smile, his attention had been on her father, not her, and she suspected that might have been due to her father's avid scrutiny. She hoped this stranger didn't offend easily and that he planned a long visit.

She was still pondering various means by which she could engage him in conversation when she realized she was riding through the gate of the hacienda. *Papá* waited for her at the door of the casa, snapping his riding whip against his boot. She sighed. He seemed more agitated than when he'd bolted from town.

She dismounted and handed her reins to a waiting vaquero and dusted off her skirt as she watched *Papá* pace before the door. With a start, she realized that the stranger's appeal was his similarity to her father. The stranger exuded the same aura of confidence and strength that she'd grown so accustomed to in *Papá* and had never seen in another man. She hoped the stranger possessed some of her father's other fine qualities, too, especially his devotion to his family: namely, her. Though she'd been orphaned in the raid on Baldwin Fort, *Papá* had adopted her and raised her as his own. No true father could have been more attentive to her needs. Love and concern for her father's unusual disquiet quickened her step.

"*Que es su problema, Papá?* What troubles you?" Out of concern, she slipped into his native tongue. She waited for him to face her, to give her that awkward pat on the shoulder that passed for a hug between them. He had never been comfortable with overt displays of affection. His was a quiet, respectful love, and if she occasionally craved physical closeness, Bernida—housekeeper, nanny, and governess all rolled into one—amply filled that gap.

"Nada, Angelina." He sighed and made an obvious effort to get control of himself. His smile seemed forced; his pat on the shoulder more awkward than usual.

"Who was that stranger?" she asked, stepping closer and tipping her head back to look up into his face. "Why do you fear him?"

"I fear nothing and no one," he proclaimed fiercely, and she winced as his whip caught her leg when he snapped it against his boot. "*Lo siento*," he muttered, and stepped inside the house to hang the whip on its worn peg. "Only losing you."

She acknowledged his apology with a smile and gazed into his troubled brown eyes as she laid a hand on his arm. She wasn't surprised to find the muscles beneath her fingers tight from gripping the whip. She stroked his arm, but he shook off her hand. "Then smile, for you will never lose me, *Papá*. I love you very much." She walked beside him into their home. "Shall we continue our game of chess, or are you willing to enrich my monthly allowance with another game of poker?"

"Minx," he growled as he escorted her into the library. He held her chair as she settled herself at the baize-covered table where bright-colored chips sat neatly stacked, awaiting the next hand to be dealt. "Perhaps I will recoup some of my contribution to last month's allowance."

"You may try," she said, as she shuffled the cards, happy to have chased the shadows from his eyes. They shared many pleasant hours in this manner, just the two of them.

"Father, why have you never married?" She asked the oft-repeated question after several hands of play and watched him flinch as he dealt the cards, saw his surprised glance, his careful study of her. What could be causing his unease? She often teased him with the possibilities inherent in their lives. In the past he had laughed and teased back. Until today. Could the stranger in town still be disrupting his thoughts? Did he threaten their future in some way?

That made no sense. The man appeared much younger than her father, though she couldn't be sure without closer examination, which she anticipated with enthusiasm. "Surely, many women have shown interest. You are still young, virile, and wealthy as Midas. You're a fine catch."

Her father shrugged, though his cheeks turned ruddy as he studied the cards in his hand. "I have no interest in marrying," he said, then added with a fond smile, "You are more than enough trouble."

"But don't you wish you had someone to share all this with?" She lifted a hand, indicating the well-appointed room. "You could have more children . . ."

"Someday, you will give me grandchildren," he said, adding with a laughing glance, "I hope."

It was her turn to blush as the memory of long, black-clad legs devouring a dusty street filled her thoughts and made her breath catch. Her blush deepened and she marveled at the fresh nuances in this old conversation. Could they all be attributed to the appearance of one man, a total stranger, or was her relationship with her father changing? Was it a sign of her increasing maturity that she could suddenly see him as a man, not just as her father?

"Yes, I hope to have children one day, and a home of my own." She caught his hand and held his gaze. "But don't you see? When I'm gone you'll be alone in this huge house with no one to watch over, no one with whom to share your days, no one to love. Though I'm sure we will see each other often, you will be alone much of the time. Are you prepared to live that kind of life?"

"Believe me, Angelina," he said, laying his cards down and giving her hand a squeeze, "the possibility is never far from my mind." He rose to pour himself a short glass of tequila.

"May I have one, too?" She rarely drank, but this afternoon her emotions were uncomfortably close to the surface. "And then, I must warn you, I intend to deplete your financial reserves. I'm feeling the need for a new gown—or two."

He paused, the amber liquor sloshing in their glasses at his sudden turn. "Why? Has someone new caught your eye?"

She rescued her glass, but avoided his gaze. "No one in particular."

At his silence, she glanced up in surprise to find him frozen in place and staring at her, his grip on his glass so fierce that his knuckles shone white in the softly lit room.

"It would not be the hombre you saw in town today."

"Are you asking or telling me?" She swept a hand

over the table, as if brushing away crumbs and gave a negligent shrug. "Come, Father, be reasonable. I did not even speak with the man."

"Do not attempt to dissemble, *querida*, I know you too well. He is dangerous," her father said, settling heavily in his chair. He set his glass down clumsily. She caught it, narrowly avoiding another spill. He captured her hand, his grip tight around her wrist. "You must stay away from him. You will not go to town again until I give you permission. Do you understand me?"

"*Papá!*" she cried, and tried to pull her wrist from his punishing grip. "Please! You are hurting me."

He shook her hand hard. "Do you understand? Answer me."

"*Sí! Comprendo.* I will do as you say."

He dropped her hand and shoved his chair away from the table.

Rubbing her throbbing wrist, she watched him pace beside the table. He ran his fingers through his hair until it rose in sharp spikes that gave him a sinister air. Finally, he leaned over the table, braced on his hands and looked deep into her eyes. His body seemed to vibrate with anger, making her wish she were much smaller and less noticeable. "Disobey me in this, Angelina, and you will live to regret it."

Her heart racing, she watched in silence as he stalked from the room. Only when the slamming of his bedroom door echoed through the house did she remember to breathe. She sucked air into her starving lungs.

"*Dios mio!*" she whispered, her heart settling into deeper, throbbing beats that thundered in the silence he left behind. Where had this demon come from? What had happened to the good-natured, easygoing man she knew and loved? She had seen him angry before, but never like this. Why had that anger been directed at her? He sometimes became irritated with her, but never had he been so fierce. Nevertheless, she thought with a toss of her head, she felt certain he would emerge from his room in the morning as he always did—wearing a chagrined smile and bearing a small surprise to redeem himself.

Despite her father's behavior, the stranger's appeal grew stronger by the minute. To soothe her *papá*, she would stay away from town for one or two days, which would allow her to come up with a plan that would provide a believable excuse for her to visit town.

Angel sighed. She hated to upset her father, but her new sense of maturity gave her unusual confidence, urging her to act independently. Father could no longer expect her to obey without question. It would be difficult for him to accept, but she must show him that she could govern herself.

For the first time in her life she was drawn to a man, and she meant to explore these new, exciting feelings. Not even her father's dire threat could stifle her burgeoning need to see this stranger's face, hear his voice, know his name.

She tossed back her tequila in one swallow, and settled in her chair, savoring the liquor's slow burn as she picked up her cards. Suddenly, she straightened and laughed aloud as relief washed over her.

What a shame her father had retired for the night. This discovery would surely have meant a windfall for her.

He'd dealt her a straight. In hearts.

Chapter Two

Jeremiah slowed his horse as he rode up the hill to the long ridge that circled Baldwin Fort on the northeast. His heart started pounding and his hands tightened on the reins. What used to be Baldwin's Fort—his father's dream and Jeremiah's childhood home—lay just over the hill. What would he see over the rise? He'd asked around town, found out that someone had bought the land, turned it into a prosperous hacienda, the largest cattle ranch in Caldwell County, though no match for the King and Kenedy ranches to the south or the state-sized latifundios in northern Mexico. The long, desolate spaces between these legendary ranches and Baldwin Fort had often been called the Wild Horse Desert, a fitting name, for nothing could live on it but longhorns and wild horses.

The only thing the land was good for was raising cattle and breeding horses. Not farming. Yet his father had been convinced that hard work, the will to succeed, and faith in God could change the face of the land. Instead, it had cost him his life. Would there be any trace left of the buildings or the wood fence they'd built to keep everyone safe, the fence that had failed to shut out hell and its fiends?

From the crest of the bluff, the long, familiar vista opened before him, bright with new-grown grass, dark with the rich green of cedars lining the creek that ran away south, skirting the casa. Cattle grazed in bunches, watched over by vaqueros slouched in their saddles, their sombreros tipped low over their faces as they snoozed in the afternoon sun. Some things never changed, and he was glad of that, for nothing remained of his father's legacy. Not a single board.

He shook his head at his foolishness. He'd ridden long and hard, pushing all the way from the Comanche's hideout on the high plains to get here, only stopping to trade for supplies—ammo, food, clothes—and information, most of which he got from strangers in saloons.

For what? To admire the scenery? He couldn't bring himself to look at the enormous house. It dominated the lush, green land that sloped away from the ridge over many miles down to Cedar Creek, source of the town's name. He needed to consider the land first.

The drunks in Cedar Creek had known a lot about Sanchez, the new owner of the land that had been the site of Baldwin's Fort, Reverend Matthew Baldwin's personal dream, founded before Jeremiah was born. The land, the hacienda, belonged to Don Miguel Sanchez, yet no one could say how Sanchez had come to be the owner; no one seemed to know. No one wanted to speculate.

He found that odd. Even among the Comanche, folks loved to speculate, especially about someone better off than themselves.

Jeremiah turned his attention to the house and surrounding buildings. No sign remained of Baldwin Fort's rugged fence or its plain wood buildings laid out in neat squares. Now a huge adobe house, a large barn, and many smaller outbuildings occupied what had been the central square, and a high, white-painted adobe wall with a sturdy wood gate ringed the buildings.

A vaquero, cradling a rifle in his arms and wearing ammunition belts crossed over his chest, rose from a chair on the casa's porch and stared toward Jeremiah. From this distance, Jeremiah could barely make out the pattern on the man's hat brim, so he couldn't tell for sure, but it felt as though the vaquero was glaring at him. Several more armed vaqueros stepped out to take a look. Their casual manner didn't fool Jeremiah; they were alert, watchful.

Why the guards? Had there been threats to the hacienda recently? The armed welcome party couldn't be for him; nobody knew he was coming. Even if someone in town had recognized him, Don Miguel Sanchez had no reason to see him as a threat.

Should he go ahead with his plan to drop in without an invitation? Or should he wait, maybe ask the local banker to come along?

No. He'd have to tell the banker who he was and why he wanted to meet Sanchez. If the banker had half the sense God gave a goat, he'd realize what Jeremiah suspected. If Sanchez and the banker were friends, Jeremiah could be walking into a trap.

You're overthinking this, Jeremiah told himself. *Go! Get it over with.* Forcing himself to relax, he kneed his horse downhill. Surprise was still the best plan. This first visit, he'd be friendly but curious, unthreatening, find out all he could about the hacienda. Until he knew more, he wouldn't understand why the Great Spirit had sent him here.

As he rode closer, he gripped his medicine bag and summoned his brothers. A wolf howled from somewhere nearby, unsettling the horses in the corrals around the barn.

The loitering vaqueros were nowhere to be seen when Jeremiah cantered through the hacienda's massive gates, but he felt them watching. He relaxed in the saddle, careful not to look like he had anything to be nervous about.

Just past the gate, several guns were cocked and the order came: "Throw down your gun, gringo."

He obeyed, then raised his hands as several weapons

came to bear on him. "I'm here to visit Don Miguel Sanchez. Is he here?" As he stared into a the rifle bores, surprise now seemed a very bad idea.

No one answered and none of them took their eyes—or their guns—off him. Jeremiah couldn't understand so much anger. He hadn't been the target of this much hostility since he'd taken Tabenanika's daughter for a walk without the old shaman's permission.

His gut tightened. He felt the men's tension like heat rising off the desert floor, shimmering in the hot afternoon sun. One wrong move, a slip of a sweaty finger, and it'd all be over but the dying.

Would an honest man need such guards? he wondered.

A rifle jabbed him in the ribs and he was ordered in guttural Spanish to dismount. Still busy pondering, Jeremiah didn't respond. The man jabbed him again and gestured, and Jeremiah realized the man thought he didn't understand their language. He'd let them think he was a dumb gringo. Right now it was his only advantage.

The glare off the white wall circling the house and its outbuildings reflected the afternoon sun, but the house itself was painted a deep rust color with dark brown shutters. It was U-shaped, with a cedar-shake roof. Black, hammered iron gates protected a central courtyard and lined the balcony above it that circled the entire second floor. This place could have held the modest wood house he grew up in and at least four more. Roses grew along the wide porch and he caught a glimpse of a large rose garden nearby. Vines covered with new green leaves climbed the sides of the house, softening the walls and making the casa more inviting.

Riding with the Comanche, Jeremiah had seen plenty of soddies and shacks, but he'd never seen a house so grand. The thought that Sanchez could be the man behind his family's murder stayed firm in his mind. All this might have been bought with their blood. He tried not to clench his jaw or grind his teeth. Thinking about his family now could cost him his life. He put on his gambling face, the one his Comanche brothers hated—because they always lost to it.

"*Vamos.*" The man used his rifle to direct Jeremiah into the house through wide double doors built of hand-planed, split logs joined together with hammered iron bars.

Compared to the simple clapboard, unadorned homes of his father's design, this house was heaven on earth. Unlike the crude log cabins and soddies that littered the plains, dropping mud on their miserable occupants in rainstorms and scorpions and tarantulas all summer, this house's thick adobe walls kept out heat, dust, and danger. His footsteps seemed muffled as he walked on thick carpets laid over gleaming tile floors down a long hall with whitewashed walls and dark wood doors. Massive timbers supported high, shining wood ceilings, making the house seem airy, full of light.

Jeremiah smelled roses and spotted several full vases beside ornate mirrors, flanked by padded chairs. The humble tipi he'd shared with Ekararo seemed barbaric, even savage by comparison. She'd made it home with bluebells, wildflowers, sage, and sweet-smelling grasses picked from the beautiful countryside and hung from the tipi walls. Ekararo, She Blushes, had waited there for him, her cheeks rosy, love shining from her eyes, her arms open wide to greet him, making it more than a tipi, making it their haven from worry and sorrow. He was glad soldiers had burned it to the ground the day she was killed. He could never have stepped inside, knowing she would never again share it.

Awash in the sudden memories, he hardly noticed the rifle jabs that directed him through the house. Who lived here? Who needed all this luxury around him to feel safe, alive? He stepped through a door and was shoved to a small, straight-backed wood chair facing a gleaming, heavily carved desk.

He started to survey his surroundings but immediately realized he was not alone in the room. From a bloodred leather throne of a chair behind the desk, the man from town who'd ridden the flashy horse eyed him, frowning. He was a tall, barrel-chested man with wide shoulders, his neatly trimmed goatee and mustache hardening an already knife-edged jaw. His gray-streaked black hair crowned a tan, strong-jawed face. His broad, high forehead hinted at great intellect, but a sharp crook in the ridge of his bold nose lent a reckless energy to his features, an impression strengthened by the challenge in his deep-set brown eyes. A muscle jumped in the man's jaw, and one black wing of an eyebrow lifted in obvious annoyance at Jeremiah's scrutiny. Sanchez resembled no man Jeremiah had ever seen or could have imagined. The man's wealth, his power surrounded them and, though he matched his host in size, Jeremiah felt small, mean. The man's large, dark eyes gleamed and Jeremiah knew he guessed what he was feeling, and was glad.

Jeremiah lifted his foot, laid it over the opposite knee, and settled against the stiff-backed chair as if it were the comfortable willow backrest in his own tipi. He removed his hat and set it on the table beside him, raked a hand through his hair. The Comanche had invented intimidation, and he hadn't forgotten a thing they'd taught him. He settled his interlocked fingers over his belly and gazed at the man, waiting.

The man cocked an eyebrow, then lifted a box, flipped open the lid, and offered its contents with a practiced swoop. The aroma of tobacco filled the room, so rich Jeremiah could taste it on the air, but he declined. He made it his policy never to share smoke with a snake until he got a good look at his skin. He hated surprises, and snakes could be very sneaky.

The man shrugged and studied the cigars. Jeremiah couldn't help staring at the man's hands as he chose a cigar, then drew it under his nose, inhaling deeply. He'd never seen hands like that on a man: long dark fingers, smooth, unscarred, with neatly rounded nails and not a speck of dirt showing beneath them. The man's eyes closed briefly, then snapped open.

Jeremiah stilled his body's jerk in reaction.

The man lifted a gleaming golden object from the box, fitted the cigar into a hole on one end, and with a loud *snick!* a sharp blade bit off the cigar tip.

Jeremiah blinked, imagining his finger caught in that hole. His stomach clenched and his nuts pulled up tight.

The man smiled. "Your name," he said, holding the cigar ready. The vaquero who'd brought Jeremiah to him leaned over the man's shoulder with a flaring match and both men focused on the process of cigar lighting. Lips working like a dying fish gasping its last breath, the man at last produced a cloud of pungent smoke that swallowed his head.

Jeremiah waited for it to clear. He wanted to see the man's face when he revealed his identity.

The man looked at him expectantly. The vaquero's hand slid to his gun butt.

"My name is Jeremiah Baldwin. Are you Señor Sanchez?"

The man didn't so much as blink as he gave a bare nod, but those fingers tightened on his cigar. "Tequila," he said, wagging his cigar at the vaquero, with a wave to include Jeremiah.

"None for me, thanks," Jeremiah said, matching Sanchez's phony smile. He glanced around the room as he waited for Sanchez's man to pour the drink. Behind Sanchez, the walls were lined with bookcases overflowing with books. Judging from their shiny bindings, few had ever been read. A long sofa sat against the wall to his left, a low table before it. Lamps on small tables here and there around the room shed enough light to make the room cozy, but not enough to read by.

The scent of burning tobacco warmed the air, combining with the tang of tequila, the soft undertones of beeswax. Jeremiah had no doubt that this was the center of the other man's empire, and the chair encasing Sanchez's solid frame, his throne.

Sanchez snatched the drink from his man, drained his glass in one loud gulp, and held it up for more.

"How can I help you?" Sanchez asked, blinking at Jeremiah as if he'd just noticed him. "I'm sorry, your name is . . . ?"

"Baldwin." Jeremiah was certain Sanchez knew it very well. "If you've lived here long, you've probably heard of my father, Reverend Matthew Baldwin, the man who founded Fort Baldwin with his congregation. Right here, on this property, in fact."

"This place was a smoldering ruin when I stumbled upon it," Sanchez said, shaking his head sadly. "There were so many bodies, we had to burn them. None were left alive. How is it that you survived?"

A jagged bolt of sorrow and guilt ripped through him, but Jeremiah sat silent, refusing to show it. "For my family's part, I thank you for tending to the dead." He took a deep breath when his feelings refused to lie quiet. His fingers clenched tighter. If he learned that this oily bastard had anything to do with the massacre, he'd take his revenge, Comanche-style. "I've only recently made my way back . . ." He looked at his hands, imagined them clenched around the culprit's throat as his final breath rattled beneath his fingers. "Too many painful memories."

"So, what is it you want from me?" Sanchez asked, his gaze sharp and searching.

"If you don't mind, I'd like to look around, see if there's anything left of the old fort."

Sanchez uncrossed, then recrossed his legs, studying his nails. "You want to 'look around'?"

Jeremiah's gaze fixed on the man's face. "I'm sure you don't want me poking around your home for long. I'll only be here for a few hours." Long enough, Jeremiah vowed, to find out . . .

Find out what? Sanchez had said nothing was left. Did he expect the bare ground to tell him who'd killed his family?

He stared at the wall behind Sanchez. The man wouldn't be satisfied with his sketchy explanation. *Damnation!* He should have given more thought to explaining his need to revisit the land. What was his interest? He didn't want the land for himself. He stifled a slight shudder. He could never live where his family had died.

"What is different now, that you can bear to face these painful memories?" Sanchez stared at him, looking innocent as he voiced Jeremiah's own thoughts.

"I need to make peace with my past." Jeremiah gave his reasons simply, hoping Sanchez would take them at face value. He couldn't say he'd been told to come here by the Great Spirit in a Comanche vision quest.

"This is the land, the place where we all lived my father's dream. It came alive here. I need to find out if there's anything left of that dream." Uneasy stirrings deep inside him warned Jeremiah that he was crossing shaky ground.

Sanchez continued to stare at him for a few seconds, then abruptly said, "Unfortunately, nothing I can say will ease your suffering. No one survived save you. You would be welcome to walk the land and search for traces of your family and their dreams, but it would be wasted effort. Nothing remains here to connect you to this place." He gestured to the door. "My man will see you out. You may find the peace you seek, but you will not find it here."

Jeremiah stood, surprised by Sanchez's abrupt

dismissal. "How can I find that peace, señor, without your cooperation? Where else could I search? Only you can answer my questions."

"What questions would you like to ask me?"

"Who sold you the land?"

"I do not discuss my personal business dealings with strangers. Please leave." Sanchez pointed to the door, motioning his man aside as if certain Jeremiah would obey him.

Jeremiah waved a hand at the room as if some of the answers to his questions were hidden behind Sanchez's books. "Your house is full of roses. My mother had a beautiful rose garden. Was anything left of it?"

"No, nothing, Mr. Baldwin," Sanchez said calmly. "Manuel." He nodded at his man, who approached with his rifle across his belly, clearly intending to shove Jeremiah out the door.

Jeremiah leaned over the desk, braced on his palms. Nose-to-nose with Sanchez, he spoke in a low, controlled voice. "Who sold you this land? You say no one survived the raid. Even my father couldn't sell it without his counselors' approval. If they were all dead, who sold it to you?"

"The bank offered the land to me. Your father had liens against the property to cover his debts." Sanchez backed away, waved his hand. Sweat broke out on his forehead, but his eyes narrowed. "Extensive debts."

"What bank?" Jeremiah demanded. Could Sanchez be telling the truth? The years before the raid had been tough, dry, and there'd been a few bad seasons, but he'd overheard his father and the other men talking. They'd sold some livestock; all was well. "There were no debts. We owned the land free and clear."

"I tell you only what the bank told me at the time of purchase." Sanchez made a shooing motion with his hand.

Jeremiah bristled. He was not a fly to be brushed off.

"If questions are to be asked, perhaps I should ask where you have been, Mr. Baldwin. How is it that you survived the raid, when no one else did? If you lived, the raiders must have taken you captive. Have you been living among your captives all this time? Did you, perhaps, become one of them?"

Jeremiah ignored Sanchez, even though his guesses came so close to the truth that Jeremiah's blood ran cold. "You still haven't told me what bank sold you the land."

"Please leave, Mr. Baldwin. This land, *mi hacienda*, is no longer your concern."

Jeremiah returned Sanchez's glare. For several seconds, neither man moved. Finally, at the sound of running footsteps, Sanchez smiled. "Ah, my men. I apologize for them in advance. They can be ruthless and a little brutal."

"You're threatening me?" Jeremiah controlled the urge to hoist Sanchez off his throne by the throat and shake the answers he wanted out of him.

Sanchez's polite smile didn't so much as flicker.

The footsteps were close now. Jeremiah reined in his temper. "I'll leave, but I won't rest until I find out what happened. You stole this land. Did you also plan the raid?" Despite the anger that blotched Sanchez's face at the accusation, Jeremiah added, "I'm going to prove it."

He left, with Sanchez's man—and his gun—following close behind. The men lining the hall didn't move to stop him. He wasn't surprised to find his horse waiting for him at the door.

Once mounted, Jeremiah looked around, hungry for some sign of his former life. Sanchez had told the truth; nothing remained. Fourteen years before, over a hundred and fifty men, women, and children had been swept away in one blood-drenched, nightmarish afternoon. Why? Hadn't anyone asked why it happened, asked who killed them? Didn't anyone care?

To no one and everyone, Jeremiah said calmly, "I care."

He didn't have to kick his horse; it jumped toward the gate when he loosened his grip on the reins. Did it, too, smell ash in the air? Did it smell the blood rotting the ground beneath its hooves?

Jeremiah rode hard, paying no attention to direction, grass and trees passing in a blur as memories came at him like startled crows, flying low and fast. His horse's hoofbeats became the crack of gunshots; men's voices, loud with alarm; children's wails; women's tortured screams. He choked on the smoke and dust fouling the air, and wiped his arm across his stinging, watering eyes. He had to find his sister. Make her stop screaming his name.

Then, just as in his memories, something hit him. The force knocked the wind out of him, bent him double. Pain exploded through his body. Daylight faded, then came flaring back—hot, red, and angry.

This was no memory! In the raid, he'd been hit in the back of the head. He'd passed out.

He straightened, alarmed at the effort it took to stay on his horse. Again, he was hit in the back, slammed forward by the pain ripping through him. This time he heard the report of a rifle.

Shot! Twice!

He hung over the horse's neck, pulled it to a sliding stop. His right leg swung easily over the horse's back, sliding through the blood on its rump, but his left leg buckled. He fell hard with his foot twisted in the stirrup.

Move! he shouted, but his leg couldn't obey.

A man loomed over him, smiling. "You!" Jeremiah would remember that face anywhere. This man's image had ridden through the nightmares that hounded him after the raid. He'd made himself remember because someday, he planned to shoot him, right between those squinty, mocking eyes.

"How unfortunate that you have such a good memory, Jeremiah Baldwin." His attacker sneered down at him. "Too bad you're not going to live to tell anyone the little you know."

"Does Sanchez know you took us boys, sold us to the Comancheros? Or were we your side bet?"

"Sanchez. Pah." The man laughed, an ugly but gleeful sound. "He knows nothing. He is weak. But you—you are strong in here." He pounded his chest over his heart. "You refuse to die." He took a running step and kicked Jeremiah in the ribs.

Jeremiah felt a rib snap and pain swallowed him, but he didn't cry out. He hadn't cried for the Kiowa; he wouldn't cry for this bastard, either.

"Ah, the big tough man, are you? No longer a frightened boy." Another kick, but Jeremiah saw it coming and shifted so it didn't hit in the same place.

"Who are you?" he gasped, between pulses of agony. He had to find out.

"Juan Delgado," the man said with a sneer. "It's a shame you won't live to tell anyone your sad story."

As Delgado pounded him, Jeremiah cussed himself for a fool. He should have known Sanchez would send a man to kill him. He'd sat in Sanchez's house, surrounded by his wealth and power. A man who needed all that to feel safe, powerful, would kill to keep it.

He reached for his gun, but Delgado stomped on his arm. It gave with a loud crack. Pain washed over Jeremiah again, but still he didn't cry out.

"You will not escape again." The man kicked him—in the side, the head. Jeremiah's head floated on waves of pain. He couldn't move, could only endure, as he'd endured many times before. He lost consciousness and for a while he was young again, sold to the Kiowa, arms and legs tied behind him, hanging belly-down in a bow while they stacked rocks on his back and women and young girls stabbed him with sharp, burning sticks. No!

He couldn't go back there. He fought to stay conscious, to keep his head clear.

Then Delgado straddled his body, grabbed the front of his shirt, and lifted him. "Many long years I have waited for your return." He pulled back his fist. Jeremiah braced himself for the punch. "Where are your Injun friends? You were a fool to come alone."

Jeremiah no longer saw the blows coming . . . his ribs, his stomach, his groin . . . The man's face swung from Mexican to Kiowa and back again. The blows, sometimes fists, sometimes burning sticks, slowed. All Jeremiah could do was breathe. Keep breathing. He had to live! Had to avenge his family, find out who, find out why . . .

Delgado stood over him, panting heavily. Beyond the agony, Jeremiah heard him say, "Now you will die." Then he heard a pistol cock.

Jeremiah dragged his unbroken arm over his chest, grabbed for the medicine bag under his shirt. It was missing! Desperate, he shouted, *Great Spirit, hear your servant! Help me!*

At once, the red fog in his brain lifted, warmth flowed into his battered body. A snarl erupted from low in his gut and he swung his leg into Delgado's. The gun jerked aside as it fired, but the bullet drove deep into Jeremiah's shoulder. His snarl became a long, pain-filled howl.

Answering howls filled his head and swelled into a chorus.

Above him, Delgado dropped his pistol and stared around him. The howling got louder, closer. His horse bolted and he ran after it.

Jeremiah listened to the fading hoofbeats and sighed. He'd survived. Again. He had to pull himself together, before Delgado came back to finish him off. The wolves would only keep him away until morning.

Juan Delgado. At last he had someone to blame for his family's deaths and the horrors he'd lived through.

Wolves rushed from the surrounding trees, their howls turning to keening whines as they approached. Jeremiah felt no fear. He raised his good hand and stroked the wolf sniffing his face, his body. All was not lost. The Great Spirit had heard his cry and sent his brothers to save him.

He lifted his head, looked down at himself, and groaned. He looked as bad as he felt. What a sorry mess. He must have blacked out sometime during the beating. Delgado had stripped him to his long johns and left him shivering in a puddle of sweat and blood. The cur had stolen his boots, his Colt, his saddle . . . hell, he'd even taken his horse.

The asshole's trying to make this look like a robbery, Jeremiah realized, again peering out of a bloodred haze. *Good thing there's no Comanche around to catch the blame.*

He'd sleep a bit—the wolves would keep Delgado and any other fiends away. But he couldn't rest for long. He had his revenge to plan.

Chapter Three

"What will you tell your *papá*?" Bull had asked when Angel appeared at the cabin he shared with Little Bird, the day after her *papá*'s ultimatum. "Don't worry. I'll think of something." Angel had smiled for Bull's benefit, though she'd been worrying about that very thing herself. "He didn't prohibit my afternoon ride. And if he finds out, I'm sure he'll be much less angry to learn I came here than to town," Angel had said, determined to be optimistic. She hadn't told Bull that she'd deliberately kept her plans from her *papá* because she was so annoyed with his dictatorial attitude.

Normally, he awoke the day after a disagreement all smiles, anxious to soothe her injured feelings. Today, he'd arisen early, no doubt to avoid having to face her over breakfast. Bernida had been tsking under her breath all morning. Angel's afternoon ride had been a blessed relief.

Once on horseback she'd been unable to resist the urge to get Little Bird's perspective on the stranger. She wasn't sure, but she suspected that two female minds were much better than one when plotting how to intrigue a man.

"I hope you're right," Bull had replied doggedly. "I don't want to have to explain to your *papá* why you can't stay away from my humble cabin."

Crack!

"Did you hear that?" At the unexpected report of a nearby gunshot, Angel had flattened over her horse's neck, then slid to the ground, keeping her head below its back.

"Quiet!" Years of living with the Comanche had honed Bull's instincts. He'd already flung himself off his horse and was pulling the horses between them and danger.

Crack! A second shot shattered the quiet. Bull shoved her to the ground and threw himself over her.

"Let me up," Angel gasped in a hoarse whisper, and pushed at him, but Bull shushed her and shoved her head down again. "Mmmph!" she said, struggling to draw breath and getting a mouthful of dirt. "I can't breathe. Get off me. Please!" Bull wasn't tall, but he was solid and strong, and very heavy. Despite the difficulty she was having breathing, she was very glad he'd insisted on seeing her safely home. As usual, his instincts were infallible.

"Not yet," he said. "Be still," he added when she opened her mouth to argue. "That was close, but not aimed at us." After a couple of minutes, he eased off her. "Stay here and hold the horses. I'll be back."

Angel had stayed flat on her belly, lifting her head only enough to spit out the dirt she had nearly swallowed.

"Stay down, and don't move!" He had waited for her to obey before moving on.

"Be careful," she'd whispered back.

Now she lay still, her senses heightened, twitching at every rustle and squawk, though there weren't many. The entire glade seemed to be holding its breath, waiting.

After what seemed like hours, but must have only been a few minutes, she carefully eased onto her knees, keeping her head down. If something—or someone—came at her, she wanted to be able to run. She winced at the noise from her rustling clothes and the brush crunching beneath her knees and glanced to either side. The air shifted around her. Had something moved in the trees?

The horses pranced, tossing their heads. She couldn't

see anything in the deepening shadows, but something, or someone, watched her from the trees.

Suddenly, a wolf howled. The horses reared. She hung onto the reins, wondering if that had really been a wolf. Its howl was unlike any she'd ever heard. There was pain in that cry. And fury. The horses reared again as answering howls rose from the trees around her. She clung to the reins as the horses pulled her to her feet while she fought to hold on. Suddenly, wolves sprang from the trees, fangs bared, running straight at her.

She screamed, expecting to be either ripped to shreds by their gleaming teeth or trampled by the frantic horses, but at the last second, the wolves veered around her, nearly brushing her as they passed. Crooning to quiet the horses, she squinted, trying to see where they went, but the wolves had vanished.

Bull came running back through the dappled light. She blinked at him, breathless and shaking. She'd never seen him so agitated.

"Come on. Quick!" He grabbed the reins and her arm, pulling her back the way he'd come. His eyes were wild, his voice low but urgent. "A man's been shot. I think he's still alive."

"But the wolves . . ." Angel cried, struggling to keep up. "Won't they . . ."

"You won't believe it," Bull said, his eyes wide and wary as he searched the undergrowth that crowded around them. "Hurry!"

She followed close behind as he maneuvered through the trees and out into a wide meadow. He slowed to let her catch up. "Look. I've never seen the like."

In a wide, heavily trampled area, a man was down—bloody, obviously beaten, probably shot—and he was surrounded by the wolf pack. They were sniffing him, nudging him with their snouts, some even making whining, whimpering noises and licking his hands, his face. She bit back a gasp as several turned and snarled at them, the fur on their spines spiking, blood dripping from their noses, their fangs glistening in the sun.

"How do we get to him?" She tried to step closer, but her horse fought her, his eyes rolling. His flanks quivered as if he'd already been bitten. If one of the wolves made a move toward her, he'd bolt and drag her with him. She backtracked and tied him to a sturdy sapling.

Bull had followed her lead. Together, a few feet apart, they slowly approached the man. The wolves snarled and crouched, ready to spring. Then the injured man lifted a hand, touched the nose of the nearest wolf, and growled softly. The wolves stopped snarling.

"It's okay," the man said, rolling his head toward them. He patted the wolf's head before his hand slid to his side. "They . . . won't hurt . . . you."

Bull shot her a surprised glance, then took a cautious step closer. The wolves backed off, some whining and obviously reluctant. As if by agreement, they moved several feet away and crouched down, tensed to spring and still snarling.

Angel waited until Bull had reached the man before moving closer. She took one look at his bloody body, covered her mouth and turned away. *Mercy!* She gagged and had to take several deep breaths to avoid vomiting. There wasn't a spot on his body not covered in blood. Both eyes were swollen shut. He had cuts on his cheeks, temple, chin, jaw—all bloody and quickly purpling. Both lips were split. How his nose had survived without breaking, she'd never know, though it looked as if his attacker had tried his best.

"Who would do this?" she croaked, stunned by his injuries, seething with outrage on his behalf. If the attacker returned to finish his dirty work, she wouldn't hesitate to shoot him herself. "What do we do? How can we help him?"

"I spotted someone running off just as I approached. It looked like Juan," Bull muttered, and she heard the same outrage she felt filling her in his voice. "Those wolves have more heart."

"Bull, you must be mistaken," Angel murmured, touching his shoulder. "Juan couldn't have done this." Juan annoyed her—a great deal, in fact—but she couldn't believe him capable of attempted murder.

A frequent visitor to the casa, Juan had made it clear he expected to marry her sometime in the near future. Unfortunately, her *papá* hadn't witnessed Juan's attempts at seduction and he refused to believe her when she asked him to discourage the man. Of all her *papá*'s male friends, Juan frightened her most. Sometimes the way he looked at her made her skin crawl. Bernida refused to be alone in a room with him and the other men gave him a wide berth, but her *papá* would hear nothing against Juan. Still, she couldn't believe Juan capable of pounding a man to a pulp. She shuddered. If Juan was the attacker, how would she tolerate his presence in their home ever again? Surely, *Papá* would agree. He would not want such a man near her.

"I didn't get a good look at him." Bull gently probed the man's right arm and shook his head. "Broken." He peeled the bloody long johns off the man's chest, muttered a curse, and replaced them after glancing at her. He stood quickly and reached for her, his face flushed. "Wait with the horses, while I—"

"Oh, honestly, Bull," Angel snapped, and pushed him aside, her fingers already working the buttons on the injured man's long johns.

"Gently!" Bull said, placing a restraining hand on her arm. "He's hurt bad."

"I've seen injured men before, though never anyone this bad who was still breathing." She opened the long johns and gasped. His entire chest was black and blue, his ribs so badly broken that a lower one poked through the skin. "*Dios Mio!* We're going to need Little Bird."

The wolves tensed, growling at something in the trees nearby.

Bull glanced over his shoulder. "She's coming." Rising slowly, he went to greet his sister.

Angel nodded, not surprised that Little Bird had come without being summoned. She often sensed when her skills were needed. Also, she'd have heard the shots at the cabin.

"Move slow," Bull said, taking a bundle from Little Bird, who sat frozen on the back of her horse, staring at the wolves. "They won't hurt you."

After tying her horse with theirs, Bird approached cautiously and settled beside Angel, near the man's head. She laid her parfleche of medicines and a couple of old blankets between them. Bull retrieved a heavier bag from her horse and fished out a large bottle of whiskey, the one Angel had given him last Christmas. He took a long swallow before he set it beside Angel.

"I'm so glad you're here." There was urgency in Angel's tone as she clutched Little Bird's hand. She spoke low and slowly, keeping a wary eye on the wolves. "I've never handled anything as bad as this."

Bird's eyebrows shot up. "You think I have?" She looked over the man, peeked under his long johns and sighed. "Are you sure he's alive?"

"He's alive all right," Angel said. "If he wasn't, they wouldn't still be here." She nodded at the wolves. "Don't make any sudden moves, and I'll pray he doesn't scream while you're working on him."

Bird glanced up at Bull. "Who would do such a thing?"

"I think it was Juan," Bull responded, taking another swig of whiskey, ignoring Angel's scowl.

"Are you sure he's gone?" Little Bird snatched the whiskey away from him.

"Yes, he's gone. Scared away by our friends," Bull added in a whisper as he glanced carefully at the wolves. He frowned as he leaned over the stranger, bracing himself with his hands on his knees. "The wolves sent him packing. A few followed him. He was moving pretty fast. Prob'ly thinks the guy's done for, or that they'll finish up for him." He nodded at the wolves.

"There's so much blood." Bird pushed gently at the man's shoulder. "Bull, help me roll him a little. I only see one wound, but I heard three shots." As Bull eased the man up, she pushed her arm beneath him. "Yes, two entry wounds in his back. Lucky for him, they missed his spine. Ah, here's a hole where that bullet left." She glanced at the shoulder wound. "How can one person bleed so much?"

"What can I do?" Angel asked. She glanced at the wolves. "Do we dare rip the blankets into bandages?"

Bird sighed, but didn't answer, her brow puckered as she continued poking, searching out the man's wounds. She bent over his protruding rib. "Bull, go back to the cabin, bring more blankets, poles for a travois, and something to splint this arm. And hurry. He's lost too much blood."

"I can't leave you here alone!" Bull's gaze slid from the wolves to his sister.

Little Bird looked into the eyes of each animal; then Angel felt her friend relax. "They won't hurt us," she whispered. "They want us to help him."

Bull shook his head, mumbling as he backed toward his horse, keeping a wary eye on the wolves. Little Bird handed Angel a blanket and they both began hesitantly tearing it into strips. Their jerking motions made the wolves jumpy, quick to growl, but they didn't attack and they soon stopped snarling. Sweat broke out on Angel's brow, dripping into her eyes as she worked. She mopped her face with her arm, noticing the lengthening shadows.

"It's going to be dark soon," she said, eyeing the wolves. "But I don't think we should start a fire. If the attacker is still around, he might see it and come back."

"I agree," Bird said, and glanced at the cloudless sky. "The moon will give us plenty of light, and the wolves will keep the killer away. Bull will be back soon."

"I should have asked Bull to get a message to *Papá*." Angel gently touched the man's bleeding hand, recognizing the insignificance of her personal concerns in comparison to his plight. "He'll worry when I'm not home before dark."

"Are you sure you want to stay?" Bird asked, leaning down to look into Angel's face. "I need your help, but if you think you should go . . ."

"No!" Firmly setting her worries aside, Angel turned to Bird. "I can't leave yet. What kind of friend would I be to leave you here, in the midst of a crisis, and in danger?" She looked over her shoulder into the distance where the fiend who'd done this could be lurking. "I'm staying. I just don't want *Papá* to send out a search party."

Bird's quiet sigh told Angel how relieved she was by her decision. Bird squeezed Angel's hand and they both turned to the injured man.

Angel raised her hands, but didn't know where to put them. The large pool of blood beneath the man frightened her. "I wish we could do more," she said, letting her hands fall into her lap. "We need to do something to help him."

Bird made two thick pads from pieces of the blanket. "If I help you lift him, do you think you can hold him up long enough for me to press these onto the wounds in his back? We've got to stop the bleeding."

"What about his ribs? So many are broken. Is it safe to move him that much?"

"If we don't stop the bleeding, his broken ribs won't matter." Bird moved to his head and motioned for Angel to join her on his other side. "The wounds are high on his back. If we lift from his shoulders, we won't move his ribs much."

Angel nodded and together they lifted. Bird pressed the first pad in place, and Angel started a wide band to hold it, passing the strip to Bird, then reaching over the man to grab it on his other side. Moving slowly, carefully, they bound both pads over the wounds and were relieved to see the flow of blood slow. By the time they got a blanket under him, Angel and Bird were both exhausted. Kneeling on either side of the man, they smiled at each other; then as if in agreement, they looked at the unconscious man's face.

"Do you know him?" Bird asked. "You get to town more than I do. Have you seen him before?"

Angel bent over the man's face, squinting in the fading light. "It's hard to tell. He's so bruised and bloody, his own mother wouldn't recognize him." She looked down his body at the remains of his black shirt and pants and felt a tremor go through her. *No! It can't be him!* The thought speared through her mind, her heart, and she cried out. Gently, she traced the line of his jaw, felt the stubble there, and looked around for his hat. Black! It was him, the stranger she'd seen in town, the man she and her *papá* had argued over. She sat back quickly. *Papá* had said the man was dangerous, yet here he lay. He certainly didn't look dangerous now.

"Angel," Bird said, pressing a hand to Angel's shoulder. "Are you all right?"

"No! I mean, yes, I think so. This is the man I was telling you about, the one I saw in town yesterday, the one *Papá* warned me to stay away from." She bit her lip to keep from gasping as she was swept by a sudden urge to hold the stranger, help him stay alive, even if by her will alone. "Oh, *Papá* mustn't find out about this. He'll be very angry."

"Are you sure you don't know who he is?" Bird asked. "He might have family nearby."

"I don't think he does. I saw him shortly after he'd arrived in town. He was just leaving the livery. He was weary, as if he'd traveled a long distance to get here. If he has family, I doubt they're close enough to help him now." Angel tried to quiet her growing agitation. After all, she'd never even spoken to the man. If only she'd stayed in town a little longer and asked Max about him. She'd agreed to her *papá*'s order to stay out of town, so how could she find out who he was? She rubbed her palms on her thighs, rocking back and forth.

"Angel, calm down," Bird said, speaking in that slow, deliberate tone of voice Angel had often heard her use on her patients.

Angel took a deep breath, then wet a cloth from Bird's canteen and began cleaning the dried blood off the stranger's face.

Bird rocked back on her heels, watching silently as Angel worked. "He was leaving the livery?"

"Yes," Angel said, suspending her wiping. "Why?"

"Any idea where he was headed?"

"Well, yes, I kind of looked at Max and he nodded toward the boardinghouse," Angel explained. "He had his saddle and his gear on his shoulder and he was just walking . . ." She shrugged and fought to keep from looking at the man's legs, remembering how quickly his long stride had devoured the street, carrying him away from her.

Bird glanced into the trees, watching for Bull. "What did he look like? A drifter, a cowboy looking for work?"

"No, not at all." Angel glanced at Bird. "That may be why he caught my interest. I couldn't begin to guess anything about him." She lifted the man's left arm to check for injuries and sighed, relieved to find it bruised and bloody but unbroken. She laid it back down carefully.

Bird watched Angel, then looked the stranger over again, her frown growing deeper. "Whoever attacked him had a reason, and a lot of anger behind it. We'll have to hide him, make it look like he died, or the attacker will hunt for him. We'll dig a shallow grave, cover it with rocks. That should keep the attacker from trying to dig him up again."

Angel's whole body jerked at the thought of the stranger dying, but she gulped and nodded. "I'll help you."

"Bull can do it. We'll be busy."

Angel shook her head. "I've never liked Juan, but I can't believe he would do something like this."

"Why not?" Little Bird began rolling up the blanket strips. "Your father knows him better than you. Has he or Juan ever talked about Juan's life before he came here?"

Angel rolled the bandages and tried to recall past conversations, wishing she'd paid closer attention, but nothing came to mind. "No, Juan's never said anything about his past. All the vaqueros and their families avoid him." Her hands fell still and her gaze settled on the stranger. "I'll ask one or two of the women what they know about him."

"No!" Bird cried, forgetting the wolves until a couple of them snarled and crept closer, fangs bared. Keeping her gaze glued to them, she whispered urgently to Angel, "Don't mention Juan to anyone. If he found out you'd been asking questions about him, he might become suspicious. If he's capable of this"—she nodded at the stranger—"who knows what he'd do to silence you?"

Angel pondered Bird's warning as they packed up all but the strips of blanket they'd need to splint the man's arm. She finished cleaning the man's face, paying close attention to the cuts that Bird would stitch closed once they got him to the cabin.

The wolves settled a bit but remained alert and watchful. They looked almost tame, but Angel knew that one sudden move or cry of pain from the injured man could change everything. As long as he remained unconscious, and she and Bird kept their movements small and spoke quietly, all would be well.

"This will make a fine story to tell our grandchildren, won't it?" Angel said, glancing at Bird with a raised eyebrow.

"If we live through it." Bird chuckled and shook her head. "No one will believe us, unless this man is there to back us up."

"Then we'll have to make sure he lives." Angel smoothed the tumbled hair off the stranger's brow.

He stirred and gave a low moan. Instantly, the wolves tensed.

Bird leaned over him with the whiskey bottle. "I don't want him moving around and starting those wounds bleeding again. And if he starts moaning, his friends will get nervous."

"Will the whiskey help?" Angel's legs were cramping from kneeling beside the stranger for so long, but she didn't dare get up and walk around. Instead, she rose unsteadily onto her knees to help Bird with the whiskey.

"Can't hurt." Bird slipped her arm under the man's head and lifted as Angel pressed the bottle to his lips. At first he didn't respond; then as the whiskey slid past his slack lips and down his throat, he moaned and opened his mouth for more.

After several sips, he blinked up at Angel. She doubted he could see much through those puffy, purple slits. She could barely tell that his eyes were every bit as blue as she'd expected. "The reverend lied. It still hurts after you die."

His eyes closed and he passed out again.

"We should have told him," Angel said, trying not to shudder as she pulled the blanket up his blood-splattered, black-and-blue chest.

"What? That he hasn't died and gone to heaven?" Little Bird snorted. "He's not out of the woods yet." She wiped off the bottle and took a long swallow.

"He's going to be fine," Angel said with a nod. "He won't die yet."

"Why not?"

Angel looked him over, taking in his strong jaw and firm lips, his long, heavily muscled body. "He'll want to know who tried to kill him and why. And then he'll make the monster pay."

Chapter Four

"*Levántate!* Get up, señorita. The sun, it is sliding down the sky. Señor Juan comes to dinner. Your *papá* says, *Andalé!*"

Angel groaned and pulled her pillow over her head as Bernida tugged open the heavy gold velvet drapes at her bedroom's floor-to-ceiling windows.

"I'm not hungry," she grumbled. As Bernida moved toward the closed draperies, she begged, "No birds! *Por favor!*"

Bernida chuckled and flung open the windows leading onto the second-floor balcony that overlooked the colorful, open courtyard at the center of the house. The small tree that occupied the corner of the courtyard near Angel's room was filled with busy, nesting birds. A fountain gurgled merrily in a large tile basin at the courtyard's center, adding to the noise and Angel's irritation.

Oblivious to her protests, Bernida flipped off Angel's covers and gasped. "*Madre de Dios!* You slept in your boots?" Her good humor vanished and she slid into a barrage of rapid Spanish that Angel didn't even try to understand, mostly about the damage she'd done to the once-pristine sheets. Bernida rarely turned her temper on Angel—she had plenty of targets among the small army of servants it took to run the house—but when she did, Angel scrambled to accommodate her, as did her staff.

"*Lo siento,*" Angel muttered, as she slid out of bed. She really was sorry. She'd intended to rest for a moment only before removing her boots and her soiled riding skirt and short, matching jacket. She hurried to do so now, before Bernida spotted the blood on them. Bernida often guarded Angel's secrets, but she drew the line at anything involving blood. Until the stranger was well, Angel needed Bernida on her side, though she would not risk Bernida's well-being by confiding all. Angel stuffed her jacket under a cushion of the settee while Bernida examined the sheets.

She couldn't stifle a moan as she bent to remove her boots. Every muscle in her body ached. You'd think she was the one who'd been beaten nearly to death. The stranger had been heavier than he looked and there had been only three of them to move him.

When Bull had finally arrived at the meadow, Angel and Little Bird had understood the reason for his delay. He'd nearly emptied the cabin, but they used everything he'd brought, right down to the loaf of bread. With Bull's help, Angel and Little Bird had reset the stranger's ribs and wrapped his chest before easing him onto the travois, all the while keeping a wary eye on the wolves, which became more and more nervous as the night wore on.

Once the three friends started the short trek to the cabin with the travois, the wolves had slipped silently into the darkness and they'd all breathed a sigh of relief. Only then did Little Bird pass around the bread and a canteen of water. Angel had watched her friend as she chewed the heel, her favorite part of the loaf. Only Little Bird would have considered the animals and waited to eat until they were gone.

Settling the stranger on Bird's bed—no easy task—left Angel limp with weariness, yet she'd balked when Bird insisted she return home.

"You must go," Little Bird had said, taking Angel's arm and urging her away from the bed. "The man who did this will be watching for any sign of the stranger. If it is Juan, he'll be watching your house, too. If he sees that you're out all night, that you return with blood on your clothes, or even if you appear fatigued, he will guess you have helped the stranger."

"He will not rest," Bull had added, his tone ominous as he took her other arm, "until he finds out where the stranger is and whether he lives. It is not safe for you to ride home alone. I will come with you. We must go now, before the sun rises."

Angel had cast a lingering glance back at the stranger, whose feet and ankles protruded from the end of Bird's bed. His broken arm had been secured to his chest in a sling, but his good arm had slipped off the bed and rested, palm up, on the floor. So large and powerful, he had looked, yet his injuries would render him weak and vulnerable for many days. He would never survive another attack. Her heart had screamed at her to stay and help her friends protect him, but her head had warned that Bull and Little Bird were right. Reluctantly, she had followed their advice.

"I will clean his wounds as best I can," Little Bird had assured her, "so go now. This is not a task for a maiden."

In that instant, Angel had pictured the stranger naked and saw herself washing those long legs—and certain other areas that suddenly intrigued her. She had ducked her head and willingly sought the door and the darkness beyond it to hide the heat in her face.

Little Bird had promised to send word on the stranger's progress. If he didn't improve, she had also promised to send for help.

The ride home had passed in a blur as Angel struggled to remain upright on her horse. Twice Bull had shaken her awake to keep her from falling, but once the house came in sight, she'd waved him off and ridden in alone. She'd managed to put up her horse without waking a vaquero, and had given the weary animal an extra ration of grain for its part in the night's events.

Now she grimaced at her boots and the mud and blood splattered up the calf-high shafts. She kicked them under the settee as soon as they were off, hoping Bernida's tirade over the damaged sheets would keep her distracted. Angel wrinkled her nose, not looking forward to cleaning the boots herself. It was not a chore she enjoyed, especially when the boots were as filthy as these, but one she'd often undertaken to hide her escapades.

What was it Bernida had said when she first came in? Oh yes, Juan was here, and staying for dinner. Bull and Little Bird had been right to suspect that he'd watch the house, though he visited so frequently, Angel couldn't recall if he had been expected tonight or not. Nonetheless, she must present a calm, unruffled facade. She must not appear fatigued or worried and, above all, she must do her best to distract him from his search for the stranger.

"Enough, Bernida." Angel sat at her dressing table and began pulling a brush through her tangled hair. "I need to bathe. *Rapido!* And then I'll need you to do my hair." She tugged the heavy mass high onto the back of her head and pulled one fat curl over her shoulder to rest on the high curve of her breast. Tipping her head to the side, she considered the effect and the new plan forming in her mind.

She wasn't a beauty, but she was no armadillo, either. Usually, she dressed modestly, not wishing to draw unwanted attention, but tonight, for the first time in her life, she would seek what most women craved.

Tonight, Juan would think of nothing but her.

"Bernida, send Father a message," she called as Bernida stomped out of the room, still muttering. "Tell him I will be a little late for dinner, but be sure to say I look forward to sharing the evening with him—and his friend."

"Stop fighting me," the voice urged. "Lie still and let me tend your wounds." The woman spoke the words of the

People, but hers was not the voice he wanted, needed to hear. Then he remembered and fresh pain stabbed through him. He would never again hear that sweet voice, kiss those soft lips, roll her beneath him, and find ease in her heat. A cry of anguish escaped him and he struggled to rise, but his body refused to obey his command and punished him for trying.

"Be still," the voice told him. "You must rest, let your wounds heal."

Wounds? He struggled to recall a recent battle. Nothing came to mind but swirling, stinking smoke that stung his nostrils as he clutched Ekararo's limp, pregnant body in his shaking arms. Then fire and heat, rising to consume him. Heat from his hatred for the soldiers who had killed her and their unborn child.

Jeremiah strained against his weakness, but darkness came again, hiding the light, stealing his strength.

When he woke to face the light, a beast rose over him, laughing as it kicked and punched him. Metal gleamed and he stared into a pistol bore. No! He reached deep for the strength to fight it. He twisted, shoved the beast off him, but the gun barked and again the darkness won.

He welcomed its numbing arms, but as he sank into the long, dark quiet, he wept for the loved ones who had gone before him. Would they welcome him when his stubborn body finally allowed him to join them? Or would they turn away and blame him for their fate, a fate he should have, could have prevented?

Suddenly, a face appeared in the dark. Not the face he longed for, but a smiling face that he had not seen for years. The face became a form, and a person he knew. She did not touch him, only stood beside him, whispering.

Set aside your fears, dear brother. This is not your time to die. Sleep. Let your mind be comforted while your body heals. All you have been promised will come to you. You are not alone. You are never, ever alone.

He sighed, and let the darkness take him.

"Smile. No, no, no. Like you mean it," Bernida ordered, peering over Angel's shoulder to watch her efforts in the dressing table mirror. Angel took a deep breath—as deep as the tightly bound corset would allow—and tried again.

"No, no! That is not the smile of a woman. You smile like a frightened virgin." Bernida fussed with the ribbons in Angel's hair, scowling into the mirror over Angel's shoulder. "Have you not seen the *putas* greet the vaqueros when they ride into town?"

Angel stared. "You want me to act like a whore?"

"No, no," Bernida said with a huff. "Only to smile like one. If you cannot smile at Juan like a lover, think of another, think of someone you would wish to smile at. Someone whose touch you would welcome. Someone you would wish to kiss."

Angel's thoughts flew to the stranger as he'd looked striding down the street. In her mind, he did not turn, but came directly to her. He dropped the saddle off his shoulder, caught her about the waist, and tugged her tight against his chest. She gazed deep into his blue eyes and her breath sighed from her throat as her lips parted for his kiss.

"*Sí!* That is the way to smile at a man." Bernida shoved her off the stool and out the door. "Now go, while you still remember how."

Poised at the top of the wide stairway, Angel fixed the stranger's blue eyes and chiseled jaw in her mind, took a shallow breath—being careful not to dislodge the rolled stockings propping her modest breasts into far more interesting mounds—and began descending. She imagined a tall, dark stranger with deep brown hair waiting for her at the bottom and her hips began to sway. Her breath came faster and her smile became easy, no longer forced.

Juan and her father stepped from his study and paused to greet her. Both men offered their usual, casual greeting, then froze, watching her descent. She took the stairs slowly with a light step, not her usual gallop, allowing her hand to trail the banister as her gaze slid over Juan.

He was handsome enough, she supposed, but in a coarse, bluff way. His features were even but unremarkable, except for the deep scar that marred his right cheekbone. The women of Cedar Creek found it very manly, proof of his virility, but no one seemed to know how he'd acquired it. He matched her father in height, but not in stature, and though Juan exceeded her father in strength, he lacked self-control. His reputation was such that he could freeze a vaquero with a glance. More than once, *Papá* had been forced to berate him for his rough handling of the young grooms, and she had noticed that their maids were so reluctant to attend him that he had begun bringing his own man when he planned an overnight visit.

Unfortunately, these visits had become so frequent of late that even *Papá* had grumbled that the man might as well move in, though not within Juan's hearing.

Juan's rancho bordered theirs on the south, but he appeared to lack *Papá*'s business acumen, for his holdings did not prosper. Perhaps if he spent less time gambling at the saloons of Cedar Creek and Austin—two days' ride to the northeast—his fortunes might improve. Angel had put forth this observation as an argument against allowing his increasing familiarity, but *Papá* had scoffed at her notions and she had tried to forget them. Certainly *Papá*, Juan's mentor, knew more of the details surrounding Juan's holdings. However, she continued to note Juan's behavior, his blasé attitude toward his rancho and the people who depended on him for their living. She had seen no reason to welcome his determined attentions. Until now. She prayed that her ruse would convince him to look elsewhere for signs of the stranger, and that he'd leave the hacienda unwatched while he searched.

The lustful gleam now shining in Juan's eyes would have made her nauseated had she not substituted his face for another. He reached out to lift the curl off her breast, but *Papá* slipped neatly between them and offered Angel his arm.

"You look lovely, my dear," he said, his voice and expression heartier than usual. His lips tightened as his gaze quickly took in the changes to her person, particularly her uplifted breasts. He motioned Juan to precede them down the hall and out to the courtyard. Juan looked belligerent, but gave a grudging nod and walked quickly away, leaving them to follow more slowly. "What are you about, *querida*? I thought you did not look kindly on Juan as a suitor."

"Perhaps I have changed my mind, *Papá*." She smiled up at him and squeezed his arm. "Is it not a woman's prerogative?"

"Only if she understands the possible consequences, *hija*."

"Look more closely, *Papá*." She took a step away from him and stopped, forcing him to turn and look at her. "Is this the face, the form, of a little girl? I am a grown woman. Perhaps it is time you recognized that fact."

He leaned close to whisper, "Beware, daughter. Girls do not become women overnight. And any woman would tell you not to tweak the tail of the wolf."

"Do not worry so, *Papá*," she replied softly, with a smile and a nod to Juan over *Papá*'s shoulder. "Our guest pretends to be *el lobo*, but is as tame as a *perro*." As she entered the courtyard and took Juan's arm, she wished she could simply kick the cur, especially if he was the man who had attacked the stranger. While doubt remained, she must pretend to accept him as a friend—or more. As Juan lifted her hand to his lips— a ploy, she realized, to give him ample time to ogle her breasts—she once again replaced him with another, a dark stranger whose kiss she had begun to crave. She smiled.

Juan appeared dumbstruck by her regard. She turned quickly away. Perhaps, in order to survive the evening, she should stop thinking of the stranger and smile less often.

"*Digame, por favor.* Tell me what has brought you here to dine with us on this lovely evening?" She settled on a wrought-iron settee, positioning herself in the center and arranging her skirts to prevent Juan from intruding too closely.

With a frown, he pulled a chair nearer and sat, his knees nearly knocking into hers. He leaned back and eyed her with a salacious leer, until *Papá* also pulled a chair near and gave him a warning glance.

She smoothed her skirts and surreptitiously glanced at her chest. Finding all still intact, she relaxed and turned her attention to the conversation and the information she hoped to pry from their guest.

"Nothing more than a desire to feast my eyes on your loveliness." Even Juan's own eyebrows shot up at his flowery declaration.

Angel chuckled. "Surely, you are far too adept at flattery, señor."

He flicked a hand at her comment as if shooing a fly. "My man tells me you rode in very early this morning and only recently rose from your bed. I feared you might have been injured, yet here you are, the very picture of health."

"Me, injured?" Angel laughed and pressed her hand to her chest. "No, no, no! I found myself restless yesterday afternoon, so decided to take a ride into the hills. I was heading home, when there were gunshots—two, no, three, I believe—and a ruckus from the local wolves. They came tearing past me and frightened my poor horse, who reared so high that I slid right off his rump."

Papá cursed and came quickly to her side. "You were not injured?"

"No, *Papá*, I am well," she said, gratified by his concern but chagrined by her thoughtlessness in provoking it. "Please do not concern yourself." She placed a calming hand on his arm and turned to Juan. "Though I was uninjured, the horse bolted and left me afoot in the dark. Once he finally calmed, he returned when I called, but for a time I was very frightened. Alone in the dark, with wolves chasing about." She squeezed *Papá*'s hand again to reassure him.

She had expected Juan to express concern also, but he sat very still, as if dreading her next words. She did not keep him waiting.

"Have any of our neighbors reported aught amiss? Could the shots I heard have been one of them hunting wolves? I had no idea so many of the animals roamed nearby. Would a death in their pack cause such unrest among them?"

"I have heard nothing," Juan replied, his rigid posture easing. He crossed his legs and caressed her calf with his foot, pushing beneath her skirts nearly to her knee. She moved her leg away and glanced at *Papá*. Ah, Juan had only dared such a move because *Papá* was preoccupied with lighting a cigar.

"I sent a vaquero to visit Bull once word reached me that you had ridden in late, also to tell him that someone had heard gunshots." *Papá* blew a pillar of smoke skyward. She welcomed the rich aroma, for it masked the nauseating scent that permeated the hacienda, especially near the house. Though roses filled every corner of the courtyard, their perfume heavy on the evening breeze, Angel still detected the scent of something rotten burning beneath their sweetness.

"You did?" She plucked a rose from a bush behind her and buried her nose in its fragrant petals, striving to appear interested but not anxious, though her heart had leaped at his comment. "What did Bull have to report?"

"He said he'd helped you find your horse." *Papá* crossed his legs and stared at her, his expression clearly saying, *Get yourself out of this one, if you can.*

"He did," Angel acknowledged with a shrug that caused the fat curl riding her breast to slide into her cleavage. Juan's gaze followed, and stayed. "I did not want to drag him into this when he has done nothing to incur your anger. His assistance was very timely; he escorted me to the ridge above the casa."

Papá nodded and turned his attention to his cigar, while Angel silently acknowledged Little Bird's foresight in suggesting they agree on a story they could all relate if asked.

"Bull saw no one?" Juan put the question in a desultory fashion, as if the conversation bored him.

"Whom should he have seen?" Angel asked, fighting the urge to fling the fat curl over her shoulder and make Juan look her in the eye.

Juan looked up, his expression wary. "Why, whoever was shot, of course."

Angel struggled to remain relaxed as *Papá* stiffened beside her. "Why do you assume someone was shot?" she asked.

Juan glanced between Angel and her father, whose hand gripped the arm of his chair. "The gunshots, of course. But, naturally," he said, resuming his normal blasé manner, "it could have been someone shooting at the wolves, I suppose."

Angel shook her head. "But the gunshots came before the wolves started howling." She glanced at *Papá*.

"In fact, one howl in particular seemed to set them off. It sounded . . . different."

"Different?" Juan asked, his tone mocking her.

"Yes. Anguished, I think." She nodded and looked directly at Juan. "In great pain."

"Perhaps a wolf was injured last night," Juan said, glancing away from her to accept a glass of tequila from a servant. "That would have gotten the others excited, I'm sure." His gaze settled on *Papá*. "I'll have some of my men ride out with me to find their dens. It's been a while since we've hunted wolf. It is time, perhaps, to reduce the size of the pack. Would you care to join us?"

"Is that really necessary?" Angel asked, nearly choking on a sip of the fruity wine. "Has anyone lost cattle or horses?"

"Not yet," Juan said with a shrug, "but why wait?" He gave her a very satisfied smile. "It shall be a preemptive effort, if you will."

Angel shrugged, annoyed by Juan's deft manipulation of her careful questioning. "I fear that all this talk of shooting may spoil my appetite. And as I missed breakfast, I'm famished." She pressed a hand to either side of her waist, noticing as she did that her breasts rose alarmingly high from her bodice. Juan noticed, too, as did *Papá*, who quickly assisted her to her feet.

"Let us forget such talk for the evening, then, my dear," he said, and propelled her toward the dining room.

Angel marveled that Juan was able to keep up.

"Until we uncover the source of the gunfire that frightened you, I want you to stay close to the house. No more afternoon rides. *Comprende?*"

"*Sí, Papá.*" With those words, her appetite was truly gone.

Chapter Five

Angel glared at the bright moon overhead and pulled the shawl closer around her face. Sticking to the shadows, she hurried into the barn. If anyone caught her out at this time of night—dressed for bed, with only a flimsy shawl for protection—she had her excuse ready.

From deep in the stable, a horse nickered. A black nose appeared over the door of the last stall and snuffled Angel's pocket.

"Bella, you are far too intelligent." Angel laughed softly as she handed over the apple she'd taken from the kitchen on her way out of the casa. "How are you feeling tonight? Are you still frightened?"

The horse bobbed its head and stamped the ground with a foreleg as if answering.

"*Sí?*" Angel patted Bella's sleek neck. "Do not be ashamed. I was frightened, too."

At a deep chuckle behind her, Angel spun, clutching her shawl over her breasts. "Juan!" she gasped, and took a step backward, only to bump against Bella. She stepped away from the horse, but didn't back deeper into the stall, knowing Juan might attempt to trap her there. "I didn't hear you come in."

"You were too busy cooing to your horse." He came closer, a specter emerging from the dark, not stopping until his chest pressed against her fists where they wound into the cloth. Heat rose from him, engulfing her senses. She ignored her first instinct: to flee. For the stranger's sake, she must continue the deception she had begun at dinner and at least appear to accept

Juan's advances, though she could not bring herself to encourage him.

"What brings you to the stable this time of night?" She lifted her chin and spoke clear and loud. Surely Pedro, who bunked in the stable to be near the horses, would hear and come to investigate.

"You, *querida*." He pressed closer and leaned in, his hot breath dangerously near her bare neck and exposed shoulder.

She swallowed hard, hiked the shawl over her shoulders, and backed into the stall wall beside her, hoping to slide around Juan and out of the confining space.

"So fragrant." He breathed deep, then nipped her earlobe. "So tender."

She gasped and jerked her head aside, her tender ear lobe throbbing. She considered throwing the stranger's welfare to the winds and running for the casa. But a real woman, the kind of woman she wanted Juan to believe her to be, would stand her ground, so she did. She just hoped he would not try *that* again.

"Surely you know why I followed you here. The man does not exist who could resist the invitation you issued tonight. Have you changed your mind?" His hands settled on her waist, pulling her hips forward to rub against the hard ridge tenting his pants. She wanted to recoil, but was trapped by her charade.

"I have never thought you beautiful, until tonight when you stole my heart," he whispered as he licked her neck.

Stunned by this revelation, she forgot to protest when he pinned her against the wall. Her hands flattened against his chest as his mouth covered hers. He tasted . . . wrong, but she played her role and tried not to reveal her inexperience. However, if this was kissing, it was highly overrated.

Her mind screamed, *No!* but Juan's tongue traced her lips, pushing, seeking to enter her mouth, even as he angled his hips lower and pressed more intimately against her. With only her robe and nightdress to provide an obstacle, his erection intruded far too intimately, almost probing between her thighs. Her eyes flew wide and her body stiffened away from his. She squeezed her lips tight, gathered her strength, and shoved.

"You forget yourself, señor!" she said, and slid along the wall, anxious to escape the intimacy.

"Forgive me." His apology seemed halfhearted. "I frightened you." He reached for her again, and smiled. "This time, more slowly."

Alarmed by the heat in his eyes, the fierce cast of his features, she again sidestepped, sidling ever closer to the stall door and avoiding his greedy hands as she composed herself. How would an experienced woman, a flirt, get herself out of a mess like this? She pasted on a coy smile and said, "Your heart is safe from me, Juan. I have no designs on it."

He stroked her arm, blocking her escape with his body, and searched her face. "That is not the message your eyes sent me tonight. It is not what your body cried out when I kissed you."

Angel slid beyond the reach of his greedy hands, out the stall, and backed toward the barn door. "Only what my heart says matters, and it assures me I could never love you."

"Love?" His low laugh mocked her and a frown pulled his brows low over black eyes gone flint-hard. Deep grooves framed his mouth, and his lips compressed. "Who said anything about love? You are become *la guasona*, one who beckons a man near only to push him away, never giving what her eyes promise, what her mouth, her body, offers."

Angel shook her head, alarmed by his intensity, but determined not to let him see the fear raised by the size of his very obvious reaction. "I am no tease. I have said and done nothing to warrant these accusations. I merely spoke kindly to a guest. Do you often mistake kindness for an invitation of intimacy?"

"I mistook nothing, *bruja*." In two quick strides he had her by the shoulders, his grip punishing as his head descended.

She struggled, certain this kiss would not be tender, like his first. This time he would take what he wanted, not try to coax it from her.

"Señorita? Do you require assistance?" Pedro, her personal groom, assigned by her father to care for her horse and provide protection when she went riding, stepped out of his quarters at the back of the barn. He cradled his rifle in his arms, the muzzle pointed upward, but Angel knew it was no idle threat. He never carried it if he was not prepared to use it.

Juan slid an arm around her shoulder as he turned to consider Pedro. She watched him size up the taller, heavier man. Did he recall Pedro's reputation for knowing how to use his fists? Pedro was also known to be fast and accurate with the large knife he carried in his boot. Juan's gaze slid to Pedro's feet, then back to his face, and Angel felt the tension seep from his body.

Her knees wobbled as relief swept over her. Only Juan's hold on her shoulders kept her upright.

"All is well, *mozo*," Juan said in a mild tone, his eyes flashing her a warning as he smiled at Pedro. "*La señorita* and I were merely talking. Return to your bed."

"No," Angel said, careful to speak normally. The short fuse on Pedro's temper was also well-known and he would not like being called a servant boy. Her horse was stamping and snorting in her stall. "I am concerned for Bella. We must calm her, Pedro. I fear that she is still nervous after her ordeal last night." She stepped out of Juan's embrace and extended her hand. "Thank you for your assistance, señor. I won't keep you up any longer." Without a backward glance, she walked away from Juan, praying that he would let her go, then leave. Pedro held Bella's stall door open for her, but kept a wary eye on Juan.

Angel stroked the agitated horse, murmuring to her.

Juan stepped to the stall and watched her briefly. "Good evening, Angel. We will continue our discussion another time." He flashed Pedro a venomous glance and stomped out of the barn.

Angel continued stroking her mare until she heard the heavy front door close behind him. Then she sagged against her horse.

"Where have you been?" she said, finally lifting her head to glare at Pedro.

"I was in San Antonio. Gordo is injured so I was asked to deliver the bull to—"

"Not then, now! What took you so long to stop him?"

"*Lo siento,*" he said with a shrug, not looking at all penitent. "All the hacienda is talking about your actions at dinner. I've been gone for a week. I had to make sure your feelings for Señor Delgado have not changed. I thought that during my absence you might have come to welcome his advances."

"Welcome?" Angel choked on the word, speaking in a furious whisper. "You have not talked to Bull today?" The two men had become friends and Pedro often rode to the small cabin carrying messages for Angel or to visit in the evenings.

"I only returned minutes before the dinner bell was rung," he explained, looking surly. He crossed his arms over his chest and scowled at her.

"I'm sorry for questioning you so harshly, but Juan frightened me," she said with a sigh, and hugged Bella's neck, seeking comfort before she must recount the harrowing events of the previous night.

"Last night, Bull and I found a man, beaten nearly to death and shot three times. We spent all night trying to save his life. Bull thinks Juan was the one who attacked him, but it happened near dark, so he isn't sure. Tonight,

I pretended to like Juan so that he wouldn't be suspicious and watch the casa. I hoped to trick him into revealing something incriminating, and to keep him from suspecting that I may have helped the stranger. We think the man's attacker left him for dead, but we suspect he may search for the body to make sure." She told him how the stranger was injured and what they had done to help him, then whispered the rest of their plan to deceive the attacker into thinking the man had died.

"What did you find out from Juan?" Pedro had followed her hurried story, nodding as she went along. He, too, kept his voice low.

"More than I ever wanted to know." The image of Juan stalking toward her, his hot gaze stripping the clothes from her body, brought a chill that stopped her breath. "But nothing pertinent."

Pedro cocked an eyebrow at her. "If you hadn't invited Juan to meet you, why are you here at this hour?"

"I came to ask you to take a message to Bull and Little Bird first thing in the morning. *Papá* has forbidden me to leave the hacienda, but I must know how the stranger fares."

"I would be happy to carry your message. I have been concerned as there has been much whispering at the casa, and the condition of your horse told its own story. I want to see this stranger. He may be someone I recognize."

"I took care of Bella myself." Angel glanced around the stall, searching for evidence of last night's activity.

"And left the brushes in her stall."

Angel started, feeling sick as she realized her error. "I'll get them," she said, but they were nowhere to be seen.

"I removed them and made sure nothing remained that would raise questions." He led Angel to the small door at the front of the barn, but she paused before stepping out.

"Please tell Bull and Little Bird that I cannot leave," she asked, speaking even more softly. "Find out if Bull has created a grave to mask the stranger's disappearance. If Juan, or whoever is the attacker, thinks he died," she explained, "the attacker will relax and go about his business."

"If Juan is this man's attacker, you may have fixed his attention by your actions tonight," Pedro said. "If he remains attentive, you won't be able to move freely between the casa and Little Bird's cabin without making him suspicious."

"I intended to distract him from his search," Angel said, deliberately sounding more confident than she felt now that she knew the direction Juan's "interest" would take. Eventually, she would ask *Papá* to discourage Juan, but not until Bull could determine the identity of the stranger's attacker. Until then, she would play mouse to Juan's cat, though she detested the notion. "I had not expected the plan to succeed so well," she admitted, realizing she should have given her scheme more careful thought before diving headfirst into it.

Pedro turned to leave, but she caught his arm. "Please also ask Bull to visit Cedar Creek and listen to the gossip and rumors, find a way to mention that he found someone shot to death and buried him. Maybe this stranger spoke to someone, mentioned his name. He stayed at the boardinghouse, not the hotel. We need to find out who he is and if he has family who can take him home."

"You wish to get him off your hands?" Pedro's tone sharpened.

"No," Angel said, offended that Pedro thought so little of her. "We need to move him to safety. Bull's story must be convincing or the stranger's attacker will see through it and return to finish what he started."

"It was not a robbery?"

"The attacker wanted it to look like a robbery—he stole most of the stranger's belongings—but to beat a man so badly that you break almost every rib, and an arm?" Angel shuddered, recalling the extent of the stranger's injuries. "No, the attacker meant for him to suffer."

"I will carry your message," Pedro said, and bent to pick up her shawl, which she had dropped during her confrontation with Juan. "But I must see to my duties here first or your father will be suspicious."

"Thank you." Angel took the shawl and laid her hand on Pedro's arm. "For everything."

"Be on your guard," he warned, patting her hand. "Juan is not a man to treat lightly."

"I know that," she assured him, and stepped out of the barn, looking around first to make sure no surprises awaited her. "I can handle Juan."

As he followed her to the casa, Pedro muttered, "If you can't, I will."

Angel threw down the book she'd been staring at and rose to pace before the floor-to-ceiling windows of the casa's library. The sun, a flaming orange ball, hung low on the western horizon, but there was still no sign of Pedro.

"You are wearing a trail in that carpet, *querida*," *Papá* warned from behind his desk. He set aside the papers he'd been reading and watched her continue her agitated pacing. "I have never seen you so fretful."

"You have never before imprisoned me in my own home." The days of confinement had worn down her spirit and Angel was past caring if she offended him. After not hearing from Little Bird for two days, she had finally sent Pedro to find out what was wrong. And she sensed that something was definitely wrong.

"You are like a caged animal denied its freedom."

"Am I really, Father? How kind of you to notice."

"I cannot bear to watch you suffer," he said with a sigh as he returned to his work, "but I must keep you safe. There are rumors that someone was shot, but no body has been found."

"What about the wolves?" she asked. "Could they have devoured the body, or perhaps dragged it to their den? Have Juan's men found any dens?"

"No, but that does not mean they do not exist."

"So I am to remain a prisoner indefinitely?"

"You may continue to ride on the hacienda within sight of *la casa*, but not beyond." He slapped his hands flat on the desk and half rose from his chair. "Now leave, so that I may finish my work in peace."

"I am not a child, Father, to be sent to my room for poor behavior. I have done nothing to warrant this . . . this . . ."

He stepped around the desk and took her in his arms. "It will not be forever, *querida*. Soon you will be able to resume your normal activities."

Angel savored the rare moment of closeness between them. She leaned her head back to look into his brown eyes and was dismayed by the concern and sadness she had put there. "I am a grown woman, *Papá*. Can you not trust me?"

"Haven't you learned that grown women have more to fear than girls?" The sadness left his deep brown eyes and a welcome smile exaggerated the crow's-feet at their corners.

"More and more each day," she said, and let her gaze slide to the window.

"Has Juan been too insistent with his attentions?" *Papá*'s voice had slid into a deep baritone, as it did whenever he was concerned for her welfare.

"He has been . . . determined," she said, careful not to unduly alarm him. She flashed him a smile but looked down, unable to meet his eyes. Hers would give too much away. "But he respects me, as your daughter, and will not take more from me than I allow."

Since their encounter in the barn, Juan had begun

arriving for dinner nightly, ostensibly to report on the progress of his search for the wolves. Though she wondered how he could accomplish the task while remaining so attentive to her, she kept her opinions to herself and focused on dodging his roaming hands. Twice more he had attempted to catch her alone, but she had kept servants close at hand to foil such a move. However, with each attempt he became more insistent and more daring, though she did nothing to encourage him and had not allowed him to kiss her again.

Only the night before he had slipped into her room well after the rest of the house had retired for the night. Angel blessed her foresight in deciding to keep her maid on a cot at the foot of her bed during his overnight stays. She trusted the wolves he hunted more than the man himself.

At that moment, Pedro rode out of the trees bordering the hacienda to the northeast. He rode hard, not sparing the horse. The uneasy anxiety she'd felt all day blossomed into dread, making her nauseated. Had the unthinkable happened? Was the stranger discovered, or worse, dead?

"If you will excuse me, *Papá*, I grow weary of this inactivity. I think I'll take a walk and then have dinner in my room, if you don't mind."

Her father patted her shoulder and returned to his seat behind the desk. "As you wish, Angel."

She struggled to walk sedately out of the room, down the hall, and outside, before allowing her steps to quicken. She waited for Pedro in the shadows and tore the message from his hand before he dismounted.

Angel, come quickly, it read in Little Bird's careful, schoolhouse script. *I need your help.*

Pedro said nothing as he unsaddled his foam-flecked horse. He slipped a halter over its head and handed the lead to a groom with instructions to walk the animal until it was completely cooled, then give it a good rub-down and an extra measure of grain. Once the groom was out of hearing, he turned back to Angel. "The stranger's fever is worse and he's delirious. Little Bird is exhausted and Bull is in town trying to find out more about him."

"I must go to her," Angel whispered, biting her lip as she considered how to accomplish it. "I'll change and gather a few things," she said, thinking her plan aloud. "I told *Papá* I planned to eat in my room, which I will do. Once the servant returns for the tray, I will slip out the back way. Have Bella waiting for me."

He nodded and started for the house.

"Where are you going?" she asked, surprised that he hadn't gone to gather Bella's saddle and bridle.

"If I'm to accompany you, I must go about my routine as usual."

"No!" she said. "Two will surely be missed more readily than one."

"If your father learns that you're gone, he'll be less likely to send out a search party if he knows I'm with you. It will give us at least a few hours and by then you may be able to return to the house with no one the wiser as to where you've been."

"You're right," she said. "I will meet you at the back of the house in one hour."

He turned to leave, but she stopped him with a hand on his arm. "Did you see him?" she asked, concern for the stranger gnawing at her gut.

He nodded. "We must hurry, señorita, if you are to be of any help."

"Make it thirty minutes, then," she said, and with a brisk nod, he followed her out the stable door, both of them walking as if they had all the time in the world. No one watching would have suspected that a man's life hung in the balance.

Or so Angel prayed as she replaced her day dress with one of her many split skirts.

At a discreet tap on her door, she froze, glad that she had locked it behind her.

"Angel," Juan's voice called out. "Are you well?"

"Yes," she replied, throwing her jacket on the bed. "Thank you for asking."

"Please open the door. Your father asked me to check on you."

Her heart raced as she racked her brain for ideas to avoid him. "I beg your indulgence, Juan, but I am not dressed."

"Surely, you have a robe?" His low whisper shouted that he hoped she didn't.

Didn't the fool realize she had no intention of opening the door? His brazen pursuit must be stopped. Soon. But tonight more pressing matters weighed on her.

"Have you lost your way, señor?"

Angel's eyes sank closed in gratitude at the sound of Bernida's strident query.

"Is there enough on that tray for two?" Juan asked, his tone condescending and dismissive.

"I was not aware *la señorita* was entertaining in her bedroom," Bernida replied, undaunted.

Angel smothered a chuckle and leaned her forehead against the door. The man was a fool if he ignored the warning in Bernida's tone. He'd be wearing the contents of that tray if he pressed his luck.

"I was sent to ascertain her condition," Juan said, as always reluctant to give up his object without a fight.

"By whom?" China clinked noisily. Bernida must have set the tray on the nearby hall table, the better to deal with Juan.

"*El señor*—" he began.

"Is enjoying his meal even now," Bernida finished for him. "He sent me to bring Angel hers."

"I merely wished to make certain she is well," Juan assured Bernida, but Angel smiled at the sound of his footsteps retreating.

A few seconds later, Bernida whispered, "He's gone. Open the door."

Angel did, completely forgetting she was still wearing her riding skirt. Her apparel didn't escape Bernida's notice; the tray tilted.

Angel turned the key in the door's lock, and rescued her dinner. She set the tray on the small table before the fireplace and settled into a comfortable chair to devour it. "I don't have time to argue, Bernie. I'm going out and since you've discovered me, I hope you'll keep it under your hat."

"Oh no," Bernida said, wagging a bony finger at her. "I've covered for you too many times already."

"A man's life is at stake. I must get to Little Bird's cabin and help her. He could die," she said, catching Bernida's finger and giving it a quick kiss. "Please don't try to stop me."

"Is he the one who was shot the other night? The one whose blood was on your clothes?"

"Yes," Angel said, discouraged to learn that she hadn't fooled Bernida one bit. She nodded and shoved the food away. At the mention of blood, she remembered how much the stranger had lost. Her hunger evaporated.

"Why are you not eating?" Bernida said, holding Angel's jacket up so she could slip into it. "I will take care of things here." She winked and shook her head sadly. "It's such a shame that you aren't feeling well."

"You're a jewel, Bernie," Angel said as she shoved her arms into the jacket, then kissed Bernie's cheek. She pulled on her boots and with Bernida's help packed an old dress and a fresh chemise into a cloth bag, then slipped out the door after her.

"Take good care of her," Bernida whispered to Pedro as she and Angel joined him behind the barn, where he was waiting with a strange horse she'd never before ridden.

"Everyone knows Bella is your mount," Pedro told her. "If she's here, your father will think you are, too."

Angel waved to Bernida as she followed Pedro, keeping to the tree line and walking their horses to avoid being seen. Once out of sight of the house, they kicked their mounts into a hard gallop. Halfway there, a howl came from the hills on their right and a trio of wolves appeared, slipping in and out of the tall grass alongside their horses. Her horse slowed, tossing its head as it fought the bit, but when the wolves didn't close in, it responded to Angel's soothing touch and words of reassurance and resumed their headlong pace.

An odd excitement sang through Angel's veins, urging her onward, but to what end, she couldn't say. Her nervous energy wasn't the result of fear for the stranger. No, it went far deeper than that. She felt herself hurtling into the future, faster and faster, dragged by destiny to a place only she could fill, a role only she could play in the life she was meant to live.

With a wild shout, she tossed her hat onto her back, where it hung from the string, bouncing in the wind, taking her fanciful notions with it. She'd been confined to the hacienda far too long. Her imagination galloped as fast as her mount. She reined in her wild thoughts, focused on the task at hand, and braced herself for the gruesome toil ahead.

Angel glanced nervously at the wolves when they arrived at the cabin. Though they stayed in the trees, their unblinking stares reflected the light shining from the cabin's only window. Angel stopped counting at a dozen. She preferred to think of them as the stranger's protectors, not a threat. Their presence only confirmed what she'd suspected ever since receiving Little Bird's cryptic note: she wasn't going to like what waited for her inside. She didn't know how she could help Little Bird, who was a far more skilled healer than she, but she was prepared to give the effort all she had.

Chapter Six

Fire! The camp, all the tipis were burning. He had to circle back and find Ekararo. Bring her away from the fire, to safety.

But he couldn't move! His arms and legs were bound. The fire drew closer and beyond it was nothing but the black, moonless night.

"Ekararo! Ekararo!" He screamed her name, but she did not answer. He fought to free himself, but he was tied fast. He couldn't run and the fire burned higher, searing his skin, turning his body into a burning ember, into soot and ash.

He shook from the struggle to free himself. Weak, he was so weak. He would not find her if he didn't rest. He forced his eyes to stay open, strained to see into the darkness.

A face appeared. A woman. A stranger. Tears ran down her face. Her lips moved, but he heard only the thunder of his racing heart and the roar of the fire.

Her hand was cool and where she touched him the fire died. He stilled, all the fight leaving his body. The fire raged on, but the thunder quieted and he heard her voice.

"Shhh," she said. "Sleep. I will help you."

Cool water dribbled over his cracked lips into his mouth. Her hand stroked his brow and he breathed easier.

"What is your name?" she asked.

His eyes closed as he whispered, "Chikoba. I am *Nemene*, of the People."

* * *

"He's sleeping." Angel sank into a chair across the table from Little Bird. For hours she'd done nothing but bathe the stranger, Chikoba, and try to get him to take some broth or a little water. Her efforts were rewarded, for his fever had dropped and his delirium had abated, letting him rest.

Little Bird's compresses had done their work; his wounds were healing, but he was too weak from blood loss to fight the fever.

"Rest while he's quiet." Angel reached across the table and gripped Little Bird's hand. "He's not out of this yet and we'll need your help."

"He's in my bed," Little Bird said and settled her head on Bull's shoulder. Her brother had returned from town during the night.

"You and Angel will fit in mine," he offered. "Pedro and I will make beds in the stable."

"Don't go yet," Angel said. "Bull, did you learn anything from your trip to town?"

Little Bird and Bull exchanged a long glance. "Let's discuss this in the morning, when we're not so worn out."

Angel glanced between her two friends. "What aren't you telling me?"

Little Bird's eyes slid closed and she gave a tiny nod.

"He told Max he's Jeremiah Baldwin." Bull watched Angel, as if he expected her to scream or faint.

"Baldwin?" she repeated. The word sounded strange to her, as if she'd heard it whispered far away. "He told me his name was Chikoba and that he's Comanche. He actually said he was '*Nemene*,' of the People. Just like you hear Comanche say it. But that doesn't make sense. He's white." *Everywhere the sun hadn't touched, that is*, she thought, and hoped her hot cheeks wouldn't betray her risqué thoughts. *And he's not used to wearing much.*

Little Bird's head snapped up and she stared at Bull. "Do you think he could be the white warrior we've heard about?"

"He must be," Bull whispered, and looked around to make sure Pedro wasn't still slouched in the chair in the corner.

Little Bird gripped Bull's hand, hard. "If so, he's been living with the Comanche for years. I remember our father talking about him when I was barely old enough to understand. The white warrior rode with Quannah and his adopted brother, the war chief."

"Duuqua," Bull said. "Best war chief they ever had."

"Dew-what?" Angel asked, struggling to follow their rapid exchange.

"Duuqua, one of the Comanche's war chiefs. He led the raid on Adobe Walls last spring."

"Are you saying this white man"—Angel jerked her head toward the injured stranger—"raided white settlers with the Comanche?"

Bull nodded. "I've seen the white warrior ride. From a distance." He gave a low whistle. "One of the best, and a good fighter, too. They say he never killed civilians, only soldiers, especially after the Palo Duro fight, when his wife got trampled and died."

"She was pregnant, near delivery," Little Bird said, taking up the story when Bull hesitated. "It wasn't an accident." She glanced into her bedroom at the man who still slept soundly. "He's been reliving it all in his delirium and he's wracked with guilt over her death. I think her name was Ekararo. That's the name he keeps calling out. We had to tie him down to keep him in bed. He reopened his wounds every time he tried to get up."

"What have we gotten ourselves into?" Bull asked, shaking his head. "There's a bounty on rebel Comanche. If the sheriff in Cedar Creek finds out he's here, we'll have to turn him over."

"But he's not just a Comanche; he's a white man." Little Bird frowned and spoke slowly, as if choosing her words carefully. "Didn't Reverend Baldwin, the man who founded Baldwin Fort, have a son named Jeremiah?"

Bull glanced at Angel and nodded. "He died in the raid. They all did."

Little Bird gazed solemnly at Angel. "Not everyone."

"Are you saying he's *that* Jeremiah Baldwin, back from the dead?" Angel demanded. A growing sense of foreboding made her stomach turn and she once again sensed herself plunging headlong into something beyond her control.

Little Bird took her hand and stared into her eyes. "It's not impossible. You lived, too."

Like the roar of a steam engine, sound and smell and emotion swept over Angel. Her ears rang as guns blasted all around her. Women and children screamed, and the smoke from the burning buildings combined with a horrible, acrid smell, making her gag. Everywhere she looked people were running, bleeding, dying . . . Angel pressed her face into the bark of the tree where she'd been hiding, before the bad men came. She squeezed her eyes shut, but lost her hold on the tree. The ground swung up and slapped her face.

Not again, she thought as she swayed and everything went dark.

"Catch her!" she heard Little Bird cry as she toppled over.

She woke flat on her back where she'd fallen and blinked up at the two concerned faces staring down at her. She lifted her head and the room spun wildly around her. With a moan, she lay back and shut her eyes. "I did it again."

"Here, drink this," Bull offered her a sip of whiskey.

"Oh no," Little Bird said, taking the glass. "Remember what happened last time?"

"Oh yeah," Bull said, moving the glass out of Angel's reach. He shrugged, looking sheepish. "I didn't know it'd make her sick."

"I hate this," Angel whispered, keeping her eyes shut as she tried to stop her whirling head.

"It was bound to happen." Little Bird patted Angel's hand where it lay clenched on her stomach. "All the worry over him"—she nodded in the direction of Jeremiah—"and your father's reaction to him couldn't have helped." She helped Angel sit up, waited to make sure she wasn't going to fall over; then she and Bull helped her to a chair.

"I wish I could remember more." Angel pressed her face into her hands and sighed.

"There's no reason to try," Little Bird said. "Let the dead lie. We have enough trouble with the living."

As if to bear out her observation, Jeremiah shouted and lunged against the ropes securing him to the bedposts.

"Stay here." Little Bird and Bull hurried to calm Jeremiah. "It's your turn to rest."

When Angel was able to stand on her own, she moved to Bull's bed and slept fitfully for a couple of hours, but the screaming and gunfire blared through her dreams, disturbing her rest. Finally, worn out from the effort, she relieved Little Bird.

"Are you sure you're rested enough?" Little Bird asked, though she looked as if she, too, might fall over any second. "Bull left a few minutes ago, but we could call him back in."

The door opened and both women started as Pedro walked into the cabin. Angel smiled and beckoned him to join her. "Pedro and I can take over for a while. Go. Rest." She helped Little Bird to her feet as Pedro took the chair beside the bed and pressed the back of his hand to the stranger's forehead to check his fever.

He shook his head when she returned, then left to get some fresh, cool water from the well.

Everywhere Angel touched the man's—Jeremiah's—body, it burned. How could swabbing his head with a cool rag stop the fever raging through his legs, his chest and arms?

After hours of bathing the man's feverish skin, Angel turned to Pedro. "I've been thinking about Bird's big copper tub that hangs on the side of the house. Why not fill it with cool water and put Jeremiah in it? With one or two pots of warm water, the coolness wouldn't be too shocking, would it?"

He scowled as he looked Jeremiah over. "He's pretty big. Tall and heavier than he looks. Trust me," he said, flexing the sore muscles in his arms, "I know."

But Angel was sure her plan would work. "You and Bull can get him in the tub, but how do we keep him there? He'll fight to get out. Little Bird won't like it if he starts bleeding again."

"His gunshot wounds are high on his back and shoulder, so they won't be in the water. The other injuries are bruises, small cuts. The water won't hurt them."

"He'll need whiskey first," Angel said, rolling up her sleeves with a grim nod. "We'll start with a little warm water in the bottom and gradually add cool. That way it won't be so shocking and he'll cool down slowly."

Pedro nodded. "I'll hold his mouth open. You pour."

Hours later, Pedro snored on a pallet before the fireplace, wrapped in a blanket, his wet clothes dripping on a line strung from the rafters. Their plan had worked.

Jeremiah's fever had abated and everyone but Angel was sleeping. She'd fallen asleep sitting on the floor beside Jeremiah's bed with her head resting near his hand, but his motion had awakened her.

Jeremiah swung his good arm as if pushing something away. "Run!" he shouted in a hoarse bellow that instantly set the cabin's occupants scrambling to secure his arms and legs, which they'd left unbound after his cold bath. They'd all hoped they wouldn't have to tie him down again.

"How much more of this can he take?" Little Bird asked, her shoulders sagging.

"How much more can we take?" Bull replied, buckling his belt as he pushed through the cabin door.

There was no time for further discussion. As if the brief respite had strengthened him, Jeremiah slid into delirium with a vengeance, plunging deeper into the horrors of his life than ever before. No longer was he reliving the recent death of his wife and child.

"Run, Christine!" Jeremiah shouted in a full-throated roar, his voice no longer hoarse and raspy. The wolves outside set up a howl. "Hide, Mother. They're not just killing the men." He arced against the ropes, pulling against the rawhide binding his wrists. "It doesn't matter how they got in, they're here!"

He continued to lunge while Bull and Pedro struggled to hold him still and prevent further injury.

"Talk to him, Angel," Bull cried. "He listens to you. Talk him down."

Bull's cry startled Angel. She'd backed against the wall and had been staring at Jeremiah's tortured face, her mind flashing corresponding images of the events as he relived them. Though disoriented, she knelt beside the bed, dragging a cool cloth down Jeremiah's arm. "Hush, Jeremiah, you're safe here."

Jeremiah's face turned in her direction and his eyes flashed open. Wide and wild, they fixed on her. "Sarah? Where's Sarah? No one has seen her. I hope she's found a tree to hide in." His eyes rolled back in his head and he went limp.

Angel and Little Bird looked at each other over his body. "Who's Sarah?" Little Bird asked.

"I have no idea," Angel said, and focused on stroking the cloth over his arms. She ignored the rapid tapping of her heart and the sense of displacement that plagued her after reliving the horrors of that day through Jeremiah. To keep the memories from penetrating her consciousness too deeply, she stared at the white bandages, a stark contrast to his deeply tanned chest. She let her gaze slide lower, something she normally avoided doing.

Little Bird had long ago stripped off Jeremiah's long johns and wrapped a large piece of blanket around his lean hips. She insisted on swabbing Jeremiah's legs, leaving Angel to tend to his upper body, though Angel had scoffed at her efforts to protect her "maidenly sensibilities." Now Angel was acutely conscious of the drag of his body hair beneath her fingers, and the way his skin rose into ropes of muscle when he strained against his bonds. She noticed how large his feet were and wondered if other parts were as big.

"Mother, get back!" Jeremiah shouted, his body arcing again as he tensed, his head thrashing. "No! Don't kill her! Christine!" As quickly as he tensed, he slumped. Beneath his eyelids, his eyes moved constantly, and his face tightened in alarm, then went slack, his mouth falling open. Angel couldn't watch the suffering revealed in his changing expressions. She was glad his eyes remained closed. The horror in his voice as he relived the events of the raid struck a chord deep within her, and she, too, felt as if she was remembering the events. She saw a beautiful young woman running from a man on horseback. It was then that she, the young girl watching from a precarious perch in a tree, had pressed her face into the bark. Angel dropped the cloth and reached up to touch her face where, high on her cheekbone, she had a tiny mark, a scar that she must have gotten when very young.

Suddenly, Jeremiah's entire body tensed, every muscle standing out in sharp relief. His back arched and he bit his lip, but he didn't cry out loud. Instead he muttered, "I will not cry. They'll get no satisfaction from me. Dirty savages."

"Do you think we need to dunk him in the tub again?" Bull asked, watching Jeremiah warily from his seat on the floor beside the bed.

Little Bird pressed her hand to the back of Jeremiah's

knee. Her eyebrows went up. "I don't think we'll need to," she said, and wiped her hand on the sheet. "He's sweating. I think the fever's about to break."

As if to confirm her suspicions, Jeremiah relaxed against the bed, every muscle in his body going limp. Everyone but Angel slumped in relief.

Little Bird reached up and lifted one of Jeremiah's eyelids, felt his forehead, his cheeks, his thigh, and smiled wide for the first time in days. "He's cooling off. He's going to live."

Angel nodded and left the cabin, seeking fresh air to clear her tumbling thoughts. Who was this Sarah he'd looked for? She pressed trembling fingers to her forehead and squeezed her eyes shut. Never before had she remembered so much of that awful day. It made her head ache, her stomach turn, and though she tried to shut out the sounds and sights and smells, the sick churning of her stomach told her there was more, much more to be remembered. She tried to push it back into the dark corners where it had hidden for so long, but it wouldn't go.

Her memories were coming back, whether she wanted them or not.

Angel woke from a dream-filled nap to find Bull, Pedro, and Little Bird eating a fragrant stew. "Any left for me?" she asked as she swung out of Bull's bed. Every muscle in her body protested and she groaned in reaction.

To her disgust, they all laughed. Gingerly, she gauged her senses and was relieved to have lost the disturbing sense of unreality. Once again, she was her normal self.

"We know how you feel," Little Bird said, gayer than usual. "Eat. You need to regain your strength."

"I will," Angel said, taking a place beside her friend and accepting a full bowl and a warm slice of fresh bread. She looked over the bounty and shook her head. "When did you do this?"

"While you were sleeping," Little Bird said. "Eat! I made some tea that will take the ache out of your bones, but you can't have it until you have some food in your stomach."

Angel complied eagerly and asked around her first mouthful, "How's he doing?" She nodded in the direction of Little Bird's bedroom.

"Still sleeping," Little Bird said, her wide smile revealing the source of her good mood. "His fever's gone and he's sweating from every pore. Once he wakes, we must keep him drinking—water, tea, coffee, soup, whatever he'll take."

Pedro finished his bowl and accepted a cup of tea, which he sipped with a deep sigh. "We must return to the hacienda. Bernida won't be able to fool your father much longer. We have been gone two days."

"Two days?" Angel cried, then reviewed past events and acknowledged his statement with a nod. "You're right. Can we wait until dusk to leave? It will be easier to slip into the house after dark. Will the wolves be a problem?"

"What wolves?" Bull asked. "They left when his fever broke."

"How could they know?" Angel asked, amazed as always by the connection between the wolves and Jeremiah.

Bull shrugged. "When I went out to the barn to sleep, they were gone."

"All of them?" Angel asked, and glanced over her shoulder at Jeremiah.

"The horses were all asleep," Bull said between slurps of tea. "They wouldn't sleep if there were wolves around."

Little Bird rose and poured two cups of tea. She handed one to Angel and shrugged. "It's strange, but not unheard of," she said. "If Jeremiah has lived as a Comanche, I'm sure he observed their customs and took a spirit guide."

"You mean, the vision quest and—"

"Prayer and fasting," Bull finished. "If he's the white warrior, I'm sure he's done it more than once. Every warrior seeks an animal as a guide. He takes on its strength—keen eyesight or sense of smell, speed, courage—whatever it may be. In the vision he receives, the animal gives him a token to carry with him." Bull gestured to his own body. "Jeremiah has scars on both forearms, some fresh, barely healed. Also, he has marks on his neck, probably from the rawhide thong of a medicine bag being pulled off. I searched the area where we found him, but didn't see one. Whoever attacked him must have taken it, along with his horse and gear."

Angel sucked in a sharp breath. "I hadn't considered that. I'm sure the attacker would want to get rid of anything that might incriminate him. What would he do with it all?"

No one answered as they sipped their tea. Finally Little Bird voiced the question: "What do we do about Jeremiah after he heals?"

"I'm sure he'll have something to say about that," Pedro muttered. "If he's had a recent vision quest, he may have been sent here. Who knows what he's here for, what might happen?"

"Vision quest or not, we know where his interest lies," Bull said with a grave shake of his head. "He was riding away from the casa when he was attacked. Did he visit your father, Angel? He may be here to ask about the raid."

"What would he want to know?" Angel asked, suddenly alarmed. "Why would he want to talk to my father? *Papá* didn't have anything to do with the raid. He arrived several days after it happened."

"I suspect Jeremiah wanted to talk to him about the

land," Bull said, glancing at Little Bird, then Pedro, who nodded in agreement.

"What about the land?" Angel asked, becoming angry. "Are you insinuating that my father may have had something to do with the raid?"

"Of course not," Bull said. "But your father was the person who discovered the raid. And he now owns the land, though I'm sure it's just a coincidence. Who knows what Jeremiah might think? Did he visit your father?"

"I don't think so," Angel said, though she couldn't shake the memory of her father bending over her, angrily demanding that she stay away from the stranger. She refused to believe he could have had anything to do with the attack on Jeremiah. "*Papá* hasn't said anything about Jeremiah visiting the casa." Silently, she resolved to find out where he'd been that day, what he'd been doing, if he had indeed received a visit from Jeremiah.

"If he did visit your father, is there some reason your father would want him killed?"

"Absolutely not!" Angel jumped to her feet and faced Bull with her hands on her hips. "My father was not involved. Not in any way."

"Don't shout, Angel," Little Bird said, taking Angel's arm. "Bull only wants to make sense out of what happened that day. He isn't accusing your father of any wrongdoing."

"I'm sorry, Bull. I didn't mean to raise my voice, but you know my father. How could you even think that he could be involved?"

Bull shrugged. "You said yourself that he was agitated after seeing Jeremiah in town that day. And he told you Jeremiah was dangerous, made you promise to stay away from him." He glanced at Little Bird, then Pedro, and finally his cool, assessing gaze slid back to Angel. "Until we know more, we should keep your identity from Jeremiah. He might not understand how you, a survivor of the raid, could be living as the daughter of a man he may suspect of being involved in the raid on Baldwin Fort. Until we know him better, find out what he's after, we can't take a chance with your safety."

"Good point, Bull," Pedro said. Little Bird nodded and murmured agreement.

"Angel?" Bull asked.

At that moment, Angel heard Jeremiah stir.

He shifted in bed and groaned. When she went into the bedroom, he tried to lift his injured right arm, then reached over with his left hand to feel the arm.

Angel was beside him before his eyes opened. "Shhh," she cautioned in a soothing whisper as she pushed his hair off his forehead. She breathed a sigh of relief, noting that he still felt hotter than he should, but that he was cooler than he'd been in a long time. She wiped the perspiration off his brow. "Lie still. You've been injured, but you're safe now."

His eyes opened and he blinked, struggling to focus on her face. "Angel?" he asked in an awed whisper; then his eyes rolled back in his head and he again fell asleep.

Angel stared at his slack face, perplexed. He couldn't possibly know her name, could he? Had he, perhaps, overhead someone call her by name while she'd been caring for him? Then she realized Little Bird, Pedro, and Bull were all smirking at her.

"What's so funny?" she asked.

"The poor guy thinks he's died and gone to heaven!" Bull slapped his thigh and laughed with Little Bird. Pedro crossed his arms over his chest and pressed his lips together, but the twinkle in his eyes gave him away.

Angel rolled her eyes and shook her head while she waited for her friends to regain control. She couldn't bring herself to chastise them for laughing. After days filled with worry and tension, they were entitled to a good laugh, even at her expense.

"Won't he be disappointed?" Bull said, chuckling while Little Bird mopped her eyes.

Angel smiled at Bull. "He certainly will be if you're the first person he sees when he wakes up."

Chapter Seven

Angel slipped through the back door of her home well after dark. Though exhausted, she'd lost the argument with Pedro over who would see to her horse. Even as she'd insisted she could take care of the animal herself, she'd slipped sideways off the horse's back. Only Pedro's quick reflexes had saved her from a fall and injuries that would have been difficult to explain.

Resigned, she sighed and handed him the reins when he helped her from the horse's back, then tiptoed up the dimly lit stairwell to her room. The past two days of sleeping in shifts on Bull's lumpy bed—plus the rigors of tending Jeremiah—had sapped her strength. She couldn't get to her own comfortable bed fast enough.

She turned the doorknob, but it was locked. She jiggled the knob, making far too much noise. She'd turned to make her way back to the stairs to search for Bernida, when someone tapped on the other side of the door.

"Who is there?" her maid whispered tentatively. Then, louder, she said, "Go away! You will waken *la señorita*."

"Bernida, it's me, Angel. Open the door," Angel whispered back, glancing up and down the hallway for intruders, alarmed that Bernida had found it necessary to maintain the pretense of her illness for so long.

The door opened and Angel slid inside. Bernida closed the door softly and quickly locked it. Too tired to argue, Angel allowed Bernida to help her remove the clothes that she feared had begun to adhere to her skin. She washed quickly from a bowl of cool water and sighed as Bernida dropped her favorite nightgown over her head. After a grateful hug, she shooed Bernida away to her own bed.

Angel sighed again as she slid between the cool sheets and welcomed the blessed oblivion that soon followed. But it was short-lived. Vivid nightmares plagued her, and she woke over and over again. Hot and sweaty from tossing and turning, she lay staring at the ceiling as her room brightened with the coming dawn, her once-cool sheets a tangled mess, her nightgown riding her waist. She squinted, trying to recall what she had seen in the dreams that had frightened her so badly.

As if from a great height, she looked down on the events that had awakened her. Men rode through the gate of a tall, crude wood fence that surrounded a community of simple wooden homes. Their guns made loud popping sounds and smoke streamed from the guns' muzzles. They were shooting everyone—men, women, and children. Startled, she'd glanced toward one of the large, two-storied homes, just as a woman stepped outside and walked to the edge of the front porch. Mother!

"No, Mother! Get back inside!" she screamed in the dream. "They'll kill you."

But her mother didn't run. She stayed on the porch and turned to look at her. Angel couldn't hear her voice, but saw her mouth move, saw her gesture and understood. Mother wanted her to stay where she was. No matter what happened.

She realized she was seated on a tree branch outside the group of homes. Frightened and anxious to obey her mother, she climbed higher and straddled a branch, hiding in the leafy upper branches. She gripped the bole of the tree as Mother called to someone in the house. Four young women came running, each carrying something. One had a rolling pin, another a large, cast-iron frying pan, the third a bristly broom, but the fourth had a rifle and a pistol. She handed Mother the rifle and, as one, they swept off the porch, each of the young women throwing her a warning glance.

"Not that way!" Angel cried out to them. From her perch she could see a group of riders coming toward them, but Mother and the four women, her older sisters, wouldn't see the men until they were upon them. One sister turned back, shushed her with a finger across her lips, then walked into hell.

Angel jerked awake. She leapt from her bed and began pacing her room. Her heart pounded like a drum inside her chest and the sweat on her body made her shiver. Sisters! The four women were her sisters. Awash in a flood of emotion, she recalled their names, their faces, and the love she still felt for each of them overwhelmed her. How could she have forgotten?

She couldn't sleep now, didn't have to dream the events that had followed. She'd seen it all happen and what she'd seen had been so terrible that she had locked all her memories away, deep in her brain. She'd forced herself to forget her sweet, beautiful sisters, and her own loving mother.

She fell to her knees at the side of her bed and wept, her body shaken by huge, wracking sobs. Though she tried to recall more of the events of that fateful day, the day Baldwin Fort was raided, her mind revealed nothing but smoke and darkness, and the sickening odor that she smelled daily: death. The scent lingered in the air around the casa, sometimes so strong that it made her ill. For that reason, she tended the rose garden— her mother's rose garden, she realized with a sob—and kept vases full to overflowing in every room of the casa.

She gave up trying to control her memories and settled in her comfortable wing chair, where she waited for the sunrise. She let memories of her family from the years before the raid wash over her, hoping the good memories would assuage the pain of the bad.

As she watched the eastern horizon brighten from

dull gray to a vibrant blush, it occurred to her to wonder why no one had told her what had happened to her family. Did *Papá* even know? He'd said nothing when Juan commented recently that it was a shame Angel had never achieved the beauty of her mother. Why would Juan have said such a thing, if *Papá* hadn't known her mother? Had he also known her sisters? She resolved to ask him at her first opportunity.

By morning, she'd found a modicum of peace, but could not bring herself to try to sleep. She sensed that these dreams were only the beginning, that more memories lurked just beneath her consciousness. For good or ill, nursing Jeremiah through his delirium had loosed her own terrors.

Jeremiah groped upward through a dense gray haze, seeking the light that winked above, teasing him out of the soft, cottony darkness of oblivion. His body had stopped hammering his brain with waves of unmanageable pain, and the nightmares had given way to dreams of a young woman. He tried remembering her features, but all he could recall was a soft smile, shining blonde hair and huge blue-green eyes. He didn't even know her name.

Blinking like a barn owl hunting at midday, he moaned as he rose above the haze. Reality arrived in the form of hunger, thirst, and pain. Pain everywhere. He tried to lick his lips to ask for water, but he didn't have enough spit. He tried to sit up, but gave that up quick. After one attempt, the whole room tilted sideways, then swung into circles.

He fell back, exhausted. The only thing working was his nose, and it smelled him. Phew! He needed to throw himself in the next stream he came to. Heck, he'd just ride in and save himself the effort.

A cup of water suddenly appeared at the end of his chin. He didn't ask how or why, just opened wide and let the refreshing coolness soften his parched lips and slide down his sore throat.

Now, why is that sore? he wondered. He cautiously tested other areas and didn't like what he found. He was a bruised, broken, shot-up, bloody mess.

He squinted up the calico-clad arm of the woman holding the cup. "Thank you."

She smiled and said, "You're welcome." In Comanche.

He blinked and stared. She'd spoken Comanche, so he did, too. "Who are you?" He looked around at the log walls, the bed made of peeled log. He lay on a grass-filled mattress. It was warm and cozy, but no tipi. "How did I get here?"

Heck, he asked himself, *where's here?*

The woman chuckled and pressed the back of her hand to his forehead. "Do not fear, you are safe. My brother, Bull, and . . . a friend found you. We bandaged your injuries and brought you here to recover." She leaned forward, the expression in her black-brown eyes turning sharp. "Do you remember what happened to you?"

"I remember getting the shi—" Too late he bit back the coarse word. "Beg pardon, ma'am."

"I am Little Bird," the woman said. "I live here with my brother, Bull."

He glanced at her skin, her calico dress, and the long, black braids that lay over her shoulders. She blushed when she caught him looking her over and cocked her head.

"Yes, we are half-blood," she said, her chin lifting. "Our father is white, our mother Comanche. She died many years ago. Our father owns a small ranch just south of this cabin. He brought us to live here, near him."

"But not with him and his white family," Jeremiah finished for her.

She shrugged. "It is an old hurt. He fears the prejudice of the other ranchers, especially Don Sanchez."

"How did you know I spoke Comanche?"

"You revealed much while you fought the fever. Maybe too much," she said, but laid a hand on his arm. "Your secrets are safe with us. You are lucky we found you. Do you remember who attacked and shot you?"

"Oh yeah," he said, his body reacting to his memories, attempting to sit upright. He groaned at the pain in his ribs and eased back. "Juan Delgado. He told me himself. I remember him from the raid. He was the one who sold me to the Comancheros. I'm betting he and Sanchez were in it together."

"Sold you?" Little Bird asked, frowning.

"Yeah, Juan stole all the boys from the fort, sold us to Comancheros. They passed us on to the Kiowa a few days later."

"How would Juan have known you were at the Sanchez casa?"

"Someone was in the hall when Sanchez had me 'escorted' out. He probably had his ear to the door. Maybe Sanchez even told him to get me."

"But why?"

"I think they're partners, working together. Probably have been for years, since before the raid." He must sound loco, but even though he couldn't prove his suspicions, he felt the truth of them in every aching muscle and broken bone.

"Did Señor Sanchez also attack you?"

"No," Jeremiah said, fighting to stay awake. Everything was looking hazy again. "He wouldn't dirty his hands, but Juan's killed before." He looked Little Bird in the eye and managed to whisper, "He'll kill again." The haze took him under again, but not before he saw the fear in her eyes. He felt bad about putting it there, but she had to know. He only hoped she and her brother didn't suffer for helping him.

* * *

"Angelina?" *Papá*'s voice at her door, followed by a firm knock, sent Angel's heart scurrying. "May I come in?"

"One moment, *por favor.*" After a quick glance in the mirror—and a grimace at the deep circles under her eyes—she settled into her armchair and sagged, closing her eyes for effect. She hated the pretense, but she must protect Bernida, who had told everyone she'd been too ill to leave her room for three days. "Come in, *Papá.*"

She didn't look up until he settled on her dressing table chair.

"*Querida,*" he said, and smoothed a stray curl off her forehead, "you do not look well. I will send for Dr. Ingmann. Bernida said it was not necessary, but now that I see you, I feel she was wrong."

"No!" Angel said, startled. "I am much better and will be fine in a day or two more." The worry on his face made her stomach twist into knots. She caught his hand and squeezed it tight. "Do not worry. I am strong, and Bernida has taken good care of me."

Though he appeared ready to argue, *Papá* nodded, then leaned away and looked her over more carefully. "You have lost weight, but do not worry. Bernida has ordered a hearty meal for you today. If you feel well enough, I will join you for dinner."

"*Gracias, Papá,* but I would not wish to spoil your meal if I am unable to keep mine down again." She scrunched up her nose in distaste and glanced at the large basin Bernida had placed on the floor beside her bed.

Papá's gaze seemed to linger on it a moment and he swallowed hard. "Yes. Perhaps I will ride into town again this evening."

When he started to rise, Angel stopped him with a hand on his arm, but couldn't bring herself to ask the difficult questions troubling her.

"What is it, *querida*? You seem sad this evening." He squeezed her hand and Angel took it as encouragement.

"I have been thinking . . . remembering the raid on Baldwin Fort. I—I had a dream last night. I remembered my mother and my sisters." She looked up at him, searching his face, his eyes, for the answers she sought. "Why hasn't anyone told me about that day?"

Papá rose and stepped to the window. Angel watched him and waited, hoping he knew something that would ease her mind. "When we discovered you . . ." He gave her a long look over his shoulder. "Let me begin again.

"You appeared out of nowhere—ragged, filthy, frightened, and hungry. Unfortunately, we had piled the bodies in the square and had begun to burn them. There were so many," he hastened to explain, "and we could not bury them fast enough. The bodies were decomposing.

"You walked up and before we could think what to do with you, you recognized one of the bodies." He crouched down before Angel and took both her hands in his. "I will never forget the look that came over your face before you began to scream. I swore a vow that you would never again wear that expression. I took you away with me and I have made every effort to keep you safe."

He squeezed her hands. "Have you been unhappy with me as your father?"

"No, *Papá*. You have made me very happy, but now I need to know what else lies hidden in my mind. What else have I forced myself to forget?"

"I cannot help you remember, *hija*."

"But Juan said—"

"Juan is unkind."

"You knew my mother," Angel said, unwilling to let the matter drop.

"I met your mother once, as did Juan," *Papá* explained. He rose to his feet, his movements heavy, almost pained. "She was a very beautiful woman."

"Yes," Angel said, her eyes stinging as tears threatened. She blinked the tears away, not wanting to upset him any more than she had already done with her questions.

"Enough talk of the past and things that cannot be changed. We must look to the future and be thankful for our many gifts. Ah!" He smiled and began patting pockets. "Before I go, I have something for you."

"A gift?" Angel's eyes popped open wide. *Papá* had always been very generous. Over the years he had given her many gifts, especially after they argued or, as now, when she recovered from an illness. She found it odd that he felt the need to reward her for recovering from illnesses. She couldn't decide if it was his way of expressing gratitude that she had survived, or if he felt the need to beg forgiveness for failing to protect her from the illness in the first place.

"After our last dinner together, I realized you have become a woman." He reached into his pocket and withdrew a deep blue velvet bag with a gold cord drawstring. She recognized the bag as the kind used by a very exclusive jeweler in Mexico City, where *Papá* often shopped when he went there on business. The strand of beautifully matched pearls he'd given her on her eighteenth birthday had come in just such a bag.

"*Papá*," she said in a choked voice, "you spoil me."

He chuckled as he set the bag in her hand. "I have been keeping it for you." When she merely sat staring up at him, he nudged her arm, not looking at her. "Open it."

With trembling fingers, she released the knot in the cord and gasped as a beautiful ruby necklace poured into her lap. Inexplicably dismayed, she pretended delight and managed a smile as she picked up the necklace. "Will you fasten it?" she asked, and rose to stand before the full-length mirror in the corner.

Papá slid a hand beneath her elbow to help her rise, then moved behind her to fasten the clasp. "It becomes you," he said, smiling at her in the mirror. His breath whispering on the back of her neck made her shiver.

"You've been keeping it for me?" she asked, trailing a finger over the jewels, which were linked together with strands of gold chain, descending to a larger stone that rested at the beginning swell of her breasts. She had seen this necklace before, but could not remember where or when.

"It belonged to your mother," he said, and leaned forward to kiss her cheek.

Angel staggered under the weight of the necklace as images cascaded through her mind, punctuated by lilting music, happy laughter, and bright, twirling skirts. In her mind, a woman danced before her, the rubies around her neck flashing as she threw back her head and laughed. The man holding her echoed her laughter, then kissed her cheek before whirling her off into the dance once more.

Angel's strength fled as abruptly as the vision, but laughter continued to echo in her mind as if mocking her. Only *Papá*'s quick reflexes and strong arms saved her from falling into and possibly shattering the mirror. With an arm around her waist, he helped her to her chair.

Helplessly weak, she welcomed his strength and let him put her where he would. "I'm sorry. A sudden wave of nausea," she said, and pressed a hand to her stomach as if to quiet its queasiness. "Please, help me take it off. I don't want to sully it should I . . ."

"Ah, I understand," he said, his face showing nothing but concern for her welfare. He quickly released the necklace's catch.

Angel clutched it to her chest, preventing it from sliding into her nightgown, though the cool metal scorched her fingers and made her whole body tremble. She pulled it away from her skin and handed it to him, making a sincere effort to smile and appear grateful. "Thank you, *Papá*. It is very beautiful."

He carefully slid the necklace back into its velvet bag and tied the cord. "You are certain you like it, *querida*? If it is not to your taste, I can have the jewels reset—"

"How could I not? Truly, *Papá*. It is beautiful just as it is." She sank into the welcoming softness of the chair, letting it absorb some of her shock, unable to take her eyes off the bag. "Thank you."

He set the necklace on her dressing table. "I will send Bernida to you, and have Pedro ride for the doctor immediately. I am concerned about you." He again leaned over her, this time to kiss her forehead. "Be well, *hija*. I will check on you tomorrow."

Angel nodded, still reeling. Her gaze remained locked on the bag as she relived the moment she'd last seen the dazzling necklace around the neck of a happy, laughing woman. That woman was not her mother, and though Angel knew her, she could not remember her given name, only her surname and her face. Her features were bold and striking, especially her blue eyes, which were the exact shade of her son's.

The necklace had belonged to Jeremiah's mother, not Angel's.

When Bernida rushed into the room several minutes later, Angel was on her knees utilizing the large basin beside her bed. She endured Bernida's coddling and scolding, preoccupied by her nausea, then by her attempts to sort out what was truth and what was a lie.

Papá had lied about the necklace so smoothly, without blinking. Could he truly not know that the necklace hadn't belonged to her mother? How had he come to have it? Had he stolen it? Had someone else given him the necklace and told him it belonged to her mother?

Had he told her it belonged to her mother in a misguided effort to give her something meaningful or emotionally significant to assuage the pain of her returning memories? Or had he mistaken Jeremiah's mother for hers?

After Bernida left, Angel sought relief from the heat of her room by stepping out on the veranda. She gripped the iron rails, every pore clamoring for the refreshment she always found in the cool gurgle of the fountain below, the rustle of leaves and a soothing breeze, and the mellow strains of guitar music coming from some vaquero wooing his señorita. Tonight, all the elements combined in their usual comforting way, but they brought her no peace.

Papá had nothing to do with the raid on Baldwin Fort and the death of its residents, particularly Jeremiah's mother. She believed that with all her heart. He must have purchased the necklace from another, someone with blood on his hands. Juan, perhaps?

What else had this person stolen? Mere objects, like the ruby necklace, or the lives of an entire community?

She could not begin to imagine. However, of one thing she was certain: she could not tell Jeremiah about the necklace. He would see it as proof that *Papá* had planned and executed the raid and, whether directly or indirectly, murdered the citizens of Baldwin Fort. She'd keep the necklace safe—though she couldn't bear to touch it—until she could prove *Papá*'s innocence.

Then she'd give the necklace to Jeremiah. It might be all that remained of his family.

Sweat broke out on Jeremiah's brow as he pushed himself upright against the rough log headboard. His good arm shook from the effort. So did the rest of him.

"*By the Sun!*" he said, and closed his eyes, waiting for

his vision to clear. He was getting sick and tired of this bed. High time he pulled himself up by the bootstraps and started doing for himself. No more having his meals brought to him, pissing in a pan, and all the other embarrassments. All because he hadn't been paying attention and had let a weasel sneak up behind him.

"You're lucky to be alive." Bull stood beside the bed, holding a plate of something that smelled even better than Ekararo's venison stew.

"How do you do it?" Jeremiah asked, and reached for the plate.

"Ah, heck, I'm just the delivery boy." Bull ignored his hands and set the plate on a small table beside the bed. He slid it close, then handed Jeremiah a fork. He crossed his arms over his chest and grinned.

Jeremiah let his first bite sit a moment on his tongue. How long had it been since he'd eaten solid food? No matter. For the rest of his days, he'd remember this as the best meal he'd ever had. "How do you read my mind?"

"Easy," Bull said, setting a mug of hot coffee beside the plate. "I imagine what I'd be thinking or feeling if I were in your shoes."

"Little Bird," Jeremiah called, hearing her knocking plates together at the stove around the corner, "you ever need a dinner guest, I'm your man."

"What about me?" Bull asked. "I shot the damn thing."

"Cows don't run very fast," Little Bird replied with a merry laugh. "Did you make sure of the brand this time?"

"Yes, it was one of good ole Pappy's yearlings. They'll never miss it."

"You sure of that?" Jeremiah asked. His father had gone to great pains to keep track of the fort's cattle.

"Hell, yeah, I'm sure," Bull said, stomping back from the stove with his own meal.

Jeremiah chuckled. "Don't get all het up. I was just

asking." He stuffed another forkful of tender meat into his mouth and nodded to Little Bird. "My compliments, ma'am."

She gave him a tight nod, acting as if she was above getting flustered by a compliment from a hungry man, but the color in her cheeks gave her away. Damn, but he loved to make a woman blush. "You've been drinking broth so long, you'd think shoe leather came straight from heaven."

"Maybe so." Jeremiah scooped up some greens and let them slide down his throat, savoring the bits of bacon and fat that added to the flavor. If he didn't need to get busy finishing what he'd been sent here to do, he'd take his time about getting well and enjoy Little Bird's cooking and Bull's company. Each of them pulled up a chair beside his bed to join him while he ate. Of course, he'd bring Bull and Little Bird an elk or a big buck to thank them for their care, but he had to get back on his feet soon and get moving before he brought trouble to their door.

"Speaking of heaven, I had the strangest dreams in my fever. I saw this woman. Twice."

Little Bird and Bull both stopped chewing, then began again, only faster. "A woman?" Bull said, and glanced at Little Bird. She shrugged and kept eating.

"Yeah, a woman," Jeremiah repeated. "Blonde hair, blue-green eyes, about this high." He gestured with his hand to keep his mind off the parts he chose not to mention, like the soft bow of her lips and the slim curve of her hips. "Pretty as an angel."

Bull choked. Little Bird elbowed him in the ribs.

Jeremiah raised an eyebrow at them. "Anyone you know?"

A wolf howled outside and Bull jumped to his feet. "Now what are they up to?"

Jeremiah reached for his medicine bag. When he

didn't find it in its usual spot on his chest, he pinned Bull with a glare. "Where's my medicine bag?"

Bull froze, as if glued to the spot. "He took it. I figured you probably had one, seeing the mark on your neck."

Jeremiah felt the side of his neck and found the healing wound. The rawhide string must have burned his skin when the bag was yanked off. "What else did he take?"

"Everything. Your horse bolted when the wolves came rushin' up, but your attacker had taken off your gun belt. I searched for it the next day but didn't find it or your gun."

"Thanks." Jeremiah tried to slide back into the bed but didn't have the strength for even that simple task. With an arm under his shoulders and one under his knees, Bull slid him down.

Little Bird came next, fluttering around him, checking her bandages and the smelly poultice on his shoulder wound. "Your shoulder's bleeding again." She shook her head. "I should have fed you myself, not let you sit up and—"

"No need to fuss, I'm fine." Jeremiah caught her hand. "You and Bull have done so much for me already. I don't know how I can ever repay you, but I'll find a way."

"Not necessary," Bull said, his voice firm. "It's plain you're a proud man, but you nearly died, so you're gonna have to let go of that pride awhile and accept our help. Whatever you need, ask for it and don't worry about repaying us. The day may come when we need your help."

"All right, then," Jeremiah said, accepting Bull's terms. "You both have my thanks and my promise that if you ever need my help, all you have to do is ask."

"Rest," Little Bird said, and smoothed the blanket over his chest.

Jeremiah closed his eyes and sighed, feeling the strain on his body tugging him toward sleep, but his mind wasn't nearly so worn out. "Would you do me one favor, then?"

"Sure," Bull said. "What do you need?"

"Next time you see Angel, thank her for me."

Chapter Eight

"I don't see the need for secrecy," Angel said, snapping her small riding quirt against her leg as she paced behind Bull's and Little Bird's two-stall stable. Here a fine-bladed grass covered the ground beneath two tall trees. Bull had built a deep-seated bench against the stable wall and near Little Bird's herb garden. It was a serene place where she and Little Bird often came to chat while they harvested vegetables, or watch the june bugs dance in the evening.

Tonight, it didn't feel at all serene to Angel. "Jeremiah's well enough to be told who I am."

Pedro shrugged. "According to Bull, Little Bird thinks it's too soon. She says he needs more time to recover."

"What? Why didn't someone tell me he isn't healing?" Angel spun on a heel and headed for the house, but ran into Little Bird, who was coming down the porch steps as Angel rounded the corner. She caught Little Bird's arms and held on until they both regained their balance.

"What's wrong?" Angel shoved a lock of hair off her face and resisted the urge to shake Little Bird, who was staring at her with a puzzled frown. "Why didn't you send word that he wasn't getting better?"

"He's coming along fine. What's this about?" Little Bird looked to Pedro for an explanation.

He shrugged and shook his head.

"Angel, he's fine." Little Bird gripped Angel's shoulders and gazed into her eyes. "Calm down. Bull and I sent for you because I wanted to find out if you've learned anything new about the attack on Jeremiah."

"No, I haven't." Knowing Little Bird hadn't told her everything—and wouldn't until she was ready—Angel turned away and began pacing. Head down, she watched each step, debating whether to add to the confusion by telling her friends about her returning memories.

"She hasn't been sleeping," Pedro said, taking the matter out of her hands. He ignored her angry glance. "Bernida says she's having bad dreams, remembering the raid."

Angel stopped before him, hands fisted on her hips. "Does no one at my home have anything better to do than gossip? You and Bernida are like two old women, sharing juicy morsels over the back fence."

Pedro flushed, but stood his ground. "Deny it."

"You know I can't." She watched him stomp away before turning to Little Bird. With a heavy sigh, she lifted her hair back from her face and stepped into a shaft of light coming from a nearby lantern, hanging from the porch. "See for yourself."

Little Bird drew a sharp breath. "How do you see between the puffy lids and those bags under your eyes? Bernida should have sent for me." She took Angel's cheeks in her hands and tilted her face this way, then that. "I'll make a poultice to take down the swelling, and give you a tea to help you sleep."

"Will it keep me from dreaming?" Angel sank onto the bench beneath the stable's eaves and patted the seat beside her.

"Are the memories bad?" Little Bird asked, taking the offered seat. She squeezed Angel's hand.

"Very." Angel let her head rest against the wall. "Did you know I had four sisters? All older than me." Her throat tightened and she couldn't continue.

Little Bird squeezed her hand. "Try to remember the good times, the laughter and the holidays. Let your happy memories comfort you."

"I try, when I'm awake. I don't have any control over the dreams." She turned her head and gripped Little Bird's hand harder. "I know *Papá* didn't have anything to do with the raid. He's always been so generous and loving to me. He would never take part in something so ugly."

"Have you asked him about it?"

"Yes." Angel released Little Bird's hand and crossed her arms over her waist. She held tight, wishing the pressure would ease the churning in her stomach. "He gave me vague answers, said he'd met my mother once."

"What about Juan? Did your father say anything about him?"

"Only that Juan was 'unkind,' whatever that means. He has told me nothing I didn't already know." Angel shook her head, anxious to change the subject and stop speculating on *Papá*'s guilt. "So why did you send for me? And why are we talking behind the stable?"

"Bull will be here in a minute. He helped Jeremiah bathe and now he's helping him get back into my bed, which he's come to hate." She sat up, her expression bright and excited. "I forgot to tell you! Jeremiah has been walking around without help today for the first time. Now that he's able to eat more than broth, he's healing quickly."

"Wonderful!" Angel cried, and jumped to her feet, ready to rush into the cabin to see this miracle for herself. "That news was worth the ride out here."

"Wait!" Little Bird cried, catching Angel's hand. "Don't go in yet. Let's talk first."

"We've been talking. What haven't you told me?" Angel faced her friend, her stomach lurching as frightening possibilities chased through her mind. Had Jeremiah's shoulder wound become gangrenous? Had he lost the use of his injured arm? "What's wrong with Jeremiah?"

"Nothing. He's fine," Little Bird rushed to assure her,

rising to face her. "But Bull and I don't think it would be a good idea for you to see him again."

"Not see him? Ever?" Angel's heart lurched at the thought. Since the day she'd seen him in town, most of her thoughts had centered on him. She couldn't explain why, but the thought of not seeing him again—ever—left a gaping hole inside her.

"He remembers who attacked him, Angel," Little Bird said. "It was Juan."

Angel's heart jumped into her throat and started drumming. "As we suspected." She searched Little Bird's face, touched by the worry she saw. "There's more, isn't there?"

"Before he was attacked, Jeremiah had gone to your house. He asked your father about the land, how he learned about it, who sold it to him. He wanted to know everything. Your father refused to show him his deed to prove that he owned the hacienda. He threw Jeremiah out and told him never to come back, that there was nothing there for him anymore."

"Do you believe Jeremiah?" Angel asked, her alarm increasing with each word Little Bird uttered. "He could be making all that up to cover his own motives. I wonder if *Papá*'s story would be the same."

"Why would Jeremiah lie?"

"To make it appear that *Papá* wants him dead, to cast more blame on him and make us suspicious. After all, if a man could order the death of a stranger, what wouldn't he do to acquire so much land?" Angel waved an arm wide, then turned away from Little Bird's sad expression. She knew her friend thought her naïve when it came to *Papá*'s character, but she loved him and knew that he loved her, too. A man with the capacity to adopt an orphaned child, a total stranger to him, and love that child unconditionally could not take another's life.

Unwilling to damage her friendship with Little Bird,

Angel decided to change the subject. Little Bird would come to understand in time. "What did he tell you about Juan?"

"He believes Juan overheard his conversation with your father."

Angel wanted to laugh. Jeremiah's logic was so transparent. How could her friends, people she respected, whose keen intellect she admired, readily accept his story? Did they hold a grudge against *Papá*? She knew that her father would not associate with people of mixed blood. He had refused to allow her friends to visit her at the casa and once he'd even asked her never to see them again. But he had backed down when she protested and agreed to let her visit them occasionally at their home. Obviously, Bull and Little Bird had been offended. "That doesn't mean he attacked Jeremiah. It was nearly dark when he was attacked. Is Jeremiah certain it was Juan?"

Little Bird shook her head. "I was afraid you'd be like this."

"Like what?" Angel shot back. "Were you afraid I'd defend *Papá*?"

"No," Little Bird said with a weary sigh. "I expected you to defend your father. I was afraid you'd be stubborn, that you'd close your ears and not even listen."

"As usual," Bull said as he joined them, stepping quietly.

"Why are you sneaking around?" Angel asked, ignoring his barb.

"I'm trying to be quiet—unlike the two of you," he said with a smug grin as he sprawled in the middle of the bench, leaving Angel and Little Bird nowhere to sit.

"Move, oaf." Little Bird pushed him off the bench and motioned to Angel to join her, leaving Bull no option but to settle cross-legged in the long grass before them, leaning back against a tree.

"Don't know why I put up with you," he grumbled.

"Because I cook and clean for you?" Little Bird said. "I've told Angel about Jeremiah's meeting with Sanchez. She doesn't believe me."

"I heard," Bull said. "I hope he didn't hear, too." He nodded toward the cabin.

"She wants to see him," Little Bird said.

"Stop talking about me as if I wasn't here," Angel said, beyond caring that she sounded irritable. "I have to know he's all right, that he's going to be well again."

Little Bird and Bull shared a long look; then Bull turned to Angel and said, "You'll have to trust us. It's not safe."

"When pigs fly and horses moo," Angel said with a very unladylike snort, glaring from Little Bird to Bull and back again. "Why isn't it safe?"

Pedro rejoined them. "The horses are quieter than you three." He sat beside Bull on the grass and looked up at Angel. "They're right. You should listen to them. They've spent more time with Jeremiah than you and they know why he's here."

"You do?" She looked between Bull and Little Bird. "What does he want?"

"He's here to find out who was behind the raid. He decided to start with the land, which led him to your father, the current owner," Bull explained. "Then Juan attacked him, which means he's on the right track so he's gotta lie low. But he hasn't given up. No, sir. He's more determined than ever to find out who's responsible for the raid and the murder of his family—and yours."

"Why does this mean I should stay away from him?"

Bull sighed.

Little Bird shook her head. "Angel, you're still being obstinate," she said. "If he finds out that you're Sanchez's daughter, he's going to hate you as much as he does your father."

Angel gasped. "He wouldn't!"

"You sure of that?" Pedro asked.

"None of us knows how he'll react," Bull said.

"I'm willing to take that chance. I'm not leaving until I see him again," Angel insisted, knowing she'd pushed her friends to their limits, yet unable to leave without seeing Jeremiah one more time. She didn't know why, but from the first moment she'd seen him walking down the street toward her, she'd known this man was someone she needed to know better. She knew she could trust him. He'd never hurt her.

"Well, good, 'cause I wanted to see you again, too." Jeremiah leaned against the cabin to stay upright. He was seeing black spots and knew he was about to melt into a puddle, but first the loud voices, then the mention of his own name, had drawn him outdoors.

Bull swore and jumped to grab a chair off the porch. He slid it under Jeremiah's swaying butt seconds before he fell. Jeremiah reminded himself to thank Bull for saving his dignity. Later.

"Do you mind if Angel and I talk a bit?" When Little Bird's fingers tightened on Angel's arm, he added, "Alone."

Pedro rose and crossed his arms over his chest. Jeremiah nodded at him. "She's safe with me, hombre. What?" he asked when Pedro didn't budge. "You a slow runner?"

Pedro snorted, but he turned abruptly and left. Jeremiah knew the other man wouldn't go far, but he wasn't concerned. He had a few questions for Angel, like why she insisted on seeing him again.

"Go," Angel told Bull and Little Bird. "I'll be fine. I could probably knock him over with a deep breath."

They left, their steps slow on the wooden porch, the door closing lightly behind them. Luckily, it squeaked when opened, so he'd know if someone was eavesdropping.

Once alone with Angel, he searched her face. She

reminded him of someone he'd known as a boy at Baldwin Fort: an older woman, the wife of one of his father's trusted council members. But Angel was her pale shadow.

And then she smiled.

Her whole face lit up from inside. The sadness left her gaze and she seemed to glow in the dusky light. Her large, hazel eyes were her best feature, along with her lean, willowy figure. She wasn't buxom, but he liked small, sensitive breasts, like Ekararo's.

His whole soul jerked away from the thought, the comparison of this stranger to the woman he loved. How could he think of the two in the same breath?

"You want to talk to me?" He winced. His voice sounded gruff, harsher than he'd intended. Hell, he wouldn't blame her if she decided to leave him alone in the dark.

She surprised him by stepping closer. Arms crossed over her middle, she looked him up and down. He liked the way her blouse fit her, full over her chest and snug at the waist of her split skirt. The legs of the skirt were cut wide, hanging well past her knees, where they met the upper shaft of a pair of black leather, low-heeled riding boots.

He knew nothing about women's clothes, the cost of cloth and such, but he knew boots. And hers were some very fine foot leather. He'd love to get a look at her horse.

He glanced up and caught her looking him over, too, with a gleam in her eye any man would recognize. Weak as it was, his whole body responded. Every damn bit of it.

He opened his mouth to warn her off, to explain that he was grieving . . . but she didn't wait for him to speak.

She leaned over him, looking in his eyes, braced her hands on the chair behind him, and kissed him.

Only problem was, she didn't know how. Her puny

little pucker was about as exciting as kissing the back
of his own hand, but he stuck with her, curious to see
how far she'd take it. Hell, she hadn't even closed her
eyes, and stared back when he opened his. Then she
sighed and her eyelids slid closed. Her pucker flattened. Something inside him rolled over and quivered.

She was a quick learner, he'd give her that. Her lips
parted and he heard someone groan. His eyes popped
open. Damn, that was *him*. She slanted her head and
pressed her lips harder, being careful to keep her weight
off his chest. He appreciated her consideration, but he
missed the feel of a woman's curves pressing against
his body while his cock rose in welcome.

She was breathing heavy. No. That was him again.
Well, hell. He was in this thing, might as well enjoy it.
He grabbed her waist with his good hand, and pulled
her down on his lap. Weak as he was, he didn't know
how long he could keep this up, but before he was
done, she'd at least be able to tell her friends—who
probably had their ears pressed to the walls—that
she'd been thoroughly kissed.

Luckily, the chair Bull had shoved under him didn't
have arms, so when he pulled her down, she sat astride
the action, with nothing but the flimsy fabric of her riding skirt between them. His britches had become so
damn tight, he was afraid the buttons might give.

To distract her from what was happening down low,
he ran his tongue along the seam of her lips and when
she sucked in a surprised breath, she got more than air.

He traced her open mouth with the tip of his tongue,
and at the same time let her feel the press of his growing desire between her legs. Her arms tightened around
his neck and she opened her mouth wider. He slid his
tongue deeper into her mouth and her tongue tangled
with his. She must have got caught up in the duel, to let
her weight settle fully onto his lap and his erection.

The sudden pressure against her woman's place

seemed to scare her. She squirmed away, her breasts heaving, her lips swollen and full, leaving him hungry and hurting. Her wide eyes fixed on his face and he could tell he'd excited her curiosity. She wanted more, a lot more.

So did he, damn his hide.

When she slid off him, he pressed down on his cock, hard, trying to ease the pain, knowing only one thing would fix his problem. He wasn't going to get it, had known from the start that he wasn't going to get it. So, why'd he let things go so far?

"I've wanted to kiss you since that first day when I saw you walking away from the livery in town." Her smile stirred his irritation.

"How would you know? You've never been kissed before," he said, struggling not to let frustration goad him into saying something hurtful. He shoved his hands into his pockets to keep from reaching for her.

"How could you tell?" Her disappointment kicked him in the gut.

"I'm a little more experienced than you," he began, not sure how to explain.

"I know you've been married, but you're not anymore." She sucked in a shocked breath and covered her mouth.

"Did I talk a lot while I was out?" What else had he blabbed while he'd been out of his head? He didn't want to hear it from this sweet slip of a woman. He'd corner Bull later.

She nodded and went still, then stared off toward the hacienda, the huge ranch that had once been Baldwin Fort. "The more you talked, the more I remembered," she said, her gaze returning to his.

"I don't understand," he said, frowning. His life had been pretty unusual. What could they have in common?

She waited, as if she knew he'd find the answer on his own, and then he did. Baldwin Fort. He grabbed her chin, turned her face toward the light from a lantern on the porch behind him.

"O'Connor," he said in an awed whisper, finally putting two and two together. That other woman she resembled was her mother! He should have known her at first glance, would have known her if it hadn't been so long ago. But which O'Connor was she? There had been five girls in the family, no boys, except for Mr. Patrick, the girls' father. His sister, Christine, had been best friends with the fourth daughter, Maude, and the youngest, Sarah, had been his private tormentor. "Sarah?"

The woman before him shrugged. "I don't know what my name was," she said, her expression turning wistful. "I forgot everything."

"You forgot who you are?" He struggled to understand, but he'd been there that day, too. He envied her the forgetting. If he'd been able, he would have forgotten, too.

"I only started remembering after hearing you talk about the raid. You were out of your head. We had to tie you down to keep you from bleeding to death." She shuddered and clasped her arms about herself. She paced a bit in front of him as she continued. "The dreams didn't start until the night I went home, once your fever broke. That night I relived my mother's and sisters' deaths."

Jeremiah didn't say anything. He remembered so many deaths; most he'd managed to bury in his mind, too. He didn't let those memories out of the corners; it was too hard to shove them back into the dark again. Instead, he looked over the woman pacing before him. Should he help her remember? Should he tell her that she'd fallen in love with him before she could walk, that she'd made his teenage years hell by following him everywhere he went? He'd never confess that he'd broken her little-girl heart and made her cry.

He couldn't blame her for shutting her mind to all the

ugliness that happened the day of the raid, and wished he could spare her the pain of reliving it. But she was a survivor, like him. They were the only survivors of a day from hell.

She'd once been the spoiled darling in a family of pampered women, and now she was . . .

Who was she, exactly?

"What's your name now?" he asked, his voice low and controlled.

"Angel," she replied, her gaze steady on his face as she told him everything. "I am Angelina Maria Sanchez, daughter of Don Miguel Sanchez."

At first he couldn't move, couldn't breathe, just absorbed her name, her situation. Then the shock and horror spewed out of him.

"I'm pretty certain he's the man behind the raid. How can you live with him? Be his daughter?" he demanded, his voice rising. He couldn't separate the sound of running feet from the pounding in his brain. Angel's friends arrived and gathered around her, wary and watchful.

"I love him," she said, her chin lifting. "He saved me and has loved and cared for me ever since. He is not the man who did this thing. I did not know about my mother and sisters, my family, until recently. I have barely remembered loving them, and they are gone."

"You loved me, too," he told her, throwing his own regrets in her face. "As a child, you followed me everywhere. And just now you kissed me. You haven't forgotten everything.

"Look at me, Sarah." He pointed at his body, weak, still healing. "Someone tried to kill me for asking questions about that day, about the people, their belongings, their land. Your *father's* friend, Juan, did this to me, probably on your father's orders. How can you love a murderer?"

"He is no murderer," she said, keeping a lid on her anger, but remaining firm. "He is my father and we will prove that he is the rightful owner of the land. He is not the man you seek."

"You always were a stubborn little twit, Sarah," he said.

"My name is Angel." She ran to her horse, mounted and kicked it into motion. In the silence she left behind, her horse's hoofbeats pounded like Comanche war drums.

"Angel Sanchez," Jeremiah said, and shook his head. "Why is nothing ever the way it looks?" he asked Bull, who offered a hand to help him back into the house. Jeremiah refused the help, needing to test his limits. He made it to his feet and, using the cabin wall for support, back inside to the safety of a sturdier chair.

"Is that true about Angel being Sarah?" Bull asked. "How old was she when she started following you around?"

"Two. I was ten." Jeremiah shook his head, remembering her baby voice calling after him to wait when she fell and scraped her knees trying to keep up. Even then, he'd admired her spunk. Over the years since the raid, when he'd allowed himself to think about it, he'd regretted her death more than anyone's outside his immediate family. He'd even wondered how she would have looked full-grown. He glanced toward the hacienda, listening as if he could still hear fading hoofbeats, and shook his head. Somehow, he had to convince her to leave before Sanchez hurt her, too.

"How'd you get her to stop?" Little Bird, too, seemed intrigued by his memories of Sarah.

"Stop?"

"Stop loving you."

"I broke her heart." The image of her crumpled, tear-streaked face still haunted him.

"Hearts mend," Little Bird said, after considering his answer with a concerned frown, "but your body won't if you don't get back to bed. You're about to fall over, you're that tired."

Jeremiah obeyed without arguing. He'd sleep for a few hours, but now that Angel Sanchez knew he suspected her father of murder, he couldn't stay here and risk Bull's and Little Bird's safety. Angel had defended her father so hotly, Jeremiah didn't trust her not to lead the man to him.

Time for him to leave the only safe haven he'd known for a long while. He wasn't well enough yet, but he'd faced tougher situations and survived. His brothers, the wolves, would help.

Deep in the night, Jeremiah slipped out of the warm cabin with a last, longing look behind him. He could never repay Little Bird and Bull for saving his life, and he hated sneaking out at night like an ungrateful skunk, but if he stayed, he risked Sanchez discovering where he'd gone to ground.

Little Bird's name appeared to fit her well, until you came up against her will. Her name should have been Iron Bird. She never would have let him leave—his body hadn't healed nearly enough—and Bull would have backed her. It had been too long since the two of them had walked the Comanche path. They'd done all they could for him. Now he needed his own medicine to finish what they'd started.

Keeping to the shadows, he slipped past the barn and smiled, hearing only snuffling and snorting from the sleeping horses. He could barely move, but still had a light step. Quannah used to have him do the advance scouting, which irritated the warriors who'd taught him their tricks. Once clear of any animals that might raise an alarm, Jeremiah crouched down and called to his brothers. He'd smelled them as he stepped out the door and knew they were near, surrounding the cabin.

Out of habit, he reached for the small leather bag

that had long hung from his neck, but his fist closed on air. His eyes shut and he promised himself he'd find another way to connect to his *puha*, his spirit medicine, tonight. As the wolves came running to greet him, he braced himself. They hurtled out of the night, leaping at him, nipping him as they shot past, then returning to butt him with their heads, showing him their joy that he was well. He returned their play, thanking them. Without their help, he would have died.

When they flopped around him, breathing heavily, he spoke to the pack leader—whining, nudging, yipping—always keeping his head low, not challenging the big wolf in any way. At last, the wolf stood and looked him straight in the eye, then turned and led Jeremiah to a nearby hill with an undercut bank. Water trickled in a steady stream down the rock face on one side of the hill, and a nearby stand of timber would give him plenty of firewood. The cutbank would catch the smoke from his fire and keep his whereabouts secret. Jeremiah looked the place over and nudged the big wolf with his head to thank him. The rest of the pack lay watching him gather branches to form a lean-to wall for shelter from the wind, and a pile of small twigs and a few larger logs for a fire. They watched, unblinking as he built a tiny tipi out of twigs and filled it with bits of broken twigs and dry leaves. When he began rubbing a thin stick between his hands with one point set in a slice of dry bark, one or two of the wolves whined and hid in the trees. The dry tinder sparked and a thread of smoke rose from the bark, Jeremiah blew gently on the tiny spark and when it flared, he fed it small twigs and dry bark until a small but substantial fire crackled merrily inside his lean-to. The rest of the wolves backed away, but continued watching from the cover of the timber.

He looked around him, satisfied that for now, he would be safe and warm. Hearing small game moving about in the timber, he made a couple of simple snares to catch his breakfast, then pulled some grass out of the bank above him and tossed it on the fire.

With a tired sigh, he stripped off his shirt, hat, and boots and knelt by the fire. Smoke rose from the burning grass in fragrant spirals that he caught in his hands and spread up his body and over his face.

Finally, he began chanting his medicine song. Almost immediately, forms appeared in the smoke and wove about him, tangling in his hair before drifting upward to hang in the air above, caught against the wall of his lean-to. Surprised, he struggled to keep chanting and make out the shapes. As if he'd asked, the smoke pulled away to form familiar faces. Surprised by what his prayer had brought, Jeremiah stopped chanting.

The face of the medicine woman, Kris Baldwin, and his brother, Duuqua, a Comanche war chief, appeared out of the smoke. Kris spoke, her voice sounding as though it came from a long distance. "Chikoba, don't speak, just listen."

Jeremiah nodded. He couldn't have spoken, didn't have a clear thought in his head. Fool that he was, he'd once questioned Kris's powers, mocked and doubted her. Never again.

"Duuqua and I have returned to my home, my time." She smiled at Duuqua and Jeremiah ached, seeing the love in that glance.

Duuqua whispered something in her ear.

Kris nodded and lifted a white parfleche. Jeremiah started, recognizing the parfleche that had been in the saddlebags when his horse was stolen by Juan. "My father gave us this when we arrived here. He said it had been passed down from father to son over many generations to be given to me." Tears filled her eyes. "I'm sorry I didn't recognize you. I was so focused on Quannah, I didn't realize you're my great-great-grandfather."

"Hurry," Duuqua urged her. "It's a small fire."

The smoke was already dissipating as the firelight dimmed.

"Chikoba!" Kris cried, and their faces flickered, becoming fainter.

Jeremiah blew on the flames, but the vision was fading. "Not Chikoba," he told her. "My white name is Jeremiah Matthew Baldwin."

"You must marry again," Kris said, speaking quickly. "If you don't, I will never be. Find a woman to love, to share your life." Her face and voice thinned, becoming whispers carried by the night breeze. "Find your new wife."

As the vision faded, his fire flared back to life. He frowned, thinking over Kris's message. She hadn't realized who he was to her, but he'd discovered it before he left the Comanche. He remembered Kris saying that she came from the future, so if she and Duuqua had returned to her time, that meant they were now together in the future, with her father. He shifted off his knees and sat cross-legged before the fire, gazing into the flames as he pondered the wonders the Great Spirit had brought to pass to help the Comanche. He'd sent Kris to help Quannah accept that he must give up the fight and surrender to the bluecoats to save the few people who had survived the long winter. And now the Great Spirit had taken her and the man she loved, a great war chief, back to the future.

He shook his head. He could get gray hair trying to understand how this had happened, but something she had said intrigued him.

Kris had the parfleche! She'd said it was "passed down." How could that happen? He'd lost it, had no idea where it was now.

Hope flared, bright as any fire, inside him. Somehow—he didn't know how yet—he would regain what he'd lost, what had been taken from him: his possessions, a wife . . . even a child? Yes! If Kris was truly his great-whatever granddaughter, he had to have a child. And since her name was Baldwin, that child must be a son.

Joy swelled inside him, until he listened to himself. *I have to have a son*. How could he do that when he could barely walk? His horse and all his belongings had been stolen. He had nothing but the clothes on his back, his hat and boots.

Ah, but the bastard who'd done this to him didn't know that he had something special, something white men didn't know about or understand.

Jeremiah tossed more kindling on the fire, then a handful of grass, and again began praying to the Great Spirit. As he chanted his medicine song, he called upon his spirit guide. At once his senses flared, sending pain shooting through his body, hitting all his injuries like fire. His eyesight sharpened, the noise of the mice and birds in the nearby timber echoed loud and he smelled their blood. His fingers and toes tingled as though they'd fallen asleep and were just coming awake. His blood pounded in his arms and legs, rushing through his veins like the wind streaming through his hair when he rode with his Comanche brothers. Pain wracked his body and he cried out, curling in upon himself as he collapsed onto his side before the fire.

Long, long the pain tore at him. Then it dwindled with the fire to a few bright embers and the voice of his spirit guide whispered, "Be still. Sleep."

Chapter Nine

"Angel! Come quick!"

The urgent summons came from a small room at the back of the stable where old or damaged tack was stored. Pedro emerged from the room and beckoned to her.

"What is it?" she asked as she stood staring into the shadows. At first, all she could see was a saddle with a pair of well-worn saddlebags flung over it. Once her eyes adjusted, she recognized the stains on the saddle blanket and gagged, covering her mouth. Dark, copper-scented, the blanket was stiff with blood.

She looked up at Pedro. A muscle clenched in his jaw and he had to unfist his hands to pick up the saddlebags. "How long have these been here?" she asked.

"They weren't here when we left for Bull's and Little Bird's last night." He slung the saddlebags over his shoulder and led her out of the storage area. "Neither was he." He pulled her to a stop at the nearest stall where a nondescript horse stood devouring a pile of hay.

She entered the stall carefully and examined the horse, which didn't even flinch when she picked up each rear hoof. "Thin, dirty, hungry . . . Look at this." She ran her hand up the animal's haunch, watching the dried blood flake away and fall off. Fortunately, it wasn't the animal's blood. Angel knew whose blood it was.

"What's in the saddlebags?"

Pedro looked inside one and scowled. "A colt .45 and a holster." He reached deep into the other bag and came up with a beautifully beaded, flat white leather bag. He lifted a flap to open it and looked carefully inside. "Clothes. Baby clothes."

Angel frowned as she watched Pedro carefully replace the items in the saddlebags. These things would have been highly prized by their owner. Hadn't Jeremiah said something about a parfleche during his delirium? Little Bird had several bags like this that she called parfleche, a bag with a flap to close it, made to hold clothing. This bag was much smaller and the beading made it beautiful as well as functional.

She looked up to find Pedro considering her gravely. "Think all this belongs to Jeremiah?"

"Mmm, I'm sure of it," she replied, then shook her head. "But how did the horse get here?"

"Your father's in town today," Pedro reminded her as he set the saddlebags on his shoulder.

"Anyone could have dumped the horse and gear. Or it may have wandered here, drawn by the smell of hay and grain. Stay here while I ask around. If it came on its own, someone had to take off the saddle and feed it."

Angel searched the horse's body for injuries and found only a few scratches on its legs and sides. Its feet looked good, too. Jeremiah took good care of the animal, which was much sturdier than it looked.

Pedro returned quickly. "No one saw a stray horse, but they have all been working in the watermelon patch."

"So, the killer—Juan, according to Jeremiah—would have had plenty of time to sneak it into the barn. By getting rid of anything that ties him to the attack, he's trying to shift the blame." Angel shook her head, appalled by the attacker's brazen actions.

"Juan may be watching the hacienda, especially the casa. How else would he know it was safe to hide the horse today, in broad daylight? He may even have someone watching you and me." Pedro walked to the door of the barn and looked out at the buildings surrounding the casa. "He may be hoping we'll lead him to Jeremiah."

"Then we've got to be extra careful, Pedro. I'll hide the saddlebags in my room. In a couple of days, I'll send one of the young vaqueros to warn Jeremiah, Bull, and Little Bird that something's up. Until then, we'll lie low, stick to the hacienda, and wait."

"Juan won't wait long. Tomorrow, your father leaves for the south part of the hacienda for spring roundup; he'll be gone for over a week. You know Juan never goes along. He'll come to check on you while your father is away. I'll wrap Bella's foreleg and apply a poultice. That will give me an excuse to stay close by."

"I appreciate the offer, but it's not necessary, Pedro. I can handle Juan." Angel stepped to the far side of the strange horse to hide her unease. What if Juan continued to press her to accept his suit, and himself, while the able-bodied men were gone? Could she fight him off if she had to? So many times recently, she had seen anger flare in his eyes, watched his fists clench and slowly relax. How long could she continue her charade?

"I promised Bull and Little Bird to watch over you. Or have you forgotten, that's also what your father pays me to do?"

"What would I do without you?" Angel wiped her hand—grimy from stroking the blood-caked horse—on her skirt. She shuddered. "Could you have one of the boys wash this animal? He's nothing to look at, but he's a good, strong horse, and all this blood . . ." She couldn't finish her comment, couldn't bring herself to dwell on the fact that the horse was covered in Jeremiah's blood. His accusations against her father infuriated her, and yet she still cared what happened to him. What was wrong with her?

"Go to your room and rest," Pedro ordered. Despite

her arch look, he added, "You're still not sleeping enough. I will send Bernida with a glass of wine."

"Make it sangria and I'll skip all the way to my room," Angel said with a laugh. Even though he was right, she should chasten Pedro for his presumption. He had no right to order her about. But today, she had too much on her mind to bother. Her thoughts chased themselves about in her head as she made her way to her room, and continued as she sprawled on her wide, comfortable bed. She stared at a spot on the ceiling, seeking slumber, her thoughts chasing themselves round and round in her head.

She couldn't stop thinking about Jeremiah's kiss last night. Or was it her kiss? Perhaps it would be best to think of it as the kiss they'd shared. She hadn't meant to go so far, but he'd felt so good, tasted so . . . How could she describe it? She pressed the fingers of one hand over her lips and let her eyes close.

Staring into his eyes, she'd savored the sensations swamping her. As quickly as she'd noticed one incredible detail—like how beautiful his eyes were up close—another stole her breath. She'd finally had to close her eyes to allow herself to simply *feel* the kiss—and him.

Oh yes, she'd felt him. Felt him prodding at her private places, pushing, always pushing, trying to breach the barriers between them. Was it ever thus between a man and a woman, working together to eliminate the obstacles that kept them from physically expressing their joy in each other?

Angel sighed and relinquished the new sensations causing such tumult in her awakening body. She longed to see Jeremiah again, feel his big hands on her body pressing her closer. Would she ever know that joy again? What would he do once he was healed? Would he leave or continue his search?

Papá had refused to show Jeremiah any proof that he'd acquired the hacienda legally, but that didn't mean he didn't have any. She knew he kept his important papers in his desk in the study. Could she find them without raising his suspicions? She did not want him to think that she, too, believed him guilty.

Having always known she was a survivor of the raid, she had asked him before to tell her about it. He'd said he'd arrived one or two days afterward for a meeting with Reverend Baldwin, Jeremiah's father. He'd refused to talk about what he'd found there, and she'd never pushed him. If she asked him again now, he would think she didn't believe him, didn't trust him. He would be devastated by her lack of faith, and she would not repay his love and kindness in such a manner. Instead, she'd find the proof herself and show it to Jeremiah. Then he'd be convinced of her father's innocence, she'd return whatever she found, and everyone would be satisfied.

She sat up straight and scooted off the bed. "Stronger measures are required."

Bernida, startled from her own catnap in the chair beside the window, frowned at Angel. "What are you planning?"

"Don't worry," Angel said, leaning forward to pat Bernida's knee. "I'm only going to search *Papá*'s study. I know he bought the land for our hacienda legally. I'm determined to find proof—a deed or some kind of legal document that states the land belongs to him. Then I'll show it to Jeremiah and this will all blow over."

"What will your *papá* think if he finds you snooping through his papers?"

"He has nothing to hide," Angel said with a shrug, pretending confidence she didn't feel.

"Then ask him."

Like Little Bird, Bernida made sense, but Angel knew that if she asked, Father would dodge her questions again or find some way to distract her. On impulse, she decided to confide her true concern. "I'm not trying to be stubborn or difficult, as Little Bird says." She pressed a hand to her neck, her throat. "I don't want to seem ungrateful," she admitted, deciding to hold nothing from Bernida. "*Papá* didn't have to take me in when he found me, but he did, and he's been a good father. I know he loves me: he's so generous and understanding. How can I repay that love with distrust?"

"Angel, to ask him for the truth about this—a part of your life—is not to betray his love. Don't you see? He betrays your trust by not telling you what you need to know. You are a grown woman. You deserve to know the truth. If he loves you, he will understand."

"I must give it more thought," Angel said, and put an end to the discussion by leaving the room. She spent the next two hours weeding her rose garden and mulling over the best way to search the casa.

Tomorrow night, she'd begin. And she wouldn't quit until she found the proof she needed to refute Jeremiah's accusations.

Flat on his belly in the short grass that topped the hill near Angel's home, Jeremiah lay as still as a snake. He'd slithered the last few yards up the hill and had expected it to hurt like hell, but his body wasn't protesting nearly as much today, not since his prayer the night before. That had been painful enough, but this morning he'd felt much better—still sore, but not weak and helpless as a puppy. Satisfied that he hadn't damaged his innards crawling up the hill, he watched the vaqueros work the remuda.

Something was up. The men were laughing and joking as they cleaned the horses' hooves, checked saddles and bridles, and curried the horses. The cook had been chasing around the open yard like a banty rooster locked in the henhouse, shouting orders as he cleaned the chuck wagon, making everyone dance to his tune. Jeremiah grinned, amused by the comparison of the short, loudmouthed cook to the small-breed cock. Why did short men make so much noise, mostly about themselves? The grin slid away and his eyes narrowed. Why would the cook be rushing around while the men labored over the remuda, the group of horses kept for the vaqueros to ride as they worked the cattle?

Pedro walked out of the barn and leaned on the high pole of a corral while he rolled himself a smoke. Even from this distance, Jeremiah saw him stiffen. His hands stilled as he shifted and looked directly at Jeremiah, who ducked low and slid a few feet down the hill. That man had the instincts of a coyote. Better be more careful. He lay on the hill, waiting for his heart to slow down while he tried to make sense of the activity at the casa.

Seemed as though the vaqueros were going somewhere, and taking the cook along. A roundup? It was the right time of year. How big was Sanchez's hacienda? How long would a roundup take? Would Sanchez be going?

To hell with Pedro. Jeremiah poked his nose over the ridge again. Pedro hadn't moved, and Jeremiah knew he'd better leave and cover his tracks. Sarah's protector had to be one part Comanche, the other part coyote. Jeremiah decided to camp nearby and watch the hacienda early the next morning. If Sanchez left with his vaqueros, Jeremiah wanted to get inside the casa.

He would search the place, and somehow, he would let Sarah know he'd been in her house. The thought of being in her home while her father was gone made heat rise in his belly. That wasn't all that rose. What was it about that woman? She'd grown from a pesky kid to an irritating woman. Only now, his irritation came from not being able to think about her without *this* happening. He looked down at himself with a disgusted snarl. He might not be ready to toss her skirts around her ears, but all she'd have to do was smile and she'd be flat on her back with her legs wrapped around his waist.

He thought about her kiss and her inexperience as he slid down the hill. If she didn't know how to kiss, she sure as hell wouldn't know anything else. A virgin. He didn't need the headache. He felt as if he were fourteen again, back at Baldwin Fort with Sarah dogging his heels, but this time he didn't feel like running away. Now he wanted another kiss, another chance to taste that hot mouth of hers and find out if the heat between them had been caused by his fever or something more. Not even Ekararo had tasted that . . .

His dead wife's name blew through his mind like a cool, fresh breeze, taking the edge off his body's driving need.

Ekararo, his mind whispered, and a prayer, a soothing blanket of calm settled about his shoulders. He pulled it close, welcoming the peace of mind and body. Guilt pierced his soul. His sweet, gentle wife, her belly still swollen with their unborn child, lay dead. Only a few moons—no, months—had passed since that hateful day, and he had no business having lustful thoughts about another woman when memories of Ekararo still filled him with agony.

She's dead! His body clamored to be heard and desire swelled again. The tip of his cock strained against his tight pants, pressing upward, drawn to the moist heat between Sarah's thighs as they'd spread over his. He'd been hard-pressed to believe she was kissing him, letting him touch her. Her kiss had bound an aching wound in his heart. She'd changed him with that sweet, surprising kiss. She'd given him hope that maybe he could love again, if he could muster the courage to try.

He didn't want to try. Not yet. Not when grief still haunted him, not when his life was so unsettled. His startling conversation with Kris had given him hope that someday he'd find a woman to love him and bear his children. Could Sarah be that woman? Given the way they'd parted company last night, he doubted it.

But that didn't keep him from thinking about her, re-playing her kiss and the feel of her body melting against him. He couldn't wish his body's needs away now that she had reminded him how good it felt to want a woman. She'd made him burn.

Jeremiah stopped at a small stream and scooped water over his crotch, his chest, his face. It was the only relief he could find—for now. Tonight he'd take care of his needs himself—if he didn't, he'd never get to sleep and if he didn't sleep, he wouldn't wake in time to watch the hacienda. Tonight he'd put Sarah out of his mind; then all he had to do was keep her there—out of his mind and out of his way.

Creak!

Angel froze, her fingers still pressed between the back of the desk drawer and the front wall of the desk. What was that noise? She'd never heard that particular sound before and she'd lived in this house over fourteen years. She should recognize every creak and groan, but she'd never heard that one before.

Creak!

She gave up searching the secret compartment she'd discovered and, pulling her nightgown and robe tight around her legs, scrunched into the corner beneath *Papá's* desk. Footsteps! Coming from the hallway, headed this way. She forced herself to breathe slowly. Who could it be? Her father and his vaqueros had all left for roundup this morning.

The study door swung open and she cringed farther into the corner. A man's legs came into view—black pants and dusty black boots on the biggest feet she'd seen since . . .

Jeremiah!

Without pausing to consider the wisdom of her actions, she popped her head out and stared up at him. At first, he didn't notice her in the darkness.

"What are you doing here?" she demanded, and found herself in a bit of a predicament. She couldn't crawl out from under the desk without embarrassing herself. If she slid out feet first, her nightgown would ride up her legs and reveal much more than she felt inclined to share. If she backed out on her hands and knees . . . well, that was not an option. And going out headfirst left her at a decided disadvantage, because when she rose to her knees her head would be level with his groin. She shook her head. Definitely not an option.

Her abrupt question had startled a curse out of Jeremiah. She couldn't stifle a low giggle.

He bent to look under the desk and his searching gaze found her. She shrank away as he stumbled backward several steps. She started to warn him about her father's chair behind him.

Too late.

She covered her eyes as it hit the back of his knees, then slid away when he started to fall. He tried to catch himself, to use the chair to break his fall, but it skittered sideways and slammed into a bookcase, causing several shelves to tip and dump their contents on the floor. Jeremiah hit the floor hard, his feet shooting straight under the desk, one on either side of her. He gave a long groan and pressed an arm over his broken ribs, then just sat there stunned, staring at her.

"Well, what do you expect?" she asked, feeling no sympathy whatsoever. "You haven't recovered. You're clearly not as agile as you normally are, and you shouldn't be out of bed, let alone skulking about a strange house in the dark. I can see what you're doing here, but I don't understand how you convinced Little Bird to let you go." She rose to her knees and began to crawl out from under the desk.

When he didn't back away, only sat staring at her with his glazed eyes glued to her chest, she glanced down. Her robe had come undone and the neck of her nightgown gaped away from her chest, revealing all her secrets. Every. Single. One.

"Oh!" She slapped her hand to her chest, luckily catching both robe and nightgown and restoring her modesty. She glanced up at him sitting there with his mouth open as if he'd been punched in the belly, and couldn't keep the asperity from her voice. "Do you think you could help me out?" She stuck out the hand not protecting her modesty. And wished she hadn't.

Like a snake striking, he caught her wrist and with one mighty tug, pulled her up to his lips and simultaneously rolled, trapping her beneath him. "You're right, I'm not back to normal. Otherwise, you'd already be naked."

When she opened her mouth to breathe—still debating whether to scream for help, lambast him, or simply enjoy her sudden good fortune and ask questions later—he plundered her mouth. She gave up thinking. Instead, she focused on meeting his tongue stroke for stroke, on tracing the fluid muscles flexing in his back, arms, and shoulders, on helping him untie her nightgown so he could . . .

Oh dear! She dissolved in a shudder as his lips closed over one breast and his hand found the other. She wanted . . . no, she needed to be closer. How could she get closer?

She sank her fingers into his hair. Cool as silk, it slid through her fingers as she pulled his head down and arched her back, offering him both breasts and watching him feast. How had she lived so long without knowing how wonderful this felt?

With an easy grace, he raised her just enough to sweep her robe and nightgown out of his way, leaving her naked to the waist. He pulled her to her knees and she laid her arms over his shoulders, not certain she had the strength to support herself as he knelt facing her. He propped her up with his hands pressed to her sides, one beside each breast. Looking down at herself, she was amazed by the bounty she presented for him to lick, suck, and savor.

She didn't even protest when he nudged her knees apart. He lifted, returning to her lips, and pulled her close to his chest. She opened his shirt and pushed it wide. The fine, curling hair she found there abraded her tender nipples, adding a new sensation that left her gasping. She rubbed against him tentatively, found the friction delicious, and pulled her shoulders back to expose more territory to this sensual massage.

He nibbled his way up her neck and once again took her mouth, sending her spiraling heavenward as she reveled in the dual sensations. His hands coursed up and down her legs, leaving her nightgown dangling about her waist. Irritated by the distraction, she tugged it over her head and flung it away, then circled his back with her arms and pulled him closer.

He groaned and whispered, "Sarah, what are you doing to me?" but he came willingly. He filled those strong, long-fingered hands she'd often admired with the twin halves of her bottom and squeezed, pulling her forward against his crotch. Feeling the coarse drag of his pants against her tender skin, she immediately set about divesting him of the nuisance, with his help.

When his swollen manhood jumped out at her, she caught it in one hand, surprised that he wasn't wearing long underwear. Then she remembered Little Bird cutting them off him. She smiled.

"I'm so glad you lived," she whispered.

He made a sound—something between a curse and a groan—and grabbed her hand. He pressed her fingers tighter around him, then moved her hand up and down. Now it was he needing support and he found it, laying one arm over her shoulder. The other hand continued to knead her bottom and she smiled when he pressed his forehead to hers and gave a long, deep sigh. "You can stop that sometime tomorrow," he whispered, and smiled.

She laughed and applied both hands, finding him a little more than one hand could manage. Then she encountered another interesting object—one she'd already seen, having peeked once or twice when Little Bird was bathing him. Now she got to touch it, and when she did, cupping his scrotum in her hand and giving it a gentle squeeze, his eyes flew open and he gripped her wrist.

"No more," he said, and kissed her. Then he pulled her hands away from his body and set them on his waist. The kiss ended all too soon and he leaned back to look in her eyes. "We're moving way too fast. We should stop."

Alarm sped through her. She knew what came next. She'd happened upon one of the vaqueros and a maid making love in the hay loft above the horse's stalls. She should have left, but she'd arrived at a very interesting moment and from where she stood on the ladder with her head barely poking above the loft floor, she'd had a clear view of the whole process. The maid hadn't seemed to mind, had even encouraged him to drive his thing into her harder.

So, if that was what Jeremiah needed to do, it didn't frighten her. Everything they had done so far had brought sensations she never could have imagined. How could he even suggest that they stop now? Just thinking of him lying over her, spreading her legs, caused a sudden rush of liquid to her core.

"Please, don't stop," she said, leaning close and pressing her breasts to his chest. He must have known how she felt, for he reached down and touched her where her body throbbed, aching to be filled, and slid one of his long fingers inside her. His arm banded her back, holding her up when her knees would have failed her. Ignoring the wetness on his hand, he chuckled at her embarrassed flush, then picked her up and carried her to the couch across the room. He tossed a soft blanket from a basket on the floor over the cushions and settled her on it.

"Come to me." She captured his hand and reached to cover her breasts with her other hand.

"Shy?" He laughed and pulled free, setting her hands at her sides. "Don't be. I want to remember you like this," he whispered, and leaned down. He nipped her breast, bringing her nipple to a firm, rosy peak. "All golden and glowing, just for me." He turned his attention to her other breast and tweaked her nipple, then kissed it to attention before finally settling over her.

"Am I too heavy?" he asked, and kissed her neck, while his hands slid down to her hips.

"No," she murmured, surprised and delighted to find his weight began to fill the need she'd been sensing since he first kissed her, the need to be closer to him, to be a part of him. "Just too slow."

He kissed her breasts again, briefly, then her abdomen, dipping his tongue into her belly button before moving lower still.

"Wait!" she cried, catching his head in her hands. "What are you doing?"

"Exploring," he said.

She tried to speak, but couldn't find the words to stop him, not sure she wanted to stop him. Everything he'd done to her had made her body sing. What other delights did he have in store? When he rose onto his knees, lifted her leg, and began kissing the length of one thigh, her hands relaxed on the blanket. The kisses he pressed to the back of her knee made her giggle. She tried to hide the sound with her hand—afraid she might wake Bernida—but he chastened her.

"Don't," he whispered. "I want to hear you, see you, smell, and taste you. Don't hide anything from me."

"But—"

"Don't worry about being too loud," he said with a

wicked grin as he examined her big toe. "There's no one awake to hear." He took her toe in his mouth and watched her while he sucked it, letting it slide in and out of his mouth while his fingers caressed the inside of her calf and her thigh, then moved farther upward.

Angel marveled at the sensations his fingers created as they parted the lips protecting her most private parts. But when he lay between her legs and began to caress her there, she tried to squirm away.

"Shhh," he said, and pressed a kiss to her thigh. "You'll enjoy this. I promise."

"You're the one enjoying it," she said, a note of accusation in her voice.

"I am," he admitted, and pressed her nether lips wide. "I admire beautiful women." He grinned up at her.

"Please," she said, "you're looking at my . . ."

"It's one of the most beautiful I've ever seen."

"Oh? How many have you seen?" she asked. How dare he seduce her into this state, then toss his other conquests in her face?

"Two."

She stared at the ceiling, counting. Herself, that was one, which left only his wife. She looked down to find him staring at her and all she could do was smile and smooth a lock of hair off his brow.

"Get ready now," he warned, using his shoulders to push her knees wider as he scooted closer to her bottom.

"What? Really, this isn't all that—" She meant to tell him his foray down below wasn't exciting her, but before she could finish, he kissed the sensitive nub of flesh above her vagina and her knees fell open wide. Any thought in her head flew out the window. She groaned as his tongue swirled about that nub, pushing, tracing, licking, then gliding lower, pressing her open and finally sinking into her. As he penetrated deeper and his tongue began thrusting in and out, her eyes rolled back in her head. She gripped his hands where he held her thighs open and lifted her hips, offering herself to him.

And he took, more and more, with skillful teasing of her sensitive nub until with a blinding flash, lightning speared through her, arching her back, making her clench and pulse inside while he continued thrusting with his tongue as the pulsing continued. She bit her lip to keep from screaming her ecstasy for the whole world to hear. Only fear of discovery, and an end to this wonder, kept her quiet.

As her body slipped from the peak of ecstasy to tingling awareness once more, she looked down to find him watching her, a pleased but worn expression on his face. She hadn't given a thought to his recent injuries, the partially healed gunshot wound in his shoulder, his still-tender broken ribs. He didn't look like a sick man, but he was most definitely in pain, and tense, very tightly controlled. His features in the dim light seemed more rugged than ever and when he moved to rise—turning his body so she wouldn't see his penis— suddenly she understood. He meant to pleasure her, but take no pleasure himself.

She lifted up, caught his hand, and stopped him. "Where are you going? This isn't finished, is it? You haven't . . ." She left off and let her glance slide lower. With a quick twist, she sat up and grabbed his hips, turned him to face her.

"How do you like it?" she asked, looking up at him from under her eyelids as she cupped his sac in one hand, his cock in the other. Marveling at her own temerity, she leaned down and took his tip in her mouth and circled it with her tongue.

He groaned and pushed her head back. "Are you sure you want this? Me? Inside you?" He gestured at his fully engorged staff.

She blinked, but nodded. "Yes, I want you." She eased back on the couch and spread herself wide. He was on her in an instant, kissing her with all the fire in his body. She responded, clutching him to her, anxious to please him as he had already pleased her.

While he kissed her breasts, he eased a finger into her passage, pushing deeper, then added another and finally another.

She moaned and her head rolled as she was engulfed by the desire—the need—to feel him inside her. "Come to me," she begged him. "I want you inside me. Now!"

"Shhh, I'm here," he said as he knelt between her legs and pressed her knees wide. "Let me know if I hurt you."

She tensed, expecting a firm thrust, but he slid into her slowly, moving himself in circles to ease his passage. Then he stopped. His eyes shut and he gripped her hips and braced her. "This may hurt a bit."

She nodded and bit her lip to keep from screaming, then grabbed his hips and pulled as she lifted upward. He plunged into her to the hilt with a sharp sting. She couldn't help wincing, though she tried to hide her reaction from him.

"Are you all right?" Sweat slid down his forehead and he blinked it out of his eyes.

She loved that he'd asked, that he'd made this taking of her virginity an exploration she'd remember all her life. Using a corner of the blanket, she blotted his face and smiled. "I feel wonderful. You feel wonderful." She wiggled.

He pushed deeper and she groaned. Not the little, quiet moans she'd been making but a full, throaty moan. The moan of a woman taking all her lover had to give. She answered his thrust, pulling back and lifting to meet him.

Instantly, he drove into her. Again and again, he pounded into her body and she begged him for more. He gave and gave and she met every stroke and thrust and gave back. Something was building inside her, tightening, coiling, moving her closer and closer to the edge.

When she hovered on the precipice, he reached between them and pressed that sensitive button—her new favorite body part—and she was flung skyward, knowing she'd never be able to quiet the cry of ecstasy rising in her throat.

He groaned as she clenched and pulsed around him. Then he plunged so deep that she thought he'd kissed her heart, but it was only his mouth, catching her cry.

Chapter Ten

Jeremiah raised himself on shaking arms and slid off the couch—and Sarah—onto the floor. He let himself go limp, sagging against the couch, too weak to react to the kiss of cold tile on naked butt.

As mistakes went, that had been the biggest he'd ever made. But making love to Sarah had been . . . the best. Ever. Even his first time with Ekararo hadn't been so . . . incredible. Yup. Incredible.

So what was he going to do about it? About her? His smile faded. She'd been a virgin. Just like he figured. He had to do right by her. He waited for the crushing guilt to settle over him, but it didn't come. Not over Sarah. His heart twisted as he thought about Ekararo. He didn't feel he'd betrayed her by making love to Sarah, but he also wasn't ready to allow another woman to take Ekararo's place in his mind. In his heart, Ekararo was still the woman he loved. His body didn't agree.

Had he wronged Sarah? He'd given her a chance to stop, but she hadn't wanted it. She'd been hungry for him. That part made him shift on the hard floor. She would have some thinking to do. If she loved Sanchez—the lying snake who was responsible for the death of her true father—she couldn't love him, too. Which one of them would she choose? Could he walk away if she chose Sanchez over him? Could he give up, forget about finding the man responsible for the raid?

Jeremiah tensed, deliberately recalling the day of the raid, the horrors he'd witnessed, the hell he'd survived during the months that followed, confirming for

himself that he couldn't stop until he'd discovered—
and destroyed—the man responsible. Not even for the
woman he loved.

That word made him sit up straight and search his
heart. No, he didn't love Sarah, but he cared about her,
wanted her to have a happy life. Those feelings might
grow into love over time, if he let them. He understood
her, perhaps better than she understood herself. After
their lovemaking, she'd drifted off, and he twisted and
watched her sleeping. Her beauty caught him like a
blow to the chest. He sucked in a deep breath, leaned
forward, and kissed her breast. She sighed and turned,
reaching for him.

He resisted the need spurring him, the urge to kiss
her awake, or better yet, let his loving wake her. But he
wouldn't start anything until they'd talked. Yes, he could
love Sarah, but he wouldn't let himself. Not yet. His mind
and heart were taken. There was no place for her there.

"Hey, sleepyhead," he said, and gave her shoulder a
nudge. "Wake up." He couldn't leave her sleeping here
naked, but he'd need her help to get her dressed and
back to her room.

Suddenly, she pulled his head down and kissed him.
He tried to resist, but she'd come a long way with her
kissing. Then those quick hands of hers grabbed him
down low and he couldn't think, let alone stop her. If he
hadn't been there before, felt the proof of it when he
slid inside her, he wouldn't have believed she was a
virgin. Nobody would ever accuse Sarah of being shy,
of not taking what she wanted.

She sat up on the couch, her legs on either side of
him, her lips all pink and puffy from his kisses, and he
had to have her again. That was a good thing, because
she slid her bottom to the edge of the couch and guided
his shaft to her, taking control.

"Wait, Sarah! We've got to talk," he said, pulling back,

pushing her hands away, trying to avoid her searing touch.

"Later," she said as she kissed his chest. "Oh, look," she said, smiling at his nipples, which she'd sucked into hard, nubby points. "What's it called, Jeremiah?"

"What's what called?" he answered, surprised he could think, let alone talk.

"You know," she said, blinking up at him innocently, though her hands continued stroking him mindless. "When you go all hard and still inside me and make me scream."

Jeremiah surrendered, grabbed her hips, and pulled her to him. He gritted his teeth and forced himself to go slow when all he wanted was to slide deep into her hot glove, again and again, until she screamed his name. "Come," he growled as he slid into her, closing his eyes when her heat closed around him. "I make you come, and then I come, too."

She moaned as he filled her, lifting her hips to help him reach deeper, gripping his buttocks and pulling, too. When his body finally settled against her, bone to bone, his rod hidden in her sheath and throbbing, she tightened her muscles inside and squeezed him tight. "Make me come."

With a growl, he gripped her hips and began the dance, pounding into her as hard as he dared, trying to remember this was her first night of lovemaking. He couldn't let himself loose, though he was sorely tempted to show this little minx exactly who controlled whom. He watched his staff surge into her again and again and again, saw her lick her lips as she watched it, too. The pleasure flushing her cheeks, glowing in her eyes, made him swell even bigger. She must have felt it, for her eyebrows lifted and she smiled and used her hidden muscles to squeeze him again.

He pumped in and out a few more times, then

yanked out of her and almost laughed as the heat and passion left her eyes.

"Don't stop now," she pleaded, reaching for him.

He pushed her hands away and flipped her onto her belly. "Have you ever watched the bulls?"

She pushed herself up on her arms and looked at him over her shoulder. "Yes, I've watched. This won't hurt, will it?"

No protest, no outrage, just curiosity. She was the kind of woman most men dreamed of finding but never did, a respectable woman who welcomed their loving, even demanded it and asked for more. Why did she have to enter his life now, when all he could do was enjoy what she willingly gave for the little time they would have together?

He pushed into her from the rear and kept his thrusts short. He gripped her hips to hold her steady, not letting his body take control of the loving, not thrusting as hard and deep as he would have liked. Her body's tentative movements told him he was right to hold back, and his body, though so long denied, found its pleasure, too, rising to the peak beside her. When he felt her muscles begin to tighten around him, knew her time was close, he lifted her back against him and looked into her eyes.

"Now, come," he said, and turned her head and took her mouth, swallowing her cries as he rubbed her clit and drove into her in short, fast thrusts, bouncing her on his thighs, flinging her into ecstasy. When she sagged in his arms, he buried himself deep, coming inside her in long, jerking spasms.

Somehow, he managed to drag her onto the couch with him and pull the blanket over them. "If we made a child tonight," he said, his voice barely a croak against her tousled hair, "don't worry, I'll take care of you both."

She stiffened and he cursed his stupidity, knowing he'd made her angry. He'd given her pleasure, so it must have been something he'd said. He didn't know what it might be, and his mind and body, so relaxed from their loving, couldn't puzzle it out before he fell asleep. All he knew was that when Sarah joined him, sleeping with her head pillowed on his arm, a chilly gap separated them.

"It's time for you to go now."

Something cold and hard clunked against him. He looked down to find his belt and pants balled up on his chest. Before he could ask why she was all riled up, his shirt hit him in the face.

She reached for a boot, but he caught her arm before she could throw it at him. "No need," he said, standing without bothering to cover himself, mostly because she kept trying to look away. And she was blushing. He kept hold of her wrist. He wasn't going to let her turn what had been beautiful into something ugly. He pulled her up tight against him and kissed her cheek.

"What's made you angry?" he asked when she quieted and let him hold her. "Did I hurt you?" A sharp ache hit him in the chest at the thought that he might have hurt her. He'd tried to take it slow, but there toward the end . . .

"No!" She seemed startled as she looked into his eyes at last, then quickly looked away again.

That tight ache in his chest eased and he held her tighter. "Good. I'd never hurt you." She didn't respond, so he kissed her ear. "You know that, don't you?"

She kicked him in the shin, and he discovered she wasn't barefoot.

"What the . . . !" He jumped backward, tripped on the blanket that had slid off the couch, and landed on his butt. He checked his shin for blood, then stared up at her.

She stood over him in her robe and nightgown—and pointy-toed, fancy slippers—with her fists planted on her hips. Her eyes drifted south and she blushed.

After what they'd done together, she could still be shy? Shy or brazen, she had something on her mind. "You planning to tell me why you're mad or you just going to keep poking at me?" He rubbed his chest, still feeling the chill of the distance between them. "What's the matter, Sarah? You can tell me to make you come, but not why you're angry?"

"You've got a lot of nerve, showing up here tonight," she said. "What were you doing in my father's study?" She threw an arm wide, indicating the messy desk.

"It's not hard to figure." He stood and pulled on his pants, being careful to slip the rawhide braid that usually rode his waist into his pocket. They'd come together so fast, he'd had to move like lightning to undo the braid and let it fall inside his pants. When they got better acquainted—*if* they got better acquainted—he'd show it to her and explain what it was and what it meant to a warrior. Her gaze followed every move as he tucked in his shirt. He took his time buttoning his fly. Did she know she was staring, that she'd licked her lips? If he hadn't been worried, wondering why she was angry, he'd have been hot all over again.

"Don't bother searching the house," she told him, jerking her gaze away from his crotch and back up to his face. Heat climbed her body, flushing her cheeks as she realized how brazenly she'd watched him dress.

"I came to find proof, a deed or some paper that shows your father owns the land—free and clear, mortgaged, doesn't matter." He finished dressing, put on his boots, hat, and coat, but felt naked without his Peacemaker. Naked and vulnerable. Once he found the man responsible for the raid on Baldwin Fort, he'd be willing to bet he'd also find his gun. Imagining her father pointing his own gun at him sent chills through Jeremiah. What if her father had come back while they'd been sleeping, or they'd been found by a maid, even Pedro? There'd have been hell to pay, but he'd willingly risk it again if it meant stumbling across Sarah, half dressed and willing.

Reminded of where he'd found her, he narrowed his eyes on Sarah and she took a step back with a hand pressed to her throat. She must have ducked under the desk when she'd heard him coming. He wasn't about to let her lay all the blame on him.

"You were searching, too, weren't you, Sarah?" He caught her to him, his head filling with plans to protect her. "Have you come to see it my way?" Excited that she'd changed her mind, he began planning. "How quick can you pack a bag? We need to get out of here before dawn. When's your father coming home?"

She shoved away from him. "What are you talking about? I'm not going anywhere with you."

He froze, standing still while the world spun out of control around him. What was she saying? "You've got to come with me, Sarah."

"Please don't call me that! I'm Angel, not Sarah. I may have been Sarah long ago, but she's dead to me in here." She thumped a fist against her heart.

The anguish on her face made his heart ache, too. He'd hurt her, pretty bad by the look of grief and sorrow on her face, and he hadn't meant to. He just wanted to help her, make her understand.

"All right, I'll call you Angel." He might not understand what else was driving her, but he understood this. In his own mind he was still Chikoba, a Comanche warrior in spirit if nothing else. "If your father finds out that you suspect him, or if he thinks you've had a change of heart, your life won't be worth spit. He'll kill you, too."

"I haven't changed my mind about my father." She kept her voice low, but her tone and her furious expression convinced Jeremiah that she meant what she said. "I'm searching for proof of his innocence, not his guilt."

His stomach flipped. Their hearts and minds were

miles apart, but his body still hummed from the pleasure she'd given him. Hell, he'd been hankering for more as she stood there tearing his assumptions to shreds. Good thing he'd decided he couldn't love her. He remembered her confession that she'd watched the bulls. Had she just been curious about sex, wondering what she was missing? Did she care for him at all?

"You're not thinking straight," he said, rejecting the notion. He tried to take her in his arms, but she pushed away. "Don't be naïve. Your father's guilty. Why else would he have sent someone to kill me? Remember that? I can't leave you here, in danger."

Sarah . . . He shook his head. Angel pushed free, her cheeks flushed and tears in her eyes.

"I shouldn't have done this tonight, but I don't regret it. Maybe I did love you as a child, perhaps that's the fascination. Maybe it's knowing that you're a survivor, too, that we're the only two left. Maybe it's . . . oh, I don't know!" she cried, then looked him in the eye. "All I do know is that I've never felt as whole as I did when you were inside me." She backed away, raising a hand when he reached for her again. "But that's not enough. I owe him, Jeremiah. Can't you understand? If he was guilty, if he'd really killed all those people, he would have killed me, too, not taken me into his home, his heart. He couldn't have loved me, but he does. I know he does." She stopped and took a shaky breath.

"I can't let this go," he said, wishing he could give her what she needed. But she couldn't continue hiding from the truth. "I can't walk away from it, because it's real and you've got to face it, too. Search your heart, try to remember what you've forgotten. Your family, my family, they're all dead and someone killed them. My money's on your father. If he didn't do it, he paid someone to do it for him."

When she began to protest, he interrupted her. "It won't do us any good to haggle over this bone any more tonight. I'll go, but if you need me for anything, let Bull know. I'll make sure he knows where to find me."

"I'll be fine," she said with a toss of her head that made him smile. His Comanche brothers would have loved her. He checked the hall outside the study. Finding his path clear, he turned back to her. He wanted to hold her one more time before he left. His gut shouted at him not to leave her there where she could be in danger. He could kidnap her, but she'd raise a fuss and he'd never get away clean. He couldn't risk it. For now, he had to abide by her wishes.

When he reached for her, wanting to kiss her before he left, she sidestepped him. The uppity toss of her head warned him that she was about to slap him down. Fine, he wanted to hear what she'd been spoiling to say ever since the last time he'd made her scream his name.

Eyes sparkling with tears—though not with menace or spite—she said, "Don't worry about me. I don't need you for anything." She laid her hands over her abdomen. "Not anything."

A light went on in his head and he felt as if he'd been kicked in the gut by a mule. He had hurt her. She thought he would only want her if she carried his child.

He considered setting her straight, but until he knew where their mutual attraction was taking them, he couldn't honestly heal that hurt. So he did what he could. He grabbed her and kissed her, long and thoroughly, leaving her breathless and wide-eyed.

"You haven't seen the last of me, Angel. Not by a long shot."

Angel trudged up the stairs, weary and heartsore, her muscles protesting in places she blushed upon recognizing. Her thoughts flew, reliving every minute of the momentous night. She hurried toward her room, anxious to look at herself in the full-length mirror beside her dressing table. Surely her appearance had changed.

She felt like a different woman, no longer a girl at all. Would Bernida notice?

"Is he gone?"

Angel started as a man stepped from the shadows at the end of the hall, not far from her door. Her heart hammered long after she recognized Pedro. "Who do you mean?"

Pedro gave her a long, hard look, head to toe. She blushed, certain that he knew exactly what had occurred between her and Jeremiah this night. Not much escaped that keen gaze. "Did you find what you were searching for?"

She assumed he referred to the papers she'd been looking for. Pedro had never been rude or snide in the past. She shook her head. "I found the secret drawer in his desk, but it was empty. He must have moved his papers, perhaps to the safe at the bank."

"Did Jeremiah find anything?"

Angel's blush intensified. "Uh, no. He didn't have a chance to look before I interrupted him."

Pedro's grin flashed white in the darkness of the hall. "Sleep well, señorita." He glanced at the window at the end of the hall where the gray light of early dawn peaked through the draperies. "Enjoy what's left of the night."

Angel let herself into her room with a sigh. She stripped off her robe and nightgown, tossed them on the glowing embers of the fire and watched with regret as the flames devoured them. She'd loved that robe. How would she explain its loss to Bernida, who never missed a thing? But Bernida also had the instincts— and the nose—of a bloodhound. She'd have taken one sniff upon walking into Angel's room and would have known what had happened.

Angel shivered through a sponge bath; the warm water in the pitcher beside her dressing table had long since cooled. She tossed the dirty water over the balcony railing, wincing at the loud splash on the tiles below.

Refreshed and clad in a clean nightgown, she lay on her bed wishing she could sleep, but her mind refused. She wanted to forget her hurt feelings and relive every moment of Jeremiah's lovemaking. He'd truly desired her, not like the first time they'd kissed, when she had been the instigator. She smiled, remembering how quickly he'd taken over, teaching her the subtle nuances of lips and tongues, and hips. Now that she had made love with him, she understood that his lovemaking had been a continuation of his kiss, which had prepared her mind and body to accept him. Without it, she might have been startled or frightened by some of his actions, and those intimate parts of him—especially his size— though she had sensed that he was holding back, trying not to hurt her unduly.

The second time they'd loved, when he'd mounted her from behind, she'd trusted him even as his vigor increased toward the end. She pressed her hands to her hot cheeks as passion once again flowed through her veins.

Unable to lie in bed while her blood sang, she went to her dressing table and stared into the mirror. She looked no different, a little flushed maybe, but something in her gaze had changed, though she couldn't say what it might be.

The loss of her virginity? Was that knowledge looking back at her? Could anyone tell by looking at her that she finally understood the one great mystery every girl hungers to unravel? Surely not.

She lounged on her dressing table chair and spread her arms wide. Her eyes closed as she savored the languid satisfaction that made her feel so serene. She knew the tension underlying it, keeping her from complete euphoria, was caused by her fear that she might never see Jeremiah again, and she had no one to blame but herself. Despite her concerns over his determination to prove *Papá* was the culprit behind the Baldwin

Fort raid, she couldn't consider the possibility that she might never be with him again. She tried to imagine another man—a faceless man—doing those things to her. Could she ever allow another man to suckle her breasts, to kiss her down there, without remembering Jeremiah's touch, his kiss?

The possibility disgusted her. But would she have a choice? Her harsh words might have discouraged him from ever coming to her again, although his parting kiss had been filled with promise. Her cheeks flushed at the thought of it.

How could she live with herself if he never returned? What if she did become pregnant? Would she want him to stand by her, claim the child? Would her father allow her to marry the man he'd thrown out of his home? Their lives would be hell, with her in the middle, torn between the two men she loved and unable, unwilling, to choose between them.

She lifted her chin, sure that her choice to stay with *Papá* had been the right decision. She must broaden her search for proof of his innocence. Only when she found it would Jeremiah accept her decision. Even so, both men would struggle to accept each other, *if* Jeremiah came to love her enough to make the effort. If she fell in love with him—and she wasn't far from it already— she must resign herself to being forever torn between them; she could never expect them to fully reconcile.

She bowed her head and prayed—not as she'd been taught by the Catholic priests her father had hired to teach her his beliefs—but the way she remembered praying as a child. Simply, humbly, she prayed for help to sort out the mess her life had become and, most sincerely, she prayed for a way to endure if Jeremiah never came to love her.

His last kiss had reassured her and soothed her hurt. She believed he'd meant it to, and she reconsidered his offensive comment. He'd meant to say that if anything like an unexpected pregnancy resulted from their night of passion, he would stand beside her. She would not have to face the consequences alone.

When had life—and love—with Jeremiah become her goal? She couldn't say, but she knew her life had changed the moment she first saw him striding down the street. She would never be the same again, and she feared the changes were only beginning.

Jeremiah stuck to the shadows, first of the house, then the trees as he left the casa. He didn't think of it as Sanchez's house, just the place where Angel lived.

Even from a distance the horses in the barn caught his scent and began stomping and whinnying. He thought about stealing one, but ranchers hereabouts still hanged horse thieves. He had enough trouble without having a bunch of angry ranchers tracking him, and he didn't want to announce that he'd been visiting. Especially tonight.

Then one of the horses neighed. Not a frightened neigh, but a welcoming whinny. One he recognized. He froze behind a tree, judging the open ground that lay between him and the barn. After another neigh— one that convinced him he needed to get to that barn— he got down on his belly and scooted across the yard. The pain and toil were rewarded when he stood before the stall looking at his horse—well fed, brushed and groomed, and happy to see him. He rubbed the horse's nose, then risked lighting a lantern to search the tack room for a saddle and blanket.

Anger rose inside him when he found his own saddle and blanket shoved in a dusty corner. Damning the threat of discovery, he searched every corner of the small room, but his saddlebags and the rest of his gear, including his gun, weren't there. The loss of his saddlebags and their contents hit him hard, like another shovel of dirt tossed onto Ekararo's grave. Guilt overwhelmed him.

Like a dirty blanket thrown over his head, it snuffed out
the light ignited in his heart when he'd found his horse,
and it tarnished the night he'd spent in Sarah's arms.

Disgust filled him. He'd betrayed Ekararo and used
Sarah to satisfy his selfish body, only to find she'd had
his horse all along and hadn't told him. Could she be in
this with her father? No, he knew he had problems
trusting people, but he figured she'd just got caught up in
their lovemaking and plain forgot to tell him.

Did Sarah know his horse had been in her stable?
How long had it been here? Had she been lying to him?
With her noble but misplaced sense of loyalty, was she
protecting her father by keeping quiet about what she
knew? He remembered her alive and thrilling in his
arms and knew she couldn't be that devious, especially
to him. He'd known women who could have done it,
but not Sarah. There had to be a reason for her silence,
an explanation. Could he give her a chance to explain?

He saddled his horse fast, before the anger inside him
swelled out of control, but he couldn't quit looking at the
blood—his blood—that had left the entire back edge of
the horse blanket stained. How much more proof did he
need that Sanchez was responsible for having him
beaten? He took a clean blanket from the tack room and
left his bloody one draped over a saddle. If Sanchez noticed his loss, Jeremiah would tell him to take it out of
the money Sanchez owed for the land he'd stolen.

He needed to think and he couldn't do that here, so
close to Sarah. Just her name made him grit his teeth to
keep from swearing. He couldn't think of her as Angel.
How could he call her Angel? It felt wrong. She'd always be Sarah to him—plain, simple, too mischievous
for her own good, and far too earthbound to be named
after something holy. He'd always think of her as Sarah,
but until she remembered everything, which he hoped
she'd do soon, he'd try to remember to call her Angel.

He decided to return tomorrow night to ask the questions spurring him. By then his anger should have cooled. Now that he had his horse back, returning wouldn't be so hard to do. He swung into the saddle, ignoring the protest from his aching body. To hell with leaving quietly. If he didn't do something, his anger would lash out like a dust devil on the high plains: mindless, hungry, eating everything in sight.

Silently, he circled the house and its outbuildings, trailed by the wolf pack that had been waiting for him a safe distance from the house.

He grinned as the ranch dogs began howling. The horses panicked at the wolf scent and charged the corral fence, breaking through and scattering at a gallop with a few of the wolves chasing them—just for fun. Angry voices shouted for quiet from the small houses built around the large casa. Roosters crowed; even the chickens started clucking.

As coups went, this one was a favorite. Too bad no campfire lit the end of his trail. He would have enjoyed sharing the adventure with his brothers and fellow warriors. He missed their laughter, the back pounding and sly winks as he ducked into his tent and Ekararo's waiting arms.

Leaving chaos behind him, Jeremiah shrugged off his melancholy as he rode over the hill and out of sight of the house. No reason why he should be the only one awake so early.

Sarah, he was sure, would sleep through the noise.

Chapter Eleven

"Whatever has been going on here?"

Angel jumped and spun to find Juan behind her, blocking her exit from Bella's stall. How did such a big man move so quietly?

"Hello, Juan," she managed to say politely, despite the sudden hammering in her chest and the catch in her throat. She refused to allow him to see alarm or annoyance, only a cool, serene facade. She set aside the brush she'd been using to groom Bella, patted the horse's gleaming neck, and slipped her arm through Juan's, careful not to soil his pristine black riding jacket. She smiled up at him. "What brings you here so early? Did you not ride in the roundup this year?"

"I never ride with the vaqueros, *querida*." He lifted her hand off his sleeve to kiss her fingertips, but paused upon seeing her nails and set it back down with a sniff. "Such dirty business."

She stifled her outrage at his shudder, preferring to think it was caused by the thought of castrating and branding calves, not kissing her hand in its current, unwashed state.

"You ignore my question, señorita. What has been going on here?" He gestured at the partially mended corral fence as they stepped out of the barn and paused to watch Pedro herd several foam-flecked horses into the corral. Three young boys strained to lift the heavy log rails of the fence and fit them into their slots in the vertical support poles.

Angel released Juan's arm, but rather than step up

and help, he shouted at the boys, "Put your backs into it. Do you want those *caballos* to break loose again?"

Shooting Juan a disgusted glance, Angel hurried to help the boys, lifting and guiding the logs as Pedro dismounted and also came to assist. She and Pedro shared a long glance, but he said nothing. She returned to Juan's side, but did not take his arm, nor was it offered. She hoped he understood the message she sent him. Until Jeremiah gave up his quest for vengeance, she chose not to act on her decision to refuse Juan. But she no longer felt comfortable leading him on.

"If you'll excuse me, Juan, I have matters to attend to inside." She started past him, intending to return to her room and the warm bath she'd requested after spending the day helping Pedro restore order.

"No, I will not." Juan caught her arm at the elbow, his grip punishing. He leaned close, his eyes narrowed and his face flushed with rancor. "You will stay right here and answer my question as any well-bred, polite señorita would do."

Alarmed, both by his tone and his manner, Angel tried to pull free, but his grip tightened.

"You're hurting me," she said, and gave her arm another tug. "Release me now."

"Not until you learn some manners." His lip curled at her efforts and he pulled her closer, forcing her flush against his chest.

She couldn't help comparing his flabby body with Jeremiah's strong, hard-muscled form. "Perhaps this will persuade you," she said sweetly, then dug the heel of her boot into the top of his foot.

Juan yowled in pain and his grip loosened, allowing Angel to escape.

"What is the problem here?" Pedro came from the barn and stepped up beside her, insinuating himself between her and Juan.

"No problem," Angel told him with a smile and a toss of her head. "Juan heard about our trouble this morning and, like any good neighbor, came to offer his services to set things right again." She smiled at Juan, too. "He can see that we have restored order, so he is leaving."

"I'll get his horse," Pedro offered, and stepped quickly to the hitching rail to untie Juan's horse.

Juan made the most of Pedro's absence. He returned Angel's sweet, phony smile with one of his own. "I will enjoy breaking you when we are wed."

"That day will never come, señor. And if you ever threaten me again, you will leave with more than your foot smarting." Angel's stomach clenched at the rage in his eyes. She had no doubt that he would make every effort to fulfill his threat, but she would never allow it to happen.

"Oh, we will be wed, Angelina," he said, rudely gesturing for Pedro to give him a boost into his saddle. His hands clenched into fists when Pedro ignored the order and remained by Angel's side. "Then you will have no one but me to protect you." He mounted his horse with difficulty and jerked the reins tight, hurting the horse's mouth.

Pedro moved to intercede, but Angel stopped him with a hand on his arm. "In the future, Juan, do not trouble yourself over our minor problems. We do not require your assistance." She turned toward the house, but the blood boiling in her veins made her reckless. "And stop leaving your rubbish in my barn. That horse, the blood-covered one? It took my grooms hours to get him clean. The truly odd thing is that someone stole him last night."

"And the saddle," Pedro added, avoiding looking at Angel.

She swung her head to face Pedro, not wanting Juan to see her surprise at Pedro's statement. Why hadn't he told her?

"What horse?" Juan's eyebrows rose, but his hand

clenched on the reins, belying his confused expression. His horse's head tossed and he began to prance nervously. "I have no idea what you're talking about. Is that what all this fuss is about? Someone stole a horse from your barn?"

Pedro stepped between Angel and the nervous animal, forcing her to back toward the house, out of danger.

Furious, Angel shoved past him, done with pretending to tolerate Juan's attentions. After seeing the venom in his eyes, she could no longer allow him to suffer any delusions about marrying her. She would speak to her father about it as soon as he returned. "Yes, you see, the thief rides with a pack of wolves. The rest of the horses smelled them and bolted. Too bad your search didn't reveal their den."

Though Juan glared down at her, Angel felt no fear, only concern for Jeremiah's safety. She would warn him to be on his guard for Juan and his men, but she had a feeling Juan faced the greater danger. Jeremiah knew Juan had tried to kill him and it hadn't been long since Jeremiah had left the Comanche. Had he shed their ways when he put on white men's clothes? She doubted it, and had no intention of warning Juan.

She turned toward the house, but before she could take a step, Juan spurred his horse into her path. Surprised by his bold move, Angel crouched and pulled her knife out of the sheath in her boot. If he made another move toward her, he'd leave empty-handed and bloody. But Juan only leaned low over his horse's neck. She should have known he would want the last word.

"Do not fear, Angel, I never miss my target twice." He pulled his horse's head around and spurred the animal hard. It squealed in pain and leapt into a run, forcing grooms, dogs, and chickens to scramble out of its path.

Angel watched Juan go with relief, though she regretted her part in his horse's suffering. As she sheathed her knife, Pedro joined her.

"Was that wise?" he asked.

She took a deep breath and let it out, her shoulders sagging. "I don't know, but something snapped inside me when he threatened me."

Pedro tensed. When his voice finally came, it was no more than a low growl. "What did he say?"

She looked up, surprised by the intensity of his reaction, to find his eyes fixed on her face with a smoldering hatred that sent a chill up her spine.

"This isn't about me, is it?" she asked, suddenly comprehending. "You hated Juan long before any of this began. You've never trusted him." She crossed her arms over her chest and cocked her head. "I think it's time you told me the truth. Why are you here?"

"I have some unfinished business with Juan," he growled, his expression easing into more familiar lines. "That is not important now. What did he say to you? Did he threaten to hurt you?"

"I see," she said, peeved that he still didn't trust her enough to confide in her. "You get to keep your secrets, but I have to tell you everything." She waved a hand in the air and headed for the house, answering Pedro over her shoulder as she walked. "He said he was going to enjoy breaking me once we were wed, and I promised him that day would never come. Then you came and—"

Her arm was caught in a firm grip, halting her progress. *Not again!* She whipped around and smacked Pedro's hand to free herself. To her annoyance, his grip held despite the blow, though his hold wasn't painful as Juan's had been. "Why do you men do that?" she asked, giving his hand a disgusted look.

"Because women try to leave in a huff before we finish talking to them," he replied, and continued to hold her. "Listen to me carefully, Angel. Do not take Juan's threat lightly. He wasn't threatening you; he was stating his intentions. He does not take other people's wishes into account. I know this from sad experience."

"What sad experience?" she asked, more curious about Pedro's past than worried about Juan's threats.

"I cannot say." Pedro shook his head. "You must listen to me."

Angel pressed her hand over the one banding her arm and squeezed lightly. "Do not worry. I trust you and Father to keep me safe."

"You must help us," he said. "Don't ride anywhere alone and stay close to the house."

"Of course," she said, and turned to go, but he pulled her back. She struggled to contain the anger rising inside her. "I heard you, Pedro."

"Yes," he agreed, finally releasing her, "but you are not taking the threat seriously."

"Pedro," she said, leaning close and whispering so no one could overhear, "you were not with Bull and me when we found Jeremiah. That sight, and the hours that followed, are not something I will soon forget." She glanced around her at the women and children milling about, pretending to be busy working, not busy watching the two of them. "I do not want to alarm the people of the casa. I will be cautious, but perhaps you should ask the men who remain to be wary also."

"They have been warned, señorita," he assured her. "But they cannot control *la señorita*, and I fear that no one can. If she does not mind herself, she puts us all in danger."

Angel glanced around the large square yard formed by the smaller buildings positioned around the main house—a smokehouse, a summer kitchen, the large bunkhouse, flanked by several small houses for the married vaqueros and their families, and on the far side, well away from the house, the large barn. At once, she saw more men than she had noticed the day before, or even while Juan was there, all cradling rifles in their arms. Even the older boys were armed, some with slingshots dangling from their pants pockets, some with knife sheaths strapped to their belts.

She turned to Pedro, alarmed. She didn't want her people hurt, didn't want them to be injured because Juan was angry with her. "How did you keep them from stepping forward when Juan became angry?"

"They were waiting for a signal from me." He nodded at the nearest vaquero, Ernesto, an older man who had long since given up the daily roping and riding required of a working vaquero to help train the boys and assist with heavy household chores. Ernesto had lived on the hacienda as long as Angel could remember.

Chastened by the concerned faces of the many people depending on her, she nodded. "I will be careful. I want no one harmed because of me, or for any other reason." She met Pedro's gaze. "I must help Jeremiah discover the truth about our families, but I will not allow him to bring harm to the people of the hacienda."

Pedro nodded, then smiled as he said, "Go bathe." He sniffed and raised his eyebrows. "Have you been rolling in the pig pen?"

"Oh!" Angel kicked him in the shin and stomped away in mock outrage, smiling at the giggles that echoed behind her. She didn't know where her father had found Pedro, but clearly Pedro, like Jeremiah, had a score to settle with Juan. Curiosity at what that could be ate at her, but she quashed the questions chasing through her head. Until he was ready to explain himself, she had more than enough to occupy her mind and her time, such as how to get a warning to Jeremiah that Juan would again be hunting him—and his wolves.

She smiled, remembering her people, armed to the teeth. Pedro would find a way.

*   *   *

Jeremiah patted his horse's neck as he wiped him down with handfuls of grass. He'd become attached to the plain, but damn smart animal. He was glad to have the horse back.

Now what about the rest of his belongings? The money in his saddlebags was long gone, no doubt, but Juan wouldn't have wanted the parfleche or its precious contents. What had he done with it? Juan hadn't destroyed it; otherwise, Kris wouldn't have it, there wouldn't have been anything to pass down to her. Had Juan given it to Sanchez along with Jeremiah's horse, and maybe his Peacemaker? He'd have to go back, and this time search more than the barn. If Sanchez had the gun and the parfleche, Jeremiah's suspicion that the two scoundrels were partners would be confirmed.

Tired of worrying over things he couldn't change, questions that wouldn't be answered until tonight, Jeremiah checked his snares and skinned the rabbit he'd caught. Cleaned, it made a damn skimpy meal, but it would have to do. Maybe he could steal a loaf of bread, some fruit, when he returned to Sarah's house tonight. Getting in would be easy. She wouldn't be expecting him back so soon.

Maybe food wasn't the only thing he'd steal tonight.

Angel squirmed on her dressing table chair. "Bernida, I am tired. Finish quickly, *por favor?*"

Bernida looked up from brushing Angel's hair dry, and Angel cringed at the hurt look on her face.

"I enjoy this time with you in the evenings, also," Angel assured her. "It is only that I am falling asleep sitting up."

"You must not go to bed with wet hair," Bernida said, brushing faster.

Angel winced as the brush snagged. "I will finish it before the fire," Angel assured her. "You must be tired, too. It has been a long day for all of us."

"*Sí*, señorita." Bernida relinquished the brush, picked up the damp linens and Angel's soiled clothing, and quickly left the room, shutting the door quietly behind her.

The soft sound felt like a rebuke because it was so foreign to Bernida's nature. Angel chastised herself for her impatience. She wasn't the least bit sleepy, only anxious, and worried. She hadn't meant to take it out on Bernida.

What would happen tonight? Would Jeremiah return to question her about the horse or the rest of his belongings? She hoped he stayed away, had even sent him a warning message through Bull, but Bull had told her Jeremiah had disappeared two nights earlier. He and Little Bird had been glad to hear that Angel had seen Jeremiah, that he was well. If Jeremiah did come again, Angel intended to chastise him, not only for leaving Little Bird's care before he was well, but for not letting them know he was all right. Then she remembered his strength of the night before and told herself to stop worrying about him on the first count. How had he healed so quickly?

Angel suspected Juan had someone watching the house. Pedro had sensed someone and his instincts were infallible. She sighed as she closed and locked the balcony door and drew the heavy drapes. At least she wouldn't be the only person not sleeping this night. Pedro had insisted on locking all the windows of the casa, which meant no cooling breeze moving through the stuffy rooms.

Should she send Jeremiah's saddlebags to Little Bird and Bull? No, she couldn't. Juan's spy would follow them and her friends' part in Jeremiah's rescue would be exposed. At this point, Juan only suspected Angel's involvement. Juan was no threat to her, but the danger he posed to her friends and to Jeremiah made her shudder. She assumed Jeremiah was once again living off the land, as the Comanche lived, since leaving Little Bird's cabin. Juan's men could stumble on him any moment.

She must persuade him to give up his quest for vengeance and leave, make a new life for himself far away from this place with all its bad memories. Yet, even as she considered how to accomplish that task, she knew his leaving would break her heart and she feared he would not leave until he had learned the truth about the raid, learned who had murdered his family. She paced beside her bed, her floor-length robe tangling in her legs as she turned. She yanked it off and tossed it over a chair.

Jeremiah seemed not only convinced of her father's guilt, but determined to publicly accuse him, to destroy his life. Only by persuading Jeremiah to leave could she protect both her father and Jeremiah. She must succeed!

She sat on her bed and gripped the mattress edge with her hands. Less than a month before, her biggest concern had been her father's overprotection. How much her life had changed! Now she must protect her father from the man to whom she'd given her innocence. She longed to confide in Bernida, but the poor woman would fly into hysterics and make herself sick with worry. No, her only confidant must be Little Bird, but Angel balked at revealing the depth of her involvement with Jeremiah to anyone until she made sense of her feelings.

He had said that she'd loved him as a child. How could that be? She'd been very young at the time of the raid, only five or six, *Papá* had said. If only she could remember more.

Oh! She couldn't continue this way or she would make herself sick. She slid into her bed, welcoming the cool touch of the sheets against her overheated skin. The sweet scent of lavender calmed and refreshed her spirits. She must not give up hope.

Her cares slid away as she remembered the strength of Jeremiah's arms about her, lifting her onto the couch. A thrill coursed through her. She closed her eyes remembering his tenderness, the care he had taken with her, the ecstasy he'd brought her. She slid into a deep, restful sleep, dreaming of Jeremiah stroking her, kissing her, loving her.

Deep in the night, her dreams intensified. She moaned as Jeremiah settled behind her, his hands roaming over her breasts, her belly. She tried to drag them to that hot, hungry core that craved his touch, but he wouldn't let her. Then, finally, finally, a single finger brushed over her sensitive button and from there slid inside her. One stroke, two, and another finger joined it, caressing in a slow circle that made her beg him for more.

His fingers withdrew and he pressed her onto her back. Her eyes flew open as he settled between her thighs. "Hello, sleepyhead," he said, then kissed her, his tongue thrusting into her mouth as his manhood slid into her.

Thrilled to realize she wasn't dreaming, Angel returned his kiss with all the passion inside her, dropping her legs wide and planting her feet beside his hips. She lifted and caught his descent, driving him fully inside her.

"Ah!" he cried. He flung back his head, his eyes closed and his body tensed.

"Hello," she murmured, lifting to kiss his neck and inhale the scent of him. She clenched his rock-hard bottom, letting her nails dig in, hoping he'd relax and begin that divine rhythm she loved—thrust, pull back, thrust again, pull back even more. She gave a glad cry when he did just that, while she met every thrust, marveling at the strength and power of his body. Then she forgot thinking to just feel him filling her, stroking deep. She took him in, all of him, and squeezed him tight as he reached between them to press that very sensitive button.

With a suddenness that surprised her, she found herself flung into ecstasy. Her entire body arched, pulled taut, while her inner muscles clenched and released again and again. Jeremiah started to withdraw and, realizing he meant to spend his seed outside her body, Angel wrapped her legs around him, pulling him deep as he came in a series of long shudders. He kissed her neck to smother his cry of ecstasy.

When he collapsed on her, he moaned. "I don't think I can move."

She stroked his back muscles, taut even in total surrender. "Stay, you're not heavy."

He lifted his head to look into her eyes. "I'm not?"

She nodded. "For now. I finally feel close enough."

He let his head fall and for several minutes relaxed against her, only his foot moving, doing something interesting to her calf. He kissed a spot between her neck and shoulder and a tingle swept her breasts. Hmmm. She wasn't asleep down there after all, and neither was he if that twitch was any indication.

"Why didn't you let me pull out?" he asked.

"It would have spoiled it," she whispered, feeling another twitch. Could he be coming to life down there already? Last night, he had taken much longer to recover. His light nip on her neck reminded her of their conversation. "I'm greedy."

She stroked down his back, feeling his response between her legs, and smiled, deciding to truly test his abilities. "You took your horse last night. I'm glad."

His head came up. This close, his eyes pierced her soul, as did the suspicion she saw there. "Why was it here?"

"It showed up two days ago."

"No one saw anything?" He lifted onto his elbows

over her and the look in his eyes softened. His hips moved.

Her mouth opened, but nothing came out. He moved again, and she felt him growing inside her. "They were all busy that day planting the watermelon patch. It's behind the house. They make a party out of the planting—" A full thrust made her breath catch and her eyes shut.

"Where's the rest of my gear?" He pulled out and knelt between her legs, his erect penis pointing straight at the place where she wanted him to be. He didn't look angry, but his features seemed taut, his whole body tense.

She lifted onto her elbows, glanced down at his groin, then studied his face. "Are you planning to withhold that until I answer?"

"No," he said, leaning forward to kiss her breasts before saying, "I'm not about to punish either of us, but I'd like to know what happened to the rest of my belongings."

"I found your saddlebags with the saddle." Her breath caught as he captured a nipple between his lips and rolled it, nipping it lightly until it stood out from her breast like a ripe raspberry. She stared at herself, marveling.

"Empty?" He surveyed his handiwork with a smile.

"What?" she asked, struggling to follow when her body had begun humming in all the right places.

"Were the saddlebags empty?" Poised over her other nipple, he waited for her reply.

"No," she replied swiftly, her breath sighing between her teeth. She grabbed his head and pulled him down, arching upward to give him her breast. "There was a bag, white leather, with baby clothes inside."

"Ah," he said, and, opening wide, took most of her breast in his mouth, then turned it, too, into a raspberry. He settled on his side behind her and pulled her back against him, snugging her hips against his and letting his shaft slide between the cheeks of her bottom. He lifted her upper leg, placed it over his thigh. "My gun?" he asked as he surged into her, driving deep in one long, hard thrust.

She couldn't think, could only feel him filling her. He didn't press for an answer, only held her as she rode his powerful thrusts. His hand closed over her breast and his lips warmed her neck and shoulder, nipping at the tender curve where they joined. Then he lifted her and positioned her astride, facing away from him. She gasped as his hard length slid deeper than ever inside her and pressed her hand over her belly, trying to feel him.

His clever fingers caressed her hips, showing her how to ride him, then slid around to delve between her legs and massage her. She closed her eyes as tension coiled inside her. Every nerve in her body strained and finally burst, exploding behind her eyelids like fireworks against a night sky. She started to scream, unable to stop the sound, but he rose up and turned her face, catching her cry in a kiss. When she sagged against his chest, he withdrew and let her fall backward, sliding her to her back beside him. Then he knelt and lifted her bottom onto his knees. He smiled down at her as he pulled her legs over his shoulders. "Hold on," he whispered, and leaning over her, thrust deep, racing for the finish in a driving gallop.

"My armoire," she murmured when the fireworks faded behind her eyelids and she caught her breath, already sinking into slumber as he withdrew to lie beside her. She rolled toward him and settled her head on his upper arm.

"What?" he mumbled, his lips lost in her hair.

"Your gun," she said, snuggling closer, still craving closeness, needing the touch of his skin, his mouth, his strong hands. "I think it's yours. Colt? Black gun belt?"

He nodded and pulled the sheet over both of them. "Where are my saddlebags?"

She lifted a limp arm and pointed. "With the gun. Bottom drawer."

"Sleep, Sarah," he said, and pulled her close, tucking her head beneath his chin.

She sighed, unable to protest, more replete than she had ever been in her life.

Shivering, she woke to find her balcony doors open and Jeremiah gone, along with his gun and saddlebags, but the pleasure he'd given her throughout the night left a vibrant hum in her veins that kept her smiling the entire day and Bernida frowning.

She would see him again. Soon. She felt certain of it.

Chapter Twelve

Jeremiah reined in his horse on the far side of the ridge, out of sight of the casa, and pulled the white parfleche out of his saddlebags. His hands shook as he removed the moccasins and baby clothes and examined them. Fortunately, the man who'd tried to murder him hadn't stooped to destroying baby clothes. He put everything carefully back in the bag.

He'd expected the wave of pain that hit him at the sight of the tiny clothes. Instead of letting it pull him down, he tried to remember happier times. As if it had happened yesterday, he remembered Ekararo and Kris sitting cross-legged in his tipi, sewing the cured deer hide. Ekararo laughed, that silly giggle that burst from her when something struck her as funny. Kris had stuck her quill in her finger and cursed—again. While she worked, Ekararo had rested the half-sewn moccasin on top of her belly. Kris had complained that she needed a shelf, too, to keep from getting a crick in her neck.

Gone. Ekararo was gone forever. Kris lived, but in another time and place. Still, neither woman would want him to grieve forever. He had to get on with his life, do his best to make them proud. Thoughts of Kris reminded him of his need to find a wife, so that his great-great-granddaughter could be born.

Hard to think of himself as a grandparent when he wasn't even a father yet. But he had to bring that to pass—marry, father a child, a son—so that Kris could be born in her time and be sent here to help the People, and love Duuqua. He grinned, glad that his friend, the man who had rescued him from the Kiowa, was with her. He was glad, too, that Duuqua would never have to live on the reservation and suffer humiliation as well as starvation alongside his Comanche brothers. He could only imagine the life Duuqua would live with Kris in her time, a proud Comanche war chief beside the woman he loved, alive and well in the future. He wondered what the Comanche must be like after being forced to surrender and live on reservations for a hundred and fifty years. What would they do with a war chief? He and Duuqua faced the same problem: both of them must learn to live like white men. Quickly.

He wished he could visit them, watch their children grow, share their life, but he needed to be here to make a new life for himself. That came first, even before a wife and children.

His thoughts turned to Sarah and became tangled in the wonder of making love to her. A child could already be growing in her belly. If she became pregnant, he'd marry her whether she wanted him or not. No child of his would be raised by her snake of a father, but he didn't want to marry Sarah while the question of Baldwin Fort remained unresolved. She'd be stuck between him and Sanchez the rest of her life.

What if she didn't become pregnant? Did he love her? Could he marry her? Or would she be a constant reminder of the sorrow they'd both suffered? Would he remember his murdered family every time he looked at her? Could he live on this blood-soaked land where they'd died, where their ashes still lingered in the air?

He didn't know, but he enjoyed making love to her. She responded to his every move, never shied away from anything he did with her, and threw herself into their lovemaking with passion and enthusiasm. Lovemaking was a big part of marriage. When he'd stopped making love to Ekararo as she became bigger with their child, they began arguing over stupid, little things. They'd never argued when they were making love regularly. He sighed, missing her and the simple life they'd shared.

He shook off the sad memories, and returned to thoughts of Sarah, so alive and real in his arms last night. He could still smell the lavender from her sheets on his skin. Outside her bed, he admired her spunk. Even as a baby, she'd gone after what she wanted. And she'd wanted him. He remembered her chasing after him and was ashamed of himself. He'd treated her badly, and all she'd wanted was to love him. Something in his heart shook loose and left him wanting to make it up to her somehow.

He didn't love her, he decided after comparing his feelings for Ekararo to his feelings for Sarah, but he enjoyed being with her, sharing her bed. If he kept that up—and she continued to refuse to let him pull out of her at the right moment—chances were good that she'd become pregnant. Soon. He'd have to work faster, find out once and for all who'd planned the raid on Baldwin Fort so there'd be no questions, nothing to keep Sarah from marrying him if a child made it necessary. His heart still belonged to Ekararo, but he'd make room for Sarah, too. He didn't love her yet, but he'd try. Knowing she loved Sanchez more than her own family would make it hard.

He had a plan in mind that would bring matters to a head right quick. He opened the bag of twenty-dollar gold pieces he'd taken from Sanchez's desk after leaving Sarah's bed. He didn't regret taking the money. Sanchez owed him plenty more than this.

It was a bold plan, but it would flush out his attacker and the man responsible for the raid. He'd have to watch his back.

He pointed his horse's nose toward Cedar Creek. No lying low at a boardinghouse this time. He'd stay in the hotel, in the busiest part of town. He'd buy himself a bath and a shave, along with some new duds, and show his face all over.

Juan would want him dead, but he was a back-shooter, too gutless to confront a man in broad daylight in the middle of town. He'd hire someone to shoot him in the back at night.

How would Sanchez react when he learned that Jeremiah was in town asking questions? Jeremiah looked forward to finding out.

One thing he knew for sure, his plan would bring Sarah on the run.

He kneed the horse into a gallop, anxious to put his plan into motion.

Angel rode out two days later and met Bull riding to find her with a message from Little Bird. Expecting bad news—she hadn't seen Jeremiah since the night they'd made love—Angel ripped open the note. Little Bird wanted to talk to her.

Angel gritted her teeth in frustration. Normally, the distance between her home and her friends' didn't bother her, but when the news could be dire, her father's prejudice rankled. He had given no explanation for refusing to allow Bull and Little Bird to visit Angel at the casa, and whenever Angel spoke of them, he refused to listen. *Papá* had never stuck to a decision so tenaciously. She could only assume that something had been done or said to offend him. She shook off her frustration, and tried to make up for her silence.

"Have you heard anything about Jeremiah, Bull? Has anyone found a body? Has anyone been shot?"

Bull shook his head, letting his horse pick its way back toward the cabin. "Naw, I heard he's been in town."

"In town? What an idiot!" she shouted. Bella's ears swiveled back and she tossed her head. "Sorry, girl," Angel said, leaning down to pat the mare's neck while she struggled to regain her composure. "What is he thinking?" she asked Bull, when the horse settled under her. "How did you find out?"

"I do get into town now and then," he said, giving her an arch look.

"Yes," Angel said, returning his look with a stern one. "I've heard those saloon girls can be very demanding."

Bull snorted. "Especially Mary Be . . . Uh, where'd you hear that?" Bull flushed under her scrutiny. She couldn't blame him for seeking companionship where he could find it. Single women were scarce as hummingbirds, and most despised half-bloods. Bull had little hope of finding a wife among the respectable women of Cedar Creek. If Bull found a saloon girl to love, Little Bird would welcome her into their family. Angel could do no less.

"I'm sorry, Bull," she said, and kneed her horse closer. She caught his hand and squeezed it. "I apologize for judging you. It's not my problem." She sighed. "I wish my sisters had lived. They would have loved you."

"Me, too." Though he squeezed her hand in return, he didn't smile. "I'll never marry. It wouldn't be fair to expect a woman, even a whore, to put up with the criticism and hatred Bird and I get."

Angel reined in. "Who's been hateful to you?" Bull and Little Bird never asked for her help, never asked her to stand up for them, but she'd already done so, many times, especially with the women in town. When a new cowboy started in on Bull, she sent Pedro to "explain" things to him. The troublemakers either left town or left her friends alone.

"I ain't hidin' behind your skirts, Angel," Bull said, tipping up his hat to look her in the eye. "Little Bird appreciates your support, but I don't need you interferin', okay? Just let it be."

"As you wish, Bull." Angel had lost this argument so many times in the past that she knew it was best to simply agree, then do what she could without Bull finding out. Nowadays, Pedro acted on his own, as Bull's friend, without her pointing out the problem. "You know I only want to help, not make things harder for you."

"You don't always see things like a man does, you know?" He nudged his horse to pick up the pace. "Like this thing between you and Jeremiah. He don't understand how you can defend your father when he's convinced your father killed your real family, includin' all those sisters you just said you regret losin'. The way he sees it, you're betrayin' their memory by takin' your father's part, but you don't see it that way at all. Do your sisters and parents even matter to you? Do you care that they died? How do you feel, knowin' your father may have planned the whole massacre?"

"Of course I care." Angel bristled, surprised by Bull's question and hurt that he and Jeremiah thought she didn't care. "My memory of them has been buried so long that thinking of them is like remembering a book I read. They don't touch my heart as strongly as my feelings for *Papá*. He's part of my daily life and has provided a home for me all these years even though he's not my real father."

Bull nodded, but said nothing. Though his expression remained thoughtful, she knew he agreed with Jeremiah that she should leave the hacienda until *Papá* was proven innocent of any wrongdoing. Only then would Jeremiah feel it was safe for her to return. But they had things backward.

"Bull, until Jeremiah can prove his allegations, I'm not leaving."

"Bird and I worry about you. You might not find out that Jeremiah's right until it's too late to get out." He shook his head. "Too many unanswered questions. Makes me nervous. Promise you'll be careful."

"I promise," she assured him, touched that he and Little Bird were so worried about her.

"Then I better tell you that Jeremiah's moved into the

hotel in town and has been stirring things up, asking questions."

"What!" No wonder she hadn't seen him for several days. She'd missed him, but hoping that he'd left town had kept her from worrying. She had, however, sent a scouting party out today toward the hills west of the hacienda, the only area with enough timber and cover for a hideout, no matter how crude. Learning that while she'd been worrying, he'd been flaunting himself in town infuriated her. How many saloon girls had *he* been entertaining?

"How did you find out?" she asked Bull.

His lips settled into a flat line and his eyes flashed angrily. He didn't answer.

"Oh! At a saloon?" Bull's belligerent look told her she was correct. "Was he with a whore?"

Bull didn't answer.

"The fool," she groused under her breath as she urged her horse into a gallop, leaving Bull to follow if he wished. She knew Little Bird would tell her the truth, even though Angel hoped to keep her involvement with Jeremiah secret a little longer, at least until she'd come to terms with it herself. The possibility that Jeremiah had been sleeping with some whore in town made the blood pound in her head. If she found out it was true, Angel would never let him touch her again.

"So, Bull told you?" Little Bird asked without preamble when Angel skidded to a stop outside the cabin and stomped inside.

"Yes, he did," Angel said, forcing herself to sit calmly and stop fuming.

Little Bird continued to rock gently, dropping the sock she was darning into her lap.

Angel said nothing, just pulled off her riding gloves, one finger at a time, fighting to control the rage burning through her. She would not vent her emotions on her friend.

Little Bird fixed her with a knowing stare. "I've prepared a special tea for you. It will keep you from becoming pregnant, unless that's what you want. If it is, don't drink it."

Flummoxed, Angel sank into her usual chair and eyed the steaming cup on the table at her elbow, then looked at Little Bird. Determined to defend herself, she tried to marshal her thoughts, but saw understanding, not accusation, in Little Bird's eyes and soft smile. "How did you know?"

Little Bird resumed her darning, shaking her head. "Pedro and Bull are terrible gossips."

Angel sucked in a sharp breath. "Pedro?"

Little Bird nodded. "His news didn't surprise me." She grinned at Angel. "It surprised Bull, though." She laughed and shook her head.

"Why weren't you surprised?" Angel relaxed into her chair and picked up the steaming tea. Before taking a sip, she hesitated. As she watched the rising steam, she considered her options. Her father's priest would condemn this, she knew, but he wasn't the one facing a potential unwanted pregnancy.

Would a pregnancy, a child, be unwanted? Was she ready to be a mother? A wife? To Jeremiah? She enjoyed making love with him, and she cared for him, but she didn't love him. Love could come, in the future, but would it grow from a forced marriage, or would caring turn to resentment? He faced an uncertain, difficult future. Dragging a wife and child along would increase his burden.

And what of the child? She would love a child, no matter the circumstances of its conception, but given a choice, she would prefer to become a mother after marrying the man she loved. She drained the cup. She wasn't sure of Jeremiah yet. Heavens, she wasn't sure of her own feelings.

"That kiss you two shared his last night here nearly

set our stable on fire." Little Bird glanced up between stitches. "And your behavior around him while he was healing . . . You've been obsessed with him since you first saw him. This way"—she nodded at the empty teacup—"you won't be forced to make the right decision for the wrong reason."

Angel frowned and considered Little Bird's comment. Her friend was trying to help. "Thank you. Is that why you sent Bull for me?"

"No, I wanted to talk to you. How are you feeling? Still having nightmares?" She dropped her darning into a basket by her feet and focused on Angel, who shifted in her chair. Nothing missed Bird's keen eyes.

"No," Angel said, blinking in surprise. "Though I hadn't noticed that they've stopped."

"I'm glad, for the sake of your health, but I'm not sure it's a good thing."

"I'm not convinced that I need to remember." Angel shuddered, unwilling to guess what another nightmare might reveal.

Little Bird nodded. "I know the dreams are painful, but you need to remember more so that the decisions you make are truly the best for you."

"I've made sensible decisions, so far." Angel couldn't help feeling defensive. "Those memories are horrible. I prefer not to relive the raid nightly."

"Don't you want to understand your relationship with Jeremiah, especially now that you've become intimate? He hurt you once before. Do you want to risk being hurt by him again?"

"He hurt me? Do you know that for certain, or are you guessing?"

Little Bird shook her head. "I would never tell you an untruth, especially if it would cause you pain. Jeremiah told me himself that he hurt you when you were very young. He said he made you cry. You could ask him about it yourself, but wouldn't you prefer to know what happened, rather than wonder if he told you everything?"

Angel smiled at Little Bird. "You have always been a true friend to me. I don't give you a tenth what you give to me. I don't deserve you."

"Perhaps I deserve you." Little Bird gazed back at Angel, her lips curving up. They both burst out laughing.

"Do you have a tea or potion that will induce memory recall?" Angel asked, arching a brow.

Little Bird chuckled. "I'm sorry. I can't help you with that. Too bad, too. I'd be rich!"

"What are you planning for dinner?" Angel rose and followed Little Bird toward the small cook stove near the cabin's only window.

"Fresh trout—Bull caught it this morning—and new carrots from my garden. Before you clean the fish, here are some of those herbs to take home with you. Just a teaspoon in boiling water, mind, and don't let it steep for more than three minutes."

Angel nodded, committing the directions to memory. Not that she expected to need the tea again in the near future, but who knew what would happen when she confronted Jeremiah in town tomorrow, which she certainly planned to do? She seemed to have difficulty resisting his manly charms.

Little Bird handed her a scrap of paper. "Here, I've written it down. I never take chances with a strong decoction. Oh, and don't make it when Bernida's around. She once told me she's used this herself, so she will recognize the scent."

Angel stared, incredulous. "Well, that's interesting."

Little Bird patted her arm. "No one's perfect, Angel. I've used it, too."

"You?" Angel stared at Little Bird's back as she pulled an empty bowl from a high shelf. "Who? When?" To her annoyance, Little Bird ignored her questions and set about peeling carrots.

* * *

"Have you ever been in love?" Angel asked, watching Bernida's reaction closely in the mirror. "Oww!" she cried when Bernida dropped the brush and tried to catch it against her back. Bernie's unusual clumsiness answered her question.

"Who was it?"

Bernida fumbled around trying to locate the fallen brush, keeping her face down or behind Angel so that she couldn't see it in the mirror. "I did not say . . ."

Angel chuckled. "You've never dropped my brush before."

Bernida straightened, frown lines making her look stern. "That does not mean . . ."

"Tell me about him," Angel said, her hopeful tone turning the request from a demand to a plea.

Bernida sighed. "There is nothing to tell. I was young and foolish. He was soon gone."

"Do you ever think of him?" Angel knew she should stop peppering her with questions—Bernida's face had gone still, revealing no emotion—but she truly hoped that Bernida's life had included more than just caring for her and Father. Angel hoped she'd experienced some of the joy she'd shared with Jeremiah.

"No." Bernida turned away to straighten the room, gathering Angel's soiled clothing and the damp towels from the long bath she'd just enjoyed.

"I'm sorry," Angel said quietly. "I should not have pressed you for answers when I can see you find the subject painful."

"I know you would not hurt me." Bernida stroked Angel's hair and bent to press a kiss to her head. "I do not like to think about it."

"I understand."

Bernida turned to leave, but stopped at the door to regard Angel over her shoulder. "Love is not always kind, Angelina. Be careful what you do."

Angel opened her mouth to respond, but Bernida was gone. She stripped off her robe and crawled into bed, resolved not to let Jeremiah hurt her as Bernida had been hurt. If she suspected that he was losing interest in her, she must end their relationship herself. But would that prevent her from suffering as Bernida still suffered?

What did she feel for Jeremiah? Everything had happened so quickly, she hadn't yet analyzed her feelings. Aside from the obvious—Jeremiah's physical appeal—she was drawn to him in some unexplainable way that continued to puzzle her. If only she could remember more about their relationship as children. Would that explain everything? What if she remembered and it was something awful? She dismissed the notion. Surely, her intuition would have warned her away from him, not urged her closer.

Perhaps Little Bird was right and Angel did need to try to recall more of her lost memories. This uncertainty troubled her, and the possibility that she could make a poor decision without the knowledge those memories contained alarmed her.

So how did one go about "encouraging" nightmares? She blew out the lamp at her bedside and lay, stiff and silent, recalling the horrible dreams about her sisters' and mother's deaths. As the images played through her mind, terror made her clutch her bedclothes and shudder. She bit her lip to keep from screaming a warning to them and coiled into herself, shaken and bereft. Each time she revisited the memories, she noted more detail. Now she could remember the smoke and the metallic taste of her own blood; she'd bitten her tongue when, in her hurry to warn them, she'd fallen the last few feet out of the tree.

Even a long sip of water from the pitcher Bernida always left in her room hadn't erased the flavors or dispelled the scents lingering in her nostrils. She splashed some of her favorite rose scent on a handkerchief and tried to sleep with it pressed to her nose. As the scent calmed and soothed her, she closed her eyes and tried to remember why it was her favorite. She recalled playing on the grass while a woman—her mother—tended the rose garden behind their home. Her mother had encouraged Angel to help care for it, but Angel had not been interested, she'd preferred to follow Jeremiah around.

Angel's eyes popped wide open. She flung back her blankets to sit on the side of the bed, her heart pounding as she considered these new revelations. As a child, she had adored Jeremiah, and he had disliked her for it. Intensely. Remembering herself trudging along in Jeremiah's wake as a child made her cheeks burn with humiliation. As an adult, looking back, she recognized the annoyance on his face as he looked over his shoulder and found her there. If he had disliked her so, why did he tolerate her now?

She'd known people who were flattered into a relationship with an admirer, despite their own inclinations. Jeremiah had never been flattered by her childhood infatuation. Looking back over their short reacquaintance, Angel realized that she had practically thrown herself at him. Again. He'd tried to tell her when she'd kissed him that he was still grieving, but she'd cut him off, thinking she could make him forget. He'd taken what she offered but would he have done the same with any woman? Had he wanted to kiss her, too? In subsequent moments of intimacy, he'd never expressed any fondness or admiration of her. Had he been using her just to relieve his needs?

Angel bowed under the mortification. Pressing her hands over her eyes, she groaned her shame. How could she have been so blind? How could she ever face him again? What if he tried to lie with her again? Should she allow it, knowing, finally understanding that he was only using her? Could she refuse him, knowing, finally remembering that she had loved him all her life? For her there had never been anyone but Jeremiah. To deny him, refuse his touch, turn from his kiss, would tear her heart to shreds. True, he had never returned her feelings, but that did not diminish them and those feelings, tardily acknowledged, flooded her being, justifying her recent, seemingly irrational behavior. Her actions had been true to her character, had she only remembered.

Loving Jeremiah as she now knew she did strengthened her resolve to put an end to his reckless need to prove her father was behind the raid on Baldwin Fort. She must make him see that proving it at this point wouldn't raise the dead or redeem them. In order to protect the two men she loved more than life itself, she must make Jeremiah see reason. She had to convince him to leave.

At any cost.

Jeremiah took the stairs to his hotel room two at a time and slammed the door behind him.

"Damn banker," he growled as he shrugged off his coat. He'd made an early-morning visit to Mr. Bulger, the owner of Cedar Creek Bank, and had been told to quit chasing ghosts and leave town.

The hefty Mr. Bulger had broken into a sweat the minute he'd seen Jeremiah enter the bank. He'd stared as if he was seeing a ghost.

The man had been involved in the raid and in helping Sanchez keep his secret. Jeremiah knew it. If he'd had paper on the Sanchez hacienda, he'd have shoved it under Jeremiah's nose. All the blustering in the world couldn't hide the fact that the banker was guilty, too. And one glance around his grandiose office suggested that he'd been paid nicely for it.

So, now what? He'd asked around town, but no one

was talking. People knew, or thought they knew, but no one was willing to take a chance and tell him.

A soft, almost furtive knock sounded at his door. He was tempted to shout, "Come in!" but didn't want to scare his visitor off. It could be someone had found the courage to come forward with information he needed.

He took off his shiny new dress boots—as big a waste of money as any he'd ever spent—and tiptoed to the door. At a second knock, he yanked open the door, grabbed the person on the other side, barely noticing she was female.

It was Sarah, but a Sarah like he'd never seen before.

"Well, surprise, surprise," he said, not bothering to keep his voice down.

She quickly shushed him. "Do you want the whole town to know I'm here?"

"Didn't you come in the front door?" he asked, suspecting the answer but wanting to hear it, and her reasons for sneaking into his room. "Did you miss me?"

She shoved him away when he tried to kiss her, hissing like a cat. Another first in a day full of firsts: he'd never heard a woman hiss before. "I came up the back stairs."

His eyebrows shot up. "This place has a back stairway?" He cocked his head, looked her up and down. "How did you know?"

"I didn't," she said, flushing. "Pedro showed me."

"That Pedro," he said with a nod, "sure does get around."

Sarah stomped her foot. He loved the way her eyes turned green, shot full of yellow sparks when she was angry. Everyone else in town was angry with him, too. Why shouldn't she join the crowd?

"I talked to Bull. He told me he saw you in the saloon."

He sat in the chair by the window, saying nothing.

"Well?" She stamped her foot. He stared at it, surprised. Who was this woman and what had she done with Sarah? "What do you have to say for yourself?"

She started pacing in front of him, her hands on her hips. Her eyes shot sparks at him and they'd turned . . . green. Not grass green, but kind of a blue green that made them shine. Or was that tears? He stopped admiring her and listened.

"If you've been with one of those whores, it'll be a cold day in Ju-ly before you touch me again."

She's jealous! He should have told her she had nothing to worry about, explained that whores knew everything that was going on behind the scenes—and in the bedrooms—in most towns, but he was enjoying Sarah angry. Full of brimstone and vinegar, she was giving off so much heat he couldn't wait to get hold of her and turn all that wasted fire to lovemaking.

"What is wrong with you today?" she asked in a whisper-shout, stopping her pacing to stick her nose in his face.

"I've had a busy morning."

"There's no need to take it out on me." Her fists slid off her hips and he thought she might hit him. "And keep your voice down!"

"Yes, ma'am," he said, barely speaking. "What can I do for you today?" He waggled his eyebrows and admired the color in her face so much he decided to increase it. "May I say that you're looking mighty fine? Migh-ty fine."

He let his gaze trail down her body, from the deep scoop of her neckline and the breasts peeking out of it, to the taut lines of her slim waist, to the flare of her hips and back to her flashing eyes. Migh-ty fine, indeed. Knowing, as he did, that every mouthwatering curve was all her, he found himself reacting to her as he always did: very strongly.

He tried to listen to what she was saying, but it was

no use. "Hold on to your hat, sweetheart," he said, then picked her up with a hand on either side of her waist and laid her across the foot of his bed.

She squawked when her hat flew off, but he pulled off his suspenders, shucked off his trousers, and climbed on, straddling her.

"Jeremiah! What are you . . . ?" she cried, pushing at his shoulders. "I didn't come here to . . ."

He kissed her mouth to shut her up, and congratulated himself on his timing. She was talking too loud. Someone would come to find out what was wrong. She would have regretted that. Hell, he would have regretted it, too.

Without breaking the kiss, he raised himself enough to drag her skirts up, exposing her . . . drawers? A little fumbling and he discovered that they were split through the crotch. A little more fumbling and he freed himself, pushed her knees wide, and moved over her.

He stopped kissing her to look down.

"You don't have to do this. I know you don't really want to. After all, you never liked me one little bit." She lifted her head to glare at him. "Are you listening to . . . ooohhh!"

With his hands free to massage her breasts, he quickly overcame her resistance and had her moaning into his mouth, especially when he inserted a finger to see if she was ready, and it came back slick with her juices. He rubbed his cock up and down her slit, found her opening; then one quick push sent him deep. He shut his eyes, soaking up her heat. Then she brought up her knees and met his second thrust, seating him fully. He swallowed her satisfied cry and winced as she grabbed his butt, her nails digging in as she pulled him to her.

"Is this all you ever think about?" she asked, tearing her mouth from his. She rocked her hips, urging him to get on with it.

"When you're in my bedroom, you better be nice.

Now hang on, I don't want to shove you off the bed headfirst." With that, he began a strong, driving rhythm that probably would have done just that, except for her legs wrapped around his waist.

As he felt her muscles ripple and her body tense, he pulled her legs over his shoulders and picked up the pace, then nipped her earlobe. "Come for me, Sarah."

He kissed his way to her mouth and swallowed her cry, then let her return the favor when he followed her over the edge.

"Shall we start over again?" he asked when he could speak.

"Why?" she replied. "Do you think we could improve on it?"

He chuckled and kissed her. "We could try." He pushed himself off her and wet a towel from a pitcher of water on a nearby table. He swabbed the stickiness from her body, then took the towel to himself before righting his clothes and again sitting at the table.

"Would you like a glass of sherry?" He held up the bottle for her to look it over. "I'm told it's the 'beverage of choice' for a lady."

"Yes, thank you. Very nice." She spared the bottle a glance, then reached to find her hat, which had tumbled to the other side of the bed. He smiled, enjoying the view. Her barely covered bottom wiggled at him, and the flames she'd just quenched flared to life again. If she didn't stop wiggling, he might as well send for a preacher.

"I wasn't sleeping with the saloon girl, just looking for information. Bull got the wrong impression, but he didn't stick around long enough to ask." He'd let her make what she wanted out of that, but Bull hadn't come to town to talk to him. He'd hustled one of the girls up the stairs without even buying her a drink first.

With a very unladylike grunt, she squirmed off the bed, hat in hand, and groaned at herself in the mirror.

After a sip of sherry, she removed her gloves and set about repairing her hair, which hung in fat curls in several places. He preferred the curls, he decided, when she'd tucked it all on top of her head again. She started to replace the hat with a very long, wicked-looking hat pin, but gave him a wary look and set the hat on the dresser across the room.

Aside from deciding not to fight their mutual attraction, it was the most intriguing thing she'd done since arriving, bar the bare bottom wiggling.

"What brings you here, Angel?" he asked, with a slight emphasis on her name.

"I've remembered more of my childhood," she said, continuing to fuss with her hat, probably to avoid looking at him.

"What have you remembered?" he asked, leaning forward, watching her closely. Why was she over there and not in his lap, where she ought to be?

"I remembered what a nuisance I was to you, when I was little. You must have hated me." She turned away from him and he thought he saw her wipe a tear off her cheek.

He turned her to face him. Sure enough, she had tears in her eyes and they'd turned even brighter green. He couldn't quit staring. With her cheeks flushed and her eyes bright and shining, she was stunning. "I never hated you, Sar—Angel. I was a kid, and my friends made fun of me, so I chased you away."

"I understand," she told him. "And I've done it again, chasing you, I mean, forcing myself on you when you told me you were still grieving." She moved away from him. "I came to tell you that I understand you can never love me. I've enjoyed the time we spent together." She glanced at the bed and blushed.

He couldn't find his tongue. Where had she come by the notion that he could never love her? Just because she'd remembered he'd been a dumb brat didn't mean he couldn't love her, appreciate her now. If she thought this—this attraction between them was one-sided, she was the dumb one. While he sorted through his thoughts, he let her have her say. Let her get it all off her chest, and then he'd straighten her out.

"Also, I've come to beg you to stop this ridiculous search and leave." She drew a deep breath after her rushed little speech.

"Did you practice that?" he asked, ignoring her glare. This couldn't go unanswered. "You know my answer. My search isn't ridiculous—it's damn necessary and important. I can't understand why no one's done it before now." His voice was rising and he didn't care, damn it. So was his temper. "They're gone. All of them. How can that happen without someone asking why or how? Did you know the bodies were burned? Burned, Sarah. There aren't even any graves where we—you and I—can take flowers, or kneel to pray for their souls. It's as if they never existed. I can't accept that."

"Why is it so important now, Jeremiah? You say you don't understand why no one has investigated before this. Who was left to do it, their murderers? You? Me? I didn't remember anything until recently, and I've still forgotten more than I recall.

"Why is it so important to you now? Wasn't it on your mind when you were raiding with the Comanche? Yes, I know about that. Are you the white warrior everyone's feared, the one who rode with Quannah Parker? Are you wanted for killing white settlers?"

He stared at her, stunned that he'd blabbed so much during his fever. He pressed his lips together. Too little, too late. "Be quiet, Sarah."

"No! I will not be quiet. It's too dangerous for you here. Juan is still looking for you, and he won't hesitate to finish the job he started."

Jeremiah fought to absorb her words, but couldn't

accept them. She wanted him to leave, after what they'd just shared? Was she really concerned about him, or about what he might learn? "Who are you trying to protect, Sarah? Me or Sanchez?"

"I don't want either of you to be hurt," she said, her eyes going wide and changing to green again. Red splotches appeared on her cheeks. "Please, don't make me choose."

He said nothing, just sat in the chair with the late afternoon sun beating on his head, his back, stunned by her plea. He didn't bother denying her crazy idea that he could never love her because he'd been annoyed by her when they were kids. That was nothing compared to this. She was willing to go on living a lie, wanted him to just disappear as if he and his family had never existed.

"I'll leave, Sarah," he told her, immune to the two fat tears running down her cheeks. His blood had turned to ice. Silently, knowing he wasn't finished with Sanchez, he added, *But I'll be back with proof of your father's guilt.*

She nodded. "Thank you," she whispered. "I knew you would see reason."

"I'm not doing it for you." He crossed the room and snatched up her hat, stuck it on her head. "Get out. And don't darken my door again. You've put yourself in Sanchez's camp. You might as well have been part of the raid, gun in hand."

She moved toward the door, but not fast enough. He pushed her out and slammed the door behind her. She didn't try to redeem herself or cry out that she'd changed her mind or even that she'd made a mistake. She didn't beg him to forgive her. He told himself he was glad; it saved him the trouble of having her thrown out of the hotel. He picked up the bottle of sherry he'd bought just for her, knowing she would come when she heard what he'd been doing, and threw it into the fireplace. He watched it shatter and nodded. He recognized that splintering sound.

His heart had made it when she broke it into thousands of pieces.

Chapter Thirteen

Angel stumbled down the back stairs of the hotel, relieved to see Pedro waiting with the buggy. She said nothing all the way home, and was grateful that he didn't ask any questions. She hadn't told him her plans, and she didn't confide that she'd succeeded in persuading Jeremiah to leave.

Pedro asked what had happened, but she couldn't talk about it. She hadn't expected success to leave her numb, dead inside.

Unwilling to debate her plans, Angel also didn't confide in Bernida, who would demand to know how she'd persuaded Jeremiah to leave. Her friends didn't need to know the price she'd paid to see both the men she loved safe.

She sent Bernida away and donned an old dress she often wore to help clean the casa, then went to her father's room. She hadn't come to clean, but to look for proof. If she could demonstrate *Papá*'s innocence, perhaps Jeremiah would not have to go. First, she tackled his bed, flipped off the heavy, down-filled mattress and examined it for hidden pockets. Nothing. Second, she got down on her hands and knees and searched for loose floorboards. She found one underneath his armoire, pried it open, and emptied it of several neatly tied bundles of money, which she quickly replaced. She had no need to take *Papá*'s money; he gave her everything she asked for, and more.

In a hidden drawer in the small desk in his sitting area, she found more money, coin this time, but no paperwork, nothing to prove he owned the hacienda legitimately, that he'd purchased it, not stolen it from people he'd murdered. In another desk drawer, she found a box full of jewelry, mostly rings, and all of it simple. No flashy pieces like the ruby necklace he'd given her, the one she'd remembered having seen Jeremiah's mother wear. The rings were simple gold bands. Wedding rings? How odd. Also in the drawer she found several empty, black velvet jeweler's bags like the one that had held the ruby necklace.

Where had this jewelry come from? Had *Papá* purchased it and taken it out of the black bags? She examined some of the pieces and found them worn, not sparkling clean and shining like new. Had he purchased the bags to disguise the fact that the jewelry was used when he gave it as gifts? Could this jewelry have belonged to the people of Baldwin Fort? Had he found the box or bought it from one of the men who'd raided the fort? She shut the drawer on the box and its disturbing contents. It proved nothing, and raised too many questions.

She straightened the desk, careful to leave everything exactly as she had found it, and stood, looking around the room to make sure she'd left nothing out of place. The bedside table caught her eye. The top drawer was ajar. Had she looked there? She sat on the bed and tugged. The drawer slid out, spewing its contents around her. Something gold flashed as it fell into her lap. She reached for it, and even as she touched it, a sense of dread enveloped her.

It was a locket on a gold chain. She held it up, turning it to catch the light of the single candle she'd brought. The piece seemed familiar, but its catch was intricate and she couldn't see well enough to open it. She bent low over it, determined to see its contents, and didn't hear the door open behind her.

"What are you doing, *querida*?"

Papá! He'd returned from the roundup early. Her head jerked up and the locket flew from her grasp as she knelt and turned to face her father. It skittered up against his dirty boot. He bent and picked it up.

"Where did you find this?" he demanded, his voice an angry growl that sent a shiver down her spine. He pulled her to her feet with bruising strength and gave her a shake that rattled her teeth. Then he shoved her into the desk chair and crossed the room to slam the door and lock it.

The *snick* of the key in the lock echoed in the silent room. Dazed, with her tongue stuck to the roof of her mouth, she watched *Papá* pace at the foot of the bed, the chain swinging from his hand, his thumb rubbing the locket's surface.

She followed its swinging motion with her eyes. Why had it captured her interest? What about it called to her so strongly? She wanted to close her eyes, force herself to remember where she'd seen the locket before, but she didn't dare take her eyes off her father. What would he do? If he chose to punish her, she wouldn't be able to prevent him. And she wouldn't blame him. She'd violated his trust, his privacy. She deserved to be punished, but wouldn't accept his decision meekly. However, this angry, prowling man, swollen with indignation, frightened her. In his agitation, he seemed completely capable of the atrocities Jeremiah believed he'd committed.

Their gazes caught, held. She looked away, realizing he knew her well enough to read her true feelings in her eyes.

"So you, too, suspect me." He didn't need her confirmation; he continued pacing. "It is unraveling, but we may still contain it."

"No, *Papá!*" she begged, not sure what he meant by the latter comment, but determined to explain why she'd been searching his room. "I believe you are innocent of any wrongdoing. You could not have done what Jeremiah accuses you of doing. You're no murderer."

"You have come to know what this Jeremiah thinks? You have spent time with him, against my wishes? I warned you to stay away from him. You will learn that I spoke the truth when I said he was dangerous."

"No, *Papá*! He is not dangerous, only very determined to learn the truth."

"Perhaps Juan is right. I have been too lenient with you, *hija*. You will learn to obey me." Taking a firm grip of her upper arm, he pulled her out of his room and down the hall to her own. Without speaking another word, he pushed her in and locked her door from the outside.

"*Papá*, please listen to me!" she cried, beating the door with her fists. "Let me explain. Please! Talk to me."

With her heart pounding in her chest, she rushed to change into a riding skirt and blouse, pulled on her boots and hat, and ran to the balcony door, determined to escape.

Papá awaited her there and with a single glare sent her retreating to the safety of her room. Though he held his small riding quirt, he didn't use it or threaten her with it, but the threat was in his eyes, in his rigid jaw, his tense body. She had betrayed him and he meant to punish her. Too late, she knew she should have heeded Little Bird, Bull, Bernida, even Jeremiah. She should have been more careful.

In minutes, Ernesto came puffing up the courtyard stairs, carrying a hammer and a bag of nails, followed by several of his compadres bearing wide, flat boards, which they nailed over her door and window from the outside. Though he couldn't see her, she nodded to acknowledge the old man's whispered apology as he left, leaving her a prisoner in her own room.

All she could do now was pray *Papá* would relent. She'd pray, too, that none of her friends, especially Jeremiah, would risk their lives to rescue her. She'd gotten herself into this mess, she'd find her way out.

Jeremiah kept his promise to Sarah and left Cedar Creek directly after shoving her out of his hotel room. Anger drove him to Austin long before he'd given much thought to what he planned to do when he got there.

Now he rode down Congress Avenue, the widest, busiest street in Austin, with his heart pounding, surrounded by white men who, until a few weeks ago, he'd thought of as his enemies. He found the General Land Office Building and rode by twice before he found the nerve to tie up his horse and step inside.

The friendly, helpful clerks he spoke to wrote down what he needed and said they'd send word when they found his paperwork. They even recommended the boardinghouse next door and told him that several years before, Sam Houston had gotten the crazy notion to relocate the capital from Austin to Washington-on-the-Brazos and had sent some rascals to steal the state's papers. Angelina Eberly, the original owner of the boardinghouse, fired off a cannon to warn the townspeople that the Land Office was being robbed. She'd been hailed as a heroine ever since. There was even talk of building a statue of her firing the cannon.

Encouraged by the warm reception and hopeful he'd soon have the proof he needed, Jeremiah mounted his horse and headed south on Congress, to the Governor's Mansion. He'd heard that Texas had money trouble, now that it had become a state, but looking at the governor's house and the massive Capitol Building being built farther down the street, he wouldn't have believed it. He joined a line of people entering the front door and walked right in.

How crazy was this, to walk unchallenged into the house of the governor? Among the Comanche, the chief's tipi was near the center of all the tipis and a stranger would have been stopped, even killed, long before he got close enough to duck inside. Didn't this governor have someone to protect him?

Jeremiah didn't like crowds, and all the people in the house, pushing and shoving, trying to get a better look around, made him nervous. He elbowed his way through the crowd and down a long hall. The farther he went, the worse he felt. Finally, light-headed and dizzy, he stepped through a door and bent over, taking deep breaths as he waited for his heart to stop galloping.

"Can I help you, son?" a big, booming voice asked.

Jeremiah jerked upright so fast, everything in the room tipped and when he leaned to adjust, he tipped, too, and went down.

While he shook his head, trying to get his bearings, the man with the big voice helped him to a chair and pushed his head between his knees.

"Head down. That's the way," the big voice, attached to a big man, told him. "Take deep breaths. James!" The man left him to stick his head out the door and shout, "Whiskey!" He slammed the door again and locked it from the inside. "Every fool in the state is out there wanting a permit for their six-shooter," he grumbled. "Don't tell me you're one of them?"

"Nope," Jeremiah said, thinking he wouldn't admit to it even if he was "one of them." "Do I need a permit?"

"It's the law, boy," the man said, leaning on the word "law" long enough to tell Jeremiah he was some kind of chief. He glanced up at the man and felt like a worm looking up at the bird about to eat it. He'd never seen a man so tall, and big, too.

The man slapped him on the back and stuck out his hand. "I don't think we've been properly introduced, son. I'm Governor Richard Coke, at your service. Who might you be?"

"Jeremiah Baldwin, Governor." Staying bent over because the room was still swaying and, since that slap on the back, he'd started seeing stars, Jeremiah stuck out his own hand and watched it disappear into the governor's. He couldn't wait until he could sit upright again. This governor was something he wanted to see.

"Why're you starin', son?"

"Well, Governor, most folks say I'm a big man, but you've got me beat and then some."

The governor guffawed. His laugh, big and deep, rattled the glass doors of a nearby cabinet. "Get on up here and let's see."

Jeremiah took a deep breath and stood, glad to have the governor's hand on his elbow as his head spun, then cleared.

"You're close, son, closer than any man I've ever met."

Jeremiah had to look up to see the governor had a pleasant face, long but not narrow, with a full white beard, topped by a bald pate. He smiled, seeing the governor only stood an inch or two taller than he. He decided to be polite and not point out that the governor had him beat in both directions, but Coke poked him in the middle and shook his head.

"Unfortunately, I haven't had a good look at my boots for years, possibly since I was your age." He directed Jeremiah to one of a pair of leather-covered chairs with wide, well-worn seats, then took the other. "Baldwin," he said, looking Jeremiah over. "You're too young to be Reverend Matthew Baldwin, but you have the look of him, and the build. Am I wrong in surmising you're his son?"

"Yes, sir, I am," Jeremiah said, unable to hide his surprise. He hoped he wouldn't regret admitting the truth.

"We heard there were no survivors of the raid on Baldwin Fort, boy." The governor's brows pulled into a V and he stared at Jeremiah as if waiting for an answer.

"That's mostly true, but during the raid, all of the young boys were rounded up and sold to Comancheros. Later we were sold to the Kiowa."

The governor's eyebrows shot up, creating a field of

furrows on his forehead. "How many of you?" he asked, leaning forward.

Jeremiah shrugged. "At least a dozen, all the boys my age—and younger." He looked down at his hands, clenched in his lap, as he recalled the weeks that had followed the raid. "Most didn't survive the Kiowa's hospitality."

"But you did." The governor relaxed back in his chair. "So what happened next?"

"The Kiowa sold me to some Comanche warriors who were on their way back to the high plains after, uh . . . visiting Mexico." The governor winced and Jeremiah guessed he knew exactly what the Comanche had been up to in Mexico. Jeremiah didn't tell him that those same warriors, led by Quannah and Duuqua, had adopted him and taught him to be one of them.

"From the frying pan into the fire?" the governor asked, his eyebrows high again as he looked over his steepled fingers.

"No, sir." Jeremiah had hoped he might someday have a chance to plead the Comanche's case. This might not be the best time to do that, but it could be the only chance he ever got. Today, he'd tell this man, this governor, what had happened. Later, he'd ask for his help. "The Comanche were good to me. I lived with them for fourteen years."

"Did you know Quannah?"

Jeremiah hesitated to admit how well he'd come to know Quannah. How would the governor react? Would he throw him in jail, send him to Florida where many other warriors and their chiefs were being held? When he'd left the Comanche, Quannah hadn't yet surrendered, though he'd heard in Cedar Creek that the Comanche had finally come to the reservation. His father had always said, "Never trust a coyote or a politician." Jeremiah didn't want to bring Quannah more trouble.

The governor said nothing, just leaned back in his

chair and looked up at the ceiling. "If we had known you were alive, son, we'd have tried to find you."

"I'm not here to cast blame, Governor," Jeremiah hurried to explain. "I'm not expecting anything from the state of Texas except a copy of the deed to Baldwin Fort."

"Why?" Governor Coke sat forward again. "What's happened to the land since the raid?"

When Jeremiah explained about Sanchez's hacienda and the attempt on his life after he'd questioned the man, the governor rose suddenly and began pacing the room.

"I've heard of this Sanchez," he said, and stomped over to the door again. He unlocked it, opened it a crack, and bellowed, "James! Whiskey!" then slammed it shut. He fixed Jeremiah with a hard stare. "According to my people, Sanchez says he comes from the Sanchez Navarro latifundio in northern Mexico." The governor shook his head. "That's one big outfit, over fourteen million acres in Chihuahua and Coahuila. Bigger than the King and Kenedy ranches combined. How much land did your father own?"

"I'm not sure," Jeremiah said, "but it was thousands of acres, more than a wet-behind-the-ears boy could wrap his mind around."

"I'll send James over to the Land Office and we'll see what's what. If there's no deed or title recorded for this Sanchez, what do you plan to do?"

"What can I do?" Jeremiah asked.

"Titles and deeds, especially in that area, are sticky, son." The governor shook his head, but he grinned as a young man banged through the door with a tray, three glasses, and a full bottle of whiskey. The governor winked at Jeremiah. "James is feeling optimistic again." He turned to James, a sturdy young man with ruddy cheeks. "Fill 'em up, James, and take a seat, but be quiet."

James quickly did as told, then began sipping with a satisfied smile. At the rate the kid was swigging, he'd be out cold in ten minutes.

"Fifteen minutes." The governor had read his mind.

"Ten," Jeremiah countered.

"It's a bet." The governor flipped a gold coin onto the table. Jeremiah nodded and took a short sip from his own glass. He should have bet five minutes on himself, he thought, choking back a cough.

The governor chuckled and took a healthy swig. "Good stuff." He tossed back the rest of his drink and relaxed in his chair, interlocking his fingers over his belly. "Titles." He shook his head, frowned. "We had a hell of a time sorting through the mess the Mexicans and Spaniards left us, but we got the worst of it straightened out. Then Bourland and Miller—the commissioners who did all the work—lost most of it when their boat sank in the gulf. Most titles, even on King's and Kenedy's ranch, are suspect."

He looked over at James, who'd dropped his glass and was now sprawled in the chair, snoring. "Light-weight."

"I've been to the Land Office, Governor," Jeremiah said, grinning at the kid, who'd passed out less than halfway through his glass and was noisily snoring.

"Good, since I can't send James." He stood and extended his hand.

Jeremiah jumped to his feet and shook the governor's hand, surprised that the meeting was over, and so suddenly.

After asking what Jeremiah had been told at the Land Office, Governor Coke said, "When you hear from them, come back and we'll talk. Meanwhile, don't mention to anyone else that you're acquainted with Quannah."

"Thank you, Governor." Jeremiah turned to leave and was glad the room remained steady.

"I'm looking forward to seeing how this works out,

son. Your father was a good man and I want to get to the bottom of this."

"Yes, sir," Jeremiah said, exhaling a long breath. "So do I." He turned to leave, but the governor stopped him, catching his arm. "You forgot your winnings." He handed him the gold coin from the table. "Don't thank me, you earned it."

"James!" he bellowed, and the kid jumped to his feet with his eyes half open. "Show this man how to get out of here the back way."

The governor's piercing gaze followed him out of the room, and Jeremiah felt all the starch leave his knees as the door closed behind him.

"Don't mind him," James advised, his voice slurred. "He's all bark, but he only bites the ones he don't like." He blinked up at Jeremiah. "He liked you."

He swayed, but Jeremiah caught him and shoved him into a nearby chair. "Lay off the whiskey, kid," he told him. "That stuff'll kill you faster than a Comanche takes hair. And, take it from me, that's damn fast."

James's eyes widened, then slid shut. After a deep breath, Jeremiah elbowed his way out the way he'd come in and didn't mind the crowding or pushing at all. He'd realized he could see over most everyone's head.

Chapter Fourteen

"Move away from the door, señorita." Angel jumped, jarred out of her thoughts by the blunt command from the far side of her locked bedroom door. She'd been busy considering and discarding scenarios for getting out of her room to seek out her father. If he only saw her, he would be unable to refuse her pleas that he listen to her, and then, of course, he would accept her explanation and end this senseless incarceration.

Angel's initial efforts, born of fear and anxiety, failed miserably. The first day she'd tripped the young servant girl who brought her dinner, but the burly guard waiting in the hallway had blocked her exit. She hadn't gotten so far as the hall. Worse still, she'd gone to bed hungry.

Demands to see Bernida hadn't made the housekeeper materialize, and notes under her dirty dishes hadn't worked, either. She'd considered overpowering the maid who brought her meals and exchanging clothes with her, but the guards that accompanied her—a different man for each meal—were too attentive and watchful. They seemed to anticipate her ideas and take delight in besting her.

Something about the voice of the guard who'd just shouted through her door caught her interest and she waited anxiously for it to open. The young girl had been replaced by a woman who kept her face averted as she moved to set the heavy tray on Angel's dressing table. Realizing the guard had moved into the room behind her, Angel grabbed the woman and, with an arm around her throat, spun to face the guard. He said nothing, only shut the door behind him.

"Who are you?" she demanded of the man. "You're not one of the regular guards."

The guard laughed and tipped up his hat, revealing his face and a broad, familiar smile. "You can have him back if you like him so much, but he's sleeping in the broom closet right now."

"Bull!" Angel's heart raced and she would have jumped for joy, except that she still had an arm around the woman's throat.

"You wanna let Bird go before you kill her?" Bull nodded at the woman Angel was choking.

"Oh!" Angel exclaimed, becoming aware of the tight hold she had on her friend. "I'm so sorry, Little Bird. Are you all right?"

Little Bird sank onto Angel's dressing table chair, holding her throat and sucking in deep breaths. She glanced at Bull and shook her head, grimacing. "Remind me why we were worried about her."

"We thought—"

Little Bird gave him a warning look that cut him short.

Angel dashed to the water pitcher on the table beside her dressing table, but it was empty. She wrung her hands. "I'd get you some water, but I've used it all and they only bring fresh in the mornings."

Little Bird looked Angel over, motioned for her to turn about, then shook her head. "You look terrible. How long has it been since Bernida washed your hair?"

"I haven't seen her since I was locked up." Angel shook her head as she looked between her friends. "Just having you here, knowing the risks you're taking, means a great deal to me, but I can't involve you in my problems with my father."

"In case you haven't noticed, we're involved. What's happened to Bernida?" Little Bird stopped rubbing her throat and drank the juice from a bowl of diced fruit on Angel's dinner tray. She raised an eyebrow at Angel when she didn't answer. "You don't mind, do you?"

"No!" Angel cried, dismayed that Little Bird had thought she resented sharing her food. "Eat it all, I don't care. I'm so sorry I hurt you. I should have recognized you."

"Don't give it another thought, Angel," Bird said, and her voice actually sounded better. "It means our disguises may get us all out of here."

"What do you mean by 'us all'?" Angel finally noticed the bag over Bull's shoulder. "You're planning to take me with you?"

Bull and Little Bird exchanged another glance, both with raised eyebrows.

"I wish you'd stop doing that," Angel said with a toss of her hair as she crossed her arms over her waist. "I may be dirty, but I'm not blind."

"Of course we're taking you with us," Little Bird said, having dropped her voice to a loud whisper. She glanced at the door. "You don't think we went to all this trouble for an afternoon chat, do you?"

"I wish you'd consulted me." Angel shook her head.

"I told you so." Bull glared at Angel, though she knew he was talking to his sister. "Why?" This time he was speaking to Angel.

"If I go with you, I'll never find out the truth and *Papá* will think that I believe Jeremiah's accusations. I don't, but I haven't been able to talk to *Papá*, to explain that I was searching his room for proof of his innocence, not his guilt."

"He caught you searching his room and locked you up, what, three days ago? How long are you going to wait for him to change his mind?" Bull demanded.

"As long as I have to." She thrust one hand out before her when he moved forward, as if to drag her with him. "I'm not going until I talk to *Papá*, and you can't risk him catching you. Go! I appreciate you trying to rescue me, but I don't need to be rescued. Truly I don't." Tears started in her eyes, but she blinked them back. If her friends saw them, they'd refuse to go without her, no matter the cost.

"Angel—" Bird began, but Angel cut her off.

"Just tell Jeremiah to get out of town. Once he's gone, *Papá* will relent."

Bull looked away but Little Bird stepped closer and held Angel by the arms. "You haven't heard, then?"

"Heard what?" Angel struggled to sound nonchalant, but her voice shook. She cleared her throat and tried again. "What haven't I heard?"

Little Bird released her arms. "He's gone. He left three days ago."

"Right after I saw him and told him to leave." Angel nodded. "Good. I'm glad. He couldn't have accomplished anything here. His 'investigation' would have continued to make trouble. It would have brought us all more heartache." She bit her lip. Now, why had she said that, used that word? She wasn't brokenhearted, and wasn't sorry he'd left. She'd told him to go, after all. So why did her heart feel bruised? Why did his departure feel like a betrayal? It wasn't as if they'd been in love. He hadn't broken her heart.

"He'll be back," Little Bird assured her with a firm nod and a hug. "Nothing's been resolved."

"No," Angel said, "he won't." She glanced between her friends, wanting them both to understand what had happened, but found the words hard to say. "We talked about it. I told him to go. That's why he went."

"If we can find him, tell him what's happened here, he'll come back." Clearly, Bird, bless her heart, was determined to buoy Angel's spirits, convince her not to give up hope. Angel hated to disillusion her.

"I don't want him to come back. I got myself into this mess, I'll get myself out." Angel ushered Bull and Little Bird to the door, making sure neither of them had left anything that would betray their visit. "Since I can't send word to let you know how I'm doing, can you check in occasionally?" She glanced up at Bull. "You seem to have no trouble breaking into the casa."

"After today, they'll be watching," he told her. "If you hear a double tap"—he demonstrated on the dressing table—"slip a note under the door as quick as you can."

Little Bird watched the two of them anxiously. "I wish this was over. Why did Jeremiah have to come and stir up old problems?"

"Somebody had to," Bull said. "It's his job to do, and he'll be back to finish it." He leaned over Angel and caught her in a tight hug. "Don't do anything crazy. I'll try to find Bernida, or find out what happened to her."

Tears stung Angel's eyes and she blinked hard, but two escaped and slid down her cheeks. "I don't deserve such loyal friends."

"True enough," Bull said as he slowly opened the door a crack to peer into the hallway. He grinned and nodded to Little Bird. "But you're stuck with us."

Little Bird kissed Angel's cheek and thumbed off the wet tear tracks. "See you soon."

Angel stood in her room listening to their fading footsteps, feeling alone and more afraid than before they'd come. Until she realized she hadn't heard that now familiar sound: the click of the door locking behind them.

"God bless you both," she whispered. After giving her friends a few minutes to get away, she shook the worst of the wrinkles out of her dress and, for the first time in three days, stepped into the hall. She went to the broom closet and opened the door.

When the guard staggered to his feet, Angel gave him a serene smile. "Tell my father I wish to speak with him. And I want a bath."

She grinned when the man hurried away, not knowing if she'd achieved her goal, but certain it would make her father stop and think. Given the opportunity to escape, she'd chosen not to take it. She'd shown him what he hadn't allowed her to say.

* * *

Jeremiah urged his horse across Barton Springs in a hurry. He needed to move fast. Sopping wet and bare-chested wasn't the way to ride through town, let alone enter the very neat, clean boardinghouse, but he didn't have a choice. He'd fallen asleep in the clearing across from the Springs after taking a dip in the water and had slept better than he had since the day Ekararo had been killed. During the night, some animal—probably a skunk—had carried off his shirt, which he'd thrown over a bush to dry. It had been a new shirt, too, that fit him almost as well as his new "waist overalls" made from something the salesman called "denim." The sales-man had recommended that he take a dip in the springs with the overalls on and let them dry on him. He'd said the overalls would shrink some to fit him better. They sure fit close this morning, but without pinching like those black britches he'd stolen, though they were still damp around the waist.

He'd almost reached the boardinghouse, taking the back streets to avoid upsetting any prissy females who might be out and about early, but he hadn't figured on running into Governor Coke.

"Jeremiah," the governor boomed, his voice ricochet-ing off the houses lining the narrow street. "Boy, what are you doin'?" he asked, staring at Jeremiah's chest.

Jeremiah had never felt so naked; his scars seemed to catch the morning light and glow. He slowed his horse to a walk and sat straight in the saddle, resisting the urge to hunch over. "Fell asleep in the meadow above Barton Springs after a swim last night, Governor. Some skunk stole my shirt."

The governor looked off in the direction of Barton Springs and chuckled. "Yessir, that's a nice little patch of heaven," he said with a wink. "Spent a little time there myself."

Jeremiah wasn't about to ask what the governor had

been doing there, and the governor didn't seem inclined to share anything more—for which Jeremiah would be eternally grateful. He was beginning to like Governor Coke.

The governor paused and raised an eyebrow at Jeremiah's bare chest. "You appear to spend a lot of time in the sun, boy. Might not want to flaunt that brown chest around here. Some folks aren't as understanding as me. Get on back to your rooms. You've got a message waiting."

Jeremiah tipped his hat and started down the street.

"Come see me later," Governor Coke called after him. "We'll have lunch and discuss how to get you out of the mess you're in." He waved and kept walking.

Jeremiah stared after him, a cold knot forming in his stomach. He hadn't fooled that man one bit. Should he cut his losses and get out of town while he could?

He stared at the governor's back, admiring his easy gait, and his gut eased. If Governor Coke had planned to arrest him, he'd already be in jail. Nope, he must have something else in mind. Jeremiah was glad he'd been invited to lunch, not dinner. He didn't think he could have waited that long to find out what the governor had decided would be his fate.

Angel eased into the steaming water of her first bath in almost a weak with a heartfelt sigh. Two maids had arrived with the hot water and armfuls of fresh linens. They stripped her bed without a word and tossed the dirty laundry in the hall, then helped her wash her hair. They spoke little and didn't respond to her questions about her father, Pedro, and Bernida, but Angel was content. Details could wait.

Once she and her room had been set to rights, one of her new guards tapped on her door and handed her a note. Recognizing *Papá*'s bold script, she ripped it open and read it in shock. He had sent Bernida to Mexico to work for his uncle. Pedro had disappeared when Angel had been "punished." No one had seen or heard from him and *Papá* had no idea where he might have gone. He had left no word, just vanished in broad daylight.

How odd, Angel mused, letting the note flutter to her lap. She rubbed her temples, afraid that her careless behavior might have jeopardized Pedro's life. What could have happened to him? Where would he go? Bull and Little Bird hadn't mentioned him when they visited. Anxiety made her stomach queasy as she debated how to discover Pedro's whereabouts. Could she trust *Papá's* word, or had he been responsible for Pedro's disappearance? She wouldn't rest until she knew that Pedro was safe, unharmed. Yes, he was canny and resourceful, but she had finally realized that *Papá* was not to be underestimated.

The note also said that *Papá* would be away for several days, possibly a week, but during his absence, she was to stay in the house. His grooms were not to let her ride and she was to be guarded at all times. She could no longer give directions or expect any but her simplest request to be obeyed.

Angel stifled her response, rose, and began pacing. She'd been reduced to the status of an unwelcome guest in her own home. No, not her home any longer. Her friends, her confidants and loved ones had all been removed. She was alone, friendless.

She stood on her balcony staring at the rolling hills beyond the casa. A lively tune, strummed on a guitar, drifted upward from the vaqueros' quarters. Laughter and clapping, happy voices shouting encouragement to the dancers, didn't lift her spirits. Even the chirp of crickets and the scent of roses rising from the courtyard gardens brought no relief. She had no one but herself to blame for her dilemma. How could she have been so naïve? She'd sent Jeremiah away, the only person who could help her escape her own stupidity.

* * *

Jeremiah paused before the door to Governor Coke's office and ran a finger between his tight shirt collar and his neck. His whole life had led up to this moment, a moment that he'd chosen to face rather than wonder about for years to come. He raised his hand to knock, but the door swung open and James, tipsy as ever, tottered out.

"Oh, itth you." He squinted at his pocket watch, then gave up. "Ye're early, but he'th ready to thee you." He hiccupped and walked unsteadily out the door.

Jeremiah watched him go, ready to steady the young man if he needed it, then entered the governor's office.

"Come in, come in!" the governor called from his desk across the wide room.

Jeremiah did so, then slid into the chair the governor indicated across his desk.

"You asked to see me? Do you have news from the General Land Office?" Jeremiah tried to hide his impatience, but nothing escaped Governor Coke's sharp eyes.

He chuckled. "Ready to have this resolved, are you? Can't say I blame you, son."

Jeremiah nodded, waiting.

The governor signed a long, official-looking document and set it aside, then drew another document out of a drawer and set it in front of Jeremiah. "I believe this is what you were looking for."

Jeremiah eagerly scanned it, relief flooding him. The deed! At last. Something inside him calmed and unwound. There was the property, described in legal terms, owned by his father as head of the Baldwin Christian Community *and* its members in good standing. "So, with my father and all his parishioners dead, who does the land belong to now?"

The governor flipped to another page and pointed. "To you, as his legal heir. See, he listed you here. But it also belongs jointly to anyone else who survived. Did anyone else survive?"

"Yes, there's one other." How would Sarah react when he told her she owned her father's hacienda? It probably wouldn't make any difference to her. Her father spoiled her, gave her everything she wanted and more. She had no need for all that land and property. How would her father react? Jeremiah looked forward to seeing that.

"Did any of the boys survive?"

"Boys?" The question sent memories tumbling through Jeremiah's thoughts like wind-driven rain. He remembered the other boys, heard their cries of pain as the Kiowa tortured them. Before the nights were over, their cries had stopped. Once again, the silence screamed through him.

"No, sir. No one survived but me."

The governor collapsed into the arms of his massive chair, seeming to shrink a little. "That's a shame."

Jeremiah used the governor's silence to give some thought to the boys whose lives had been cut short prematurely. He'd known those boys. They'd been his friends so long, they felt like family. Not a day went by that he didn't think of one of them and regret not only their deaths, but the way they'd died. If he had to die, too, trying to find out who was responsible, he'd do it happily. He glanced up from staring at his clenched fists to find the governor watching him, his eyebrows pulled together in a worried frown.

"I think we're of a like mind on this matter, Jeremiah. I want to know who did this almost as much as you do, and I'm willing to sweeten the pot for you. You get to the bottom of this and I'll pardon you for everything you did when you rode with the Comanche."

Like a gust of sweet, fresh air, the governor's offer filled Jeremiah with hope. As if a heavy, dark blanket had lifted off his shoulders, he gripped the chair's arms to keep from floating out of his seat and stared at the governor. "You'll pardon me? I haven't even told you what I've done."

The governor waved a hand. "Details, my boy, details. One pardon covers all. My sense of it is, you've been through hell and made your way the best you could. Only natural for you to make a couple wrong turns, especially without a father there to guide you." He leaned forward, propping his bent arms on the desk. "No other deed has been filed on that land, and I smell a rat. I'm not expecting you to handle this by yourself, nossir. I'm sending a couple of my best Rangers out there with you. In fact, you may know one of them." He rang a brass bell and a door opened.

Pedro walked in with another man, but Jeremiah saw only him. Pedro's secret didn't stop Jeremiah from confronting the man. "You! A Ranger? What about Sarah? Who's with her?" He told himself she wasn't his problem, but that didn't stop the worry.

"Angel?" Pedro asked with a frown, and Jeremiah nodded. "She's not going anywhere right now," Pedro told him, settling into the chair beside his. "Sit down and relax, we've got some decisions to make."

Chapter Fifteen

Jeremiah sipped his second watered-down whiskey, leaning on the bar of a Cedar Creek saloon, and wondered when all hell would break loose. He'd done so much talking the last two days that his throat hurt. It shouldn't be much longer 'til word got to Sanchez that he was back in town, with proof that Sanchez's hacienda rightfully belonged to him. And Sarah, too, of course, but he hadn't bandied that about. He didn't want her life on the line as well. Just knowing that demon she called *Papá* had locked her up while he was in Austin made him want to ride out there, kick in the door, and take her away, keep her safe. But Bull and Little Bird had warned him that he'd only get himself killed. Then how could he help her?

A mean-looking hombre shoved through the saloon's swinging doors and pulled up next to Jeremiah at the bar. He ordered mescal, bolted it down, and left. Jeremiah wasn't surprised to find that he'd left a folded slip of paper under his elbow.

Come to la casa *tomorrow afternoon. Bring your papers. Fail me and she dies.*

It was just as Jeremiah had feared. Sanchez would not hesitate to harm Sarah.

He tossed back the rest of his whiskey and sashayed down the street to his hotel and up the stairs to his room, making sure he talked to everyone he passed. Once inside, he tossed the note to Pedro, who read it in one glance, then turned back to watching the street. He nodded to the Ranger across the street, the one who'd kept an eye on Jeremiah's back as he strolled down the street. A third agent slept soundly in a bedroll in the corner. He'd drawn the short straw, the night watch.

The hotel's back stairs weren't going to be a secret much longer if he and the Rangers kept using them. Jeremiah stripped down to his long johns and crawled into bed. He had to follow the orders in that note, even if he found himself at a disadvantage. He had to make sure Sarah was unharmed.

Angel stumbled into *Papá*'s study, shoved there by another of his surly guards. Where had all these rough men come from? Why were they here? What was happening elsewhere on the hacienda? Were the people also being treated harshly? These restrictions chafed at her sense of responsibility, her need to protect and nurture the people under her care. How could she protect them when she couldn't even control her own situation?

Papá flicked his hand and the guard left the room, but not without first giving her a look that stripped her bare and left her shivering. Was he being allowed to interact with the young girls on the hacienda? Who was watching out for them? *Papá* had never concerned himself with their needs, she knew. Her fear for her welfare and the welfare of her people threatened to overwhelm her, but she must remain strong in the face of his intimidation. As of yet, he'd done nothing but restrict her activities, confine her to her room. She would never have believed him capable of this. Her trust in him had been sorely tested, even her love. She didn't know what he might do anymore.

She waited, determined to control the tremors chasing up and down her body. She sensed that the guard and men of his ilk fed on the fear of their victims. As their leader, was *Papá* driven by the same impulses? Tears burned her eyes, but she blinked hard and squeezed them shut, hating that her home, her haven, had become this hellish, fear-filled place she longed to escape. What could she do, what must she say to repair the damage that had been done, to restore *Papá*'s trust in her, to return to a peaceful, loving coexistence? She longed for the tranquil life she'd enjoyed only weeks ago. So much had happened, would those days ever come again?

She shuddered and forced her thoughts away from the future and her fears. First she must face today and conquer the problems it presented. She breathed deep, reaching for the courage she needed, and turned her gaze on *Papá*.

As if he sensed her change in spirit, his attention snapped to her. Frowning fiercely, he looked her up and down, then fixed his gaze on her face. She returned his piercing stare with a slight smile.

"What is so amusing?" he growled in a voice that should have frightened her.

"This. Us." She waved a hand between them. "How did we come to this, *Papá*? How did one small misunderstanding become this yawning chasm? Will we ever be able to cross it, to find peace with each other again? Will we ever trust each other as in the past?"

Papá said nothing. Only a slight tremor about his lips revealed that he felt any emotion at her words, but that he quickly restrained.

Angel's heart squeezed. She could not love this side of him, the side capable of turning from her affection, offered freely.

Papá turned back to the papers on his desk. "I expect a guest shortly, your friend Jeremiah Baldwin. He comes alone." He opened a desk drawer to his right and Angel stiffened. That was the drawer containing his pistol. Surely, he wasn't planning to kill Jeremiah!

With her heart hammering in her throat, she watched him withdraw the pistol and some shells and carefully load the gun, then set it on the desktop.

Empty-handed, he stood and rounded the desk. "You can save your friend's life." He stroked a finger down her cheek and wiped off the damp trail from a tear she hadn't even noticed. "Tsk, tsk, tsk." He shook his head and frowned. "This won't do at all. You must convince Jeremiah that you have chosen to stay here with me, that you love me and cannot bear to be parted from me. But, most importantly"—he took hold of her chin and turned her face up to his blazing eyes—"you will tell him that you don't care for him, that he must cease his accusations against your dear *Papá*. You must send him on his way."

He released her chin and sat again at his desk. "If you cannot do so, I must take care of matters my own way." He picked up the gun, wiped a speck of dust off the barrel, then replaced it in the drawer.

"Do we understand each other, Angelina?"

She did not respond, mesmerized by the cool indifference in his eyes, sickened by the suspicion that he truly had ordered the attack on Jeremiah.

"Do you understand me?" he shouted, his expression filled with rage. "Say it!" He half rose from his chair. "Tell me you can do this."

"Yes!" she cried, surprised she could speak, let alone breathe, for her heart threatened to claw its way out of her chest. "Yes! I will convince him."

Papá smiled and lounged back in his chair. "I knew I could count on you, *querida*."

The endearment hung between them like a rotten fruit. Angel returned his phony smile. "You have nothing to fear from Jeremiah."

Without asking permission, she left the study with the smile frozen on her face until the door of her room closed behind her. Then her features crumpled and she sobbed freely. Finally, she splashed some water on her face to cool it and calm herself.

You can do this, she told herself, clutching her arms over her chest. *What's a lie, if it will save Jeremiah's life? That's all that really matters.*

She had faced worse—much worse—in her life, events so horrible, she'd shut them out of her memory completely. This, by comparison, would be simple. She could do it. She must do it. She sank to her knees beside her bed and ran a myriad of dialogues through her mind, seeking the right words and practicing them again and again. She must convince Jeremiah that she did not care for him, that she was perfectly safe and happy on the hacienda. Bald-faced lies.

For once she sent Jeremiah on his way, there would be no one to protect her from her father.

The next afternoon, as he rode to Sanchez's casa, Jeremiah felt as if he were riding buck naked. His back prickled, telling him he was being watched, and not only by the Rangers. Had they noticed it, too?

Relax, he told himself. Pedro and his friends had impressed the hell out of him since he'd hooked up with them at Governor Coke's office. If that savvy old man trusted them, why shouldn't he? Was it the plan that had him sweating?

He considered, then rolled his shoulders. Nope. The plan was solid, except for the threat to Sarah. Did she know what Sanchez had written? Did she know she was in danger? Not for the first time, he wished he knew how she really felt about him.

He tried whistling to shake off his edginess and got so caught up in the tune—an old one he'd whistled as a boy, before the raid—that he was riding through the hacienda's massive gate before he knew it. Like the first time he'd "visited" Sanchez's casa, he got the bore-end of a rifle greeting in the back, until he stopped cold and gave the pushy hombre holding it—the same rattler-eyed snake who had delivered Sanchez's note to him in the saloon—his meanest stare. The snake had the good sense to back off.

Jeremiah's heart started pounding so loud he hoped he'd be able to hear Sanchez over it and the ringing in his ears. Was Sarah here, too?

Where else would she be? he asked himself. According to Pedro's informants—people who lived and worked at the casa—she was confined to the house. He needed to see her, make sure she was all right, that she wasn't being abused.

The snake shoved him into the study, where Sanchez waited for him, cigar and tequila in hand. This visit wasn't going to be as cordial as his first. Jeremiah waited impatiently while Sanchez sipped his tequila and enjoyed a long drag on the cigar.

"You wanted to see me?" To hell with it. He didn't give a damn if Sanchez knew he'd gotten under his skin.

"Did you bring it?" Sanchez asked with a satisfied smirk after another long drag.

"I want to see Sarah first."

Sanchez's calm, dark gaze settled on his face. "You'll see *Angelina* when I say, not before. Now give me the papers."

Jeremiah pulled the deed out of the breast pocket of his duster and passed it over. He had a hard time letting go of it, but Sanchez ripped it out of his fingers and smiled as he read it.

"Yes, very pretty." He nodded and glanced up at Jeremiah. "Official-looking, too."

"It is official," Jeremiah said, fighting to keep from leaping across the desk, going for Sanchez's throat. He didn't like the look on Sanchez's face. "It's a legal document, filed and sealed."

"Such a shame, then, that it accidentally caught fire." Sanchez's cigar, pressed to the edge of the deed, set it aflame instantly.

"No! You can't do that!" Jeremiah lunged for it, but Sanchez waved it out of his reach, chuckling as he watched the flames devour the paper. The snake kept a firm hand on Jeremiah's shoulder and another man stepped out of the shadowed corner behind Sanchez, his rifle pointed at Jeremiah's chest.

"What a pity," Sanchez observed as he set the last of the document in the fireplace grate and made sure all of it burned. It didn't take long.

Jeremiah gripped the arms of his chair so hard that his knuckles turned white. When the burning was done, he gradually eased back into his chair. He'd been afraid Sanchez would pull something like this, but with Sarah's life on the line, what choice did he have? "Now may I see Sarah?" He'd told Sarah he'd call her by the name Sanchez had given her, but that courtesy didn't extend to Sanchez.

Sanchez nodded to another guard lingering at the door. "Let us be clear on what will happen when my daughter arrives. You will say nothing, only listen. You asked to see her, not speak to her. She would be very upset if one of my men had to hurt you in her presence."

Bastard. Jeremiah nodded, though it took a mighty effort not to leap that desk and strangle the man. So what if the snakes killed him? Sanchez was evil; he deserved to die for what he'd done and was about to do to Sarah. Why couldn't Sarah see it?

"You sent for me, *Papá*?"

Her sweet voice almost undid him. Jeremiah gripped the chair arms harder than ever, bracing for the moment that he'd have to look her in the eye and pretend not to feel anything for her.

She rounded the corner of the desk to greet Sanchez—who'd stood and beckoned to her when she entered—with a kiss on the cheek. Jeremiah tried to stand, but the snake behind him shoved him back into his chair.

She glanced over her shoulder at Jeremiah and her eyes went soft. Answering heat rose from Jeremiah's toes, sweeping up his body to his face.

"Oh! Jeremiah. What brings you here?"

Jeremiah grimaced at her cool tone. If he hadn't seen the expression in her eyes, he'd have thought she didn't give a damn about him.

Sanchez shot him a warning glance. When Jeremiah opened his mouth to answer, Sanchez spoke for him. "A little business." He glanced at the ashes in the fireplace. "It's been concluded nicely," he said with a smirk. "But Mr. Baldwin was concerned for your welfare and insisted on seeing you."

Jeremiah went still when she turned toward him. He was shocked by the change in her appearance. She looked pale, dark circles ringed her eyes, and she'd lost weight. Worse, her eyes seemed flat, her expression dull. She'd lost her sparkle, her glow. His chest ached, as if he'd been punched over the heart.

"As you can see," Sanchez said, and Jeremiah hung on his every word to keep from snatching her away from him, "she is quite well. She is pale, yes, but she's spending less time outdoors these days. Aren't you, *querida*?" He bent to kiss her, but she turned her cheek. She winced as his hand tightened on her arm and she looked at the floor, the desk, but not Jeremiah, as her lips tightened.

Jeremiah took a deep breath and shoved his hands into his pockets where they couldn't clench into fists. He wanted to shout, *I'll get you out of this, out of here!* But he didn't want to make more trouble for her. When he did risk a glance, her face remained serene, unruffled.

"Is it true?" he asked instead. "Are you happy here?"

Sanchez glared at him for speaking, then pulled Sarah tighter against him, making Jeremiah want to rip her away from the older man. All the while, Sanchez's smug gaze was fixed on Jeremiah. The man was watching him battle his emotions and enjoying himself.

Sanchez patted her shoulder. "We have been angry with each other, yes, but things are better now. We will have no more problems in the future. *Es verdad, mi hija?*"

"Yes, *Papá*, you speak the truth. I will do nothing to anger you. I love you and wish only to be your true and loving daughter."

"Ah, Angelina," Sanchez cooed, and folded her into his arms.

Jeremiah took a deep breath and managed not to gag. Sanchez seemed sincere, but it could all be an act. He'd even squeezed out a couple of tears.

"Go now," Sanchez said, and waved Jeremiah away. "You see that my daughter cannot possibly come to harm under the care of her loving father. Leave this hacienda and never return to bring doubt and misery upon us again."

Sanchez's two henchmen closed on Jeremiah, guns drawn, and he had no choice but to obey. He didn't protest. The sight of Sarah in Sanchez's arms sickened him. He wanted no more of this place, these people.

"Sickening, I tell you." Jeremiah slumped against the porch railing of Bull's and Little Bird's cabin.

Little Bird shook her head. "All we can do now is wait and see what happens, how he treats her. I'm glad Pedro has someone in the casa who'll keep us informed. I'm so worried about her. She can't even get a note to me, or get one from me. Every now and then I dress like a peasant and drop by to sell some of my vegetables and eggs."

"But they don't need extra produce, do they?" Pedro asked.

"You haven't seen Bird's vegetables," Bull said, his chest lifting as if he'd done all the work himself.

"Oh yeah?" Jeremiah challenged, just to see Bull puff up a little more.

"Eggs the size of a bull's—"

"That's enough, Bull," Little Bird said, then added with a laugh, "Although that is a good comparison."

Pedro and his Rangers laughed. "Don't take any chances," Pedro warned her. "My contact in the casa sees her every day. She'll tell me if there's a problem." He looked at Jeremiah, who'd begun pacing. "I think things may be better for her, especially if you think Sanchez's show was sincere."

"I could kick myself for saying it, but it's hard to pretend tears. Two big fat ones rolled down his cheeks. I was surprised they didn't crack his face."

Everyone chuckled, but nodded, their expressions hopeful. He didn't tell them that watching Sarah embrace the man who'd murdered their families had almost killed him. How could she be so naïve and trusting? He had to remember that Sanchez had lied to her all her life. It would take more than being locked in her room for a few days to convince Sarah of Sanchez's guilt.

For now, he would focus on breaking Sanchez, rather than convincing Sarah of his guilt. Juan, Jeremiah believed, would come to a bitter end as they worked their plan. No one knew where he'd gone to ground, so they'd decided to begin attacking the hacienda, rustling cattle and horses, burning outbuildings, scaring off vaqueros, Sanchez's biggest asset. The Mexican vaqueros were far better cowboys than these white boys who thought they could rope and ride. If they tucked tail and returned to Mexico, Sanchez would have a hard time replacing them with men who could handle the work.

Pedro agreed with Jeremiah's plan. Juan would turn up when the time came, and they'd take him down then.

"We found that hidden canyon you told us about and

set up camp," Pedro said, drawing Jeremiah out of his bitter thoughts. "We'll work from there, begin the second part of the plan while you're gone. You leave tomorrow?"

Jeremiah nodded. "I'm bringing extra horses, so the ride won't take so long."

"You could take the train part of the way," Pedro reminded him.

"But my friends can't," Jeremiah replied, "and I don't want to draw attention. There's no need to go over the plan again. I leave first thing in the morning and I'm counting on you to keep control here while I'm gone. By the time I get back, you'll have the hacienda spooked. My friends won't have to do much. I want them involved as little as possible."

"Understood," Pedro said. Jeremiah gripped his forearm, Comanche-style. Pedro nodded and smiled grimly. "Stay out of sight."

"Lie low," Jeremiah said with an answering grin. He recalled the times when he and Quannah and Duuqua had done this, said almost the same words as they left for a raid. Damn, he'd missed the rush in his blood. He wanted to throw back his head and give a blood-curdling Comanche yell, but that would get his spirit-brothers, the wolves, all riled up, and it wasn't time for them. Yet.

"Enjoy your lunch, señorita." The maid lifted the lid from the plate of food and held it high to show Sarah the note stuck under the lid. She replaced the lid and Angel nodded, keeping her face impassive as the maid quickly left the room.

The door had no sooner closed than Angel ripped the note from its hiding place and tore it open.

I hope you're well, Little Bird had written. *We haven't forgotten you. If you need us, send a message the same way you received this one.*

Angel didn't bother fighting the tears that stung her eyes. Her friends had not given up on her, but she wondered if she deserved their loyalty. She prayed that Bull and Little Bird wouldn't do anything foolish. She wouldn't put it past her father to threaten them as well.

She just hoped that her loving display with *Papá* had convinced Jeremiah to leave. Afterward, she'd felt unclean and had hurried back to her room where she'd requested a hot bath. She'd sat in the water until it chilled her, scrubbing at her arms, her chest, her face, trying to wash away the layer of dirt she felt covering her. Lying to Jeremiah—even to save his life—had been much harder than she'd anticipated, and she'd known it would be difficult. She wouldn't be surprised if the words she had uttered had left a stain on her very soul.

As the days passed, and she learned that Jeremiah had indeed left the area, she was happy for his sake. He, at least, was safe from the growing trouble at the hacienda. But her own life was constrained and without purpose. She longed to be able to saddle her horse and ride where she wished on the hacienda. She missed her visits with Little Bird and Bull, especially now.

Since *Papá* had forbidden her to ride, she'd begun tending her mother's rose garden. Her memories seemed closer to the surface there, particularly her early childhood, and she no longer turned from them, but struggled to remember as much as possible.

Most of her memories had resurfaced, but one dark, forbidding memory continued to elude her. Every time she tried to recall being rescued by *Papá*, she was wracked by tremors. She remembered hiding in a dark, cool hole in the ground, but couldn't recall for how long. She'd stayed there during the day, only venturing out after dark to search for food. Once she'd satisfied her hunger, she'd searched for her friends, the others who had lived in the fort, but she'd found no one. Then one day, she'd heard a voice and walked out. She remembered walking down the long street, past the ashes and rubble that had been her home and her friends' homes, through a hole torn in the high, wooden fence that had surrounded the fort, following the smell to one of the fields beyond the fence.

That was it, the point where her mind went blank and refused to show her the events that followed. Horrific events, she knew, for her body shook with fear, she broke out in a sweat, and often woke up curled in a ball under her blankets. She wasn't yet strong enough to remember, but she would. She would not rest until she'd remembered every detail of her life with her first family, and the raid that had taken them from her.

She knew the exact moment she'd resigned herself to the bleak future. It had been when she'd seen Jeremiah again. When she'd been forced to act as though she was choosing her father over him. She'd seen the disgust on Jeremiah's face.

At that moment she'd known that she'd killed any feelings he'd had for her. He no longer desired her and he didn't love her, probably never had, never would.

In her dreams that night she remembered the day he made her cry. She'd been following him, struggling to keep up. She'd called his name and he'd shouted, "Go away!" The older boys with him had laughed and called her his "little sweetheart." Jeremiah's face had turned all red and mean and he told those boys, "Shut up."

Then she'd fallen, tripped over a branch he'd thrown at her and landed on a jagged rock. She'd sat in the dirt, holding her throbbing, bloody knee and trying not to cry, but it hurt so much she couldn't stop the tears. Then Jeremiah saw her and finally, he stopped and came to her. She stopped crying, certain he would pick her up and kiss it better and everything would be all right.

But Jeremiah didn't help her. He leaned over her and said in a mean, nasty voice, "Serves you right, Sarah.

Maybe now you'll leave me alone. Stop following me! I hate you!"

His words had hurt her more inside than the cut on her knee had hurt her outside. The tears she'd been holding back tumbled down her cheeks. Her older sister, Megan, had found her at the foot of her favorite climbing tree—the one that let her see the entire fort and find Jeremiah anywhere he might be—and carried her home.

Angel shook off the wisps of remaining dream and examined her knee. Only her memories, and a small scar, remained from that day. She kissed her fingertips and pressed them to the old wound, then set her chin on her knee with a sigh.

Little Bird had been right to encourage her to remember as much as possible. Angel's cheeks burned with shame as she remembered how she'd thrown herself at Jeremiah—again. What must he think of her?

Well, she'd stopped chasing him now. Her father had made it very clear that Jeremiah must leave, and he never would if he thought she cared for him. After the act she'd put on, he must dislike her intensely. She could no longer fool herself into believing he might someday care for her.

The realization came with unbearable pain. She felt hollow inside, as if a giant fist had reached in and yanked out her vital organs. But pushing Jeremiah out of her life had been the right decision, for his sake.

Chapter Sixteen

"A message, General Mackenzie, from Governor Coke." Jeremiah handed over the letter, his heart beating like a drum in his chest. Would the general recognize him now that he wore white men's clothes, not buckskin? Whenever they'd come face-to-face in the past, Jeremiah had worn war paint over his face, black with wide horizontal red stripes, but Governor Coke had warned him that the general was sharp-eyed and smart as a skunk. He didn't miss much.

Mackenzie took the letter and didn't even look at Jeremiah, until he finished reading. "You must be one of those Texas Rangers the governor's so fond of," he said with a sneer. "Where's your badge?"

Jeremiah made a show of searching for one, but Mackenzie wasn't that interested and waved him off, grumbling about Texas governors flexing their muscles in somebody else's territory. If Jeremiah hadn't known that the note only introduced him and asked that the general allow him to visit Quannah, he'd have thought the governor had asked for Quannah's release. His conscience twinged a little. If the governor had known Jeremiah's plans, he might not have written the note at all.

Jeremiah shrugged. Governor Coke must have suspected that more than one or two Comanche warriors might slip off the reservation to join Jeremiah when he visited, but they hadn't discussed the details. Jeremiah blinked, realizing how cagey the governor had been. Since they hadn't discussed it, he could deny being involved.

Still chuckling and shaking his head, Jeremiah found

himself back on the porch of the general's office, staring at the dust bowl that was Fort Sill. It was nothing but two long, plain wooden barracks framing the sides of a flat, dirt parade ground. There were no Comanche to be seen.

A lower-ranking soldier followed him out of the general's office and looked him over. "Now, why would a fine-lookin' fella like you wanna see a stinkin' Comanch' chief, I'm a-wonderin'?" He leaned closer and sniffed. "You don't smell Injun. You an Injun lover?"

"Boles!" a sharp voice barked, and the soldier snapped into a rigid salute that looked painful. "Get along and mind your own business."

The newcomer smiled and extended his hand. "Lieutenant James Gordon, at your service." He took Jeremiah's hand in a firm grip and gave it an even firmer shake.

Once he got his hand back, Jeremiah resettled his hat and flexed his fingers, giving the lieutenant a wary once-over. This officer might be one to keep an eye on. Jeremiah knew his type. Too brisk, too cheerful, he was one of those men who did everything by the book. His father had had a few men like that in his "flock." He'd made it a point never to turn his back to one of them.

"I'll escort you to the Comanche." The lieutenant gestured to Jeremiah's horse and stepped off the porch with him, watching as he mounted.

Jeremiah thought for a minute the man might be going to give him a leg up. He hadn't needed help mounting a horse since he was eight, or was it six? "I hate to take up your time, Lieutenant. I can find my way, if you'll tell me which direction to point my horse's nose." He did not want company on this trip. Quannah had never been one to guard his tongue and there was no telling what he'd say when Jeremiah rode into his camp. Jeremiah looked the man over, taking in his clean, snappy uniform. Had this officer ridden with Mackenzie at Palo

Duro? Had he been one of the men who rode down Eka-raro?

Jeremiah's blood simmered, and he knew he'd better put some air between him and these soldiers and the many reminders of all that had been taken from him.

Several miles passed before Jeremiah calmed enough to try conversing. He slowed to a canter, mentally composing and discarding comments that might get the man talking about things he wanted to hear.

"You boys must be relieved not to be out chasing Quannah anymore." He tried to sound friendly, but had trouble getting his mouth around the words. He burned to grab the lieutenant off his horse by the front of his pretty blue coat and shake out everything the man knew about the Palo Duro fight. Though that might make him feel better, it would also get him arrested, maybe even hanged. Better to dig quietly. As he'd hoped, the lieutenant was more than happy to talk about capturing the Comanches.

"Yessir, he led the army on a merry chase." The lieutenant shook his head and smiled. "All the men are glad to have the Quahadi on the reservation where we can keep an eye on them."

Jeremiah was surprised by his use of the Comanche name for their warriors. Most soldiers just called the warriors "dirty Injuns." "I heard the fight at Palo Duro was a bad one. Were you there?" Jeremiah's hands flexed on his reins, but he forced himself to relax. He would control himself if the lieutenant came up with the wrong answer. He hoped.

"No, I missed it. I arrived a month ago."

Jeremiah relaxed.

When he and the lieutenant finally arrived at the Comanche camp, Jeremiah could only stare. The Comanche's once-beautiful tipis were gone, burned at Palo Duro along with all the People's possessions. These dingy, soot-stained canvas tipis seemed to capture the dust and dirt, unlike the buffalo-hide tipis. He'd bet they didn't keep out the cold wind, either. Children still ran about naked, chasing one another and being scolded by their mothers. They stopped to stare at Jeremiah, then ran and hid. No one recognized him, not even the warriors squatting in circles outside a small wooden building, gambling and shouting.

"Thank you for your escort," Jeremiah told him. "I can handle things from here."

"I can't leave you here without protection, Mr. Baldwin," the lieutenant protested. "The army can't be held responsible—"

"I don't need the army to be responsible for me," Jeremiah said, instantly realizing he'd spoken too harshly.

Just then, a tall Comanche man emerged from a small building nearby, stopped dead, then hurried over, calling out in Comanche as he came.

Jeremiah hoped Quannah would be discreet, especially as it looked as though he was about to squeeze the breath out of him in front of the lieutenant, but Quannah hadn't changed a bit. Switching to English—which Jeremiah didn't register as he was busy watching the lieutenant's face swing from surprise to suspicion—he gave Jeremiah a bone-cracking hug and pounded his back.

"At last you find us, brother. Where you hide so long? Why you here now?" He ignored the soldier completely and, with an arm around Jeremiah's shoulders, pulled him away. "You ride with bluecoats now? Forget how to find old friends?" he asked, his tone less friendly.

Jeremiah didn't bother with an answer to Quannah's pointed questions. His old friend knew him better than that.

He looked Quannah up and down, taking in the long, hide-wrapped braids that dangled over a white man's shirt worn under a neatly buttoned vest. Matching trousers replaced the leggings Quannah had always worn, but moccasins still covered his feet.

"What is this getup?" Jeremiah asked him, catching a pinch of the black trouser leg between two fingers. He could see through the cloth when he tugged it away from Quannah's leg. "Stay out of the wind. Your nakedness will frighten away the maidens when these blow off."

Quannah snorted. "You not hear? All Comanche women want to marry me." He peered through his pant leg. "This not bad. Come. I show you blankets, gifts from Great White Father in Wash-in-tun." Quannah shook his head. "Only lint. Reservation man say we must thank the Great White Father for white man's gifts. I say he steal from the Comanche. Mackenzie promise warm blankets, new tipis, plenty food. Huh. Children cry all night. Can't sleep with empty bellies." He nodded at the rest of the warriors sitting around, wherever they could find shade. "At night we hunt with rocks and knives. Set traps. Make snares. But no animals live in this." He kicked at the ground and a cloud of dust flew up. Jeremiah listened, sensing that Quannah needed to release the anger bottled up inside him.

"No hides to replace clothes, no meat for women's stew pots." His shoulders slumped. "They ask me, 'Be judge. Tell *Nemene*, the Comanche people, to obey law.'" He stared into Jeremiah's eyes. "How do I punish man who leaves to find food? To live, he must steal from white men who have plenty.

"They give us flour, sugar, and lard and say, 'Eat well.'" Quannah laughed. "Comanche eat meat, not white dirt. Give us cattle, deer. Let us hunt! Finally, after much talk, much complaining, they take us on hunt, but we find no game. Many suns we ride. See not one antelope, no deer, no elk. Even skunks not live here." He kicked the dirt again and spit on it.

His heart aching for the challenges facing the People, Jeremiah led Quannah aside. "I can help you. Let's walk."

Quannah nodded, then pulled a pipe out of his sleeve and lit it. Jeremiah took a long pull when it was offered to him, surprised to learn that he'd missed the acrid taste. Mainly, he'd missed the companionship, but he wasn't here to smoke a pipe and enjoy Quannah's company. He needed Quannah's help and to make sure he got it, he had something to offer in return.

He spent hours arguing with Quannah, but finally got him to agree to his terms. When one of Quannah's wives came to fetch them for the evening meal, Quannah's spirits had improved so much that he jumped up and gave his wife a firm kiss and a pat on the rump. She giggled and ran ahead of them back to the largest tipi in camp, where five other women waited, smiling and laughing behind their hands.

"How are your wives?" Jeremiah asked. "They look happy."

"They happy I not go raiding anymore." He sighed and rolled his eyes at Jeremiah. "Too many women make a man weary." He smiled at a blushing maiden as they strolled past, then grinned at Jeremiah. "Maybe one more?" He laughed and hugged each of his wives, spoke to each child, and settled by the fire. "Kris say I have seven before I die," he whispered behind his hand. "Only five now, but still plenty time."

"You take your time, Big-time Chief Quannah," came a shrill feminine voice from inside the tipi. Jeremiah recognized it as belonging to Duuqua's aunt. Padaponi ducked out and swatted Quannah's hand as he reached to tug on her short-cropped, chin-length hair.

Jeremiah gave a glad cry and swept her up in his arms, then swung her around. She clutched his neck, swearing a blue streak, but began sobbing when she recognized him.

"Chikoba!" she cried, and the women and children

joined her glad cries and began dancing around them. "You scare the mean out of me. You look like a white man, but under here"—she pressed her hand over his heart—"you still my boy."

"Always." He hugged her close to whisper in her ear. "I have seen Duuqua. He is safe and happy." As he'd expected, news of her blood nephew, her sister's son, brought cries of joy.

"And Kris Baldwin?" she asked, looking anxiously between him and Quannah.

"Kris is with him. Her medicine has taken them back to her home. We won't see them again, but they are very happy," he added.

"It is well," she said with a nod that made her double chins wobble. "I am happy they do not share our troubles." She walked around behind Quannah and squeezed his shoulders.

He reached up and patted her hand. "Our troubles not so bad," he said, sharing a long look with Jeremiah. "Tonight we happy. Our brother has found his family again."

The small fire died down long before anyone was ready to stop talking and turn in. Jeremiah and Quannah, the last to leave, sat beside the glowing embers making plans, then made their way to their beds.

Jeremiah had barely shut his eyes when Quannah shook him awake. "Come! The men are ready to leave."

Jeremiah rolled to his feet and rubbed both eyes with the heels of his hands to clear the cobwebs. He frowned at Quannah, who'd picked his way out of the tipi through his sleeping family. How could the man be so alert in the middle of the night? Quannah had always been the last man up, and grouchy as a bear for hours. Ah, but this was more excitement than he'd seen for months. Jeremiah put his gun back on, turned his boots upside down, and shook them. A small scorpion dropped out of one and scurried for cover.

He snatched up the insect by its stinger and took it outside, where he released it well away from the tipis. He ignored the other men's smirks and rude comments about his change from Comanche to white. Quannah slapped him on the back. "What you do with your friend?"

"Put him in your blankets."

Quannah pretended to be afraid, but Jeremiah shook his head and turned to the men, all shivering under their flimsy blankets, wearing cheap pants like Quannah's. He hoped Bull had plenty of clothing. It was about to go missing. He and Quannah reviewed the plan with the men, made sure they all knew where to find the horses Jeremiah had bought from a nearby ranch and hidden, and when and where to rendezvous. Then they started leaving in groups of two and three, each group heading a different direction.

When dawn came, all the men had been gone for hours. Jeremiah mounted up and looked down at Quannah. "Don't worry. Everything will go the way we figured. Once the reservation agent finds out the men are gone, he'll send soldiers out to search. When they don't find the warriors, they'll ask you to track them down. You'll be the hero and they'll fall all over themselves to reward you. Better think about what you want."

"I hope you right and they not shoot them or send them to jail in Floh-ree-duh." Quannah still wasn't convinced, but he sighed and nodded. "I trust you."

"Now wake the women and go butcher those cattle." Quannah had driven a hard bargain, but Jeremiah had known he would and he'd come prepared. One of the groups of men would be driving twenty head of cattle back to the reservation. Jeremiah rode now to buy another hundred, enough to feed the Comanche until the men coming with him could get back with cattle from Sanchez's hacienda. "Try to leave a few to start a herd."

Quannah smiled and slapped the rump of Jeremiah's

horse. He'd been happy to let his men help Jeremiah take back what had been stolen from him, as long as there was something in it for him and for his People, too. The hard part had been explaining why Quannah couldn't come, too. The governor had stressed that part. The Comanche chief couldn't be seen to have left the reservation except under government orders.

Leaving the Comanche again seemed harder now than it had been the first time—especially with them sick and hungry—but Jeremiah hoped the steps he'd taken would put them on the right trail, get them started on fixing their own problems.

Watching Quannah smile and laugh with his wives, Jeremiah remembered times he and Ekararo had shared a fire with Quannah and his family. Though the memories made him sad, they also made him think of Sarah, and feel anxious because of the way they'd parted. He wanted to talk to her before the rift between them became a canyon they couldn't cross.

Jeremiah rode hard to reach the ranch where he'd bought the livestock the week before. The owner was happy to sell him more cattle, though he tried to find out who'd be coming to drive them to their new owner. Jeremiah dodged his questions and paid him with the last of the money he'd taken from Sanchez's desk. He wasn't worried about his empty pockets. There'd be plenty more cash once they started selling Sanchez's herd.

He was glad his father wasn't around to see what he was doing. Reverend Baldwin wouldn't have approved, even though it was his family's blood that had purchased everything Sanchez owned. As far as Jeremiah was concerned, that blood sanctioned every move he made.

The rancher gave him permission to bunk the night in an empty line shack near his southern property line.

Jeremiah accepted, though he wouldn't sleep inside. He'd rather lie on the ground nearby. He fell asleep thinking of Sarah, rembering her sweet heat closing around him as he thrust into her. He sucked in a deep breath and smiled, looking forward to getting back to her.

The moon rode high in the sky when his horse's whinny woke him. Peering into the shadows, Jeremiah spotted a lone wolf standing there, gazing at him. When the wolf saw that Jeremiah watched him, he turned south and walked away, then looked back over his shoulder at him. It sat and howled several times, then scratched at the ground and howled again. Jeremiah didn't know how the wolves always knew what he wanted or needed. He'd always had to guess what they wanted by their actions. What was this one trying to tell him?

"Ask." The answer came as a thought from out of nowhere, like a feather floating out of the sky and into his mind.

If he was to ask the spirits something, he would need a medicine fire. He gathered some partially burned wood from the ground near the shack, added some dry brush, a few twigs and small branches, and soon had a nice blaze. He found some sage nearby and pulled off a few twigs, uprooted some grass, and took off his gun belt and his shirt. He didn't worry about unwelcome visitors. The wolf would keep varmints away. His wolf-messenger lay on its belly beyond the light cast by his fire. With its muzzle resting on its paws, it lay perfectly still, waiting, its eyes following Jeremiah's movements.

He knelt beside the fire facing east, packed some tobacco into the bowl of the small pipe he always carried, and lit it. He took a deep draw, tipped his head back, and exhaled, watching the smoke disappear above him. Then he began singing his medicine song as he offered smoke to the Great Father above, Mother Earth below, then the four winds. As Jeremiah chanted, he added the fresh sage, then the sweet grass onto his fire. He shoved his hands into the cloud of sweet-smelling smoke that billowed skyward and bathed in it knee-to-head, still chanting.

Across the fire the wolf stood and approached. Jeremiah stared and rose to his knees as its head seemed to grow larger and larger until it hung over him and his fire, looking down on him, its eyes flashing. Then it spoke, startling Jeremiah so that he fell backward, braced on his elbows.

"Son of my spirit, listen well! Though you have left the People, you have not forgotten them. The Great Spirit is pleased and sends you blessings. Behold!"

The wolf head faded and became instead Kris and Duuqua, and in Duuqua's arms lay an infant with black hair and his own blue eyes. "I wish Chikoba could see Karrie," Kris said. Duuqua took hold of one of the infant's arms and waved it, then looked directly at Jeremiah. "He does," he said, and leaned over to kiss Kris. "She is named after Ekararo, my brother."

"Wait!" Jeremiah cried, but the vision faded and showed him instead Sarah's bedroom. He frowned, thinking the vision must be wrong. The room looked different, but he'd only seen it once. Clothes covered the floor and dust dulled the sheen of the furniture. Light streamed through the space between the curtains, but Sarah still lay in bed. Was she sick? Had she been hurt? A young maid set a tray of food on the table beside Sarah's bed, then tried to wake her.

"Go away," Sarah told her, "and take the tray with you. I'm not hungry." The maid shook her head, but turned and left the room. Sarah lifted her head and looked directly at him. Jeremiah recoiled from the sight. Her eyes were lifeless, her hair limp and dirty. As he watched, she settled back into her bed and her heavy breathing told him she'd fallen asleep. He saw her sleep through the day, watched the shadows made by the sun's journey across the sky change as the day passed by. Sarah rose once, twice, stepped behind the screen to use the chamber pot, but returned each time to her bed.

What's wrong with her? She must be ill, he thought, staring across the fire into the face of the wolf, which had regained its normal shape and size.

Yes, the wolf answered him, and again he felt the voice enter his mind. *She is sick, in her mind. She needs help.*

What about her father? Jeremiah asked, amazed that he was talking to the wolf. Was this one of the "blessings" his spirit guide was talking about? He couldn't give it much thought now, but knew he'd be puzzling over it long after.

Her father remains angry and keeps her confined to his house. He wishes to punish her further, but fears you.

Good! Jeremiah crowed. He wondered why she hadn't tried to contact Bull or Little Bird. He knew her friends would have helped her escape.

She has given up hope, the wolf said.

Jeremiah jerked, staring at the animal. *You can read my mind?*

It is part of your gift.

But I can't read yours, Jeremiah said, thinking this "gift" ought to work both ways.

Be thankful, the wolf said, his eyes shining. *My thoughts are too savage for humans.*

Jeremiah nodded. *How can I help her? It would take days for me to reach the hacienda. If it's only her mind that's sick, not her body, she'll be fine until I get there.*

She thinks of harming herself, the wolf told him. *Use your powers. Stop her.*

How? Jeremiah considered several ideas, could think of nothing that would help Sarah quickly.

No, the wolf said, and snarled impatiently. *Like this.*

Suddenly, Jeremiah felt his body slump to the ground. He looked down at himself and scowled. What the hell had just happened?

The wolf stood over his body and howled again, looking south. *Go!* it cried. *Save your mate.*

She's not my mate, Jeremiah replied, even as he felt himself gathering.

Is she not?

The wolf's last word stretched along the wind as it carried him south and east to the ridge overlooking the casa. As he crested the horizon, Jeremiah saw Bull and the Rangers driving about fifty head of cattle to the hidden canyon. Behind him, many miles to the north, his Comanche brothers settled in hidden places to wait for night's coming to hide their journey. He could not call on any of them to help Sarah. It must be he.

First, he wanted a closer look, so he continued onward and entered her bedroom. She slept, but now he smelled her unwashed state and knew Sarah had given up on life. He closed his eyes and slid into her thoughts. She grieved and dreamed of dying.

Shocked and sick at heart, he left her room. The entire house smelled of fear. Bull and his men had been successful. Sanchez must be struggling, for the scent was strongest in his rooms—the study and his bedroom. The perfume of fresh roses was gone, replaced by the odor of dead, rotting flowers left in vases. With nothing to overpower it, the house reeked of that other smell, the stink of burning flesh.

Jeremiah hovered in the hall outside Sarah's room. What could he do? What did she need? What had brought her so low? Did she think he wasn't coming back? He hadn't left for good, though she'd told him to go. She'd given up. How could he convince her that there was hope, that he was coming back, that she would find happiness?

He returned to her room and called to her, trying to

wake her. As if he'd turned suddenly light as air, he floated into her dream and took the shape of the wolf. He found her with a rope around her neck, about to step off her balcony railing. With a mighty lunge, he caught her arm in his mouth and dragged her to the floor of the balcony. He lay beside her and licked away the tears streaming down her cheeks. When she didn't respond, he nudged her face with his muzzle, rubbed his head along her arm, trying to show her that he cared, begging her never to do such a thing, even in her dreams.

She lay beside him, not moving, her eyes squeezed shut, tears leaking from under her lashes. He licked them off both cheeks, but they kept coming. He growled a little, low in his throat. Angry and desperate, certain he couldn't hurt her since he was only in her dream, he snapped at her chin. Her eyes opened wide and she stared at him. He tried to tell her he cared, he begged her not to give up, but his gift only worked with wolves. She couldn't hear him.

But she saw him. Her hand lifted and she scratched between his ears. Jeremiah's wolf eyes rolled back in his head and he had the urge to roll over and wag his tail. Damn, he was starting to think like a wolf. He'd better get back to his body soon.

Anxious to help, he tried to think, but his mind was locked up in fear. If this dream went on much longer, would he be able to return to his own body? Whatever he did needed to be dramatic, loud. It must wake her up and challenge her. With one last swipe of her cheek, he left her dream, but he didn't go far.

Chapter Seventeen

"*Levántate!*"

Angel shook off the annoying hand and pulled her pillow over her ears. She'd been dreaming the strangest dream about a wolf that had Jeremiah's blue eyes. His fur had been warm and silky. Her fingers still tingled from scratching between his ears.

"*Por favor,* señorita." The hand shook her harder.

"Go away! Can't you see I'm sleeping?"

"No, señorita. *Lo siento,*" the strident voice apologized, the hand kept shaking.

"What?" Angel sat up, whipping her blankets off as she rose. The young maid jumped back, startled but relieved.

"Come." The girl tugged on Angel's arm. "*El Patrón no esta aqui.* Your *papá* is not here. You must help."

"Help what?" Angel let the girl rush her into her robe, wondering where *Papá* could be. Her heart began pounding and she felt flushed and light-headed. For weeks, she'd done nothing but sleep and eat, read a little, sleep some more, and cry. Oh yes, she'd done a great deal of crying. Father refused to see her and she no longer begged to talk to him. She would be a prisoner in this house until he deemed she'd been sufficiently punished for disobeying him.

Her monthly courses had come and gone since her last "encounter" with Jeremiah. She would have no lasting reminder of him. Whenever his face popped up in her brain—as it did with annoying regularity—she replaced it with a fictional character from whatever book she was trying to read. Soon he would no longer be real to her, only another painful memory to forget.

Nor had she let herself think about her dead family. What could she do for them now? Heavens! She couldn't help herself. The last wall in her mind, the blank space she couldn't fill, remained blank, black, empty. She liked it that way. Much less painful.

She turned back toward her bed, but the little maid stepped in her way and pushed her toward the door.

"Wait," Angel said, slowing to pick up her other slipper, the one that wasn't on her foot yet. "Stop pushing." She scowled at the girl over her shoulder, but the maid shook her head and pushed.

Angel sat on the bottom step of the stairs. "Not another step barefoot." The girl cut loose with a rapid stream of Spanish, mostly bad words. "Uh-uh-uh," Angel admonished as she pulled on her slipper. "No swearing."

The girl's lips pressed together, but her eyes flashed fire as she plunked her hands on her hips and regarded Angel with something akin to malice.

Whatever could be so dire? The casa ran so smoothly, its staff hardly needed . . . "What on earth?" She cast a loving gaze around her at her beautiful home, only to recoil in horror. It wasn't beautiful anymore. It was . . . filthy. The lovely round table in the entry held its usual vase of cut flowers, but instead of a beautiful, sweet-smelling arrangement, dead flowers hung their heads and their stems rotted in slimy green water. Everywhere Angel looked she found thick dust, muddy footprints . . . Was that *manure*? Tracked in from the barn, no doubt.

How could *Papá* allow this to happen? Her gaze narrowed on the footprints, noticing that they looked very close to the size of her father's foot. And that bigger one next to it must be Juan's.

"Where is he?" she asked, turning to the maid, her fists clenched in her skirt. She didn't give a rat's droppings what *Papá* said about her authority in the casa.

Someone had to take responsibility since he didn't seem to care.

"*No es importante*," the girl said, gesturing to the filth around them. "Come." She tugged on Angel's arm.

"What do you mean it's not important?" Angel shouted at the girl, who pushed her out the wide-open front doors. A rooster ran over her foot, crowing his fool head off, followed by two chickens and a grubby child. Angel froze in shock. Utter chaos greeted her.

A stream of servants ran by her into the house, screaming, "*El Lobo Diablo!*"

Just then a wolf—an actual wolf—ran out of the stable, snarling and snapping at the heels of two young grooms. Once outside, it stopped and watched them run. Angel could have sworn it smiled past the chicken feather stuck in one corner of its mouth.

Angel spun on her heel and ran to her father's study, where she snatched her favorite gun, a Winchester, from the cabinet on the wall. She loaded it as she hurried back outside. "Move, move!" she cried, and the people, seeing her take aim at the wolf, leaped out of her way.

Her first shot hit the dirt in front of the animal. The wolf skittered backward away from the ricocheting bullet, but flying dirt and rocks hit him. He yelped, saw Angel, and tucked tail and ran. Angel took aim at his backside, missed because he zigged at the last moment, then began reloading just in case he doubled back. But when she braced the gun against her shoulder and squinted to take aim, the wolf had disappeared. He was nowhere to be seen.

She hadn't imagined him. Had she?

Several other people were staring in the direction he'd run, too. They looked at her, wide-eyed and frightened, then made the sign of the cross as they ran away. She looked again, but there was nowhere that wolf could hide. How had it disappeared? She shook her head and searched the swaying grass stretching in all directions.

Still no wolf. Maybe she'd projected her dream onto a dog, or . . .

No, she told herself, *you saw a wolf.* Everyone saw a wolf. There had to be some explanation.

Angel looked around the casa's yard, breathing heavily and seeing stars. How could she be out of breath from so little exertion? She'd only run to the middle of the yard. Her people cheered and chattered.

"*Andale, andale,*" she told them, ignoring their cheers. She didn't deserve accolades. "Quickly! Let's clean up this mess."

Ernesto limped up to her and bobbed his head. "Thank you, *Patrona*. The wolf, he frightened everyone. Even me." He hung his head. "To see such a one raiding the casa while the sun is shining . . ." He shook his head. "He must be *Diablo*, sent by the devil himself."

"What has happened here, Ernesto?" Angel asked. "Where is my father?"

"He has been gone for many days, señorita. There is trouble on *la hacienda*—cattle are gone, horses taken, many buildings burned. It is war, but no one knows who we fight."

Angel had a pretty good idea who was behind it. Jeremiah. "Well, that's no reason to let the place fall down around our ears," she told him. "I am putting you in charge. Send the women to me, then have some men fix the henhouse while the boys catch the chickens. Have the other men repair the fences and set things back in order, *por favor.*"

Ernesto hurried off to do her bidding and she joined the women already gathering in the house. Once she'd given instructions for the casa's cleaning and left one of the women in charge, she hurried upstairs to change into her clothes. Her maid followed her and, once Angel was dressed, brushed her hair back and tied it at the nape of her neck.

"*Bienvenido,* señorita. Welcome back," the maid said

in a sudden rush of emotion. Tears trickled down her cheeks. "*Estoy preocupado por ti.*"

Angel hugged her, ashamed that she had caused her people to worry about her. "Wipe away your tears. I'm back."

"*Sí, sí. Es la verdad,*" the girl said, searching Angel's eyes. "Truly, your spirit has returned."

Angel felt a tug on her soul at the girl's words. In her sorrow, she had subjugated her true self, shut her emotions away so that she didn't have to deal with the problems in her life. Well, no more of that, she assured herself. She couldn't hide in her room while everything precious to her crumbled to ruin. People depended on her and *Papá* either didn't care enough to take on the responsibility or didn't understand what needed to be done to keep the casa running smoothly. He could shout to the moon until he was blue-faced that she had no authority, but she had long since accepted responsibility for the casa and its people. She understood this. Her people understood. *Papá* would, too, when once again he enjoyed a clean home, fresh clothes, and good, warm meals.

And while he was enjoying all that, she would find Bernida and bring her home. Not because she wanted Bernie to cook and clean and work for her, but because Angel loved and missed her.

Jeremiah watched Sarah, the old decisive Sarah he knew, with a smile. He felt bad about scaring all her people, but he'd needed to get her moving quickly. That new feeling started up again, the one where all his innards clumped into a bunch. As if he rode the wind, he returned to where his body lay sleeping beside his fire. He slid back into himself slick as a whistle. In fact, it felt a little like blowing through a whistle, only backward. Instead of blowing out, the air—and his soul with it— was sucked back in.

He sat up and shook himself, feeling for aches and pains, but found none, just a little fuzzy feeling around the ears, which were still sensitive. When he scratched, he was glad to find that he didn't feel like wagging his tail.

You have done well, the wolf said, and turned to leave. *Use your gift wisely*. In moments, it disappeared into the rippling heat haze on the horizon.

Jeremiah dumped some water from the small creek nearby onto the fire and watched a thin line of steam rise into the air and disappear. He'd gone from here to a point five or six days' hard riding away in a flash. The realization didn't alarm or frighten him. In fact, it seemed natural, as if he could have done it any time, if he'd only known how.

Best put that kind of thinking aside. What he'd done came from a powerful gift and he'd be smart not to use it lightly. He hoped he'd made an impact on Sarah. Sure, he'd only saved her in her dream, but her dream had felt pretty damn real, as if she was acting out her plan in advance.

If she was planning suicide—and he prayed she wasn't—he trusted the Great Spirit to warn him if she lost hope again.

"Angelina!" Papá threw open the door to her bedroom.

Angel jerked her blouse shut and turned her back to him, hurrying to finish dressing. "Do you no longer remember how to knock?" She glared at him over her shoulder, surprised by his dirty, dusty appearance. Never before had he intruded on her privacy. "Please turn your back or leave until I finish dressing."

"I do not care if you are naked." He grabbed her arm and swung her around to face him. He leaned in close, his dark eyes narrow and threatening, his fingers squeezing her arm tight. "Why are you doing this?"

"Doing what, *Papá*?" She forced her trembling fingers

to work the buttons up the front of her blouse, but didn't dare move toward her skirt, which lay on her bed.

"Destroying the hacienda." He began pacing, throwing his hands about in his agitation. "Stealing cattle and horses, from under our very noses. They hit always where we are most vulnerable. Minutes after we leave one place to run to another, they take the cattle we just left. How do they know where to strike, unless someone is telling them?" He took her by the shoulders and shook her. "Why have you turned against me?"

"*Papá*, stop! Please." Angel pushed herself away from him. With tears gathering in her eyes, she backed away, rubbing her stinging arms. "I am not helping whoever is doing this to us. To *us*, *Papá*. How would I know to tell them where to find the cattle? I am no longer allowed to leave the casa, remember? I have not turned against you."

He stared at her, his eyes bleak, his face flushed, and his body sagged as if in defeat. When he stepped toward her, she flinched and twisted away, but he only took her in his arms and held her.

"*Lo siento, querida*," he whispered into her hair, rocking her slightly as he held her. "I am so sorry. I have been wrong to punish you harshly, to lose my trust in you, and now to blame you for my problems." He leaned back and took her face in his hands. "Can you forgive me?"

He kissed her forehead and searched her eyes.

Angel stared up at him, not sure what to think of this new, emotional person in *Papá's* body.

"You must stay close to the casa, *querida*," he went on, finally stepping back and looking into her upturned face. "These banditos are unpredictable and move *muy rapido* from one place to the next." He crossed himself, looking out the window of her room. "*Madre de Dios!* They do not seem to be real men. They move like the wind."

"How do you fight the wind?" she asked, reminded of the wolf that she had seen disappear into thin air—once with her own eyes, and once in her dreams. But that had been over a week ago and the wolf had not returned.

"*El Lobo Diablo*," her father said in a hushed voice. "That is what the vaqueros and their families are calling it. We have lost all the single men. They won't stay and fight what they cannot see. The men with families may soon follow them. I have sent everyone who wants to leave to my family's latifundio in Mexico, where I know they will find work and where I can find them again once we catch these bandits and kill them."

Angel's breath caught. "Surely there is no need to kill them, *Papá*. Can you not leave their punishment to the law?"

He stared down at her, looking surprised and disappointed. "They have stolen from us, Angelina. Yes, they must die for what they have done to the hacienda. I am forced to take drastic measures."

Her blood ran cold. "What kind of measures?" How easily her father spoke of killing to protect his wealth.

He sighed and ran a hand through his hair, leaving a messy trail behind. She noticed that his hair had begun to silver at the temples and sides. Even his mustache, always boot-black, had started to gray. New lines bracketed his mouth and creased his forehead. The events of the past weeks had taken their toll on him.

"*Jefe, con permiso.*" Ernesto tapped on the open door, asking permission from *Papá* to interrupt their conversation. He bobbed his head repeatedly, obviously embarrassed to interrupt their private conversation and catch her partially dressed. He kept his face averted as Angel grabbed up her skirt and slipped behind the screen to pull it on over her drawers. "Señor Juan is come to see you."

"*Esta aqui?*"

Angel heard the concern in her father's voice.

"He was to guard the cattle tonight with his vaqueros."

Ernesto said nothing, but shuffled out of the room. Juan must be very angry to make Ernesto interrupt their conversation. What was wrong now?

Turning abruptly, her father made to follow him. "We will talk later, Angelina."

Angel watched him go, wondering why he was hurrying to respond to Juan's peremptory summons.

Sudden shouting disrupted her thoughts and she heard *Papá* shout her name, and "No!" Then Juan said something in a lower, quieter voice. She did not hear *Papá* answer.

Angel tiptoed down the stairs, not intending to eavesdrop, merely alarmed by the rancor in the men's voices. She shooed off a maid and the cook, who lingered in the hallway outside the closed study door, their eyes wide and frightened. When they saw her, they blanched and slipped away.

"It is not enough," she heard Juan shout. "Bulger offers a pittance for nearly a third of the hacienda's land. You can never replace your stock. It will take years to rebuild."

"With your help—"

Juan interrupted *Papá*. "I will not help unless you agree to my terms."

"What do you want?" *Papá* asked. Angel cringed, hearing the defeat in his voice.

"You know what I want," Juan said, "we have discussed this many times. Why do you delay? As my wife, she will never risk our plans again. She will learn obedience, something you have never succeeded in teaching her."

Shocked, Angel moved closer to the door and heard *Papá* say, "*Sí*, I agree to the marriage. You and Angelina will be wed in two weeks' time. Now are you satisfied, Juan? Will this seal your lips once and for all?"

Angel covered her mouth to stifle her protest. A few months ago, she would have stormed into the room and shouted, "No, Juan! I will never marry you!" Since then, she had learned caution. Tears welled in her eyes as she turned from the door. She blinked at the maid, who reached to put an arm around her, sympathy shining from her wide brown eyes.

Angel pushed away from her and hurried back up the stairs to her room. How could *Papá* do this? Why would he agree to this marriage? He knew she hated Juan, that she could never marry him.

As if she'd called him with her thoughts, *Papá* came running up the stairs. He stopped short, seeing her there as if she waited for him, her face streaked with tears. His lips thinned and all emotion left his face as he walked to her.

"You heard," he said, not asking. His voice chilled her to the bone.

"I will not marry him." She did not raise her voice, but let her words convey her anger and determination. "How could you agree to Juan's demands? You know I hate him."

"That is not what I know." His voice seemed flat, emotionless, as limp as his body. This man bore little resemblance to the one she had loved all her life. "I have watched you encourage him, fan his lust, make him desire you above all things. How can I deny him now?"

"He lies!" she cried, desperate to make him see, understand how much she disliked Juan. "He is the man who almost killed Jeremiah. Bull and I found him, shot, badly beaten, bleeding to death. When Jeremiah recovered, he told us it was Juan who attacked him. I saw what kind of man Juan is, *Papá*. I know he is dead inside. I refuse to marry him."

Her father's eyes narrowed and all lassitude evaporated. He drew himself up and fixed his angry gaze on her face. "*You* were the one who saved him? You helped my enemy? What have you done?" He glared at her, waiting for her response, his face flushed, his hands flexing.

"No, *Papá*," she said, searching his eyes, his face. "What have *you* done? What hold does Juan have on you to make you do his bidding?"

He recoiled and slapped her hard. "This! This is how you repay my love, all the years of care and kindness. You are as deceitful as your mother."

Angel reeled from the blow and fell backward. Her head hit the wall hard. Flashes of light blinked through the sudden dark surrounding her, then her vision cleared enough to allow her to see her father standing over her. She lay curled on the floor, clutching a hand to her throbbing cheek as she watched her father, not sure what he might do next.

"Here!" Gold sparkled in the dim light as he pulled something out of his pocket and threw it at her. "Wear this. It will complete your transition." Without looking back, he walked to his room and slammed the door behind him.

On the carpet before her lay the locket she had found in the table beside his bed. She picked it up and, finding it partially open, pried it wide. Inside was a painting, a miniature of her mother's face. The opposite side was empty, but her mind showed her the locket as it had once looked, when it had held the portrait of her father—her true father. With an earsplitting scream the black wall hiding her last memories came tumbling down.

She stumbled to her feet, clutching her cheek with one hand, the locket with the other, and blinked through the tears streaming from her throbbing eye while the last terrible memory broke free in her mind. She slammed the bedroom door and turned the key in the lock, then collapsed on the carpet as the dark horror overtook her.

* * *

Jeremiah dropped his saddle beside his men's and sat in front of it. He looked around the circle of weary—and wary—faces. "How many head are left?"

"Less than a hundred cattle, maybe twenty horses." Pedro wiped his eyes with his bandana and lay down nearby, propping his head on his saddle. "Your wolf spooked the vaqueros. Hell, it spooks all of us, too." He rolled his head and squinted at Jeremiah. "How d'you do that anyway?"

Jeremiah shrugged. "I told you. It's a gift."

"Yeah, from the Great Spirit or your wolf guide, I get it." Pedro closed his eyes and shook his head. "Still don't understand it, but I'm glad it's on our side."

"It helps on nights like this when we're watching the hacienda," Bull said. "It don't spook me none, nor these Comanche fellas, either. We understand spirit stuff."

The Comanches laughed and poked Bull. One of them made a face with bulging eyes and puffed up cheeks, and flapped his arms like wings. Bull kicked some dirt at him. The rest of the Comanches laughed.

"Well, some of us do," he said, and glared around the circle. "Bird figured it out first. Nothin' gets by her."

Jeremiah smiled with the others as Bull bragged about his sister's talents. Bull was right, Little Bird had understood what was happening to him. She'd explained it to the others, who wouldn't have accepted his version, and spared him their ridicule.

"Tomorrow we'll start separating the last of the cattle in the pens and drive them south to sell. The Comanche have their horses and Quannah's got them all hidden where the soldiers won't find them. He sent word that the cattle you sent are in pens on the west end of the reservation. If anyone spots them, he'll tell them he's leasing that land to a local rancher or that they're strays from the last cattle drive."

"When's he coming to play the hero and round up

the renegades?" Pedro propped his head on his crossed arms and tipped his hat down over his face.

"Early next week." Jeremiah also stretched out on his bedroll, dead tired. Once his head hit his saddle, it wouldn't be long before he'd be snoring like the other Ranger. "He's looking forward to it."

"Hate to admit it, but Governor Coke's pretty damn smart." Pedro chuckled.

"I hope James never gets wind of it," Jeremiah said, cocking an eyebrow at Pedro. "That kid's drunk all the time. No question he'd blab the story."

"We Texans do like a good story." Pedro laughed and peeked out from under his hat brim. "Who'd believe him? He's a drunk."

"Yeah, but a drunk who works for the governor and—"

A loud, unearthly scream split the quiet night. A woman's voice cried out in pain, and fear. *Sarah*.

"Oh no." Pedro jerked upright and stared about them as if the person who'd screamed was there, in the dark beyond the firelight. "That sounded like—"

"Sarah." Jeremiah had risen to his knees and wasn't surprised to see the black wolf loping toward him out of the gathering dark.

"Follow with two horses," he told Pedro, and felt himself shifting, his body falling to the ground as he rose into the air. "Meet me at the cabin . . ." He hoped Pedro and Bull had understood, but he couldn't wait to make sure.

Sarah was in danger, and this time not from herself.

Chapter Eighteen

Sarah peered out the broken root cellar door, shaking from hunger and cold. Safe! She was safe. No one was nearby. She could leave her hidey place to search for food. She'd eaten the last apples and carrots, even though the apples had been mushy and the carrots all hairy and bendy. It was summer, so everyone had been eating vegetables from the gardens. Nobody wanted old apples and carrots left from last year. She didn't, either, but her tummy didn't mind.

It hadn't been dark long, but each night it took her longer to find food. Tonight she'd start looking early, while the moon still shone in the sky.

She tiptoed from the cellar, looked for the mean men, then ran very fast to a big tree and pressed herself against it. Only two more trees and she could hide in the burned-down house where Mommy had helped the ladies bake bread. The bread had all burned up, but she'd found some flour and that yellow flour Mommy used to make corn cakes. Sarah didn't know how to make bread, but when she put them together in a pot and added a little water they turned gooey, like Mommy's oatmeal, and she could eat it with her fingers. But she was tired of pretend oatmeal. She wanted fried chicken, or turkey, or boiled eggs. Right now she could even eat liver and onions, but she didn't know where to find food like that. If she had to kill a chicken, she thought she could, but she really didn't want to kill anything. And she hadn't seen any chickens.

Quiet as a mouse, she moved black, burned boards

*away from the cupboard where the ladies had hid the
sugar and the honey. It was 'posed to be a secret, but
once she had hidden under the big table and saw where
the ladies kept it. She knew it had to be there, if the fire
hadn't burned it all up. Pushing hard, hard, hard, she
made the biggest board fall, but sparks flew and she had
to hurry, stamp them out quick, then hide when the board
made a lot of noise falling. She didn't want the mean
men to catch her.*

*From under a pile of burned wood, she watched and
waited. When no one came, she started hunting again
and found it! The cabinet was still there and full of honey.
She didn't bother with the flour and cornmeal, just grabbed
two jars of honey and ran back to her hidey-hole in the
root cellar.*

*She woke up sick, crying from the pain in her tummy.
It hurt like the time she ate too many jalapeño peppers
when Jeremiah dared her. He hadn't left like the other
boys when she threw up. He said she smelled awful, but
he helped her wash her face in the creek and took her
home.*

*She'd waited too long, remembering. She jumped for
the door but didn't make it.*

*Peee-yew! She had to wash her shirt. If Mommy saw
how dirty she was, she'd tan her bottom good. Sarah
started out the door, but stopped and stared. She couldn't
go out! It was daytime. Those bad men who had shot her
sisters and took Mommy away would hurt her, too. She
had to stay hid. But her hidey-hole was too stinky now.
She had to do what Mommy always said she should do:
use her head. Her head said git out! It stinks in here! So
she ran to the creek and sat in the water. She took off her
shirt and shook it underneath the water to get rid of the
icky stuff on the front, then used it to rub her face clean.*

*She felt so much better that she lay down in the water
and kicked her feet and swished her hair, but she didn't*

*take off her drawers. She had promised Mommy she'd
never, ever take off her drawers outside.*

*Suddenly, she heard the bad men laughing and shoot-
ing their guns and a woman crying and screaming.
Mommy? It sounded like Mommy.*

*Another man yelled, "Stop! Don't do this." A gun went
off again and then it was quiet. Too quiet.*

*Sarah ran to the fence, toward the bad smell. She'd
stayed away from that place. It scared her. Something
dark and ugly waited there to hurt her. But her mommy
was there! She'd heard her!*

*She squeezed through the broken fence and ran as
fast as she could. Then she saw it, a big black pile in the
middle of the hay field. What was it? She stared, seeing
black, bare bones, heads and fingers with no skin, and
that awful, awful smell. She covered her nose with her
wet shirt. Her face was wet with tears.*

*A man stood between her and the big black pile. He
reached up to the top and yanked; then there was a big
whoosh! and something blue and white on top caught
fire. Mommy's favorite apron, and Mommy was in it.
She had to help her mommy!*

*Sarah screamed, "Git away from my mommy!" She
ran at the man and shoved him away, but when she tried
to climb up to Mommy to pull her off the pile, the man
picked her up. She kicked and fought, but the man
wouldn't let her go. He wouldn't let her help Mommy.*

*"Hush, now, angel," he said, and pulled her away from
the mean men who tried to take her away. They said, "Kill
her! Kill her! All must die, you said so yourself." But he
took her away. When he finally set her down, he reached
out to wipe her tears, and hanging from his hand was
her mommy's locket. He stole Mommy's locket.*

*"That's my mommy's. Give it to me," she'd told him,
but he had said, "No, it's too big for you, little angel.
That's what I will call you," he said, and smiled at her.*

"You will be my little girl and I'll call you Angelina." He'd lifted her onto his horse and climbed on behind her and he'd taken her away. Sarah had screamed and fought and bit his hand, but he'd been very strong and he hadn't let her go. She'd been too tired to fight anymore, so she'd screamed and screamed and screamed . . .

"It's all right, Sarah," a voice said into her dream. "You're safe now. Don't scream anymore."

A warm, furry head rubbed her cheek and a heavy body lay down beside her. Cold, she felt so cold, and she was shivering. She clung to the warm body, hugging it close, and let the animal lick her face, her neck. Abruptly, the scream echoing in her head stopped and in the silence it left behind, she heard the heavy thud of her heart. She was alive, but she kept her eyes shut tight and clung to the comfort she'd found in her dream. She didn't want to let it go, but she knew, eventually, she'd have to. She risked a peek, hoping to keep dreaming but needing to see what this animal—for there was no mistaking it as anything but an animal—looked like.

A black wolf stared back at her, its blue eyes fixed on hers. It poked her with its cold nose and she could have sworn it smiled. Then it spoke in a man's voice, but in her head, not with its mouth. "You're fine, Sarah. This is the last of your memories of the raid. It's the worst one, but you can deal with it now. You're not a child anymore. You're older, stronger, and you'll know what to do. Let me help you. Don't shut me out."

He looked like a wolf, but in her heart, he felt familiar, like someone she knew well and loved. "Jeremiah?" she asked, and he butted her with his nose and blinked. She scratched between his ears and he growled, his eyes rolling up in his head.

"You always were a smart little thing," he said, but he started to feel cooler. "Stop scratching," he said, his tongue lolling out and his head settling on her chest. "I like it too much." When she stopped, the vision faded, leaving her clutching air and shivering. "Come find me," he called to her as he left.

She blinked and awoke, alone and huddled in a ball on the bare floor of her bedroom. Her mind, her soul, felt bruised, but clear. Recalling the horrible memories she'd buried for so long, she understood why she'd been so afraid of them. Her mother had been shot, almost before her eyes. And she knew now, without a doubt, that the man she'd called *Papá* for so many years was indirectly responsible. She recognized his voice as the one begging the men to stop, shouting, "No!" He'd been too weak to control them, to save her mother. But why was he there in the first place? Did he have anything to do with the other deaths? She didn't know, and her mind, her very soul, ached from thinking about it.

She'd faced the last black wall and torn it down and, thanks to her wolf friend, it hadn't destroyed her soul. She would survive the raid, physically and mentally intact, though she would always be haunted by the sound of her mother's last cries.

Her poor, beautiful mother. Tears welled in her eyes and she let them fall, filled with anguish for her mother's death. She cried for her sisters and her father and the children who had been her friends, and even those who weren't. All the people, so full of divine purpose, trying to carve a better life from the hard, unforgiving land. They hadn't deserved to die, hadn't hurt anyone, hadn't intruded where they weren't wanted, hadn't threatened a single soul. Why had they died?

And how was Miguel Sanchez involved? She couldn't bring herself to call him *Papá,* nor would she continue calling herself Angel. Had he stumbled on the scene afterward? She guessed, based on her rambling memory, that she'd been hiding for at least a week after the raid. Why was her mother still alive after everyone else had been killed? The possibilities brought more tears and anguish. She had to find out why, what had happened to trigger the raid. What had Miguel Sanchez done?

Had he adopted her out of guilt and remorse? Perhaps that was why he'd been unable to hug her, hold her as a true father would. Maybe he believed, down deep inside, he didn't deserve her love.

She sat up and her hand dragged over something on the floor beside her. The locket! Her mother's prized possession. Sarah picked it up reverently and studied her mother's beautiful face. With her memories completely restored, she knew that she resembled her mother physically, but where her mother's hair had been a lustrous gold, Sarah's was a dull ash blonde. Her mother's eyes had been a brilliant green that sparkled when she laughed, and when she cried, but Sarah's eyes were hazel—neither green nor blue. Her own skin was pale, but her mother's had been a warm, golden color, especially when she'd been out in the sun.

Her mother had been beautiful, yes, but emotionally needy. She'd craved attention, especially from men. Angel remembered her parents fighting, her father shouting that her mother must stop flirting with every man she met, and her mother crying in her apron, then going to bed. Her father had explained to Sarah's older sisters that her mother couldn't help herself. She'd been raised by her grandmother, who'd never forgiven Sarah's mother for being born and causing her daughter's death. Her mother's father had enlisted in the army, running from his grief, and her grandfather had died in a farm accident when she was very young.

Her mother had been raised without a man to look up to, Sarah realized, feeling compassion for her. She couldn't remember if her mother's father—her grandfather—had died in the War of Northern Aggression, but she knew that he'd died before she was born.

How difficult it must have been for a young girl to have no one who loved her. Sarah had been fortunate to have Bernida to care for her and love her as if she'd been her own mother. Even though Miguel Sanchez had seemed unable to show his love, he'd made time for her and included her in his life. Her poor mother had been virtually alone, ignored all her life.

Sarah struggled to recall what Sanchez had called her mother before he'd thrown the locket at her earlier. Deceitful? She frowned. Had he been misled by her mother's flirtatiousness into thinking that she cared for him? Even if he had, her mother hadn't deserved such a horrible death. There was no excusing what *Papá*— Miguel Sanchez—had done or caused to be done to her family. No excuse at all.

She didn't know what to do, how to handle this new information. Only one person could help her make sense of it.

Sarah put on the locket, tucked it into her blouse, and dressed to ride. She had to get away from the casa and all its reminders of grief and loss. She had to find Jeremiah.

After all her weeks of imprisonment in the casa, it turned out to be surprisingly easy to escape. Her father was holed up in his room, and there was no sign of Juan. Sarah was just wondering how she could get one of the horses out of the barn, when a dark form stepped out of the shadows in the empty courtyard.

Sarah spun toward it, then gave a muffled cry and flew into Pedro's arms. "Pedro! I've missed you so much. Where have you been?"

"Shh, shh." He returned her hug then hurried her out of sight of the casa. Behind the barn, two horses were waiting. "Don't worry, I haven't forgotten you, *Princessa*."

"Where have you been?" she whispered. "I've had so much trouble without you here to watch over me."

"Your father took matters into his own hands and told me to leave." Pedro lifted her onto one of the mounts, then swung up on the other. "I would not have left you alone, but I had no other choice." Motioning her to silence, he led the way out of the courtyard.

"Where are the guards?" she asked.

"They won't be waking up 'til morning," he answered with a grin.

"What is that?" Sarah asked once they were safe with Bull and Little Bird in their cozy cabin. She pointed at the gleaming badge on his chest. "You're a Ranger?"

"Don't that beat all?" Bull thumped Pedro on the back. "Here he's been all along, investigatin' San—uh, your father—just like Jeremiah."

"Not 'just like' Jeremiah." Little Bird shook her head at Bull. "No one's been seeking the truth as aggressively as Jeremiah."

"Will you take me to him?" Sarah smiled up at Pedro.

"Nope." Pedro turned away, pouring water into a basin and washing the dust off his face.

Sarah frowned. "Why not?"

"Because he's coming here." His eyes gleamed at her over his bandana. "I would have told you if you'd asked."

"But he can't!" Sarah cried, all her nervous energy rushing through her like a river headed for a fall. "It's too dangerous. This will be the first place *Pa*—Sanchez— looks." Knowing her reluctance to refer to Sanchez as her father would raise questions, she braced herself.

"Finally!" Bull shouted as he slapped her on the back. "What happened? What made you see the light?"

"We had a terrible fight." Sarah turned away, gathering her thoughts and trying to control the flood of emotions tumbling through her. "He said something that made me remember . . . everything."

Little Bird put an arm around her shoulder. "I'm sorry the memories were so painful. Was it very bad?"

"Yes," Sarah said with a sigh, "but the strangest thing happened while I was remembering. There was this—"

"Wolf?" her three friends asked at once, sharing smiling glances.

"Jeremiah?" Sarah didn't need to see them nod to know she'd guessed correctly, and understood why they all looked a little awestruck.

Bull and Pedro explained that they'd heard a scream, and Jeremiah had known it was her, though Pedro had also guessed. The black wolf had appeared out of nowhere; then Jeremiah had gone limp and fallen asleep, just before telling Pedro to meet him here. The wolf had disappeared, like mist before the wind. Pedro had left two men to watch over Jeremiah's sleeping body and hurried to the hacienda to find Sarah and bring her to the cabin.

"If he doesn't show up soon, I'm gonna start to worry," Bull said, frowning into the dark.

A loud, long howl came from nearby, startling everyone.

"He's here," Pedro and Bull said, simultaneously.

"Wait," Bull told Sarah and Little Bird.

"When are you going to get over yourself?" Sarah shoved out the door ahead of him.

"Wi-men," he grumbled as he followed Little Bird out of the cabin, rubbing his arm where Bird had punched him as she, too, pushed by.

Jeremiah came striding out of the dark, leading his horse.

Pedro shook his head as he walked up and took the reins of Jeremiah's horse. "This animal confounds me. I don't understand why it isn't afraid of you, and this wolf spirit . . . thing."

"We have an agreement." Jeremiah swung off the horse and gave Pedro his usual forearm-squeeze greeting, before turning to Sarah. He searched her face, frowning as his hands settled on her waist. "Are you all right? You've lost too much weight."

She nodded, suddenly too overcome with emotion to speak. When he extended an arm, she stepped into his embrace, wrapping her arms around his waist, smiling when he kissed her forehead.

He swept an arm under her legs and picked her up. She gasped when he grabbed his saddle horn with his other hand, stepped into the stirrup, and swung onto the horse. She blinked in surprise as he settled in the saddle with her in his lap, but couldn't resist grinning at Little Bird, who stood a few feet away, smiling at her.

"Now where you goin'?" Bull asked, frowning first at Jeremiah, then Sarah, then Pedro. "Where they goin'?"

Jeremiah kneed the horse and shouted back, "You'll figure it out, Bull."

Sarah laughed as they galloped into the dark. She didn't care where they were headed as long as they were together again. "It was you then, in my dre— oomph."

Jeremiah's lips closed over hers, stealing her breath. Her first instinct was to object, to demand answers to her many questions first, but she wanted this, too, probably more than he did. She needed to explain why she'd sent him away, two times, but she also needed confirmation that he did care about her.

When the horse slowed to a walk, he wouldn't let her keep any distance between them, turning her to press her chest against him as he plundered her mouth with lips and tongue. Hungry and needy, she returned his fervor, fencing with his tongue, until, finally overwhelmed by his passion, she wrapped an arm around his neck and yielded all.

Immediately, his lips gentled and he caressed and

nibbled, then slid to her ear and nipped her lobe. "Do you have any idea how much I've missed you?"

"Mmm-hmmm." She smiled under his lips, then glanced into his eyes. Her heart caught at his expression. He wasn't teasing. He'd truly missed her. Her flirtatious reply died in her throat and she whispered the truth. "I've been so lonely without you. How did I ever live before you came?"

"I hope you never have to figure that out."

The short distance to the cut bank near Bull's and Little Bird's cabin where he'd built a brush shelter had never seemed so far before. Jeremiah hoped the horse knew where he wanted to go, and that it remembered the way. He was too caught up in Sarah's sighs and her willing arms to guide it.

Long before the horse finally stopped moving under him, he'd unbuttoned her blouse and feasted on her tightly budded nipples. She was firm and small, but incredibly sensitive. Jeremiah didn't mind the trade-off. He handled her carefully, feeling her ribs closer beneath her skin, but she wouldn't let him be gentle. She wanted his passion and she drove it higher with every touch, every sigh, every request and demand for more.

She moved with the horse's gait, her hip rubbing his full shaft. She wasn't satisfied to feel it there, she had to hold it, stroke it, until he begged her to stop or he'd spend. She switched to stroking his chest, his belly, and then his arm as he snaked his hand through her clothes to find the warm, wet core of her and thrust a finger inside. One stroke, two, and on the third, she screamed. He nipped her breasts and let her cry ring out, holding her as she came undone. When she sagged in his arms, he kneed the horse, urging it to move faster.

When it stopped, she straddled his waist and settled over him, still wearing her split skirt. He groaned as his cock strained against the buttons, seams and fabric holding him from her. He gripped her buttocks, longing to feel her soft, warm skin against his hands.

"Get down," he urged her. "I need to be inside you. Now."

He supported her so she could lean away from him and pull her leg between them. Then she twisted and slid down his leg to the ground. He hit the ground right behind her, dropped the reins over the horse's head, and grabbed Sarah around the waist. He lifted her high, kissing up her torso from her belly button to her bare breasts. Her open blouse hung from her shoulders, flapping in the night breeze. She shrugged out of it and cried out as he took one breast, then another, fully into his mouth and sucked hard. She tasted like sweetened cream. He couldn't get enough of her.

Her skirt came loose and slid down her legs, followed by her drawers. Still holding her waist, he lifted her a bit more and dipped his head to take a long sip from between her thighs. She cried out and stiffened, her fingers tightening in his hair.

"Not fair!" she cried when she stopped holding her breath. "Let me down."

He leaned against the bole of the huge pine tree beside his shelter and let her slide down his body, feasting on her as she went. He caught her under the buttocks with one arm and held her pressed to his waist as he dealt with his buttons. At last, his pants fell to the ground and he kicked them off, impatient with the cumbersome weight. With his free hand, he grabbed his cock and held it steady, letting Sara slide down, pressing the tip home.

It was almost more than he could stand. He tossed his head back and tried to fight his instinct to grip her hips and . . .

Sarah loosened her legs and slid fully onto him, taking all he had to give in one searing plunge. They both cried out and stilled. He willed the moment to go on forever, never wanting to forget the warmth and heat of her body and the joy of being inside her again. Sarah tightened her legs around him, lifted, and plunged.

He lost control as the beast inside him growled and fought for release. Gripping her buttocks in his hands, he bounced her up and down on his shaft and froze when her inner muscles jerked, then squeezed him tight. His eyes shut as lights burst behind his eyelids, but he held his seed as she rode out her ecstasy. When she recovered, he bounced her upward again and let her slide down his full shaft once more.

He smiled into her eyes as they widened and her eyebrows lifted. "Want to ride some more?" he asked, his voice barely a growl.

"Oh yes," she said, and kissed him, thrusting her tongue into his mouth, matching his rhythm as he bounced her up and down on his cock.

When he felt her body tighten and her sighs turn to cries of need once more, he turned and, still buried inside her, carried her into the shelter, where he laid her on the blanket-covered bed of pine needles.

"Again, Sarah." He lifted her legs over his shoulders and kissed her, putting all the love he felt but wasn't ready to speak into his kiss. "Come for me again." He rubbed her sensitive bud, lifted himself over her, and drove deep, letting the beast take control, knowing she welcomed his passion, his powerful thrusts, his pounding, pulsing need as he caught her up and flung them both into the star-studded night sky.

They cried out as one, their ecstasy silencing the night creatures and echoing from the rocks and hills nearby.

Sarah snuggled into Jeremiah's side once he flopped onto his back. "Tired?" she asked, knowing she sounded smug. She was near exhaustion herself, partly because she'd become unused to strenuous activity. Since he'd left, she'd barely stirred outside her room, not even leaving its confines for meals. Over the last week she'd helped the vaqueros' wives clean the casa, but she was still weaker than she liked. This romp in the pine needles, while thrilling, had sorely depleted her resources. She needed to eat.

As if he'd read her mind, Jeremiah produced a small, towel-wrapped package from a box above his head. "Little Bird leaves me dinner so I don't have to risk going to their cabin. There's plenty for both of us."

Sarah blessed her friend and vowed to thank her later as she ripped into a juicy, fried chicken leg.

Jeremiah grinned at her. "That's a pretty big appetite you've got there."

She shrugged and hesitated before taking another bite. "I haven't felt like eating lately, but tonight I'm famished."

"Good," Jeremiah said, tearing the heel off a crusty loaf with his teeth. "You've lost some flesh."

Sarah's smile disappeared. "Are you saying I'm too skinny?"

Jeremiah gulped. Oh, man, he'd walked right into that pile of manure. He leaned forward, pushed his hand under her hair, and pulled her face to his for a slick, smacking kiss. "I'm the man who kisses your breasts, remember? I'm not criticizing, but I noticed the difference."

"Hmmph." She stuck her nose in the air as she bit into some cheese. "You've got some of your muscle back." She grinned at him from under her lashes. "You're much stronger."

"You like that, huh?" He waggled his eyebrows at her and sat up straight, then made his chest muscles dance.

She laughed and pressed her fingers against his chest. "I can feel the muscles clenching and releasing. How interesting."

"Your buttocks do the same thing, and you do it inside, too, when you come."

She glanced up, her cheeks turning bright pink. "I do?"

"You can't tell?" He loved to make her blush. The high color made her cheeks bloom like roses and her eyes sparkle bright green.

"No," she said, and ducked her head to pick through the remaining pieces of chicken. Her sudden shyness intrigued him. How could she be so shy after everything they'd done to—and with—each other? There wasn't an inch of her body he hadn't kissed. "All I know is that I clench all over and then everything bursts inside me."

"That's pretty much how it feels for me, too."

"Was it like this with your wife?" She gasped, covered her mouth, and turned away. "Don't answer that, I shouldn't have asked, but you talked about her a lot when you were delirious. You must love her and miss her terribly."

"Hey," he said, "come back here." He grabbed her hand and kissed each fingertip. "I loved Ekararo as much as any man can love a woman, but she's dead and I have to move on. She would understand, and I think she would like you."

"You do?" Sarah smiled at him and he kissed her index finger again, then sucked it all the way into his mouth.

Her mouth fell open and her eyes widened. "That tickles. Is that how you feel when you're inside me?"

He sucked on her finger again, ran his tongue around its tip. "Not even close. You feel much, much better."

For a few minutes, they said nothing, just finished devouring the food Little Bird had provided, feeding each other tasty morsels, eating out of each other's hands.

"Have you remembered everything?" Jeremiah asked, mainly wanting to know if she'd remembered how it had been with them when she'd been young and he'd been a teenage boy with all the sense of a dirt clod.

"Yes." She swallowed the last bite of cheese. "Water?"

He pulled a full jar of water out of the same box the food had been in. "Little Bird thinks of everything."

"She's incredible." Sarah took a long gulp and he watched her throat work, wondering why she'd turned nervous again. Had she remembered something she didn't want to tell him?

"I was pretty hard on you when we were kids," he admitted, wanting their past out in the open, not festering between them. "I hurt your feelings, made you cry, and I've felt bad about it ever since."

Sarah laughed, not a happy sound, but a sound of disbelief. "I'm sure you never gave it a second thought."

Jeremiah sat up, cross-legged, but she glanced at his penis and blushed, so he raised one knee to hide himself. When she looked back at his face, he told her what he'd wanted to tell her for years, but never thought he'd have the chance to say. "I'm sorry, Sarah, for every harsh word I ever said to you. You were a baby, a little girl. You didn't love me to embarrass me in front of my friends. You just loved me, pure and simple. I wish I'd been half as honest with you."

Sarah blinked at him, her eyes glistening with unshed tears. "I was a real nuisance," she admitted with a sad smile. Her clenched fingers rested on her bent leg. Hell, if she didn't relax them soon, she was going to break a bone.

He took her hands in his, straightened her fingers, kissed the tips. "I was a brute, a typical, self-centered boy with about this much sense." He held up a finger and thumb, nearly pressed together. "Can you forgive me?" He kissed her fingertips and gazed at her over them, waiting.

She looked down and a lone, fat tear slid down her

cheek and plunked onto Jeremiah's hand. She gasped and reached to wipe it off, but he lifted his hand to his mouth and licked it away. "Come here," he said, trying to make it sound like a request, not the order it was. "I see a few more places I need to kiss to make up for my lack of sense." He kissed the tip of her nose, leaving it wet and pink.

She wiggled it and laughed. "You don't need to—"

"Oh yes, I do," he said, and kissed her chin, teasing it with tongue circles. Next, he kissed his way to her earlobe and nibbled there, breathing into her ear while she giggled and begged him to stop.

"I can't stop," he growled, moving to her belly button and delving into it with his tongue.

She cried out and yanked her legs up. "Stop! Please!"

"Do you forgive me?" he asked, licking his way down to the backs of her knees, which he kissed thoroughly, using lots of tongue.

"Oh!" She caught her breath as he licked his way up the backs of her thighs, over the curve of her buttocks. Then he lifted her onto her knees and pushed her knees wide, baring her bottom and all her secrets to his touch.

She flinched and gasped when he stroked her most sensitive spot, but only groaned and spread her legs wider when he kept up the torture. Surprised that she didn't pull away or refuse him, but settled onto her chest, the beast inside him tore free. As her inner walls began to tighten, he rose to his knees and replaced his fingers with his cock, then drove himself home.

With her head propped on her forearms, she glanced back at him and smiled, her cheeks flushed with passion. He rubbed her buttocks and felt his own climax rushing at him. Then she pushed up on stiff arms and drove him deeper into her hot, wet channel than he'd ever been. With a blinding rush, he shot his seed deep into her body and felt her muscles clench around him.

He caught her hand and pressed her fingertips to the place where their bodies met.

"Feel it," he urged her, pressing her fingers between his cock and her clenching muscles. "Now you know how you feel when it happens, and how I feel, too." Sealed together, they rode out their mutual satisfaction and fell into each other's arms.

Chapter Nineteen

When she woke late the following day, Sarah wasn't surprised to find another box of food and a note from Little Bird.

> *Angel*, the note began, but "Angel" was crossed out and "Sarah" was written above it. *I've sent some of my special tea just in case you want it. I'll be waiting to hear from you.*

Sarah lifted the towel over the basket of food and found a stoneware jug with a note attached that read *For Sarah Only.*

Shaking her head at Little Bird's perspicacity, Sarah swished the liquid inside, then poured it onto the ground outside the shelter. She replaced the cover on the food, waiting for Jeremiah to awaken to eat with her. Food could wait. The poor man was exhausted, she thought with a shy grin. They'd made love throughout the night and on into today with no sleep, only brief naps snatched in between passionate bouts of lovemaking.

Several times, he'd surprised her with some new move or position and she could tell by the way he watched her that he expected her to balk, to shy from the intense intimacy. As the night progressed, he'd stopped hesitating and watching, waiting. She'd shown him that she trusted him to gauge her needs and give her the pleasure she'd come to crave, and expect, in his arms. Now he watched her avidly, for she knew, she sensed, that her pleasure increased his own.

Still, remembering some of the things they'd done made her blush, but not from embarrassment. She wished he'd wake up, so they could try some things again and maybe explore some others. Making love with Jeremiah thrilled her more every time they came together. Even those rare times when he simply ravished her, unable to hold back and take his time. The knowledge that she—plain, simple wren that she was— could make this man lose control sent her tumbling over the edge along with him.

She treasured this time alone with him, knowing it couldn't last. Soon she would have to face Sanchez and demand an explanation, the truth. He owed her that. Not knowing how that confrontation would resolve itself, she was determined to make the most of this idyll.

She wanted to explore Jeremiah as thoroughly as he was exploring her, but she wanted more than his body. He knew everything about her—her body, her life, her needs. She wanted to know as much about him, and he hadn't shared his story with her. She needed to know what had happened to him after the raid. What horrors had he lived through? Had he survived in spite of them, or because of them?

"What are you frowning about now?"

She didn't need to look to recognize his touch on her back, her arm. She went gladly when he pulled her down beside him, and she sighed as he tucked her into the curve between his arm and shoulder, close against his warm body.

"So many scars," she said, running a hand over his chest and tracing a particularly vivid one with her finger from his rib up to his collarbone. "You haven't told me what happened to you after the raid."

"I don't want to spoil our time together with ugly stories that don't matter anymore." He pulled away from her, reaching for the canteen. "I'll be right back."

She lay back and flung an arm over her eyes to block

the midday glare peeping through the holes in the ceiling of their brush shelter. She smiled, and hoped it didn't rain anytime soon. His living space was so crude compared to what she had always known, and yet it felt like a palace to her—warm, comfortable, and the people— She grinned. Only the best.

She sobered, hearing his approaching footsteps, remembering his response to her request. How could she reason with him, explain that his silence was unfair?

When he returned, he knelt beside her and pulled her up to sit facing him. "I was unkind just now. You deserve to know as much about me as I do about you. My memories are old and I've put them behind me. They're not fresh and new like yours." He sighed and sat beside her, his arms resting atop his bent knees as he looked into the distance. Was he seeing the past?

"All us boys were taken alive, though some of us were injured in the taking. I only saw Juan once, giving orders to the Comancheros, but I swore I'd never forget his face, and I didn't. They tied our hands in front of us, tied us together, and made us run in a line. We tried to help the injured ones, even carry them, but they wouldn't let us and some of the smaller boys died the first night. When I fought the Comancheros, one big, ugly man hit me in the head with his rifle butt. I didn't wake up for hours.

"Little Tommy—you remember the redheaded Paladin kid?—he fell off a horse the second day and hit his head on a rock. They kicked him to make sure he was dead, then left him where he lay. More boys died the second night. Then the Comanchero leader sobered up enough to realize he was losing money and kicked out a couple of men.

"The third day, we met up with the Kiowa and the nightmare really began. The Kiowa that bought us enjoyed inflicting pain. They worked us like dogs all day, then played with us all night. Their favorite game was

'Make Him Cry.'" His fists clenched and he crawled out of the shelter.

He turned away from her when she followed, but he continued. "They'd tie me up at night, hands together, feet together, and then they'd kick my feet out from under me, roll me onto my stomach and tie my hands and feet together behind me."

She cringed as he gestured with his hands, showing her the bowlike shape his body had been forced into.

"Then they'd lift me and hang me over a tree limb and start stacking rocks on my back, the biggest rocks they could find, trying to break me, to make me scream or cry or beg them to stop. Anything. One of the women, a white captive, loved the game. She'd stand by my head and stroke my hair and tell me it was okay to cry. No one would blame me, she said over and over. I ignored her, 'cause I knew the boys who listened to her, the ones who cried, were killed. They disappeared during the night, but I saw their hair, their scalps on the women's scalp poles."

He again turned his back to her, but Sarah hugged him from behind, feeling sick inside at the pain he'd suffered. Almost, she regretted asking him to tell her, but she knew he needed to talk about it, get it out in the open between them. She let her body tell him what she couldn't find the words to say: She thought no less of him as a man for having endured these horrors as a boy, for being unable to seek revenge for himself and the other boys.

"What about the Comanche? Did they hurt you, too?" she asked when his silence drew out.

He glanced over his shoulder at her. "The Comanche?" He seemed surprised by her question, and shook his head. "No, the Comanche were good to me. They taught me to be a man, a warrior. It was a good life, a free life, and I learned a fair bit about horses and riding, too.

"They taught me how to love and care for a woman, to provide for her needs, to put someone else's needs before my own. The Comanche love their families. Everything they do, every thought they have is all about their families."

Sarah's angst over his suffering gave way to relief that he'd known some joy those fourteen years he'd been gone. "I'm sorry that your time with them ended badly, with the death of your wife and unborn child."

"I am, too," he admitted, taking her in his arms. He pressed her head to his chest and held her, still gazing into the distance over her head.

"I'm sorry you were never able to avenge the boys who died," she said on a sad sigh.

He pulled back and searched her eyes. "What makes you think that?"

"I assumed . . ."

He chuckled and pulled her back into his embrace. "I rode with the Comanche for several years. The Comancheros and Kiowa feared me. I remembered their faces. Whenever I came across someone I remembered from the raid, I gave him a chance at a fair fight, but the Comanche had taught me well. None of them beat me, and no one broke me." His chest rose on a swiftly drawn breath.

"The guy with the rifle butt?"

"Died in a fair fight. He's the one who gave me this scar." He pointed to the one she'd traced earlier.

She nodded, understanding the pride he took in that fact. As a mere boy, he'd been tortured beyond most men's endurance and he'd never broken, never given his captors the satisfaction of making him cry. As a man, no enemy had been able to stand against him.

"What about the women?" she asked, searching his face, hoping to see mercy and compassion there. She found none.

"I never touched a woman or girl who'd tortured me,

but my Comanche brothers weren't so forgiving. They learned to recognize the way I looked at them, and then the women disappeared. They told me later that they'd kidnapped any woman I looked at like I wanted to butcher her for the stew pot. They'd question the woman, then sell her to the Comancheros, who sold the women in Mexico. They were never seen again."

"Your brothers truly loved you." She couldn't criticize the men for their brutality, not knowing that the women had tormented Jeremiah when he was alone and afraid. They should have been whipped.

"Sometimes they were," Jeremiah said.

Sarah glanced up at him. "Were what?"

"Whipped."

"You read my mind!" she cried, and shoved away from him with a palm to his chest, not sure she liked his new skill.

He caught her and hauled her back. "You make it easy. Your emotions play across your face."

"Oh, you! What else should I think? You walk into my dreams—even my nightmares—as a wolf." She slapped both palms against his chest. Her fingers curled into the springy hair that covered the wide, muscular expanse and she gave a sharp tug.

"Ouch!" He pulled away carefully and gave her bottom a sharp slap. "Now you're going to pay, woman."

Sarah squealed and ran from him, but he caught her easily, slung her onto one hip, and carried her to the nearby stream.

"Jeremiah! Don't you dare throw me in that water. Jeremi-ugh!"

Her cries faded to noisy gurgles as he waded in waist deep and sat down, dragging them both under. She came up splashing and kicking. He fended her off until he'd maneuvered her into the deepest part of the streambed; then he pulled her to him, kissed her deeply, and showed her another type of water activity altogether.

Sarah threw herself into their love play, giving her all to the passion consuming them, hoping he could read in her heart and her mind the words she couldn't find the courage to say. She wouldn't risk having those new, tender shoots trampled when she must again leave him to confront the man who claimed to be her father. Until then, she'd spend every moment of the day loving Jeremiah.

She hoped it would not be her last chance.

Jeremiah woke to something rustling outside the shelter. Why hadn't his horse whinnied? Then he remembered.

Sarah. He reached out, seeking her warm body, his cock already rising as he reached for her, but her side of the blanket was empty. "Sarah?" She didn't answer, but the rustling outside stopped.

He didn't bother searching for clothes, just ducked outside, into the dark. With his wolf vision aroused by anxiety, he found her quickly, between his horse and the tree, scrabbling around on the ground. He walked over, snatched up her blouse, and shoved it at her. "Leaving without saying good-bye?"

He leaned a shoulder against the tree and crossed his ankles at the knees. Yeah, he was flaunting his manhood, but he loved the way she reacted to his body. She glanced up, her gaze going right where he wanted it, then up to his face. And back to his swelling cock. Even after two days of making love, his cock raised its hungry head every time she was near.

She licked her lips and he bit back a grin. If he ever saw her look at another man like that . . . he'd kill him. Without blinking.

Whoa, there, he warned himself. *Let's find out what's going on here first.* He grudgingly admitted he needed to have a talk with Sarah soon and find out if she was thinking the same thing he was thinking. He was gone, doomed, head-over-heels, bring-on-the-preacher in love with her, and damn happy to have her back in his arms, his bed, his life. And that's where he wanted her to stay.

Surely she wasn't planning on going back to Sanchez after everything they'd shared?

"It's almost dawn," Sarah said, glancing east. She started buttoning her blouse, her cheeks turning the same color as the sky above the hills.

"Let me help," he said, and pushed her hands away. "If you ride hard, you can get home before breakfast."

Sarah stared up at him, astounded. "How did you—"

"Oh, please," he scoffed. "This is your pattern. You do it to me every time. I swear you think more of that man than you do your own life, let alone me."

He stared at her, his eyes cool, silently daring her to argue with him, talking over her sputtering protests, not giving her a chance to defend herself. "Or is it the haci-enda you love? Even without the livestock, the land's valuable. Is it money, Sarah? Is it more important to you than my love?"

His eyes widened and his mouth fell open as he realized what he'd admitted.

"So!" She leaped at his obviously inadvertent revela-tion, the one she'd longed to hear, though she'd imag-ined him delivering it on bended knee, with flowers. "You love me."

His eyes closed and he nodded. Scowling as he crossed his arms over his naked chest, he watched her like a hawk eyeing his next meal.

"Then you'll understand why I have to go back and confront Sanchez now that I've remembered every-thing. Don't you see? That's the only way I'll be able to live with these memories." She couldn't hold back the shudder that chased through her as the memory of her mother's death flitted through her mind. "I have to know *why* he did it, why he adopted me, why he agreed to give me to Juan to . . ."

Jeremiah went dangerously still. "To what, Sarah?"

"To marry!" she admitted. "I don't know what Juan's holding over his head to make *Pa*—Sanchez—agree to it. He always promised me he wouldn't force me to marry a man I hate.

"If you love me, you'll understand that I have to know the whole story, not just the bits and pieces from my childhood memories. I need to know all the details—from him."

He grabbed her by the shoulders and she braced herself, certain he was about to shake her. But he only leaned close and spoke in a deadly quiet voice. "What do you think he and Juan will do once they confess everything? Do you think they'll let you live? They'll kill you, Sarah, like they killed your family and my family and everyone else in Baldwin Fort."

"*Pa*—" She shook her head in frustration. "Sanchez won't kill me and he won't let Juan do it either. He adopted me, remember? He loves me." Desperate to make him understand why she had to confront Sanchez, leave him, she tried another line of reasoning. "I just have to go back one last time. Then I can be with you."

He spread his arms wide. "Fine. Go, if that's what you want. Do what you must. All I can do is ask you to be damn careful while you're there. I hope you won't regret this, Sarah."

Sarah sighed, feeling hollow inside, knowing she had upset him. "I do love you, Jeremiah; it seems I've always loved you. I wish you could understand that I have to do this, and, no, I don't want you to come with me. Sanchez won't talk to me if you're there. I have to do this alone."

She watched him close himself off to her, saw the light dim in his eyes. He said nothing, only watched as she mounted the horse Little Bird or Bull must have brought during the night. She struggled to control her mount, which was tense and nervous probably because of their loud disagreement, or Jeremiah's proximity.

When she finally got the horse under control, she looked at Jeremiah, still glaring at her in all his naked glory. Her mind flashed through the last two wonderful days she'd spent in his arms and she felt her body heat and ready for him. Was he right? Was she putting her life at risk by returning to the hacienda?

She couldn't let herself dwell on that now.

Instead, she blew him a kiss and rode hard for the casa, hoping she'd made the right decision.

Jeremiah watched Sarah ride away, her hair flying out behind her, riding as if his wolf brothers were chasing her. The Comanche in him admired her seat. She rode better than any of the Comanche women he'd known, and they were damn good. He couldn't fault Sanchez for her upbringing. Guilt had brought out the best in the man.

But how long would guilt keep him from harming her once he realized she knew the whole truth? Not long, he'd bet.

Quickly, he pulled on his clothes and mounted his horse. Without wasting another moment, he set off after Sarah. If she thought he was going to let her beard the lion in its den all alone, she was loco.

Halfway to the hacienda, not far from the place where Juan had tried to kill him, he spotted the wolves flanking him through the trees. What now? He hadn't called them. Why were they here? As if they'd heard his question, they closed in. His horse tossed his head as they came. Though the animal didn't fear the wolves, he liked to keep them at a distance. *Sarah*.

Her name came to him clearly and he saw the black wolf in the distance, leading the wolf pack. Jeremiah tensed, expecting that odd lifting feeling he always felt before he left his body and became the spirit wolf, but it didn't happen.

The black wolf glanced back over his shoulder without stopping, and again its thoughts were clear. *Not this time*, it said in its low growl. *Today she does not dream. Hurry!*

Jeremiah urged his horse faster and felt the animal lengthen and stretch under him. He leaned low over its neck, tucking his legs in tight, becoming one with the horse. Its ears flattened back to hear Jeremiah's words of encouragement, and they flew across the waving grass.

Jeremiah's blood pounded in his ears, keeping pace with the horse's ground-eating stride. How could she be in trouble already? Sanchez and his men must have been waiting for her. They'd want to know where she'd been, whom she'd stayed with. She'd tell them, but if they tried to make her tell them where to find him, she'd refuse. Or lie. Then they'd get mad, and he knew these men—men who had killed hundreds to get what they wanted—would stop at nothing to make her tell them what they wanted to know.

Jeremiah cursed his stupidity—and her stubbornness. He never should have let her return alone. If only he could use his gift, transform himself into the wolf and stop them. But nothing he could do in spirit form would keep her safe. He had to be flesh, solid bone and muscle to be of any use. A wolf flashed by to his right, a mottled streak of flying fur. His horse was slowing, but the wolves could run at a steady pace much longer and faster.

Go! he shouted to the black wolf. *Run as fast as you can, don't wait for me. Stall them, scatter the horses, frighten the people, but don't risk your own lives. Keep them busy until I get there.*

The black wolf gave a yipping bark and the pack poured on the speed, leaving Jeremiah in their dust. He slowed his horse a bit to let it catch its breath and heard hoofbeats approaching. Pedro and Bull had seen him riding hell-bent for the casa and were riding in that direction, too. They veered toward him upon seeing him slow down, but he waved them ahead and urged his horse after the wolves.

Keep them talking, Sarah. Let them brag about their dirty deeds until I get there. He knew she couldn't hear him, but hoped she'd know what to do. She could survive this, he knew she could. Pride swelled inside him for the gutsy woman his little tormentor had become. She'd always been part of his life, part of him. He'd fought that knowledge at first, too young to understand, but she'd always known.

Well, he was finished fighting it. If they survived this day, he'd finish his duty to his family, his Comanche brothers, and Governor Coke. When he returned to Sarah, he'd be a free man with something to offer her. He only hoped they both lived to see that day.

Chapter Twenty

"We've been waiting for you, Angelina."

Juan's voice made Sarah's stomach turn. She continued unsaddling her horse. "My name is Sarah, Juan. Please remember it." She pushed past him to take her saddle to the tack room and brought back a currycomb.

"Leave the horse," he snarled, knocking the implement out of her hand. He grabbed her arm and pulled her toward the house.

"Get your filthy hands off me. You don't own me. You never will." She didn't care if she antagonized him. It was time he learned she was no meek filly to be whipped and pushed around.

He glared at her and she glared back, unwilling to let him intimidate her. The swift swing of his right arm caught her unawares, leaving her no time to dodge his open hand as it connected with her cheek. The ringing slap echoed in the stable as she flew sideways and crashed into the horse, which shrilled and danced away.

Angel scrambled out from under the horse's hooves and clutched the wall of its stall to pull herself back to her feet, ignoring the sting in her cheek and the tears streaming from her left eye.

"You will learn to obey me, Angelina, or suffer the consequences." He dragged her toward the house, his bruising hold on her arm much stronger than she'd expected. "Your father is waiting."

He took her to the study and pushed her ahead of him into the room. She stumbled to the desk, barely catching herself before slamming into it. Across the room, her father sat tied to a straight-backed chair, a bloody gag in his mouth, his face cut and bruised, his normally fastidious clothing torn and blood-splattered.

"What have you done to him, Juan?" she demanded, spinning to face Juan. She got another slap that knocked her to her father's feet. She shook her head to throw off the stars spinning behind her eyes and stood. She didn't wipe away the blood dripping from her nose when she faced Juan. "Did he stand up to you, too?"

She glanced around the room, counting three armed men in addition to Juan. "Has it come to this? Have your secrets been revealed? Does my father know what you did to Jeremiah and the boys from Baldwin Fort?" She hoped to goad him into talking so she could work her way behind the desk. She took a careful step toward the desk and braced her hand on it, making it look as though she needed support. She glanced at her father and sagged onto the desktop, moving in the direction of the right-hand drawers.

Her father's eyebrows lifted, only enough to communicate that he comprehended her plan. He struggled in his chair, tried to talk behind his gag, moving himself away from her. One of the guards hit him in the head with his rifle butt and his head lolled forward, onto his chest. Sarah fought the urge to go to him. She had to keep Juan talking.

"Did you tell him"—she nodded at Sanchez, who hadn't lost consciousness from the blow, but was having trouble holding his head up—"that one of the boys you stole might have survived, that he lived with the Comanche, became one of their warriors?"

Juan laughed. "You have me to thank for your lover's life, *puta*."

"I am no whore," Sarah shouted, then pretended to sway on her feet. She stumbled a little, feigning dizziness, and turned to place both hands on the desk to steady herself.

"No," he agreed, "that was your mother, wasn't it?"

"Liar!" she screamed, not faking the rage that enveloped her, but keeping her goal—the second drawer of Sanchez's desk—clearly in mind. "She was a beautiful woman. Men fell in love just looking at her. If she smiled at them, they were smitten. It wasn't her fault men are so gullible, so stupid."

Juan laughed, a high-pitched giggle that grated on her nerves. "Do you hear, Sanchez? The woman didn't love you after all. Such a shame." He shook his head in mock sympathy. "I don't blame you for giving her to me, and your men."

Sarah gagged. The thought of her beautiful mother struggling in the arms of a gang of ruthless men sent her to her knees. She groped for the wastebasket under the desk and was violently sick. When she could breathe again, she dragged her arm across her mouth and glared at Sanchez. He stared back at her, tears streaming down his face, shaking his head, pleading for understanding with his eyes. She wanted to fly at him, rip his eyes out, then do the same to Juan, but she couldn't be weak now. She must be strong. She must live.

For the first time in her life, she had no one to depend on but herself. She'd been so sure her father wouldn't let her be hurt, despite everything Jeremiah had said.

"So this is the hammer you have held over his head," she said, looking at Juan with contempt and loathing. "He'd have done anything to keep me from finding out what he did and why."

She looked at Sanchez as she groped behind her for the desk chair, remembering what had happened the last time she'd been in this room. Here, she'd given up childish infatuation for a woman's fulfillment. The thought comforted her, gave her strength and focus. She sat heavily on the edge of the chair and laid her head on her folded arms.

She looked up, letting the tears slide freely down her cheeks. "Is this why you agreed to make me marry a *peon* like Juan?"

When Juan looked at Sanchez in surprise, Sarah snatched open the secret drawer beneath the desk and pulled out the pistol. She knew this gun, recognized the weight of it in her hand. Sanchez had used it to teach her to shoot. She gripped it in both hands, the way he'd taught her and took aim at Juan's chest. At this distance, she couldn't miss.

Juan swallowed hard. No doubt Sanchez had boasted how well she could shoot. "Now, Angel," he said with a nervous laugh as he waved his own pistol at her, "you are only one against four. You can't shoot us all."

"Maybe not," she admitted, her voice calm and steady, her aim fixed. "But you will never know, because you're first, Juan. You'll be dead."

He motioned to the vaquero closest to her. "Do not come any closer," she told him, standing and backing up against the wall. She kicked the chair between her and the man on her other side.

Suddenly, from outside came the howl of wolves, followed by the squeal of frightened horses. Chaos erupted and the men's attention turned to the doorway as another of Juan's thugs burst in. "Wolves!" he shouted. "Dozens. *Andale! Andale!*"

Sarah seized her moment and pulled the trigger, aiming at Juan, but he'd anticipated her move and ducked. Her bullet went through his shoulder. His men, their attention torn between the door and Juan, took too long deciding to shoot at her. She ducked behind the desk and got off a shot at the closest man before he pulled his trigger. This time her aim was true. She rolled onto her back and fired at the man about to shoot her from behind and winged him. She shot again as he went down, but missed.

"Get her!" Juan shouted. "Kill her!"

Shots sounded outside, then in the hallway, and first Jeremiah, then Pedro, burst into the study, firing as they came. In seconds, Juan's men lay dead and Juan, wounded, raised his hands in surrender.

Jeremiah scooped her off the floor and into his arms. "Are you all right?" He gently explored the bruises on her face and cursed under his breath. "Juan did this?"

"He's very brave when faced with a lone woman."

"Look out!" Pedro cried. During the shooting Sanchez had tipped his chair and fallen to the floor, landing beside one of Juan's dead men. He'd gotten hold of the man's knife, cut himself free, and now raised the knife, aiming at Jeremiah's back.

Simultaneously, Juan pulled a small gun from his sleeve and took aim at Sanchez. At once, Juan fired at Sanchez, Sanchez threw the knife, and Pedro fired at Juan. When the smoke cleared, Juan lay dead, and Sanchez's knife, sunk nearly to the hilt, trembled from the wall inches from Jeremiah's back.

Sanchez cursed, still alive, but bleeding badly. Sarah hurried over to him and lifted his head and shoulders into her lap. Jeremiah cut off his gag and stood over him. Sanchez ignored Jeremiah, focusing instead on Sarah. "I have much to tell you, but not enough time, I fear."

"Don't waste your breath." She ripped open his shirt and lifted his hand from the wound, which bled profusely for such a small hole. "My memories have returned. I remember everything."

His eyes closed and he nodded. A tear escaped to roll down his cheek. "I am sorry, *querida*. I wished to spare you that."

"Why did you do it?" she demanded. "How could you do such a terrible thing?"

"I'm dying," he said, gripping her hand with the last of his strength. "Please give me your love, your forgiveness."

"I have no more love to give you. You took too much over the years with your lies and deceit. I wanted to love you, but you always held yourself aloof from me."

"My guilt," he said, then coughed up blood and whispered, "I couldn't. I knew I didn't deserve your love. But I . . . did . . . do . . . love you."

"As I loved you." She held his hand and felt the last of his breath sigh from his body. He went limp in her arms. She let his body slide to the floor and stood. She felt no sorrow, shed no tears. Instead, it seemed a heavy weight had been lifted from her shoulders. She turned to Jeremiah. "I need some fresh air."

The other Texas Ranger and several Comanche braves burst into the study. The Comanches wanted to take hair, but Jeremiah talked them out of it. Pedro gave orders and the dead men were soon removed to the stable. The other Ranger rode for town to telegraph news of the confession and deaths to the governor and to ask the Cedar Creek sheriff for some deputies.

Jeremiah and Pedro flanked Sarah as she approached the door of the casa, not letting her step through until they had checked the courtyard. When they stopped abruptly, she pushed past them, then she, too, came to an abrupt halt.

"Throw your weapons over here. Now hit the ground!" Bull shouted, motioning with his gun at the ten or twelve men lined up in front of him. "Try anything sneaky and I'll let the wolves eat you."

Pedro burst out laughing and Jeremiah followed. Sarah could only manage a wan smile.

Little Bird arrived near dusk and took over the task of treating Angel's bruises and the injuries of the casa's people, who'd been hurt running from the wolves. The wolves left once Juan's thugs were tied and locked in a small storage shed until the Rangers could deputize enough men to transport them to jail in Austin. The governor wanted to question them personally.

Sarah let Little Bird coddle her, grateful not to have to deal with the aftermath personally. Instead, she took a long, hot bath and ate dinner in her room. She noticed that her sangria tasted a little odd, which was confirmed when she dozed off before she finished eating.

Little Bird was becoming too high-handed with her tonics and medicines, Sarah decided as she fell into a deep sleep.

Jeremiah lay beside Sarah, content just to hold her through the night. Little Bird had objected, but he'd pushed her out of the room without a word. What kind of man did that woman think he was? He wasn't about to take advantage of the woman he loved when she wasn't capable of loving him back.

Still irritated, he stripped off his dirty clothes and tossed them out the door to Little Bird. "Get someone to wash these for me, would you?" Then he made use of Sarah's cold bathwater. It left him smelling way too flowery, but at least he was clean.

He finished up the food Sarah hadn't eaten, but avoided the bloodred fruity wine after one glance and sniff.

No, thanks, he thought. He needed to wake up well before dawn to get the prisoners mounted and moving toward Austin, several days' ride northwest.

Sleep came fast once he stripped off Sarah's clothes and pulled her into his arms. He rested his chin on top of her head, closed his eyes, and yawned.

Damn, if he didn't smell as good as her hair.

"Come in, boy, come in!" Governor Coke didn't wait for Jeremiah to obey his hearty command. He grabbed his arm and pulled him into his office, then stuck his head out the door before shutting it to holler, "James!"

"None for me, Governor, thank you." Jeremiah took his usual seat across from the governor's big, comfortable-looking chair, too tense to slug down a whiskey. He wanted his wits about him, just in case the governor—one of the cagiest men Jeremiah had ever known—tried to wiggle out of their agreement. He wanted to skip the niceties. He'd been away from Sarah for too long already and was saddled up and ready to ride for the hacienda. But the governor was not a man to be rushed.

"You're sure?" the governor asked, looking surprised. He looked Jeremiah over as he settled in his chair. "Relax, boy. I already had lunch." He laughed heartily at his joke, then eyed Jeremiah with concern. "What's eating you, Jeremiah?"

Jeremiah shifted in his chair, knowing he should be more at ease with the governor by now. They'd met many times and the governor had always been pleasant, but Jeremiah had seen firsthand how governors worked. The power they wielded made his knees knock. His future depended mightily on this next half hour with Governor Coke.

"Begging your pardon, Governor," Jeremiah said, swallowing hard but looking the man in the eye, "I've got a lot riding on this meeting."

"That you do, that you do." The governor slapped his knee and shook his head. He gave Jeremiah his eagle-eye look, peering out from under his heavy brows without blinking. He only did that when he wanted to make his point crystal clear. "I keep my word, as long as the man I'm dealing with keeps his."

Jeremiah returned the governor's look, knowing he had nothing to be ashamed of on that score. "Yessir, I realize that, and admire you for it, too."

"Hell, boy," the governor hollered, "I don't want your admiration. I see us more as friends." He stuck out his hand, which Jeremiah quickly shook, feeling relieved. "A man needs all the friends he can get, Jeremiah Baldwin. Have you got friends?" He leaned forward, pulling Jeremiah closer with the hand that still had hold of his, and whispered, "Other than the Comanche, I mean."

"Yessir, I do," Jeremiah said, trying not to flex his fingers, which had been well squeezed in the governor's firm handshake. "I count Pedro and Ranger Johnson as friends."

"Good men. Anyone else?"

"Well, yes, there's a woman . . ."

"Now we're getting somewhere!" The governor jumped to his feet and pounded him on the back. "You sure you don't want that drink?" He stomped to the door and shouted for James, then settled back into his chair. "Anyone I know?"

"I doubt it, sir." Damn, but Jeremiah wanted the small talk over, wanted to grab his pardon and get the hell out of Austin. The city was too big, too busy. He longed for open range, where a man could see for miles and smell what was coming before it was on top of him. He'd been here over three weeks. The wheels of government moved too slow, but they'd finally moved and in his favor. With Juan and Sanchez gone, the men who'd ridden with them couldn't talk fast enough. Like a flock of magpies, they'd blabbed every foul deed they'd ever done or heard of anyone else doing. It had taken days to sort the facts from the fiction. Additional arrests had been made, including the fine, upstanding Mr. Bulger, owner of Cedar Creek Bank, who had also been involved in the planning and execution of the raid on Baldwin Fort. Sanchez had been paying both Bulger and Juan from the money he'd raked in hand over fist running one of the biggest haciendas in the territory.

Jeremiah and the governor reviewed the facts that

had been disclosed about the raid on Baldwin Fort. They'd learned that Sanchez—a member of the family that owned the Sanchez-Navarro latifundio, a huge cattle operation in Mexico that measured its land in hectares, not acres—had been banished for killing a cousin in a fight. He'd first seen Baldwin Fort as a guest, but soon decided the land was intended to be his. Apparently, the land had once been owned by a long-dead ancestor, but had been lost in the confusion surrounding Spanish deeds and Mexican titles long before Texas became a republic, then a state.

Sanchez's arrogance, his sense of entitlement had overloaded his good sense and he'd planned the raid on Baldwin Fort. Not wanting to dirty his elegant hands, he'd put Juan Delgado, a hotheaded nobody with grandiose dreams, in charge of the raid. Sanchez's only order was that everyone be killed but the beautiful Mrs. O'Connor, who had smiled in his arms as they danced in her parlor the night he'd been a guest at the fort.

Juan's men had fallen all over themselves to tell how Mrs. O'Connor had spit in Sanchez's face and how Sanchez, puffed up like a snake about to strike, gave her to Juan. But Juan hadn't wanted her and he'd given her to the Comancheros. Sanchez had been furious. Then, before Sanchez could stop him, Juan had shot her and had his men burn her body. Sanchez had never intended for her to die. Guilt over her death had driven him to adopt her young daughter. He'd devoted himself to her welfare and had disbanded the Comancheros, not wanting the girl, who'd lost her memory, to suddenly remember the truth about herself and her family.

Jeremiah's return had begun the unraveling of their tapestry of lies, and once it started, it couldn't be stopped. Juan had tried to avert disaster by attacking Jeremiah, but failed, ironically because of the girl Sanchez had adopted.

The governor's eyebrows rose. "That woman you're interested in, she wouldn't be Sarah O'Connor, would she?"

Jeremiah shrugged, not surprised that the governor had figured everything out. "Sanchez called her Angelina, but she's taken back her real name."

"And will she soon be trading O'Connor for Baldwin?"

"That's up to her." Jeremiah returned Governor Coke's questioning gaze with a bland look and settled his hands, fingers interlocked, over his belt buckle.

The governor gave him that eagle-eye look again. "Don't you take no for an answer," he advised.

"Begging your pardon, Governor, but Sarah's been pushed around too much already. I'm not going to push her into this, too. I want it to be her choice, or she'll never stick with it."

"Very smart, very smart." The governor sipped his whiskey, which James had finally delivered during their review of the case. "So, if you're thinking marriage . . . ?"

Jeremiah nodded. "I am."

". . . you'll be wanting to get home to this lady, and bring her some good news for a change."

"Yessir." Jeremiah nodded again. His eagerness to do just that had him perched on the edge of his seat.

"Well, then, boy, I won't keep you any longer." The governor went to his desk and picked up a stack of official-looking papers, one boasting the seal of the State of Texas. "Here's your new deed, made out the way you wanted, even though I think it's a big mistake, mind you. And here's your pardon for all the raiding you did with your Comanche 'brothers.'"

Jeremiah accepted it, feeling weak with relief. He put it in the new leather satchel he'd bought just for this occasion. "Thank you very much, Governor. I couldn't have done it without your help."

"It's my pleasure, son." Governor Coke pumped Jeremiah's arm, his grip firm and unyielding. "But don't go just yet. I have a proposition for you."

"If it involves me putting on a badge and riding with the Texas Rangers, I have to decline, sir."

"Why?" Governor Coke still had hold of his hand, but he wasn't pumping anymore. "Texas needs good men like you. The Comanche respect you. Those renegades will run like hell back to the reservation if they hear you're after them."

"I aim to keep their respect, Governor, by not hunting them. If you want to keep them on the reservation, tell that government agent who's supposed to be watching over them to quit stealing from them. Their agent's buying bony cattle and lint blankets, paying full price for cheap goods, then sharing the difference with his friends."

"You don't say," Governor Coke replied, his eyes narrowing, his grip on Jeremiah's hand still firm.

"I suspect it goes deeper than that—it's worth looking into." Jeremiah shook his head at the governor's expression. He pitied the man who crossed Governor Coke.

"By the way, boy, did you see the headlines on to-day's paper?" Governor Coke finally released Jeremiah's hand to pick up the newspaper on his desk.

Quannah Parker Rounds Up Renegade Comanche, Jeremiah read, and grinned at a picture of Quannah leading the men who'd helped him haze the Sanchez hacienda. Quannah Parker? Before he knew it, Quannah would be some kind of folk hero. "That was a great plan, Governor. Gotta hand it to you."

"You won't reconsider that badge?" the governor asked, following Jeremiah to the door of his office.

"Not a chance, sir." Jeremiah turned back to shake the governor's hand once more, but saluted him instead, hoping to spare his fingers.

"Don't be a stranger, son!" Governor Coke followed

him out to the wide, columned porch and waved him off.

Jeremiah heard him call, "God bless you, boy," as he headed south on Congress, making for Cedar Creek, and the woman he hoped would welcome him with open arms.

Chapter Twenty-one

"Levántate!"

As always, at Bernida's too-cheery greeting, Sarah groaned and stuffed her head under her pillow. She'd been dreaming such a delicious dream and Bernida had interrupted it at the worst possible moment, as Jeremiah settled between her thighs.

"The day, it is getting no younger, *princessa*." The heavy drapes were swung wide, and Sarah squeezed her eyes shut as the room filled with brilliant sunshine and the annoying chirp of birds. "You have much work to do today. The people wait for you to tell them what to do. *Andale!*"

"Just a few more minutes, Bernida," she pleaded. If she kept her eyes closed and the pillow over her head, she could . . .

Bernida? Sarah's eyes popped open. Was she dreaming? She couldn't be dreaming. Bernida wasn't in this dream. She tossed off her blankets and scrambled out of bed.

"It is you!" She grabbed the little woman standing beside her bed and spun her around, hugging her tight, crying and laughing at the same time. She stepped back to look at her, while Bernida pulled out a handkerchief and wiped away Sarah's tears.

"Blow," Bernida said, holding the cloth to Sarah's nose.

"Where have you been?" She hugged her close again. "I've missed you terribly. Nothing's been right since you've been gone."

"Ha! You have been too busy to miss me ordering

you around," Bernida said, but her bright cheeks and shining eyes told Sarah that she was pleased to hear her praise.

"Seriously," Sarah said, pulling Bernida down to sit beside her on the bed. "Where have you been?"

"*Su papá*, Señor Sanchez, he tell me to go, but I do not want to leave you while he is so angry." She shook her head and sighed. "He push me out the door, say he will kill me if I do not go, but I could not. Finally, he had Mr. Juan take me to *la familia de su papá's*. His family's home. In Mexico." Her eyes grew round and wide. "Mr. Juan sent them a letter which say I am bad servant, no to be trusted." She shook her head sadly. "They make me work in the kitchen, but I show them I am very good servant. Then they like me too much. They no let me go. When we hear that Mr. Juan and Señor Sanchez are killed, they let me leave. But they begged me to come back."

"Of course." Sarah smiled, blinking back tears of joy. "But you belong here, with me. Oh, Bernie—" Sarah gave her such a hug that the whole bed bounced. "I'm making so many changes. The casa was damaged, outside and inside. And the gardens have been destroyed. Many of our friends have sent plants and people to help us restore it, but we may have to buy most of our food for the winter. Only the watermelon patch survived."

"*Muy bien*," Bernida said with a laugh. "A very good thing, for the Watermelon Festival is next week. Without our watermelons"—she shrugged—"no festival."

"Everyone loves it so much, they would find a way to hold it, even if they had to send to Houston for more."

"Do not worry, *Patrona*, we make everything right again, even better."

"Why do you call me *Patrona*?" Sarah asked. "You have never called me that before."

"All your people are calling you this," Bernida said, shooing her off the bed, then straightening the bedclothes. "They are proud and happy you not hurt by Mr. Juan or Señor Sanchez."

Warmth flooded Sarah and she felt herself blushing. "Thank you for telling me. Everyone has worked hard to restore the ranch. Our neighbors have returned stray animals they found wandering on their property. Little Bird's and Bull's father, who bought Bella, gave her back to me as a gift. All of the cattle and quarter horses are gone, but I have a plan, so this is not wholly a bad thing."

Feeling lighthearted and impetuous, Sarah hugged Bernida again, even though the housekeeper's arms were full of dirty clothes. "And now you have returned. Only one thing could make me happier."

"One man?" Bernida asked with a sly wink.

Later, as Bernida brushed Sarah's hair and tied it at her neck, Sarah stopped her. "You said Juan sent you to Mexico, but you didn't say how you got back. Did the people in Mexico pay your way?"

"No, *Patrona*. Señor Baldwin sent money to pay for the stages and the train ride. He say you need me very much."

"He did?" Sarah asked, incredulous. "How did he find you?"

"One of Mr. Juan's men, the man who took me to Mexico, he told Señor Baldwin when they question him in Austin."

"Oh, I see," Sarah said, assuming the man must have taken Bernida to Mexico, then returned to the hacienda. She turned back to the mirror, but avoided Bernida's questioning gaze by fiddling with a scent bottle on her dressing table as she considered Jeremiah's actions. His kindness and consideration reassured her. At least she knew he'd been thinking of her. "Do you know where Mr. Baldwin is now?"

"You have not heard from him?" Bernida asked, concern furrowing her brow. "His note say I am to help Little Bird take care of you until he comes."

"It did?" Sarah asked, feeling her spirits lift, though she planned to point out to him that she was a grown woman. She didn't need a nursemaid. Hadn't he noticed?

"*Sí, Patrona,*" Bernida said, smiling as she handed Sarah a wide-brimmed straw hat. "*Es la verdad.*"

Sarah's high spirits floundered when she pondered why Jeremiah hadn't sent *her* a note. He'd written to Bull, to Little Bird, even to Bernida, but not a word to her. Nothing had been settled between them. She'd finally awakened after drinking Little Bird's drugged wine in the late afternoon the day after the shoot-out in the study. Little Bird had been waiting for her and Sarah had blasted her up one side and down the other for giving her the sleeping draught without first discussing it with her. She would not have taken it, not while Jeremiah was still at the casa.

She'd awakened naked and fuzzy-headed. Though she'd soon figured out the fuzzy head, she couldn't remember taking off her clothes. Then she noticed the rumpled, slept-in condition of the other half of her bed. Once she realized Jeremiah had spent the night in her bed, she'd tried to remember if they'd made love, but couldn't recall a thing after going to bed fully clothed. Since she didn't have any tenderness or sore muscles, as she usually did after a night with Jeremiah, she was grateful he had subjugated his own needs and let her sleep.

The lost opportunity to resolve their differences—and make love—fueled her irritation with Little Bird, but she couldn't stay angry longer than it took to express her frustration. Bird had done what she'd thought was best, but she promised never again to give Sarah any medication without her knowledge.

She again offered Sarah some medicinal tea, but Sarah declined. If Jeremiah never returned, she hoped—in the deepest, most secret part of her soul—that he might have left her with child so she would always have a precious reminder of their love.

As the days of his absence turned into weeks, her hope dwindled, but the hacienda and its casa kept her too busy to mouse in her room as she had done before.

One night, nearly a month after Jeremiah had left, Sarah and Bernida were busy preparing for bed, engaged in their nightly hair-brushing ritual. A cool breeze drifted in from the open balcony door and Sarah had become drowsy listening to the nightly chorus. A lone wolf howled in the distance, raising goose bumps on her arms.

She snapped to attention, listening for another howl, but heard only silence. She hurried to the balcony and saw nothing, but a thrill raced through her.

"Quickly, Bernida," she said, keeping her voice calm but firm, not wanting to alarm Bernie, just hurry her along. "Get the other maids and light a candle in every window. I think we're about to have company. And then you may all have the rest of the night off. Oh, and, Bernida," she called as Bernie hurried away, "I will be sleeping late tomorrow. Very late."

Bernida gave her a wide smile and a nod and rushed away.

Jeremiah heard the howl of a wolf in the distance and smiled. His brothers had smelled him already. With the wind at his back, it was small wonder.

He'd had plenty of time to think on his feelings for Sarah. He had no doubt now that he wanted her for his wife, wanted his sons and daughters to have her nerve, her spunk, her—what had Pedro called it?—tenacity. Yeah, that was it. A fancy word that meant sticking to your guns and not taking no for an answer.

But he still wasn't sure how she felt. Could she forgive him for forcing the truth out into the open and causing

Sanchez's death? Did she feel guilty for her part in Sanchez's death? Did she regret loving Jeremiah? He'd
soon find out, and he was braced for the worst.

Anxious to stop the worry eating at his gut and making his head pound, he kneed the tired horse, pushing
it a little faster. Up ahead, he saw the casa. The sun had
set behind the western hills and the brilliant sunset
had faded, turning the sky behind the casa to purples
and deep blues. The casa was all lit up, glowing in the
falling dark. Was it on fire?

Heart in his throat, he kneed the horse again. It galloped another mile or two, but slowed to a walk, then
stopped. Jeremiah sat on his horse, staring, certain
he'd seen the house like this before. The casa had been
whitewashed and shone like a church on Sunday morning. Candles glowed in every window, as he'd dreamed
in his vision quest when he first left the Comanche. He
kicked the horse hard and set it running as the door
opened and a woman stepped out.

He'd know that form anywhere. Sarah waited for him.

Tired to the bone, he swung off the horse and walked
toward her, taking his time. Someone pulled the reins
from his numb fingers and he let go of the horse with a
muttered "Thanks."

Sarah waited, not running to him or throwing herself
at him, just watching his face and smiling. Light glowed
behind her, shining through her nightgown and robe,
outlining her long, slim legs and tiny waist, making his
heat rise and his body stir.

Later, he could never remember the last few steps of
that long walk, only the smile on her beautiful face, the
feel of her stepping into his arms, and the sweet pain of
his heart expanding. He thought it might burst in his
chest when she wrapped her arms around his neck and
said, "I've missed you."

The most beautiful words in the world, next to the
ones that followed: "I love you, Jeremiah."

Joy washed over him, so bright and shining that he didn't know if he could hold it inside. All he could do was kiss her and tell her he'd missed her, too, and that he loved her, too, as he carried her up the stairs and down the hall to her room.

Candles lit every corner. There were even candles in the fireplace. So much light! Light everywhere, even inside, warming him heart and soul. His worries and doubts fell away, and he no longer felt the heavy drag of uncertainty. Instead, he felt light and as wispy as the robe he gently pushed off Sarah's shoulders. Her nightgown followed the robe, gliding down her body to catch on the tips of her breasts, but she gave a shake and it drifted to the floor. She smiled and stepped naked out of the pool of fabric and reached for his shirt, but he lifted her and carried her to her bed, laid her down, and came down over her.

"Wait." She laughed, her hand caught between them as she tried to undo the buttons on his pants. "I can't—"

With an impatient growl, he stood and shucked his pants, boots, socks, everything, then turned to admire her. She waited with open arms, her skin gleaming in the candlelight, her smile warm and welcoming, impatient as she looked lower and saw that he was ready.

"You're beautiful," he whispered.

Her eyes went wide and she glanced away, shaking her head. "Don't make fun, Jeremiah. I'm plain and too skinny, and—"

He pressed a finger over her lips and shushed her. "You're beautiful. So beautiful you make my heart ache."

Her smile started slow and grew 'til it was brighter than all the candles in the room. She pulled him to her, sighing into his kiss, her arms binding him to her. He never wanted to be set free. He'd been born to be her captive.

Long, long he stroked her body and kissed every inch of warm skin. She did the same, even swirling her tongue around his nipples. He smiled at her pleasure when his body responded like hers.

When she pushed him onto his back and kissed her way down his chest to his cock, he thought his heart would explode in his chest. She took him in her mouth and his heart stopped beating, then started up again with a slam as she sucked him, twirling her tongue around the head of his shaft until he cried out for her to stop.

He flipped her onto her back and pushed her legs wide, kissed her thighs, took one long, slow lick up her weeping center, then drove into her. She lifted to meet him and screamed his name. He thought he'd never heard anything sweeter until—a few throbbing strokes later—she screamed it again and wrapped her legs tight about his waist as her whole body tightened around his.

He plunged into her heat once, twice more, and must have howled his release, for the wolves outside answered, rending the quiet night with their chorus.

He collapsed beside her and they slept through the night wrapped in each other's arms. He woke to find her stroking him erect again and kissed her. Then she surprised him and slid astride, taking him deep and riding him hard.

His plans for their morning—including discussing their future, and asking her to leave her home—would have to wait.

But not for long.

Sarah fought for patience as the day stretched on and on. Her wonderful night in Jeremiah's arms had ended too soon for her liking. She recalled straddling him and taking him deep inside her, her hair flying about them as he gripped her hips and taught her how to ride him fast, then faster and deeper. She'd wanted to stay in bed with him forever, but her people needed her.

The only thing that kept her going was the sure knowledge that he loved her. He'd told her so, over and over, and not only while they were making love. She had told him she loved him, too, and she did. But she was worried. How would he react when he found out what she wanted to do with the hacienda? Now that he had taken the land back, would he be willing to do as she asked? She must find an opportunity to ask him, before someone—like the man representing the conglomerate from England—did it for her. They had plenty of time, she told herself; there was no rush. But the problem weighed on her mind and kept her preoccupied throughout the long day as she led her people, answering by rote their questions about the tasks she'd set for them.

Jeremiah was busy, too, though he'd taken several opportunities to seek her out and steal kisses when he thought no one was watching. Her people laughed and clapped and cheered him on, making her blush. She'd even heard a few of the men howl when they thought he wasn't looking. Instead of being angry, he'd grinned, thrown his head back, and shown them how to truly howl like a wolf, then winked at her. He was fast gaining their respect and admiration.

Suddenly, strong arms caught her from behind and swept her feet out from under her. She cried out in fear, then realized Jeremiah had hold of her. She closed her eyes and squealed in glee as he twirled her, letting her feet slide to the ground. As she waited for the world to stop spinning, he turned her to face him and kissed her as though he was afraid he might never see her again.

"Don't make any plans for tonight," he whispered, his breath tickling her ear. "We're going for a ride."

She watched him walk away, his stride long and sure, almost carefree. She blew him a kiss, wondering what he had in mind, hoping her own news wouldn't spoil his surprise.

"Have you told him yet?" Little Bird asked from behind her.

Sarah jumped and slapped her hand over her heart. "Do you have to do that?" she asked.

"You're going to have to tell him sometime. Why not tonight, on your *ride*?" Little Bird grinned at her.

"I'm sure he has something planned, so it will have to wait, but I promise to tell him soon."

"Good. Bull and I want to set our plans in motion and we can't do that until we have Jeremiah's approval." Little Bird stood looking at Sarah, who realized her friend was waiting for her to acknowledge her comment. She never would have suspected Little Bird could be so tenacious when she wanted something.

"I understand you're anxious to get started. I'll present the plan to him soon."

Little Bird gave her a hug and a kiss on the cheek. Then trotted off to find Bull.

A rider, leading a string of two horses, trotted up to the barn. Sarah hurried over, recognizing Pedro. Jeremiah greeted him when he swung off the horse and she gave him a big hug. "What is this? It looks like you're going on a long trip."

"As a matter of fact, I am." Pedro looked worried and anxious. "Could I talk to you two privately?"

Jeremiah looked at Sarah with a questioning arch of his brow. "Let's find some shade in the courtyard." She stepped between them and took an arm on either side. "How about some lunch while we talk?"

"I wouldn't turn it down." Pedro sank gratefully into a chair.

"I hope you can stay the night at least." She was relieved when he nodded.

Sarah sent one of the children for Bernida and led two of her favorite men to a small table beneath the largest shade tree, well away from any windows and doors or inquisitive ears.

"The house is looking more beautiful than ever,

Sarah," Pedro said, glancing about the courtyard with a critical eye. "You've replanted the roses, I see."

"Yes," she said, and plucked a newly opened bloom from a bush near her chair. "They're beautiful again, aren't they?" She buried her nose in the flower, enjoying its spicy scent.

"She's been working day and night," Jeremiah told Pedro, and squeezed Sarah's hand. He rubbed a thumb over her calloused fingertips and raised an eyebrow at her.

Jeremiah lounged back in his high-backed, wrought-iron chair, looking like a giant on a doll's chair. She hoped he didn't try to rock back on the chair's back legs. When he saw her watching him, he straightened in the chair and grinned at her. "Sorry, I'm used to a willow backrest. Much more comfortable."

Sarah and Pedro chuckled. "You'll have to show me how to make one," she said. "I've seen them here and there, but never got to try one out."

Jeremiah shook his head. "Sorry, that's woman's work. Comanche males turn up their noses at weaving, scraping hides, carrying water, you name it. All the backbreaking chores belong to the women."

"So what do the men contribute?" Sarah demanded to know, outraged on behalf of the poor, uneducated women.

"They hunt, and keep everyone safe." His unconcerned shrug spoke volumes.

Sarah folded her hands in her lap and sighed. "You're going to miss that life, aren't you?"

"You have no idea," Jeremiah said, and waggled his eyebrows at her. "Sitting in the shade all day, gambling, drinking, eating . . ." He leaned back and put his hands behind his head. "But I don't see why I have to give it up. Do you?" He turned to Pedro.

"Don't drag me into the middle of this," Pedro said,

laughing at both of them. "You two will have to work that out between you."

Bernida wheeled a small cart into the courtyard and they applied their attention to their meal until Bernida left again.

"What's on your mind, Pedro?" Sarah asked. "I know you didn't come all the way from Austin to have lunch with us."

"You're right." He turned to Jeremiah. "You remember the man that took Bernida to Mexico on Juan's orders?"

He nodded.

"Well, let's just say it's not the first time Juan's sent him to Mexico with a woman." He spoke low and urgently, as if he couldn't spare the time to speak at all.

Sarah glanced at Jeremiah, but he stared intently at Pedro. "Someone you know?"

"My mother and sister," Pedro answered with a strained smile. "They've been missing for more than a year, but we've found them. That's why I've been here, Sarah, more to keep an eye on Juan than you."

He turned to Jeremiah. "When Juan's men were questioned in Austin, one of them confessed to that crime, too. The man admitted that they sold my mother and sister to the Comancheros. He told us where to find them. I'm on my way to Mexico to bring them home."

Sarah stared at Pedro, horrified by his revelations. "So how can we help you?"

"Governor Coke signed Juan's ranch over to me to thank me for my service to the state and the Rangers. I'm officially retired."

"Congratulations," Jeremiah said, and extended his hand to shake Pedro's.

"Thanks." Pedro nodded. "But I need a favor. I know it's a lot to ask after what you've been through."

"How can we help?" Sarah asked.

"Anything you need," Jeremiah said. "You've done so much for us, how could you think we'd refuse?"

"Can you keep an eye on the rancho for me while I'm gone, maybe have some of your womenfolk clean it up a bit? Juan and his men left a hell of a mess."

"Don't worry about a thing," Sarah assured him. "We'll take care of it for you. You won't recognize the place." Now she understood why Juan had always come to the casa and had never invited her or Sanchez to his home.

Later, as Pedro prepared to leave, Jeremiah pulled him aside. "If you have any problems in Mexico, you can find me here."

"*Vaya con Dios.*" Sarah gave Pedro a long hug and kissed his cheek.

Pedro smiled grimly as he shook Jeremiah's hand. "I'll take God along, but I'd rather bring a few of your wolves."

Chapter Twenty-two

"Okay, open your eyes."

"Where are we?" Sarah clutched Jeremiah's hand tight as she sought something familiar to help her get her bearings. "I don't think I've ever seen this place."

"It's pretty well hidden," he told her. "This is where the Comanche made camp while they were here helping me steal Sanchez's stock. Years ago, some of us boys found it while we were playing 'cowboys and Injuns.' Christine and I used to come here to get away from the Reverend."

Sarah's eyes popped open. "You called your father the Reverend?" She giggled when he nodded, looking guilty but not ashamed. "Why? We all thought you—his family—were devoted to him."

"He was a stern man. One who commanded more respect than love," Jeremiah admitted.

"I'm glad you mentioned your family," she said, and reached into her pocket for the black jeweler's bag she'd tucked inside before leaving the casa. She held it out to him and ignored his questioning frown. "You may remember this," she said, and poured the ruby necklace Sanchez had given her into his hand. "I do. Your mother wore it to a dance when I was young."

He held it a moment, as if weighing it in his hand, then gave it back. "Hold it for me while I light the fire." Crouching over a tipi of twigs, he struck a spark off the flint he pulled from his pocket and soon a crackling fire brightened the dark around them. What looked like a small altar lay between him and the fire, and on it a brightly painted pipe rested beside more twigs and a palmful of grass.

"Now let me see it." He held up the necklace, letting it dangle from one hand. "Yes, I remember the last time she wore it, the night Sanchez was our guest. Your parents had invited us to dinner. We danced in your parlor afterward. That was when Sanchez met your mother."

His words stripped away Sarah's joy at being here with him, sharing one of his Comanche rituals. "I remembered her dancing and laughing, but not the details."

"My mother danced with the Reverend and your father. Your mother danced with Sanchez all night," Jeremiah went on. "Patrick, your father, cut the evening short. I remember my mother and father arguing about her all the way back to our house. Mother wanted my father to 'handle it,' to reprimand her, but Father said Patrick was capable of dealing with his own family and refused to interfere."

"I think my parents argued about it, too." Sarah gazed into the dark beyond the fire's light as if she saw her parents' angry faces there. "I remember him shouting at her, but it wasn't the first time they'd argued about that. Mother seemed to need attention like plants need water. Especially from men."

"She couldn't have known what would come of it." He settled his arm around her shoulders and pulled her up against his side, but his offer of comfort felt forced, wary. "Don't blame her for Sanchez's evil nature."

"Of course not," Sarah said, and his tension slipped away. Had he thought she would protest his opinion of Sanchez, blame it all on her poor mother? Knowing what Sanchez had done, she believed he had deserved to be punished for his crimes, though she was very thankful it had been Juan who killed him. She wouldn't have wanted that stain on her soul.

She did not regret her efforts to prove Sanchez's innocence. No matter his reasons, he had been good to her, had given her a home and affection and cared for her. She'd had no reason to suspect him of treachery, and when he was accused of murder by Jeremiah, she'd behaved as she believed a dutiful daughter should. Now, however, having remembered her life before the raid and learning the truth from Juan's own mouth, she had no regrets for the way Sanchez and Juan had died or for her part in it. She only hoped that Jeremiah understood why she'd been unable to break free of Sanchez sooner.

She pulled her shawl close around her body, feeling a chill chase up her spine. "Mother was so beautiful and loved us all so much. I'm trying to remember more of the happy times to blot out the bad memories."

He kissed her cheek. "Good. If you ever need a happy memory, let me know. I've got plenty."

"Jeremiah, I want to talk to you about the hacienda." She glanced up at him, anxiety over what she needed to say making her tremble.

"Yes, we need to talk, but not yet. The fire is small and I need to show you something, share something about me before we talk of the future." From a small bundle by the fire, he picked up a twig and tossed it on the fire. Then he knelt, removed his shirt, and caught the smoke from the fire in his cupped hands, bathing himself in its smoke.

She rose onto her folded knees and swept some of the fragrance toward her body, inhaling it deeply. At first it stung her eyes and made her want to cough, but that need faded, replaced by the heady scent of the plains, warmed by the sun after the rain. "Mmm," she said, and repeated the motion, copying his movements. "That smells nice."

He nodded at her and smiled, then tossed a handful of grass onto the flames, which hissed and crackled and sent another scent puffing skyward.

Sarah watched him drag this smoke toward him, too. He swept it up his chest and over his head several times; then she did the same. He picked up a pipe and packed it full of the remaining grass, then lit it with a glowing stick from the fire and puffed it to light. After a long inhale, he held it up to the sky, then the earth, then held it up in each direction. When he began chanting, she sat very still and listened to the Comanche words. Was this what he'd wanted to show her? Should she say something? Was he finished?

He startled her when he raised his arms to the sky and began talking, still in Comanche. She'd learned a few words from Bull and Little Bird and recognized some of them as he spoke. He seemed to be praying to the Great Spirit, and, though she had no idea what he was saying, she bowed her head. As if he realized she didn't understand, he began praying in English.

"Great Father, who lives above and sees all who move upon the breast of Mother Earth, look down upon us, your servants and hear my prayer.

"I thank you, Father Above, for giving me revenge upon the murderers of my family and all the people who died in the raid on Baldwin Fort. No longer will the blood of our families cry from the ground where it was spilled. No longer will their spirits walk the earth in despair.

"Grant them peace, Father. Let them rest their heads upon your chest, and help us, their children, to find our way. Bless the love that grows between us, as we grow in strength and wisdom sent from above. Help us to know where our journey will take us, that we may prepare for our life together.

"Great Father, though I am only a poor servant, please heed my prayer."

Sarah lifted her head and glanced at Jeremiah, who was staring across the fire, a smile on his face. She followed his gaze and gasped as she looked into the yellow eyes of the biggest black wolf she had ever seen. Her first instinct, to jump up and run, died quickly when Jeremiah reached over and squeezed her hand. She hadn't even brought her knife, knowing she was going to be with him, thinking he would keep her safe.

Jeremiah squeezed her hand harder and she saw the wolf's face stretch and grow. It swallowed the fire and, hanging above them, it spoke.

"Your prayers have been heard, Jeremiah Baldwin. You have done well, my son, and used your gifts well. Your woman is frightened, but you have done right. Teach her the ways of the People so that she can help you teach your sons and daughters.

"Your life and the life of your mate are no longer in danger. You no longer need your 'special gift,' but should you find yourself threatened in the days that lie ahead, call on me and it will be restored to you.

"You need not ask where your journey will take you. Consider the words of the woman you call Kris Baldwin, sent to help the People find their way.

"Farewell, my son. Do not forget the ways of the People or the needs of those who are yet to come."

The wolf shrank, its eyes swallowed by the flames, its black, shining fur becoming part of the night.

Sarah blinked, staring into the fire, feeling her whole body begin to shake. Suddenly, the fire flared higher and a baby cooed. Sarah started as a woman's face took shape in the smoke rising from the fire and was joined by a man's face.

"Chikoba!" the woman called, and she smiled at Jeremiah.

"Kris," he answered. "It is good to see you again. How are you and how is my many-greats-granddaughter?"

"Karrie is well. Fat and happy." She held up an infant wearing a beautifully beaded white buckskin tunic that didn't quite cover its chubby, kicking legs. "See? Already she wants to run."

The man leaned over her shoulder, looking concerned. "*Aihe*, brother," he said, "how goes the battle?"

"It is over," Jeremiah said with a smile. "The fight is won. What's that on your head, Duuqua?"

"Nothing." Duuqua touched the bandage on his temple. "A scratch."

Kris bit her lip and tried not to laugh, but a giggle escaped. "He hit a tree, trying to drive my car."

"Too many metal boxes in your world, Kris Baldwin. I miss my horse. Chikoba, you should see the television, and refrigerator—"

Kris kissed his cheek. "Another time, babe. It's a small fire."

His lips snapped shut and he gave her a look that promised retribution, but in a pleasurable way.

Sarah couldn't help grinning, too, though she did not understand this strange ritual. The love between these two was easy to see, and strong. Who were they? How did Jeremiah know them?

"I want you to meet Sarah O'Connor." He pulled Sarah closer with an arm slung around her shoulder. "She's—"

"You've found her!" Kris cried before he finished. "Take good care of him," she said, speaking to Sarah, her eyes filling with tears. "He is loved by many."

To Jeremiah, she said, "I'm so glad you've found each other. Be happy."

"Farewell," Duuqua called as the fire blew out, then flared to life again, crackling happily.

Sarah glanced up at Jeremiah, who was still smiling at the fire. "I hope you plan to tell me what all this was about?" she said, throwing an arm wide to include the fire and the altar. She didn't know whether to be curious, flabbergasted, or a little of both.

What she did know was that she was very confused. "Who, exactly, are you?"

"I'm the man who loves you," he growled, then caught her up and swung her around. Her head spun and she returned his kiss, his passion, his love. They returned to the casa to make love all night. Near dawn, she remembered she'd meant to talk to him about the hacienda. Tomorrow would be soon enough. They had the rest of their lives to work out the details.

Jeremiah slipped out of Sarah's bed before dawn the next morning. After dressing, he stood gazing at her tousled hair sticking out from under the pillow covering her head. Fighting the urge to laugh, he lifted the pillow off. Seconds later, she reached out, grabbed the covers, and pulled them over her head, then gave a sigh and started breathing deeply again.

He pulled on his shirt, wondering if a lifetime would be long enough to learn everything he wanted to know about her, starting with: how did she breathe at night?

After watching him pray last night, she'd pelted him with questions until he'd shut her up, distracting her with kisses. When she woke up this morning, he knew she wouldn't let him dodge her anymore. He drew his saddlebags out from under her bed, brushed off the dust, and pulled out the white parfleche. He settled cross-legged on the bed and flipped off her covers, then waited for the kettle to boil.

He didn't have to wait long.

"Bernida!" she growled from somewhere under all that hair. "It's not even morning yet."

"You're right about that, but I'm not Bernida."

She jerked awake, tossed her hair back, realized she was naked, and slapped a pillow over her chest. Then she recognized him and threw the pillow at him. She squinted at the crack between the drapes and threw another one at him. "What is wrong with you? It's still dark outside. Please tell me you're not an early riser."

"Guilty." He tossed the pillows onto the floor beside him, partly to cushion his fall if she got angry enough to push him off the bed, partly to keep from being hit with them again. "I've got something to show you and I couldn't wait any longer."

"Oh no," she said, snuggling back under the covers. "No more smoking fires and big black wolves with yellow eyes and long white fangs that talk, of all things." She tried to pull the covers up, but he had them pinned under his knee.

She frowned at his leg, then him. "You're not going to let me sleep, are you?"

He shook his head. "It's time we got on with the future, our future, and there are some things about me you have to understand before we can do that."

"All right," she said, and sat beside him, her back to the headboard. She motioned for a pillow, then another, and another as she shifted about, getting comfortable. "I'm ready, and very anxious to hear you explain all that . . . happened last night."

Jeremiah took his time telling her how Kris Baldwin had come to live among the Comanche, pausing to answer any questions she had, hoping she could accept what he believed: that Kris Baldwin had come from her own life in the future to help the Comanche in the past. He explained his original distrust of this strange woman who bore his sister Christine's name and even looked like her, though his sister was dead, killed the day he was captured. He thought Kris was a liar, a thief, or worse, someone sent by soldiers to deceive and betray the Comanche.

His brother, Duuqua, hadn't trusted her, either, at first, but she'd captured his heart and he'd come to believe her story, though he'd wanted to believe she'd been sent by the Great Spirit to show the Comanche how to kill the soldiers.

"They fell in love, didn't they?" Sarah bounced eagerly on the bed, getting caught up in the story.

"How did you know?" Jeremiah asked, surprised not only that she accepted his tale, but that she had figured out what had happened before he could tell her.

"I was there last night." She raised an eyebrow at

him. "It was obvious. They're very much in love. But who is Kris to you?"

"She's from the future and she's my great-great-granddaughter."

"So that precious little baby is your great-great-great-granddaughter?" Sarah's eyes rounded and she stared at him. He could almost see the details sinking into her mind.

"That's right, and she's named after my first wife, Ekararo, or She Blushes. They call her Karrie."

"Oh, my," Sara said, and sank into her pillows. "This is a lot to take in."

"I have proof," Jeremiah said, and opened the parfleche.

"That's right!" Sarah cried, taking the clothes as he pulled them from the leather bag that was decorated to match the tiny tunic and moccasins. "These are the baby clothes Pedro and I discovered in the barn after you were shot. I'm so glad Juan didn't destroy them."

"I am, too." Jeremiah rubbed the finely tanned white deer hide between his fingers, remembering how long and hard Ekararo had labored over it.

"So what did Kris mean when she said, 'I'm glad you found her'?" Sarah was looking at him, searching his eyes.

"She must have recognized you, or your name at least. You're her grandparent, too."

"This is all very strange." Sarah looked up from the baby clothes and fixed him with an incredulous stare. "She knows what lies ahead for us?" She looked up at him. "Did she tell you?"

"No, but I know that whatever it is, I want you to share it with me. I want you to be my wife, Sarah. Can you forgive me for bringing the past out in the open, exposing your father? Can you put all that aside and marry me?"

Sarah studied his face, reached out, and stroked his

cheek, then kissed him. "Yes, Jeremiah. I can. I would be very happy to marry you."

He gave a joyful shout, relieved to have that behind him. "I love you, Sarah, more than I thought I ever could."

"More than you loved Ekarao?" she asked shyly, blushing.

"Differently," he told her, and kissed her palm. "Eka-raro will always be special because she was my first love, but you'll be my wife for the rest of my life, and you'll be the mother of my children. No other love is as strong as that."

Sarah looked away, biting her lip.

"What is it?" he asked, turning her face to his. "There's nothing you can say to me that will change my mind or turn me away from you. You know that, don't you?"

She nodded and scooted closer, wrapping her arms around him.

He held her with her head pressed to his chest and waited for her to gather her thoughts. She wasn't leaving this room until she told him what was troubling her.

"You fought hard to take back your father's land," she began, and looked up at him. "And now that you have it . . ."

"Didn't you read the copy of the deed I brought back with me?"

"I started to, but someone interrupted me and when I returned to finish, you'd put it in the new safe. Why?"

"I put the land in your name, Sarah. I don't want any part of this place. Every day I'm reminded that my family died here, but there are no graves to mark their lives, no headstones to mark their passing, just screams on the wind and the stink of death in the breeze."

Sarah rose onto her knees, tears starting in her eyes, and smiled at him. "I'm so relieved," she said, pressing her palms over her eyes to stop the tears. "I didn't know how to tell you—I don't want to stay here, either. I saw and smelled their burning bodies. I know what you smell on the breeze. I can't stay here, knowing what it is, reminded of that blackened pile of bones with every breath I take."

"Let's make a fresh start, in a place that's green and beautiful." Jeremiah hugged her tight, offering comfort as she wiped away her tears. "Kris said Oregon's a beautiful place. She would know. She grew up there."

"The Baldwins, her family, lived in Oregon?" She rose to her knees to face him, a look of wonder lighting her eyes. "I'd love to see more of the country."

Jeremiah had never seen her so happy, never felt such joy himself.

"We'll sell the hacienda and find some land of our own."

She looked a little alarmed. "I've been keeping a se-cret from you," she admitted, glancing down at her hands, which lay clenched in her lap. "Bull and Little Bird have asked to buy the casa and two or three hun-dred acres. They want to start a 'dude ranch,' a place where wealthy people can come to experience ranch life firsthand—you know, hunting, fishing, roundups, cattle drives, all of it. Their father is going to help them and they're anxious to get started."

"That sounds wonderful, but will it work?" Jeremiah was surprised that she'd not only thought over what to do with the hacienda, but had already set some plans in motion.

Sarah nodded and went on eagerly. "I want to do something for our people. Most of them have worked for the Navarro-Sanchez families all their lives. I want to give them the chance to own land of their own by break-ing up the hacienda into smaller ranchos and letting them pay us for the land over time. They could form a cooperative and work together to minimize the risks."

For a few seconds, Jeremiah said nothing, too amazed and proud of her to speak.

"Say something," she said, leaning toward him, her

whole body tense as she waited to hear what he thought of her plans.

"I'm so proud of you." He gathered her in his arms and hugged her tight, then set her away from him so he could see her face. "I want to know all the details. Tell me everything."

"Well, I promised Bull I'd let him tell you himself," she said with a laugh.

Jeremiah smiled. "I can hardly wait. Honestly." He took her hands in his and sighed. "I was so worried that you wouldn't be able to accept all this, my strange experiences, friends, all of it, but you've opened your mind and your heart. I couldn't love you more. But, Sarah, what about us? What do you want to do?"

"All I want is to be with you." She shrugged. "I'm sure we'll figure out something. It'll take a while to finish dividing up the hacienda. We could take a trip to Oregon and look around."

"You're right, but let's think about some of our options. Pedro tells me you're good with horses." When she nodded eagerly, he said, "So am I. I'd like to raise horses, really good cattle horses, but not for the army. I'll never forgive the bluecoats for what they did to Ekararo." He looked into her eyes. "And children. I'd like lots and lots of children."

"Yes, lots of children." Sarah refolded the tiny baby clothes and put them back in their bag. "Let's keep these safe, preserve them as best we can, and pass them down to Kris through our children and grandchildren. When she sees them, she'll remember the people who came before her, who struggled, fought, and lived to make her life and the lives of her children possible."

Once the precious clothes were packed away again, Sarah tucked them safely into the bottom of her armoire, then dove back into bed.

Jeremiah caught her to him to keep from getting poked with an elbow or knee and slid down into the bed.

"Are you sure this is what you want?" he asked.

Sarah propped herself up with her elbows on his abdomen and smiled. "Absolutely." She leaned down and licked his chest, then looked up and smacked her lips.

"If I'd known all those years ago that you tasted this good, I would have worked harder to catch you." She returned to her love play with a wicked grin.

"If I'd known you were so good at licking, I would have let you."

"When shall we get married?" she asked, looking distracted, though he knew she was anything but.

He tumbled her under him and kissed her soundly. "After lunch?"

She thought a minute, then wrapped her arms around his neck and kissed him tenderly. Looking him in the eye, she said, "Yes, but no later."

He stared down at her. "Why not?"

"Your first child's already on the way," she told him, and pulled back to watch his face.

Stunned, he stared up at her, then leaped out of bed, carrying her in his arms. Cradling her tenderly, he stood in a slim ray of sunlight peeking through the drapes, letting the joy swell inside him.

"When?" he asked, his voice a hoarse croak. "When did it happen?"

"The brush shelter," she whispered, "those two blissful days we spent together."

"Have I told you today that I love you?" He kissed her tenderly.

"Yes, but I'd love to hear it again."

"I love you, Sarah O'Connor."

"And I love you, too, Jeremiah Baldwin."

A wolf howled nearby, though people on the hacienda later swore the howl came from *inside* the casa.

☐ **YES!**

Sign me up for the Historical Romance Book Club and send my FREE BOOKS! If I choose to stay in the club, I will pay only $8.50* each month, a savings of $6.48!

NAME: _____

ADDRESS: _____

TELEPHONE: _____

EMAIL: _____

☐ I want to pay by credit card.

☐ **VISA**   ☐ **MasterCard**   ☐ **DISCOVER**

ACCOUNT #: _____

EXPIRATION DATE: _____

SIGNATURE: _____

Mail this page along with $2.00 shipping and handling to:
Historical Romance Book Club
PO Box 6640
Wayne, PA 19087
Or fax (must include credit card information) to:
610-995-9274
You can also sign up online at **www.dorchesterpub.com**.
*Plus $2.00 for shipping. Offer open to residents of the U.S. and Canada only.
Canadian residents please call 1-800-481-9191 for pricing information.
If under 18, a parent or guardian must sign. Terms, prices and conditions subject to
change. Subscription subject to acceptance. Dorchester Publishing reserves the right
to reject any order or cancel any subscription.